Books by Kresley Cole

The Game Maker Series
The Professional

The Immortals After Dark Series
The Warlord Wants Forever
A Hunger Like No Other
No Rest for the Wicked
Wicked Deeds on a Winter's Night
Dark Needs at Night's Edge
Dark Desires After Dusk
Kiss of a Demon King
Deep Kiss of Winter
Pleasure of a Dark Prince
Demon from the Dark
Dreams of a Dark Warrior
Lothaire
Shadow's Claim
MacRieve

The Arcana Chronicles
Poison Princess
Endless Knight

The MacCarrick Brothers Series
If You Dare
If You Desire
If You Deceive

The Sutherland Series
The Captain of All Pleasures
The Price of Pleasure

KRESLEY
COLE

The Professional

THE GAME MAKER SERIES

**SIMON &
SCHUSTER**

London · New York · Sydney · Toronto · New Delhi

A CBS COMPANY

First published in Great Britain by Simon & Schuster UK Ltd, 2013
A CBS COMPANY
This paperback edition, 2014

1 3 5 7 9 10 8 6 4 2

Simon & Schuster UK Ltd
1st Floor
222 Gray's Inn Road
London
WC1X 8HB

www.simonandschuster.co.uk

Simon & Schuster Australia, Sydney
Simon & Schuster India, New Delhi

A CIP catalogue record for this book
is available from the British Library

PB ISBN: 978-1-47111-386-4
TPB ISBN: 978-1-47113-767-9
EBOOK ISBN: 978-1-47111-387-1

Interior design by Jaime Putorti
Printed and bound by CPI Group (UK) Ltd, Croydon, CR0 4YY

Warmly dedicated to Lauren McKenna,
my incomparable editor. Ten years, three genres, twenty-two books.
Couldn't have done it without you, lady.

"If you run, I will catch you. It's what I do"
−ALEKSANDR "THE SIBERIAN" SEVASTYAN,
BRATVA ENFORCER, FORMER PRIZEFIGHTER

◆

"Heading off to a Russian gangsterland.
With a twisted enforcer who's hotter than the sun.
What could possibly go wrong?"
−NATALIE MARIE PORTER, GRAD STUDENT

PROLOGUE

From: NataliePorter@huskers.unl.edu
Sent: Saturday 2:51 PM
To: caseworker03@russian-ancestry-DNA.com
Subject: Don't keep me in suspense. . . .

Dear Mr. Zironoff,

Sorry to e-mail you yet again, but I was so excited to learn of the potential DNA match you discovered last month. After six years of searching for my biological parents, I'd love to hear back from you, even if the lead didn't pan out. I've tried calling, but your voice mailbox is full. I don't have enough money to start over with a new investigator, so could you please respond?

Sincerely,
Natalie Porter

From: NataliePorter@huskers.unl.edu
Sent: Thursday 1:14 AM
To: caseworker03@russian-ancestry-DNA.com
Subject: Response needed!

Dear Mr. Zironoff,

I'm starting to get worried, so please write me back. You gave me such hope that I would soon find my mother and father. I can wire the last of my savings to you. Anything.

But I need you to respond.

Sincerely,
Natalie

Sent: Thursday 1:15 AM
To: NataliePorter@huskers.unl.edu
Subject: Mail delivery failed

The following address(es) failed: caseworker03@russian-ancestry-DNA.com
Mailbox is FULL

CHAPTER 1

"Mommy issues. Serial cheater. Humor void. Two-pump chump." With each guy who entered the campus bar, I ticked off my initial impression to my drunken friends.

I had an uncanny knack for sizing up males—I was a regular "manalyst." My secret? I always went negative, and the guys, well, they always accommodated.

The girls at the table—several of my roommate's friends and a couple of mine—looked at me like I was a fun sideshow act, their carny pal. Drinks were perpetually free.

After the week I'd had, my dinner of salt, tequila, and lime was hitting the spot.

My best friend Jessica murmured at my ear, "You better be careful, you picky prude, or else you'll take your hymen to your grave. Like a skin tag."

She alone knew that I'd never given it up—and why. "Low blow, Jess," I said without any heat. Like her, it took a lot to get me ruffled, which was one of the reasons we made such great roommates.

Other than that, we were as different as we could be. Whereas she was leggy and tan with twinkling blue eyes and cropped black hair, I was short and top-heavy, with long red hair and pale-as-a-porcelain-sink skin.

I was a workaholic studyaholic, pursuing my history PhD. After years' worth of incompletes, Jess had finally dipped a toe into the core courses of her major—leisure studies—and decided college was "a racket" for "wretched fucks." Though it was mid-semester, she was heading out tomorrow for a tour of the Greek Isles with her wealthy family.

Another round of tequila shooters arrived, sent by a trio of frat boys a few tables away. We raised our glasses, then dutifully licked, pounded, and sucked. The tequila, not the boys.

While other women might look at these superficially attractive guys and see potential mates or even fun one-night stands, I saw impending headaches. Other girls got hot and bothered by their lines and pickups; I just got bothered.

But I hadn't always been that way.

"Do the frat boys, Nat!" our friend Polly cried. She was a sturdy corn-fed Nebraska girl—her family's farm was in a small town outside Lincoln, just a few miles away from ours. Well, not ours anymore, since Mom had sold out last year.

"Too easy," I said, having already sized up the trio. The first guy had been constantly checking sports scores on TV while his leg jogged. The second was a bleary mess whose own friends rolled their eyes at his drunkenness. The third one's grooming and clothing were fanatically perfect, and he kept checking his appearance in the mirror behind the bar.

"From left to right, then?" I said. "Inveterate gambler, habitual drunk, and—how should I put this?—the third is *ill-equipped*."

I sighed. Yep, those guys were too easy to read. Where was the excitement? Here I was at the same Lincoln bar I always went to, with the same crowd I always hung around. I had an early work shift tomorrow at one restaurant, a late one at the other, and classes to take and to teach on Monday. I'd been averaging five hours of sleep a night for the last few weeks. What was I even doing here?

I guessed I could sleep when I was dead.

"I've chosen my quarry for the evening," beautiful Jess said. "Ill-equipped is mine." As per her usual, she would pick up another conquest and take him back to his place—so she could leave when finished with him. "His type," she continued blithely, "usually make up for any shortcomings with their mouths. True story."

I told her, "And *you* better be careful, Jessebel, or else you'll collect another admirer who clings like lichen."

"I can't help it that this is the Bermuda Triangle"—she pointed at her crotch—"when guys venture there, they tend to stay."

I tapped my chin. "Oh, I thought you called it that because it's sucked in lots of seamen."

Between guffaws, she said, "That's a completely fair statement!"

We could laugh about it now, but I'd lived with the aftermath of her affairs: the desperate gifts, the late-night phone calls, the stalking.

What was the point of all the drama? Of all that angst? Dating, love, and sex were all overrated—as I'd repeatedly tried to explain to Jess. She would get this secretive smile and say, "You're gonna get blindsided one day. I only hope I'm there to see it. . . ."

When the laughter died down, Polly said, "Do *him*," with a wave at the door.

"Fine." Exhaling with boredom—*earn your booze, carny*—I turned toward the entrance. And saw the baddest-looking man I'd ever encountered.

His eyes were a vivid gold, stark against his thick black hair. He wore it longish, the ends brushing his collar. He had a roman nose that had likely been broken and a razor-thin scar that sliced down across both lips. A fighter?

Yet that didn't fit with his expensive clothing: a tailored black coat and dress shirt, dark gray slacks, black leather shoes and belt. Through Jess, I'd learned enough about fashion to recognize fine threads. His outfit probably cost more than my entire wardrobe.

When he stood at the bar and ordered a drink, I saw that he had three rings on one hand, a ring on his other thumb, and a wicked-looking tattoo peeking out from his starch-stiff collar. His style was a mix of privileged and street.

He was tall, with a lean, muscular build, and looked maybe twenty-nine or thirty, but his face was weary, as an older man's would be. With those rough-hewn features, he was ruggedly handsome, yet not classically so.

There was an aura of ennui about him, but he also seemed hyper-alert. What the hell? My internal manalyzer whirred with confusion. *Does not compute!*

I could feel my friends staring at me, but I was at a loss. "I . . . I got nothing." Was he a brawler or a rich playboy or both? I was also sensing top notes of *European*—along with strong under-tones of *dangerous!*

He was like a history book written in a script I'd never seen. Fascinating.

Jess pinched my side, drawing my attention to her smug grin. "You can close your mouth now, hooker." In a patronizing tone, she said, "Welcome to my world—where first meetings are always in slo-mo and the song 'At Last' repeats on a loop."

No, no, her world was angsty and overwrought. So why had my gaze darted back to the man?

"That's one hot piece of tackle—in a cage-fighter/*GQ* model mash-up kind of way." Jess wasn't going to let this go. "Probably gets more ass than a toilet seat. But he got you to look twice, which makes him a rare and wondrous creature, this bar's very own unicorn. Requires closer investigation, don't you think?"

I could question him, type him, then discard all thoughts of him. I was just tipsy enough to consider it. "I should go up and introduce myself?"

She nodded. "Unless you're a twat. Now, go forth with confidence, for you look cute-iful tonight."

Jess's style was *SEXY GLAM!* Mine? *See-me-love-me, mother-fleckers.* Yet tonight, I was wearing a hip-hugging suede skirt and a slinky red top—one of Jess's fashion-forward, low-cut numbers. For once, my bra wasn't a minimizer.

This outfit had come about because the clothes I'd normally wear—jeans and a turtleneck—were all in an overflowing laundry hamper. I'd worn the black knee-high boots Jess had bought me, to show appreciation in front of her.

I rose, smoothed my wavy hair over my shoulder, then tugged down my skirt, prompting Jess to give me a loud slap on the ass for encouragement. As I passed their table, Ill-Equipped and Habitual Drunk raised their glasses to me, which didn't hurt my confidence.

Once I was halfway over to Badass, his eyes locked on me. His gaze grew heated, and immediately the area felt smaller, warmer. I squelched the urge to fan myself. For the first time in my life, I was a little . . . *giddy.*

When I sidled up to him at the bar, he turned fully to me. Up close, he was even more intimidating, even more attractive. Taller than I'd thought.

His spellbinding eyes were the color of amber, irises ringed with black.

As I noted additional details—scarred knuckles, tattoos on his fingers under those rings, chiseled jawline clean-shaven—I perceived the heat coming off his big body. Then I got my first mind-numbing hit of his scent.

Crisp, masculine, intoxicating.

Blindsiding.

Speak, Nat. I had to look up to face him. "Uh, hi, I'm Natalie." I offered him my hand to shake. He didn't take it. *Okay . . .* I swallowed. "Can I buy you a drink?" Was that a vodka rocks he'd ordered? He didn't look like a 7&7 type of guy.

He canted his head, studying my face—the same way I studied men's expressions. Still he said nothing. Maybe he didn't speak the language. UNL had a lot of overseas students. "Drink?" I pointed to his untouched glass and mimed a shot.

His expression gave away so little, it was like I was talking to a wall.

As my cheeks flushed, I muttered, "Sooo, this went well. Good talk, buddy." With a mortified smile, I turned around—

A callused palm closed around my elbow, his rings cool compared to his skin. The contact was so electric, I shivered.

"Wait," he said. Had there been a subtle *v* sound to that *w*?

My heart leapt—maybe he was . . . Russian. I turned around, a genuine smile on my face now. "Are you from Russia?" I added, *"Zdrav-stvooi-tee."* Hello.

He still cupped my elbow. How could his hand be so hot? I

stifled imaginings of him cupping other parts of me, those hands spreading heat in their wake. . . .

"You speak my language, then?"

Bingo, a Russian! "A bit," I said with delight. I could grill him about the country, learning more about my birthplace! "I took a class or two." Or five. My master's had required fluency in a second language, and I'd chosen Russian.

He swept his glance around, his stance alert, as if someone might throw a punch at any second. Then he met my gaze once more. "Of all the men in this bar, you choose me to approach?" His English was very good, though heavily accented. "Are you looking for trouble?"

With a confidence I didn't feel, I teasingly said, "Maybe I am." I sounded breathy—I still hadn't caught my breath since he'd first touched me. "Have I found it?"

He glanced down, seeming surprised that he was still holding my arm. He abruptly released me, growing angrier by the second. "No, little girl. You have not." With a disgusted look, he turned away and stalked out.

I stared at the door, battling my bewilderment. *What just happened?* I'd seen interest in his gaze, hadn't I?

Yet then he'd acted like a vampire who'd discovered I was a fucking sunbeam.

CHAPTER 2

"What the hell, did you bite him?" "Did you insult his manhood?" "Let me smell your breath."

I'd stayed at the bar long enough to take my ribbing, because it was deserved and because I was a good goddamned sport. In general, I tried not to take myself too seriously—I called myself "the manalyst," after all. My life's motto: Joke 'em if they can't take a fuck.

A few shots later, I'd made my farewells and drunkenly set out for home, the pad I shared with Jess about five blocks away.

Tons of students were out, blowing off steam before midterms. It was a chilly fall night, with a full moon overhead. I pulled my jacket tighter. This close to harvest, the smell of ripe corn carried on the air—always a time of excitement for me since I was a farm girl at heart.

Yet another hand-holding couple passed me, and I gazed after them with a little wistfulness. Even if I had zero tolerance for men and their drama, I wouldn't mind having someone to snuggle up with this winter.

Someone to notice that my hands were cold and to hold them between his own.

Don't think of the Russian, don't think of . . .

Too late. I didn't exactly see myself strolling around campus all *fa la la* with a guy like that. But there'd been *something* about him—

A sudden sense that I was being watched hit me. Running a palm over my nape, I swept a glance around me. I only saw students meandering the streets, crowding into and out of various bars.

Probably just the tequila getting to me. Or stress from this week's insane work schedule. Safety-wise, the only scary thing about this campus was its deadly dullness.

Shaking off my unease, I dug my phone out of my pocket and checked e-mail. Nothing from Zironoff. I was beginning to think I'd gotten scammed by my investigator. It wouldn't be the first time one of them had ripped me off. Had I blown a year of tips on that DNA dickwad?

There was an e-mail from Mom, wondering why I was work- ing so much, worrying. If she ever found out about my quest, she'd take it personally, and we didn't need any more friction be- tween us.

Finally home, I meandered up the walk that wound through our yard. Our place was a cute mid-century bungalow, owned by Jess's parents. She called it the Bunghole, a perfect indication of her maturity level.

Inside, I shed my coat on the way to the kitchen. Chilled Gatorade, my secret hangover preventative, awaited me.

Hearing a sound from the front of the house, I called from the fridge, "Jess, that you?" I sounded *tanked.* "Whatcha doing back?" Maybe she'd struck out for once? We could commiserate.

No answer. I shrugged—the Bunghole emitted more banging and moans than a porn set.

I closed the fridge. Half of the door was covered with glossy pics from Jess's pervasive fashion magazines. My half was covered with postcards. She sent them from all the exciting locales she visited each break. Though I had an open invitation from her family and yearned to travel, I was constantly working. I'd never even been outside of the Midwest.

I'd never seen a seashore, much less the Eiffel Tower.

If I had a dollar for every time I'd gazed at these cards while promising myself, *One day* . . . well, I wouldn't need to work three jobs.

After downing my Gatorade dose, I swerved to my room, knotting my hair atop my head for a bath. Minutes later, when I eased back into the steaming water, another wave of drunken disappointment settled over me.

Now that I'd crashed and burned on my first pickup, I had to wonder how guys kept hitting on women, forever risking rejection. I mused over all the men I'd turned down—had I torpedoed their mojo?

I just couldn't figure out why that Russian had been so angry. And what the hell had been so off-putting about me? I wasn't a beauty like Jess, but I'd had male interest ever since I'd sprouted mammaries.

Curious, I ran my palms down my legs. They were fit from standing for hours on end while waiting tables, just as my arms were lean from hefting trays.

My hands ascended to my hips. Admittedly, they were wide, but my waist was narrow. And my breasts? They were fairly big, bobbing now in the water, coral-colored nipples puckering just above the surface. My rack had been on display tonight; that Russian hadn't given it a second glance.

But what if I *hadn't* repelled him? What would those hot, rough palms of his have felt like kneading my chest? At the thought, I experienced a surge of arousal so strong it startled me. My nipples stiffened even more. When the bathwater lapped at them, my breath hitched.

I'd talked to him for less than two minutes, seen him for less than ten, and his effect on me was this strong?

To hell with it—he could spurn me all he wanted to, but he couldn't keep me from fantasizing about him. With a mental *Screw you, Russian,* I reached between my legs to stroke, picturing his broad shoulders, his square jawline, his mouth. Those hooded golden eyes.

Even in the water, I could tell how slick my pussy had grown, my forefinger gliding along my lips, parting them. When I reached my clitoris, I found it swollen and supersensitive.

Sighing with need, I began to rub the bud in slow circles. My lids slid shut, and my knees fell wide against the sides of the tub. With my free hand, I petted my breasts, thumbing my nipples till they strained. . . .

I debated fetching one of my trusty vibrators from under the bed. But then I pictured the Russian kissing down my torso with that scorching expression, and realized B.O.B. could sit this one out.

Though I'd never had a guy go down on me, I could all but see the Russian's dark head between my thighs as he began to lick. Another stroke had me undulating in the water, gasping. His lips would be firm against my weeping flesh as he hungrily tongued me. He'd want me wetter and wetter, and I'd oblige.

In this fantasy, my aching clit wasn't throbbing against my finger, but against his greedy tongue.

As my body tensed for my orgasm, every inch of me seemed to gather in on itself, like a star about to explode. I rubbed my palm over my taut nipples, another shot of stimulation. So close, only a couple more strokes . . . I cracked open my eyes to watch myself writhing in the throes. Corner of my vision, strangest thing . . . through the steam, I thought I saw the Russian.

In my doorway, gazing down at me with smoldering eyes.

Broad chest heaving as he gnashed his teeth.

Muscles tensed as if he was about to fall upon me.

I squinted through the haze. Surely my muddled mind was imagining this? Was I *that* drunk? I was right at the razor's edge of coming, my toes already curling. As I met his mesmerizing imaginary gaze, my sneaky finger decided to give my clit one more shudder-inducing flick.

He exhaled sharply, big hands opening and closing. His expression said that he was about to seize my body and eat me up, bit by little bit.

So close . . . Then it registered that he was *actually* standing in the doorway of my bathroom.

The Russian had broken into my house and was spying on me, like some psycho!

I shot upright, drawing a breath to scream, but he cut me off: "Cover yourself, Natalie." His voice was rough, his brows drawn tight. "We need to talk." With a vile curse in Russian, he strode off.

Cover myself? Talk?

Night-stalker-serial-killers didn't say shit like that!

I was so confounded, I couldn't manage a scream. My mouth moved, but no words came out. I scrambled from the tub, reaching for a towel, and secured it around me. Even in the midst of this turmoil, I hissed in a breath as the terry cloth rubbed my nipples.

Casting around for a weapon, I plucked off the cover of the toilet tank, hefting it over my shoulder in a batter's pose. From the safety of the bathroom, I called, "I don't know what you're doing in my house. But you need to leave *now*. Or I'll call the cops!"

"I was sent here by your father," he replied from my bedroom.

I swayed, and my makeshift weapon faltered. Considering his Russian accent—and the timing—I knew he had to be talking about my biological father. Still I said, "My dad died six years ago."

"You know that's not the one I'm referring to."

In a rush, I demanded, "What do you know about him? Who *are* you? Why did you break into my house?"

"Break in?" Scoffing sound. "Your key was under a plastic rock. For anyone to find," he added in a chiding tone. "Your father is a very important—and wealthy—man. He's assigned me to be your new bodyguard."

"Bodyguard! Why would I *need* one?"

"Anyone in a family with a ten-figure net worth"—I gasped at that—"needs protection."

"You're saying he's a . . . billionaire?" Was I getting punked? Maybe that was in rubles or something.

"Correct. His name is Pavel Kovalev. He just learned of your existence a short while ago, through the investigator you hired."

I now knew my father's name.

I'd initially wanted to learn about my birth parents because I possessed an overdeveloped sense of curiosity. Then it had occurred to me that I might have gotten my sense of curiosity *from* my parents.

After that, I'd imagined a man and a woman in their forties, mired in endless wondering about the child they'd given up to a Russian orphanage twenty-four years ago. The thought had pushed me to take on yet another job, to keep digging relentlessly. I'd searched not just for my sake, but for *theirs*.

But he'd never known I existed? Then I frowned. "My investigator? Zironoff? He hasn't returned my e-mails or calls."

"He was made aware that we would be handling this inter-
nally going forward."

"Oh." *Thanks for the heads-up, dickwad.* At least I hadn't gotten ripped off again. No, I'd . . . succeeded.

After six years of searching.

I tottered from shock—and residual tequila. I returned the
tank cover to its spot before it dropped on my head like a cartoon
anvil. "If you're my bodyguard, then why were you spying on me
in the bath?" I snagged my pink robe, hastily swapping it for the
towel. "Huh?"

Silence. When I didn't hear *anything*, I had a weird spike of
panic that this man—a new source of answers, an alleviator of
curiosity—had vanished as quickly as he'd appeared. "Are you
there?"

Trying not to think of how short my silk robe was—and
what he'd just caught me doing—I poked my head out of the
bathroom; no sign of him. So I cautiously padded toward my
room. "You didn't answer my question. Hey, why are you in
my closet?"

He emerged from the walk-in. "Where is your luggage?"

"What does that have to do with anything?" I didn't have real
luggage. I'd packed for school in laundry baskets and boxes.

He raked his eyes over me in my robe, lingering on choice
parts of me. Seeming to shake himself, he snagged my sizable
book bag, dumping library books on the floor. *The History of Sexuality, The Boundaries of Eros, A Thorn in the Flesh.*

"What the hell, Russian?!" If he'd noticed the titles—my
general field was the history of women and gender—they didn't
faze him.

When he tossed the empty bag to me, I barely caught it. "Pack necessities only. Everything else will be provided for you."

I gaped down at the bag then back up. "I'm not doing anything, not until you tell me where you think I'm going. And why this can't wait until tomorrow. For all I know, you could be a human trafficker!"

"And *this* would be my m.o.?" He exhaled with a kind of surprised impatience, as if no one had ever argued with him before—as if he'd done this to a hundred other girls, and every one of them had started packing with a *Yes, sir*. "My name is Aleksandr Sevastyan. Call me Sevastyan." Like Sebastian with a *v*. "I've worked for your father for decades. Kovalev is keen to meet you." He added almost to himself, "I've never seen him so eager."

"How can he be sure I'm his daughter? Zironoff could've made a mistake."

"Nyet," he said, enunciating a hard no. "You offered up your DNA. Kovalev already had his on file. There is no mistake."

"If he's so eager to meet me, why didn't he come himself? Why not just call me?"

"As I said, he is a very important man in Russia, and at present, he's caught up with work concerns that can't be handled by anyone but himself. He trusts me implicitly." Sevastyan moved to my bedroom window, peering out between the blind slats with the same wariness I'd noticed in the bar. "If you pack a bag and get on a plane with me, he will meet you at his estate outside Moscow in less than fourteen hours. This is your father's wish— one I *will* be carrying out."

My manalyzer might be cocked up, but my bullshit detector was still pinging clear; against all odds, I was starting to believe this guy.

Reality began to set in. "But I've got shifts tomorrow." Which I wouldn't need if my search could *end*. "And my classes!" As soon as the words left my lips, I felt silly. What would this towering, tattooed Russian understand about a Husker's advanced degree? What would he care?

Surprisingly, he said, "Your schooling is important to you. We understand this. But your father wants you in Russia now. Not next month or next week. You leave tonight."

"Does he always get what he wants?"

"Without fail." Sevastyan checked his expensive-looking watch. "Our flight leaves in an hour. I'll explain more on the way to the airport."

Airport? Flight? I'd never been on a plane. Yet I could be in Russia in less than a day. *Don't think of the postcards, don't think . . .*

Even Jess had never been to Russia!

Then I straightened. "Again, what's the rush? And news flash—I don't have a passport! How am I going to get into Moscow without one?"

"I'll work that out. It's not a problem." Sevastyan shut off the lamp beside my bed, dimming the room.

"How can that not be a problem?" I glanced at the tattoos on his scarred fingers and had a sinking suspicion, but tried to ignore it. *Nope, not possible . . .*

"I understand that all of this is a lot to take in. But things are different for you now, Natalie. Some rules . . . no longer apply."

I squared my shoulders. "Not good en—"

"Let me make this simple for you," he interrupted. "I'm walking out of this house in five minutes. You can either walk out with me, packed and dressed, or leave in that little robe"—his piercing eyes swept over me, over my nipples pressing against the silk—"thrown over my shoulder. Your choice."

His tone and bearing left no doubt that he was dead serious about kidnapping me. This ruble-billionaire's bodyguard was going to finish his job—period. Still, I dared another question. "Why haven't you said anything about my mother?"

When his eyes narrowed, I again got the impression that not many people challenged this man.

"*Four* minutes."

I folded my arms over my chest. "I can't just sign on for this, Sevastyan. Not without more answers."

"Which I promise you will get when we are under way."

Worst case scenario: if I didn't like what he had to say, I could run from him at the airport, straight into the arms of security guards.

Sevastyan crossed to stand in front of me. The soft light caressed his hard features. They were almost *too* masculine. His rugged jaw was wide, the bridge of his aquiline nose slightly askew, giving him a roguish look. But on the whole, he was devastatingly attractive, with that dangerous aura about him.

"You must trust me, pet," he said as he reached forward to gently grasp my chin.

At his touch, that dizzying heat filled me once more. It was just the liquor at work, I assured myself, or exhaustion catching up with me. Or my unsuccessful bath time.

"You know my intent isn't to harm you," he murmured. "Otherwise, I could have led you from that bar earlier, taking you somewhere for us to be alone." My breaths went shallow at that. "Would you not have left with me?"

In—a—heartbeat.

He leaned down to say at my ear, "That's right, *Natalya*. You would have followed where I led."

"Um . . . uh . . ." I was still recovering from the sound of my name in his raspy accent when I felt his warm breaths. Oh, God, had his lips ghosted over my ear? If his scent and heat had affected me, this grazing contact made my legs weak.

He drew back, expression inscrutable. "So why don't you stop acting like you haven't already made up your mind to come with me."

"P-pardon?"

"You were decided as soon as you heard the words *Russia, father,* and *go.*" His firm lips thinned, making that razor-slice scar whiten.

"That's not necessarily true—"

"Time's up, pet." He bent down to loop an arm around my ass, hoisting me over his shoulder.

CHAPTER 3

"*P*UT ME DOWN!" I screeched, wriggling over the Neanderthal's shoulder as he strode out the front door. Cold air swept up my robe, chilling me in unfamiliar places. "You can't do this!"

He tightened his grip on my ass. "Doing it." His tone was casual; he wasn't even out of breath.

Another futile round of squirming. "Please put me down. We'll go back inside"—*I'll run away*—"and then I can pack, just like you said."

Three passersby ambled down the sidewalk, huge no-neck guys in letterman jackets. Husker football players! They stopped and gawked.

Hanging upside down, blood rushing to my head, I opened my mouth to scream for their help—then hesitated. Did I believe what Sevastyan had told me? Was I dealing with an overbearing asshole of a bodyguard—or being abducted? If I screamed, the jocks would kick Sevastyan's ass, which wouldn't help me get to Russia—

This decision, just like the previous one, was yanked out of my hands. Sevastyan turned to face them, slowly shaking his head. Whatever look he gave them made three massive football players *hotfoot the other way.*

As they vanished, I pounded on Sevastyan's back in frustration, stunned to feel a holster. He was carrying a gun! I didn't have time to register my shock before he was shoving me into the front passenger seat of a luxe Mercedes.

As soon as he shut the door, I lunged for the handle, but he'd already clicked the lock, holding it down with the remote.

At his door, he gave me a look of warning through the window. He knew he'd have to release the lock button to get in, giving me a chance to escape. The unlock game. I would time it perfectly, reflexes like lightning—

Shit! He'd opened his door, then jammed the lock button back down before I could open my side!

He slid his big body into the car. "Better luck with that next time."

"This is kidnapping!"

"I told you my intentions. Gave you a countdown." He started the engine and pulled away from the curb. "Understand me, Natalie, I do exactly what I say I'll do. Always." He smoothly executed turn after turn, as if he knew this town as well as I did. "And right now I'm telling you that I will get you safely to your father in Russia."

"How do you think you'll get me through airport security like this?" I waved my hands to indicate my robe. "I don't even have my purse!"

"We're going to a private airport. And by the time we land in Moscow, you'll have all new clothes brought to the jet."

New clothes? Jet? Was he serious?

His gaze landed on my legs, on my half-bared thighs. And

with that one dark glance, my skin flushed. I couldn't help recalling the way he'd looked down on me in the bath.

Like a hungry predator eyeing tender prey.

Like I was already a caught thing, his to enjoy. I shivered.

"Are you cold?" he asked. "You look . . . chilled."

Chilled? Oh. Because my nipples were still jutting. Yes, I was cold, but my body was also suffering the aftereffects of my foiled masturbation attempt. To be so close, drawing in on myself . . .

In some ways, I felt the same now. Tense, drawn, my skin prickling with awareness each time he looked at me.

When I didn't answer him, Sevastyan turned on the heater, and hot air blasted against my chest, over the hypersensitive tips of my breasts. I nearly yelped when I felt the seat warmer toasting the cleft of my ass. In the close confines of the car, I got another hit of his mind-numbing scent.

So much stimulation. Could he see me trembling?

Once we were on the main highway heading out of town, the car purring along at eighty miles per hour, he commanded, "Put on your seat belt."

I didn't like this tone at all, heard it constantly at my server jobs. "Or *what*?" I narrowed my eyes. "And did you really call me *pet* earlier?"

"When I tell you to do something, it's in your best interest to do it, *pet*." Without warning, he reached over to yank my seat belt into place, roughly grazing my breasts with his forearm, filling my head with his scent. I squirmed on the hot seat, feeling dazed by this arrogant man.

I remembered one time when I'd been written up for public intoxication after a football game; I'd been mentally yelling at myself to sober up, willing myself to recover my wits so I could talk the cop out of the expensive citation. *Stop chuckling, Nat, and answer the nice officer! Not OSSIFER, dumbass! Do NOT touch his shiny, shiny badge, do not—DAMN IT, NAT!*

I felt like that now: under the influence.

Sevastyan affected me in a way I couldn't shake. I was experiencing a bewildering attraction to him, some inexplicable connection.

And no matter how bad an idea it was, I kept wanting—metaphorically—to touch his badge.

No, no, no—I needed to concentrate on getting information out of him. "Do you keep your promises, Sevastyan?"

"To you and your father alone."

"You promised me answers."

His hands tightened on the wheel, those sexy rings of his digging into the leather. "Once we are on the plane."

"Why not now? I need to know more about my parents."

He didn't deign to respond, just monitored the rearview mirror with that wary alertness.

I remembered his earlier demeanor, checking the street through my bedroom blinds. "What's up with this paranoia? We're in Lincoln, Nebraska; the most dangerous thing that's ever happened here was when this Russian asshole kidnapped an unwitting co-ed—*in her robe.*"

The speedometer hit triple digits.

"Are we . . . are we being followed?"

Another glance into the rearview. "Not at present."

"Which indicates we might have been in the past—or perhaps could be in the future?" This was too bizarre. "Am I in some kind of danger?" Questions about my parents and past faded as dread about my immediate future surfaced.

With reluctance, he said, "Kidnapping for ransom is always a fear."

I narrowed my eyes. "I don't buy that. What you just described sounds like a *chronic* problem, or a theoretical one. Yet you broke into my house and demanded that we leave in five minutes, which sounds like an *acute* problem. So what happened between the time I saw you in the bar and the time you entered my home?"

Sidelong glance. "I think you have your father's cunning."

"Answer me. What happened?"

"Kovalev called and gave me the order to get you on a plane. Which means it's as good as done."

A sudden thought struck me. "How *long* have you been my bodyguard, Sevastyan?"

"Not long," he hedged.

"How—long?"

He hiked his broad shoulders. "A little over a month."

And I'd never known. "Have you been following me around? Watching me all this time?"

A muscle ticked in his wide jaw. "I've been watching *over* you."

Then he would know me better than I could even imagine. So what would a man like him think of me?

When he turned off the highway at an obscure exit, I cried, "Wait! Where are we going? There's no airport out this way. Not even an executive one."

"I had to arrange an alternative departure point."

Alternative? I'd promised myself that if I didn't like his answers, I'd flee into the arms of a security guard. I'd gotten no answers, and now had serious doubts about running into any guards.

After a few miles, he turned onto a dirt road that bisected a cornfield. We drove and drove until a clearing appeared ahead, what looked like a crop-duster airstrip. At one end, a jet awaited, beacon lights flashing, engines radiating heat in the night air.

To take me to Russia. This was all . . . real.

Sevastyan parked near the jet, but didn't open his door. "I understand you have questions," he said in a milder tone. "I'll answer any I can when we're in the air. But you must believe me, Natalie, you won't regret taking this step. You'll enjoy your new life very much."

"New life?" I sputtered. "What are you talking about? I happen to enjoy my current life."

"Do you, pet? *You* sought *him*," Sevastyan said. "Relentlessly. Something was driving you."

I glanced away, unable to argue with that.

"And now you'll never have to work again, can buy anything you like. You can travel the world, see all the places on those post-cards on your refrigerator."

My dream. "This is a lot to take in, and I don't like making big decisions under pressure."

"Will it suffice for you to know that Kovalev is a good man, and he wants to make up for all the years he's missed with you?"

"If our situations were reversed, could you take this step?"

He nodded easily. "When I first started working for Kova-lev's organization, I trusted that my life would be better with him in it. I've never regretted my decision." He must've seen I was still unconvinced. Exhaling with frustration, he ordered, "Just stay here."

He climbed out of the car and crossed to the jet with long-legged strides. The pilot—a tall, muscular blond in a uniform— met him at the bottom of the stairs, gesturing and speaking heatedly. I caught the cadences of Russian, but couldn't make out the words over the humming engines.

Out of habit, I surveyed the man, noting that his well-worn belt was cinched tighter than its regular notch and his shoes were meticulously polished. Recent illness? Lots of downtime? Then I saw his hands, saw the same kinds of tattoos that marked Sevastyan's fingers.

At that, my niggling suspicion couldn't be stifled. I'd studied all aspects of the land of my birth enough to know about the Russkaya Mafiya—and how they favored tattoos like that.

And really, what were the odds that a billionaire over there *wasn't* tied to organized crime in some way? Not to mention that Sevastyan had kidnapped me, with the intention to smuggle me—passportless—into the country. How could somebody do that without a shady, look-the-other-way bribe?

Had I scrimped and toiled and searched, only to connect myself to a mobster?

The pilot continued to vent. My thoughts continued to race.

Then silent, menacing Sevastyan took one ominous step forward; the pilot backed down, hands raised.

A single step had cowed that big pilot. Maybe Sevastyan could've taken those three jocks. Because he was dangerous.

And he wanted to drag me into his world.

Follow the chain of logic, Nat. If Kovalev was *mafiya*, then no good could come of this hasty midnight jaunt to the motherland.

Did I believe I was in some kind of danger? Maybe. Did I trust Sevastyan to protect me? Not more than I trusted myself.

At that moment, I decided to *decline* the "new life" that some strange man on the other side of the world envisioned for me. If Kovalev wanted to talk to me, he could pick up the phone!

And Sevastyan? I still felt that bewildering attraction to him, that weird sense of connection. I forced myself to ignore it.

With him occupied, I cracked open my door and slipped

outside. I drew my robe tight, stealing closer to the cornfield. Naturally the one night I needed to escape the mob, the moon was a bright ball in the sky. At least the field would provide cover. This close to harvest, the stalks were tall and dense, the leaves lush.

Almost there. My breaths smoked. Almost—

"Natalie," Sevastyan bellowed, "do not run!"

I took off in a sprint, charging into the rows.

CHAPTER 4

*C*orn leaves slapped my face, raking my hair. My bare feet kicked up loose soil.

How much of a head start had I managed? Was he already crashing behind me?

"Stop this, Natalie!"

I gave a cry. My God, he was fast! I'd felt like prey before; now I literally was. This man was running me down, bent on capturing me! I dug deeper, sprinting even faster—

One second I was fleeing at full speed, the next I was flying. He'd lunged for me, snagging me around the waist. At the last instant, he twisted and took the impact on his back, crushing stalks beneath us.

"Damn you! Let go of me!" I struggled against him. Like fighting a steel vise.

Before I could blink, he'd flipped me to my back onto a mat of leaves.

"Get off me!" I battered his chest with the bottoms of my fists.

Huge and furious above me, he wedged his hips between my

legs, snagging my wrists in one big hand. "Do not ever run from me again." The moon shone down on him, highlighting the tight lines of his face. He seemed to be grappling with his fury, drawing on some inner iron control.

"Let me go!"

Over the familiar scents of rich soil, fragrant crops, and cold night, I detected his scent: aggression and raw masculinity. His shirt had gaped open, and I could see more of his skin, with the edge of another tattoo just visible past the material.

"Sevastyan, release me. *Please*."

At that word, his grip on my wrists loosened a degree. "I don't want to hurt you," he said in a gravelly voice. "Only to protect you." Behind that inscrutable mask, so much was going on, but I could read so little.

Under the moonlight, his prominent cheekbones shaded his lean cheeks. His collar-length black hair gleamed like a raven's feather, the ends tripping across his jawline. Wavering almost hypnotically.

"You must remain with me," he grated, his gaze on my lips, his brows drawn tight. He looked like he was struggling not to *kiss* me.

Kiss? What was happening here? Confusion began to drown out my panic; I had nothing to draw on as a reference for my predicament—because I'd never been in a situation like this.

A sexual situation I didn't control.

I was embroiled in dangerous circumstances with a mysterious stranger, but I felt no fear. I felt . . . anticipation. And I suspected the lack of control was fueling it.

Was danger turning me on? The tension between us seemed to shift; as smoothly as a machine switching gears, my confusion morphed into hazy heat. I hadn't known I had this in me! *Who am I??*

When my gaze dropped, I spied the shadowy bulge in his pants. He wasn't indifferent to me! He might've disdained me in the bar, but he couldn't disguise his erection straining to be freed.

At the sight of it, arousal muddled my thoughts like a fog rolling into my mind. I'd heard the expression *stupid with lust*. I was getting there.

"Sevastyan?" That feeling of connection surged within me. Desire, need, and something more. "What do you want from me?"

No answer. All I could hear was our breaths.

In this position, he could unzip his fly and be inside me in a heartbeat's time, covering me on the ground. Like animals in the dirt.

Him. Inside me. Here.

The mere thought made my body vibrate with a need so strong, I suspected I might allow him to do anything he wanted to me. My staggering level of arousal began to unnerve me more than this entire situation. I had no control with him, needed to get away!

I shook my head hard. "You let me go *now*." I squirmed in his grip, digging my bare heels into the ground to propel myself back. Managed maybe a foot.

He looked at me like I was insane to defy him. So why wasn't I terrified of him? No, I was *furious*—at him, at my out-of-control body. Another heel-digging lunge back.

With his free hand, he gripped my waist and yanked me back against him, forcing my thighs wider.

His gaze descended, his eyes going wide before narrowing intently.

I felt cold air between my legs, just as I saw that my robe had come open at the belted waist. Everything below was exposed. My pale skin glowed in the moonlight, the trimmed thatch of red curls stark in comparison.

I was too stunned to react, pinned by his gaze. His lids grew heavy, his nostrils flaring. His broad chest seemed to struggle for breath. I was naked from the waist down but had no way to cover myself. I twisted my arms to free my wrists—until I saw that look of his.

Dark, hungry, molten. Dangerous. As before, I felt like his captured prey, his to enjoy.

My fury dwindled. When my body decided to soften beneath his, he gave a curt nod, as if I'd pleased him, and his free hand landed on my bare hip. Skin to skin. He groaned at the contact; I shivered from the electric heat of his rough palm. Hadn't I imagined those hands kneading me everywhere?

Shaking, I watched as he straightened his ringed thumb from my hip until it reached my mons. He brushed the tip of his finger along the edge of my curls. It was so slow and unexpected, so tender, I couldn't bite back a moan.

He touched me as if with . . . reverence.

I no longer saw signs of that iron control; instead he looked *lost*.

Like I probably looked in that moment.

His cock pulsed in his pants, drawing my attention. At the sight of that long, heavy length, my pussy clenched for it. I murmured, "Sevastyan?" as my hips rolled. "What are you doing to me?" He'd somehow spellbound me, making me feel empty and desperate.

For the second time tonight, I was heading toward an orgasm.

Still riveted to my sex, he grated words in Russian, something about how he couldn't be expected to deny himself in the face of this. How *no one* should expect him to.

I'd never been more confused in my life. "Are you . . . are you going to kiss me?"

With his accent thicker than I'd heard it, he rasped, "Would you want a man like me to take your mouth?" His thumb ring glinted when he gave another slow stroke.

Good question. I answered myself when words spilled from my lips: "Try it and see."

"You think I'd stop with a kiss?"

"You assume I'd want you to?"

My reply seemed to wake him from a daze. As if burned, he jerked his hands away, his expression transforming from lost to disgusted. Again, he told me, "Cover yourself." Now he was as furious as I'd been before, but I had no idea what I'd done.

I swatted the ends of my robe down as he levered himself to his feet.

When he seized my hand, yanking me up, sanity resumed— as if the Natalie I'd known all my life had decided to rejoin us.

What kind of madness had just possessed me? I clutched my robe with a shaking hand. I'd just let this man touch me, this *stranger*, and had been rolling my hips for more.

If he'd made a move to fuck me on the ground, I thought . . . I thought I might have let him.

Fist clenched around my upper arm, he dragged me along. "If you run from me again, I will catch you. It's what I do." He locked his gaze on mine. "And then I'll spread you over my knees and whip your plump ass until you know better."

I stumbled at that, but he hauled me back up. Striding on, he scowled down at my bouncing breasts.

Braless in silk. Nothing left to the imagination. "I won't run if you don't force my hand! I don't want to go with you. I know what you are. You're *mafiya*. Which means my father is too." *Deny it, deny it. Laugh in my face.*

Sevastyan set his jaw, dragging me along faster.

No denial. My father, this man, that pilot were all *mafiya*.

"You can't force me to go to him—ow!" Sudden sharp pain dug into my bare feet; I'd stepped on a strand of briars.

Without even slowing his stride, Sevastyan swooped me up as if I were weightless.

I had no choice but to wrap my arms around his neck. "Just wait—I don't want to get caught up in anything like that!" My mouth was inches from his throat, from his bobbing Adam's apple. His heat seeped into me, and I could feel his heartbeat; though he was no longer running, it sped up sharply when I murmured, "Sevastyan, *please*."

"You're already caught up," he said, the words like a sentencing.

We emerged from the field. Desperate, I whispered, *"Pozhalu-ista, nyet."* Please, no.

"Natalya," he rasped, "I won't let you go. I *can't*. Resign yourself."

As we neared the plane, the pilot raised his brows at me. I could only imagine what he was thinking. I was in Sevastyan's arms, my hair a tangle, my nipples protruding.

When the blond smirked, Sevastyan grated in Russian, "You leer at *his* daughter? I should give him your eyes for that."

The pilot swallowed; I gaped. With crystal clarity, I understood that Sevastyan was capable of such brutality.

Then he was carrying me up the steps. Shit, shit, shit! Oh, God, this was happening!

The pilot followed us up, pressing a button to close the outer door. By the time he'd closeted himself in the cockpit, the door had sealed closed with a hiss.

Trapped.

CHAPTER 5

As Sevastyan deposited me into one of several seats, I grappled for words, but stunned disbelief and a roiling anger rendered me mute. He'd forced me onto this plane against my will. Was *kidnapping* me.

I wanted to say, "You're not going to get away with this," or even "You're going to pay for this." But I suspected both would be lies.

"We leave directly," he told me, his voice inflectionless. "Put on your seat belt."

Despite how pissed I was, I wouldn't argue with him this time. In my mind, *private jet* was just another way of saying *baby plane*. And hadn't this crop-duster-esque runway seemed short? I knew sub-nothing about flying, but surely that wasn't normal?

As I strapped myself in with shaking hands, I surveyed the luxurious interior. There were twelve seats, along with a plush sofa, a big-screen TV, a stocked media console, and an extended dining table. Polished wood accented all the amenities.

Nothing but the best for the mob.

Sevastyan didn't sit. He stared out the windows, still vigilant.

I wondered what he would look like relaxed. "I'm in immediate danger, aren't I?"

Gazing out into the night, he gave me an unconcerned shrug. As good as a *yes*. Before I could ask more, the engines grew louder. I clenched the armrests of my seat, nails sinking into the buttery soft leather. When we started easing forward, I found myself telling Sevastyan, "I've never flown before."

Our speed increased so rapidly, I was thrown back into the seat. The jet thundered down the runway. Outside the window, the cornfield zoomed by. Even Sevastyan took a seat on the sofa across from me.

"I-I've been on a train."

He spread an arm over the back of the sofa. "It's *just* like that."

"Was that a joke?"

Face grim, he said, "Unlikely, pet."

"You really need to stop calling me th—"

The nose of the plane was rising! I squeezed my eyes shut.

But taking off was surprisingly smooth. When the pressure eased and I realized we were in the air, I cracked open my eyes and popped my ears. Gradually, I released my death grip.

Several things competed for my attention. I couldn't decide whether I wanted to watch the fading lights of Lincoln, the full moon glimmering off the right-side wing, or Sevastyan trying to relax.

My mysterious companion won out. He stretched his long legs in front of him, then rolled his head on his neck. At some point, he'd refastened the buttons of his shirt. Clearly, whatever temporary insanity had occurred in the field had passed.

When we leveled off, the lights of the cabin dimmed, reminding me that I was sequestered with a larger-than-life type of man—one who had pinned me to the ground and felt me up only minutes ago.

Just as I opened my mouth to ask him what that was all about, he said, "As promised, I'll answer your questions. But you need to wash yourself first."

I followed his pointed gaze with my fingers, found a leaf in my hair. I peered down at my dirty legs and bare feet. I didn't embarrass easily, but now my cheeks flushed with heat.

"There are showers in both of the suites."

Chin raised, I unfastened my seat belt, rose with an indifferent air, then started toward the back. Over my shoulder, I said, "When I return, prepare for an interrogation."

In a dry tone, he replied, "I'm not going anywhere, Natalie."

◆

*F*ifteen minutes later, I emerged into the main cabin—clean, sober, and dressed in one of Sevastyan's button-down shirts.

After a shower in a large marble enclosure stocked with high-end toiletries, I'd padded back to the suite's bed and stared down at my abused robe. The back had looked like modern art, in a pallet of greens, yellows, and blacks. And it had reeked of corn, a treacly sweet smell. No way I could wear it again.

I'd surveyed the suite, lighting on an expensive piece of luggage. Sevastyan's. He'd helped himself to kidnapping me, so I'd felt justified borrowing a shirt. Slipping on the starched button-down, I'd shivered, enveloped by his crisp scent, covered from my neck to almost my knees.

With nothing between my skin and the material, I hadn't even been surprised when arousal swept over me again; in the shower my skin had been hypersensitive. . . .

Now Sevastyan raked his gaze over me, head to toe, giving me an *are-you-fucking-kidding-me?* look.

I frowned in turn. Everything was covered. "I'm just borrow-ing it until I get my promised new clothes, okay?" When I sat at the opposite end of the sofa, he pinched the bridge of his nose.

"Tension headache?"

Without looking at me, he answered, "You could say that."

"I can't imagine the pressure you must be feeling," I said in all truthfulness. "Do you do this kidnapping stuff a lot?"

Scowl from the Russian.

"It's a fair question, considering that you and my father are involved in organized crime."

Without missing a beat, he asked, "Why do you persist in thinking that?"

"Your tattoos. The pilot's. I've researched your country enough to know about the Russkaya Mafiya and their love of ink. Plus, that would be the absolute worst outcome to my years-long quest." I tapped my chin, musing, "And yet totally in keeping with my fortunes over the last few weeks—"

"A worse outcome than never knowing Kovalev?" Sevastyan asked, irritation scoring his tone. "You speak about things you don't yet understand, little girl. But you will. . . ."

CHAPTER 6

"*T*hings I don't understand? Like crime?"

Stony gaze.

"Oh, God, he is *mafiya*." I grew queasy at the idea. Why had I ever hired that investigator? My biological father was a thug. "What have you gotten me into?"

"You sought him," Sevastyan repeated.

"You're not really a bodyguard, are you? You're probably his, what? His professional hit man? His enforcer?" I gave a nervous laugh. "That's why you have those scars on your knuckles—from beating people senseless, right? And exactly what business is Kovalev 'caught up' in?" My hysteria building, I said, "A turf war against a rival gang?" Yes, it took a lot to ruffle me, but once I lost my cool, I tended to go big.

Sevastyan didn't answer, so . . . *ding, ding, ding*. A turf war. And I was on my way there.

He finally said, "Are you done?"

"Tell—me."

"Your father is part of the Bratva, the brotherhood. It's like a

criminal aristocracy. He's *vor v zakone*, the head of our organiza-
tion, answering to no one."

The blatant pride in Sevastyan's tone made my queasiness in-
crease. "So I'm a freaking *mafiya* princess, then? That's the real
reason I'm in danger, isn't it?"

"Your father is embattled. Adversaries would love to see him
fall. And there is another *vor* who might hurt you in order to hurt
Kovalev. Or use you to coerce him."

"Again, that sounds like a *chronic* problem."

Sevastyan studied my face, as if debating how much to tell
me. "After I left the bar, I found out that two very dangerous
men flew from Moscow hours ago, heading to America—sent by
Kovalev's bitterest enemy. There's a good chance they were coming here."

Fuck. This little *mafiya* princess was in trouble. "You're taking
me straight to the source of the conflict! Turn this jet around, and
let me disappear! I could go out west, get lost."

He glanced over at me, must've sensed I was about to freak.
"I was sent here to keep you safe. If you do as I say, then you'll
have nothing to fear. And there was another reason we felt it im-
perative that you leave tonight. When you return to Russia, those
men will follow you—instead of questioning your loved ones."

"They would hurt Mom? Jess?" Alarm for them razored
through me.

"Without hesitation. Unless we signal that you've left Lincoln—which we will do in Moscow."

"I have to warn them! Just in case." Would Sevastyan let me
call?

"There's a phone in the cabinet beside you."

"How much can I tell them?"

"That depends on how much you trust them not to tell others. You have five minutes."

Remembering the last time he'd said that, I didn't waste time arguing. With the headset clutched in my damp palm, I rang my mom. What could I tell her? Things were already tense between us.

Those last few years with Dad's illness had been tough on her, on us both, and after his death, we'd drifted apart. Then, this past summer, she'd remarried, moving upstate with her new guy. But I was happy for her. She and her hubby had an RV. Apparently, RVing was a lifestyle choice. They went to "roundups" with other RVers.

I got her answering machine. Luckily, she was on the road for a week. I left a message, trying to sound casual. "Hi, Mom, just calling to check in. Have fun at the . . . roundup," I said, feeling like a rube in front of Sevastyan. "Love you."

Jess answered on the fourth ring, snapping with impatience: "Having my box eaten right now; this better be good—"

"Jess! I've only got a couple of minutes to talk."

"Nat, is that you?"

"Yeah, and I need you to listen to me. You can't go home tonight."

"Why can't I go back to the Bunghole . . ." Jess trailed off, then gasped. "Oh, my God! Did you hook up with that DUDE FROM THE BAR? The unicorn!"

Sevastyan quirked a brow. Of course he'd heard.

"In a manner of speaking." Yes, I was presently wearing nothing but his shirt—with my body still thrumming from his touch—but not by choice!

Making her voice syrupy, Jess crooned, "Awww, our little Nat's gonna lose her skin tag tonight."

My eyes went wide, darting to Sevastyan. "Shut it, Jess! Look, here's the deal—that guy was sent here to take me to Russia because my biological father is some kind of *mafiya* criminal-lord type."

"Huh." Completely unfazed, she said, "Actually, that explains a lot about you." Then, to her boy toy, she said, "I don't remember telling you to stop."

"Will you pay attention? I'm on a jet heading to Moscow—"

"Get the fuck out!"

"—and some rival goons might go by the house. Can you stay away until after your trip?"

"You mean I'll be forced to buy all new clothes and luggage for Greece? My parents will believe this excuse as much as all my others." Growing serious, she said, "Are you safe?"

I gazed at Sevastyan's face, searching. "If I don't call you in a week . . ." I trailed off. Then what? Notify the embassy? What hope would they have against the Red Mafiya? "I *will* call you in a week."

"Just be careful, babe," Jess said. "Oh, and tell the unicorn that if anything happens to you, I will skull-fuck him, 'kay? How do you say 'desecrate his motherfucking corpse' in Russki?"

Sevastyan tapped his watch.

"Gotta go, message received—and stay safe yourself." Hanging up, I turned to him. "It's morning in Russia. Why don't you give me your boss's number, so I can explain some things to him?" *Customer service in your organization requires a complete overhaul.* "Share some of my thoughts."

"Kovalev's in a congress." At my nonplussed look, Sevastyan explained, "It's like a summit meeting for *vory*."

"Don't you think my going to Russia will just magnify this problem?"

"We have men there, safeguards in place. Your father's compound is a fortress."

A *mafiya* compound? I could just see it: some gray and dingy Soviet-era monolith. Inside, the décor would be a riot of gaudy knickknacks, selected on the basis not of taste, but of price. And Kovalev . . . I pictured a hulking brute in a tracksuit, wearing so many thick gold chains that his neck looked like a ring toss. He probably kept white tigers and had a diamond-encrusted toilet.

Ugh. I frowned at Sevastyan. "Forcing me back there wasn't always the plan?"

He shook his head.

"So if those bad guys hadn't headed to the States, would you have kept spying on me from afar?"

"I would have remained in place—*protecting* you—until your father could travel here to meet you."

"If you were my sole bodyguard, when did you sleep?"

"While you were in class or at work. When I knew you'd be around others for a while." That meant he'd gotten even fewer hours than I had. He cocked his head. "I can sleep when I'm dead, no?"

Exactly what I'd thought. "This is a lot for Kovalev to put on your shoulders." I couldn't imagine a task like that—having another person's life in my hands.

"I would do anything he asked me."

"Is devotion like that common in your . . . organization?"

"He's been a father to me since I was young. I owe him my life," Sevastyan said in a tone that told me he would *not* be unpacking that comment.

"Then in a way, you're like my much, much older brother."

Another scowl from the Russian. He didn't like that remark *at all*. "I'm only seven or so years older than you are."

I waved that information away. "And my mother . . . ?"

"I must let Kovalev explain that. It's not my story to tell."

"At least tell me if she's alive."

I might've seen a flicker of pity in Sevastyan's eyes. I assumed the worst, grief hitting me like a swift stab to my heart. All these years of wondering . . . Now it seemed that I'd never meet her, never speak to her.

Stemming tears, I asked, "Do I have any siblings?"

"None."

"Grandparents?" Mom and Dad had been older when they'd adopted me, and my grandparents had passed away over my childhood.

He shook his head. "Only your father and a distant cousin you'll meet." He rose, then crossed to a marble counter in the middle of the sitting area. With the push of a button, a panel retracted to reveal a stocked wet bar with a full range of bar and stemware. He poured two drinks into cut-crystal glasses. A vodka rocks for himself—and a chilled Sprite for me?

"No warm milk?" I accepted the glass and drank, surly because it tasted so good.

Returning to his seat, he ran a finger around the edge of his glass, but he hadn't taken a sip. Just as his drink at the bar had been untouched. "I don't have your preferred tequila."

"Preferred? I drink whatever folks buy me. I've been on a budget."

Had my comment amused him? "The last *budget* you'll ever have, I assure you."

Because he expected me to spend the family blood money. Reminded of my situation, I said, "I'm having a hard time believing two strange men would really hurt me."

"They target relatives. When Kovalev started out in the Bratva, their code prohibited members from having a family, from having anything they cared about other than the brotherhood—because family is a weakness that enemies can use against you."

As I tried to imagine such a brutal world, Sevastyan continued, "That's why Kovalev sent your mother away. He didn't know she was pregnant. Not until you started this search."

"You said my DNA matched his. But why would his have been available?"

"There were others before you, claiming to be fathered by him. Initially, I came to Nebraska to discover if this was some type of scam." Gazing into his glass, Sevastyan said, "Kovalev never wanted it to be true before you."

"Why not?"

Sevastyan faced me again. "The others were deceitful gold diggers, cold-blooded and seemingly committed to unemployment. You held down three jobs, all while finishing your master's degree with honors. You even learned to speak Russian. You *wanted* to find him, but you didn't *need* to. At least, not financially." Had Sevastyan sounded . . . admiring?

The thought warmed me. Until I remembered that my DNA tied me to a mobster. "There could have been a mistake in the match. A clerical error or something."

Sevastyan raised his glass to his lips, only to lower it without taking a drink. "Your resemblance to his mother is uncanny."

I looked like my grandmother. I found myself softening, but not enough to soothe my misgivings. "So what does my father do? In a criminal sense. Run girls? Guns and drugs?"

Sevastyan gave me a look as if my question was the height of ridiculousness. "The bulk of his business is related to real estate and construction. But he also mediates disputes between gangs, and he sells protection to business owners. He does a brisk trade blackmailing politicians. No girls, no guns, no drugs. That's part of why we're having this conflict—because he doesn't want that in his territory."

"Because it would bring down his real estate values?"

Sevastyan looked like he was grappling for patience with me. "Because it would bring down the quality of life for the people he protects."

That was surprising. "Okay, so maybe he's not a diabolical, moustache-twirling villain. But I still don't want to get mixed up in this. I just want to finish my doctorate, to have a career."

With my history degree. Though I didn't necessarily want to be a professor or writer. Had I continued with my PhD because it'd been the path of least resistance?

"Do you think your father wanted to uproot you from your life? Blame Zironoff for this. If not for him, you'd be asleep in your bed right now."

"My investigator? What did he do?"

Again Sevastyan's drink almost made it to his mouth, but he set it down. "The greedy little prick demanded money from Kovalev to keep secret his discovery. But we found out he'd already told our enemies about your existence, offering your whereabouts for a price. He willfully put you at risk."

I swallowed. "Did you hurt Zironoff?"

Eyes gone cold, Sevastyan said, "He took your trust—and your hard-earned money—then used your blood to blackmail a *vor*. He jeopardized the life that I've sworn to protect. Tell me, Natalie, should he not have been punished for the damage he'd done—and prevented from doing more?"

I could read the writing on the wall. Sevastyan had ganked Zironoff. A true mob enforcer. A professional killer.

Leveling his gaze at me, he said, "Understand me, girl, I will eliminate any threat to you, pitilessly."

I wondered how many other men Sevastyan had killed. I wondered why I still couldn't manage to be afraid of this man. Instead, I found myself feeling . . . protected.

"Zironoff set you up to be murdered, but still you won't understand." He exhaled a weary breath. "I can't wait to hear your moral American outrage."

I tried to drum some up. But Zironoff had gone to a group of lethal thugs, planning to profit off my dream of finding my relatives. He'd leaked the confidential information I'd entrusted to him, knowing I might be killed.

So I shrugged. "*Do svidaniya*, Zironoff." So long and good-bye.

Sevastyan's gaze flickered over my face. Observant, watchful. Then one corner of his sexy lips curled.

My heart thudded at his half smile. If he ever truly smiled, I'd probably have a coronary. Quelling the urge to fan myself, I asked, "So, do you have a mob name? Like Alex the Butcher or Al the Shark or something?"

"I'm from Siberia; they call me the Siberian. End of story."

"Simple yet elegant, goes with everything. Were you born into 'the life' or did you steer your major?"

Flinty gaze.

"Okay, so what's Kovalev's mob name?"

"Older *vor* call him the Clockmaker."

"Because he cleans clocks? With his fists?"

"Your father has a wry sense of humor as well. You have much in common with him."

"Really?" I tilted my head. "You've learned a lot about me, huh?"

"I know everything about you, academically, financially, socially. I know that you had stability growing up and a caring couple to raise you, which relieved Kovalev's mind greatly. I know that you're driven and clever. Probably too much for your own good."

I recalled that feeling I'd had of being watched earlier tonight. "You followed me home from the bar." Mere hours ago.

"I did."

"Have you been in my house before tonight?" Had he found the collection of vibrators under my bed, or noted that half of my Internet bookmarks were for porn?

"Of course. I was thorough." His demeanor was so matter-of-fact, even as he sat here admitting that he'd violated my privacy on the regular.

My entire life had been laid bare to this man. Between gritted teeth, I said, "Any highlights you discovered that you'd like to share?"

"Don't worry—not every detail will make it back to Kovalev." Smirk. "Such as the arsenal you keep under your mattress."

Arsenal? *Dying here.*

"Or what I caught you doing to yourself in your bath."

Now that I wasn't in fear for my life, embarrassment scalded me. Sevastyan had caught me diddling the da, spelunking, dialing the pink telephone. "Why did you open the door to my bathroom in the first place?"

"I heard a sound." He raised an eyebrow. "A *whimper.* I thought the worst."

"You seem to have a talent for keeping me at a disadvantage. Maybe when we get to Moscow, I can investigate your apartment? Look under your bed? How about I watch while *you* masturbate?"

At that, tension shot through him as if he'd been gut-punched. "Guard your tongue, pet." His fingers were wrapped so tightly around his glass, I thought the crystal would shatter.

"Or you'll do what? Throw me down in a cornfield and feel me up?"

He clenched his jaw, as if battling for control of himself. "That shouldn't have happened."

Stop arguing with him, Nat. Go—to—bed. Was I so intrigued/aroused by this guy that I'd do anything with him, even fight?

"If you hadn't run—"

"Oh, don't you dare put that back on me!"

"A half-naked redhead was spread beneath me, rolling her hips in welcome. I don't have ice in my veins."

I arched a brow. "Don't you?"

"Not in that area of my life," he amended. "Even though you're far from my type, I was affected." He used his right forefinger to twist the thumb ring on that same hand. I'd noticed he'd done that before when he'd seemed uncomfortable. A tell? That could come in handy. "Any man would've been, so don't read more into it than that."

"Far from your type." How could that comment wound me? "You're not exactly mine either, *Siberian*." Probably not the best idea to taunt the assassin. I rose. "You seem determined to humiliate me and pick a fight. I'm not interested in either." I turned away and marched down the aisle. "Wake me up when we get there."

He called after me, "The only thing I told Kovalev about your personal life is that you have no current lover to leave behind. I won't mention how eager you were to remedy that situation tonight."

I stiffened, turning at the door of one of the suites. "Why were you so angry at the bar?"

He finally drank that vodka down, which gave me chills for some reason. "I didn't like seeing the daughter of a great man throwing herself at me, trolling for *trouble*."

"Throwing myself? Are you insane? I introduced myself and offered to buy you a drink." My ire kept mounting. "And I really hope you're not going to try to slut-shame me—because I will go off like a bottle rocket!" It was times like this when my virginity embarrassed me.

He stood, then stalked up to me. With his every step closer, my breaths shallowed. What would he do? I had no idea—excitement warred with uneasiness.

He towered over me, toe-to-toe, and I craned my head up to meet his heavy-lidded gaze. Whenever he was angry, his eyes appeared hard and glinting, like cold amber. Otherwise, they were molten gold, like now. . . .

"Of all the men in the bar, you picked me for a reason, little girl." His voice had gotten huskier, his accent rougher; I responded to it as if he'd touched me. "And it wasn't to talk about classes."

Inner shake. "I picked you because you were a mystery. I can read men with ease, but not you. That made me curious."

He rested his hand on the wall above my head, surrounding me with his heat. "When a woman singles me out"—he leaned down to murmur at my ear—"it's because she wants to get fucked. She looks at the scars and tattoos and knows she'll get *fucked hard.*"

I gasped, melting for him.

"Is that what you wanted of me, Natalya?" His warm breaths traced over my ear, hardening my nipples even more. I shifted my weight from one foot to the other, squeezing my thighs together.

"Th-that's not why I approached you." That *might* have been why I'd approached him.

"Little liar. You think I can't tell when a woman wants me

buried deep inside her?" He eased back to study my face. "And when you didn't get what you wanted, you settled for a nice . . . hot . . . bath."

I swallowed, beginning to pant.

Voice hoarse, he said, "Were you thinking about me when you touched yourself?"

Between breaths, I said, "I'm not telling you that."

"You just did, pet." He straightened, as if a trance had been broken between us. With a vile curse, he turned from me. "Just go to bed."

I watched his broad back as he strode away to pour another vodka. With a curse of my own, I slammed the cabin door behind me.

That man was going to drive me insane before we ever reached the motherland!

In a huff, I yanked down the cover and crawled into the sumptuous bed. Then lay there staring at the ceiling, feeling out of sorts, *hating* that I was forced to wear that man's clothing.

Hating that it turned me on.

Why him? Why was I so strong in every other aspect of my life and so weak with him? After so many years of holding out for Mr. Right, I would have given my virginity to Sevastyan in the dirt.

In high school, I'd never imagined I would be a twenty-four-year-old virgin, because I'd been so curious about the deed. And, damn, I'd been *game.*

But the drunken boys I'd fooled around with had been ham-handed and slavering, never inspiring me to go further. Sex, it had seemed, wasn't for me. At least, not with guys like the ones I'd known.

The problem with growing up in a small town and going to a

tiny school? There hadn't been a big selection of males to choose from.

When I got to college, I'd felt like I'd won the lottery—star-struck by the assortment of men. My curiosity hadn't lessened, and I'd been sure I'd lose my virginity before homecoming.

In preparation, I'd learned all about sex, through voracious reading, rooming with Jess, and my own breathless research. Oh, and my burgeoning interest in high-quality lady porn.

I'd hooked up with guy after guy, but inevitably each one would do something to prevent me from sealing the deal.

The one who'd fingered me like he was digging to China.

The one who'd prematurely ejaculated into the condom he'd been rolling on, then been too embarrassed to ever call me again.

The one who'd wanted me on top, dominating him, when I was pretty sure my tastes ran in the exact opposite direction. (Confirmed by my recent encounter in the cornfield?)

Was it too much to ask for an attractive, dominant guy with sexual skill, one who wasn't a minute-to-win-it two-pump chump?

When I hit twenty, I'd thought, *I've waited this long . . .* I'd figured I might as well hold out until I experienced blazing, blinding lust for a man who met all my qualifications. But no man had.

Until tonight.

Sevastyan ticked all my boxes—yet he'd sneered that I wasn't his type.

Okay, was it too much to ask for a guy who met my qualifications, who liked me—and who *wasn't* an asshole?

Sighing, I gazed out one of the windows, saw the moon and the stars closer to me than they'd ever been. Because I was on a plane, heading toward a great big unknown. To my "new life."

Damn it, I needed to get my mind off Sevastyan and think

about what tomorrow might bring. Just hours ago, I'd despaired of ever finding my biological parents. Now I was on my way to meet my father. Would he like me? Would I like him—despite his occupation?

Maybe I should look at this trip to Russia as a mini sabbatical from my life, a short time-out from my larger game. Like Jess's vacation. Tomorrow I could call to arrange for incompletes in my classes and get a pal to cover my teaching. The server jobs had been so grueling and shitty that I wouldn't waste a long-distance call on either.

Yes, everyone needed a break now and then.

The drone of the engines began to lull me, and the worst of my frustration started to fade. I felt like I was floating on the soft mattress, between silken sheets as light as air. Though I'd thought I was too keyed-up to sleep, I soon passed out.

And dreamed of Sevastyan.

In a sizzling reverie, he lifted me from my bath, cradling my naked, soaking body to bed. There, he followed every drop of water with his mouth before settling between my thighs. . . .

"Natalya," he groaned right at my flesh—all hot breath and slicked tongue. *"Natalya."* He raised his face, licked his sexy lips, and asked, "Are you dreaming of me?"

Huh? Dreaming? I opened my eyes—and found the Siberian staring down at me.

CHAPTER 7

*M*oonlight illuminated his beautifully rugged face, making my heart lurch. "Sevastyan?" He was lying beside me, head propped on his hand, a position that belied the tension coming off him.

He wasn't wearing a shirt. I nearly moaned to behold his bare chest, packed with rigid slabs of muscle. His smooth skin sported wicked-looking tattoos. High on both of his pecs were large eight-pointed stars, intricately shaded. Two Russian domes adorned one brawny arm; on his other, a patterned band encircled his bicep.

Those markings and the latent power in his body left me spellbound. "What are you doing in bed with me?" *And why can't I manage to be afraid of you?*

His breaths came quickly. He reminded me of a rubber band pulled taut, ready to snap. "I heard you moaning," he grated. "Came in, saw you rocking your hips beneath the covers."

I flushed, averting my gaze—which fell on his flat stomach, on the dark line of hair trailing from his navel. I had the mad urge to nuzzle it.

"Just when I think you're shameless, your cheeks heat."

I forced myself to face him. "You've explained what *I* was doing. What the hell were *you* doing?"

"Watching you and getting harder by the heartbeat." He pressed his hips closer to my side, letting me feel his sizable erection against my thigh.

I gasped, my body going soft when treated to the unyielding heat of his.

No, no, this man was an asshole! I reminded myself of his ricocheting mood swings. "You can leave now." I was proud of how resolute I sounded. "I'll try not to disturb you again."

As if I hadn't spoken, he rasped, "You make . . . you make these *sounds*. Your whimper, your moan. I hear them, and thought leaves my brain."

"You've been drinking."

"*Nemnozhka.*" A little. "I've been replaying how I saw you in the bath, stroking yourself with these fingers." He peeled my right hand from the cover—which I'd been clutching like a roller-coaster safety bar—then pressed my fingertips against his face. "I only wish you'd finished yourself in front of me."

I wished I had too! Then maybe I wouldn't be overcome with lust right now, falling even further under his spell.

His hooded eyes flicked over my face, then lower. "What were you dreaming of to make these so hard?"

I followed his glance down. My nipples were stiff against the fabric of the shirt I wore.

"Tell me, pet, why were you on the verge of a wet dream?"

I couldn't resist him before; now, on this bed, hearing his rumbling, seductive voice, I feared I was defenseless. *No! Be strong, Nat.* "Why do you insist on calling me pet?"

"Maybe because you make a man want to collar and keep you."

"Right." I knew he was just being a smart-ass, but the idea gave me shivers.

"Tell me about your dream."

"Why should I? You'll just give me that disgusted look and go all icy again."

"Icy? That's the last thing I feel right now."

I swallowed when he began unfastening the buttons on the shirt, spreading the lapels just shy of baring my breasts.

"What are you doing?" I demanded. But I wanted them bared, wanted him to see them and desire me.

Hey, I was on vacation from my life, right? So why couldn't this man be my fall holiday fling?

He took the starched edge of the shirt and lightly scraped it over my left nipple. *Oh, God, oh, God . . .*

"I caught just a glimpse of your nipples when you were in the bath. Do you know that my mouth watered to suck them?" He'd wanted to put his mouth on them. Picturing that scrambled my thoughts.

Another scrape.

"Y-you need to stop that." I hadn't thought the tips could get harder. They tightened almost painfully.

"Yes, tell me to stop and to leave you alone." *Scrape.* "Tell me that I frighten you, and I'm not to touch you." *Scrape.*

I choked back a moan. "You don't frighten me. And the only reason I don't want you to touch me is because you won't follow through, and I've been sexually tortured enough tonight."

Including now, I'd been on the verge of orgasm three times— all because of this man.

He gave a low, sexy laugh. "You think I've tortured you? Maybe

I should show you what real torture is." His tone was forbidding; so why was my pussy clenching with anticipation? "Then perhaps you would rail at me to find me in your bed."

"Is that what you want?"

"It's what I would have expected from you. And if you tell me to leave you, I will."

"Answer me, Sevastyan. Is that what *you* want?"

He didn't say a word; *scrape*.

"Ahh!" I licked my bottom lip, struggling for words. "You confuse me so much! Since you refuse to tell me anything, I'm going to tell you *everything*. I find you extremely attractive. When your eyes are like this, all gold and smoldering, you are pretty much irresistible to me. I think you were right; I did approach you in the bar because I wanted to have sex with you."

His firm lips parted. Then he shook his head hard, as if to dislodge whatever idea had just taken hold. "You wouldn't have done so if you knew me better. I *am* an enforcer, a contract killer, and I pity you for piquing the lusts of a man like me."

In a soft voice, I said, "But you piqued mine too. So what do we do now?"

"If you knew the thoughts in my head, you would not be so welcoming. You wouldn't like it in my bed. I have particular interests, and I demand obedience."

"Obedience." Was that *my* titillated tone? "Like my doing whatever you command?"

He nodded, eyes alight at the prospect.

Why did that sound so unbearably erotic? I'd never relished being ordered around at my jobs. But in this context—in bed with a domineering man—the idea excited me. "Why do you demand it?"

"I don't like surprises. If you do as I say, there will be none."

I nibbled my lip, giving this some thought. "What kind of interests?"

"I need to do filthy things to your body, Natalya. And I know I never can." His voice was almost . . . forlorn.

Filthy? That sounded so freaking hot. "Why can't you?"

"You are taboo to me. No woman is more so."

Because I was the boss's daughter? Was this why Sevastyan had been running hot and cold with me? "We're in this cabin alone. No one ever has to know what goes on between us. Maybe we should try to get this out of our systems before we land."

He looked like he was actually considering my proposal. "Have you ever relinquished control of your body to a man?"

Breathless, I shook my head. I'd wondered what it'd be like to be dominated; this man could relieve my curiosity. And that was the great thing about vacation flings: you could go crazy, do things you never would otherwise, and suffer zero consequences.

Right?

Did I have the nerve to try this? I recalled when I was twelve, the neighboring farm boy had dared me to jump off a train trestle into the creek below. Atop the tracks, I'd been terrified, shaking like a fledgling. But I'd forced myself to step off that ledge into nothing.

Into a free fall.

I remembered screaming with fear all the way down. Then I remembered kicking up through the water and breaking the surface, triumphant, to cast that boy a *suck it* grin.

All the terror had been worth it, just for that reward. Would the same prove true tonight?

"Could you give me absolute obedience, Natalie?"

Gut check. Could I step off the ledge once more? My honest

answer: "I won't know until we try." I reached for his chest, stroking over a tattoo. His muscles rippled to my touch.

When my thumb brushed his flat nipple, he inhaled sharply. "I've warned you of what I'll expect, I've warned you about what kind of man I am. And you still push? I'll give you a taste that will send you fleeing from me. This *will* be out of your system—because you will fear me. . . ."

CHAPTER 8

*F*ear him? I swallowed audibly. Did I dare go along with this?

"Spread your thighs," he commanded, rising above me.

It seemed I was still under the influence—of him; I tentatively opened my legs.

He positioned himself between them. Clutching the shirt lapels in his fists, he snatched open the rest of the buttons, yanking the shirt from me—until my naked breasts quivered before his predator's gaze.

My body was completely bared and defenseless, and his behavior should have made me nervous. Instead, I had to concentrate to keep my hips from undulating.

"If you want more, then put your hands behind your neck."

I blinked up at him. "What?" Make my position even more vulnerable?

"Do it, and do not move them. *Sdavaisya*." Surrender.

"I-I don't know."

"I didn't *ask*."

I hesitated, but then curiosity and this aching horniness demanded I do as he said.

When I laced my fingers at my nape, he said, "Good girl." For long moments, he stared at me with such a possessive gaze, it was almost palpable. Finally his hands descended on me, gripping my waist. When his fingers almost touched, I was struck by how much larger he was than I, how much larger he was than anybody I'd ever fooled around with. Would he think me too small?

He rubbed his rough palms up my sides, pronouncing me *"ideal'naya."* It meant perfect, or, more specifically, unimprovable.

I sighed with pleasure. "I thought you didn't like the way I look."

He raised his face, all consternation. "When did I *ever* give you that impression, pet?"

"Far from your type? Ring a bell?"

"I meant that—literally. You are different from the women I've been with." More to himself, he said, "Night and day."

I imagined him with cool, statuesque beauties from the north, felt like a runt in comparison. That feeling was short-lived— because he moved his attention to my breasts.

Cupping them from the bottom, he nearly circled them with his big hands. Avoiding my nipples, he kneaded with a practiced touch that was just this side of rough. But I loved it, arching to him.

Again and again, he palmed me, plumping the mounds until the rest of my body begged for contact—which he seemed determined to withhold.

"What are you doing to me?"

"Sexually torturing you." He tightened his grip on my breasts.

They began to swell, the skin heating and reddening. My nipples stiffened and distended, until the sight of them was lurid, turning me on even more. I looked from them to his transfixed gaze, then back. Still he massaged; still my flesh swelled.

When I felt his heavy breaths on the sensitive tips, I squirmed with a perfect mix of misery and delight. I noticed the sheets were damp beneath me and realized I was going to come like this. My eyes went wide with discovery. I could orgasm without a single touch on my neglected pussy.

I thought I'd known what my body was capable of, yet now it was behaving in unfamiliar ways. He seemed to know what it could do better than I did.

Never lessening his grip, he leaned down, letting his breaths torment the peaks even more. Avoiding contact with them, he darted his tongue to flick kisses along the sides, all around the tips.

If he touched my nipples I would scream. If he didn't touch my nipples I would scream. "Sevastyan, kiss them!" I was panting with distress, writhing from this excruciating arousal. I twined my fingers behind my neck, but I didn't know how much longer I could last before I touched myself. "*Do* something."

"Like this?" With a sinister look, he blew on one tip, then the other.

A cry broke from my lips, my back bowing to get me closer to that frustrating stimulation.

"Still." He pinned me down, giving my breasts an even harsher squeeze. "Submit to me."

Just the word *submit* made me tremble, made my clitoris throb. Until I was helpless not to touch it. Releasing my hold at my neck, I trailed my hand down.

"Ah-ah." He snatched my hip, shoving me to my side, baring my ass to him.

"What are you—"

With one of his callused hands caging my neck to hold me in place, he used his other to slap my bottom. With enough force

to startle me. "If you don't obey me, you'll be punished. Understand?" Another harsh slap.

He'd told me I would fear him; with each swat, alarm began
building inside me. I swallowed hard against the hand at my
throat.

"Understand?" His palm cracked across my ass again.

"Ow!" That one hadn't been a love tap either. "Yes!"

"Say, 'I understand, Sevastyan.'"

"I-I understand, Sevastyan." But I didn't. His eyes were flashing with excitement, his chest heaving; the tip of his bulging cock
had moistened the material of his pants. He got that turned on
from whipping me?

Did I? Obedience was one thing, but this was corporal. Yet
I was as wet as I'd ever been, my ass tingling so deliciously that I
craved another slap.

Which couldn't be right. How could I *crave* something I should
fear?

Between breaths, he said, "Don't like a man giving you a correction?"

My body screamed, *Yes!* But my mind resisted. The truth? "I'm
undecided."

That made him scowl anew. "Hands, Natalya."

When I twined them behind me, he positioned me on my
back again. Grasping my breasts once more, he lowered his head,
mouth almost to my nipple.

Suck it. Make me come. "Please, your mouth." I could hardly
utter my thoughts. "Your tongue."

"If you were mine, I'd pierce these. Force you to wear my
gold."

Pierce. Mine. Force. *His* gold.

Every word was dripping with domination. He was talking

about *piercing* me—and merely imagining it made me undulate up to his clothed crotch for relief. But he kept that beautiful bulge in his pants from touching me.

His hot hands continued to squeeze. Just when I thought my tits couldn't get any bigger, any pinker, any more sensitive, when I was rocking my hips in abandon, he rubbed his stubbled chin over one nipple.

"Sevastyan!" I was almost levitating with pleasure, babbling, *"Please, please, please."*

"What would you give me to suckle you?"

Easy. *"Anything."*

Voice rough with lust, he demanded, "Would you be my slave? I'd want to bind you, make you helpless. I'd use you in unspeakable ways."

As long as he made me feel like this—with my ass on fire and my breasts so swollen I could hardly think of anything but my own inflamed flesh. "Yes, yes!"

"You'd feel the bite of leather across your breasts, its sting between your legs."

I arched to him. "Okay!"

His grip tightened even more. "This was supposed to punish you, to punish me. But you fucking love it. You *need* it, even if you don't know how badly."

My head thrashed, and I murmured over and over, "I love it, need it."

"Put your hands over your mouth. Muffle your scream."

My what? Still, I did as he said.

In Russian, he muttered, "God help us both." Then he sucked one of my engorged nipples between his firm lips, into the waiting heat of his mouth.

His wet tongue lashed the peak as his teeth grazed—

My orgasm ripped through me. Violent, scorching, startling. Melting me as waves of pleasure contracted my untouched pussy—clenching inside, clenching so hard. Bucking my hips, I pressed my hands tight over my mouth to muffle my ecstatic screams.

The release was so intense, two tears spilled down my temples.

He sucked my other nipple, and the waves returned, my core convulsing.

Rapture . . .

When I was spent, he released me and drew back on his knees. I struggled to catch my breath and marshal my thoughts—failed on both counts—so I gave him a tentative grin.

As his gaze swept over my body and then to my curling lips, he looked like he struggled with rage—with actual rage. Which couldn't be right.

I scrambled up to kneel before him, my breasts feeling so lush. My nipples were damp and throbbing against his rock-hard torso. I whispered, "More."

I could feel his body shaking. So why wasn't he throwing me down, plunging inside me?

My hand tripped down his body. When I palmed his huge, hot cock, he made a growling sound. As I traced it with my fingers, I found the wet spot from his pre-cum, and shivered with want. "More."

Between gritted teeth, he said, "Fuck—you."

"I don't understand. What did I do?"

He grabbed the length of my hair, wrapping it around his fist. *"Ty ne dolzhna byla byt' takoy."* You weren't supposed to be like this.

Tugging my head down to the side, he slanted his mouth over mine. He kissed as wickedly as he did everything else, with sensual flicks of his tongue stroking mine. I threw my arms around his neck, pressing our chests together.

His skin felt like it burned with fever, his heart thundering. When one of my nipples glided across one of his, he groaned into my mouth, deepening the kiss.

Tongues tangling, breaths mingling. Slow, sinful, shattering. Until I was brazenly rubbing my body against his.

Yet then he broke away. "You don't know better, but I'll teach you." I heard him tear open his zipper. He used his grip on my hair to tug me down to my hands and knees; with his other hand, he yanked out his shaft. Bigger even than I'd imagined. Exquisite.

Under my captivated gaze, his veined length bobbed. I watched it pulse even harder. A bead of moisture clung to the head, glistening in the moonlight, and I was hungry for it.

He merely waited while I stared, his hand shaking in my hair. If he'd wanted to frighten me away, why hadn't he forced my mouth onto it? Shoved it back in my throat?

He muttered words in Russian, his voice so hoarse I had trouble understanding him. Something about *needing* to drive me away, while *faltering* to.

I wanted to pay attention, to ask him to explain, but that bead taunted me. Unable to help myself, I eased forward and swiped my tongue along the tip, tasting his arousal, stoking mine to a fever pitch all over again.

A guttural sound broke from his chest. I glanced up, saw his head thrown back, the muscles in his chest rippling with strain. His arm muscles twitched.

I'd given blow jobs before, but was by no means an expert. Yet I'd always thought enthusiasm trumped lack of talent. Encouraged by his reaction, I sucked him into my mouth, tracing those veins with my tongue.

He began to rock his hips in a sensuous rhythm, slipping his shaft deeper between my lips. Holding me in place with his grip in my hair, he leisurely fucked my mouth.

With his free hand, he brushed his knuckles along my jawline, then the shell of my ear. As if he couldn't help himself.

One hand gripped my hair, demanding I obey; his other caressed my face as if to thank me for it.

The contrast was maddening. This man was maddening. And he tasted so sublime, I found myself tending him . . . lovingly.

"Beautiful little Natalya," he grated, "with her eager mouth." More tender strokes along my cheek. "I've imagined you doing this."

I pulled back to run my lips down the side of his shaft. "When you were watching me?"

He grunted in answer. So I'd been walking around minding my own business, and this gorgeous Russian had been fantasizing about me giving him head? That turned me on like crazy!

When I increased my suction, I tasted another shot of precum, and wanted more, more. Stiffening my tongue, I delved the tip right into the center of the plump crown.

"Ahh!" he yelled, rolling his hips sharply, filling my mouth with cock.

The head hit the back of my throat. I might've gagged, but I was too hungry, had only been awaiting it. He'd wanted me to submit; my mouth and throat *had*, relaxing for him to use.

"Take me down, then." Another sharp buck at my mouth. When my lips met his zipper and I moaned for more, he repeated, "Fuck you."

I didn't understand him, was too far gone to care. As I sucked in delight, my hand grazed down my body to cup my wetness, rubbing my clit with the heel of my hand.

"Ah-ah, Natalya." He pulled me off his dick, then tore open his belt and pants, shoving them down his legs. My eyes drank in the sight.

The cords of muscle in his powerful thighs. The dusky perfection of his heavy testicles.

I reached forward to fondle the sac he'd bared for me, making him buck uncontrollably.

Then, in one deft move, he was on his back and I was turned around to straddle his head, with his shaft like a rod in front of my face.

Was he going to lick . . . with me in this position . . . while I . . .

He murmured in Russian, "Just a taste. To cure me." I perceived his breaths against my slick folds. His fingers spreading my wet lips. When he'd opened me, I felt his gaze on that most private part of me—

"So beautiful."

Then came his wicked tongue.

Bliss. "Oh, God," I breathed as he licked and laved. I'd never had anyone go down on me. Or *up*, as it were. I moaned, wondering, *How exactly have I lived without this?*

He fisted his cock, bending it toward me. Between licks, he said, "Suck." When I reclaimed him with my lips, he gripped the curves of my ass and forced me closer to his mouth.

As if feasting, he tongued me greedily, breaking away only to command me, "Harder." Down came his palm across my ass, making me arch like a cat in heat.

I hollowed my cheeks, and in return, I felt the lightest graze of his teeth over my clit—just as his finger began rimming my opening. *Oh, God, oh, God . . .* Awaiting the penetration, I spread my thighs wider over him and went still, which earned me another slap across my ass, reminding me to get busy.

He was controlling me utterly, and I couldn't get enough of it.

When his finger inched inside, I rocked back, wantonly rubbing my clit over his mouth, wriggling for more. As he probed deeper, filling my tightness, his shaft pulsated even harder.

With his tongue snaking and his finger pumping in and out of my core, he made growling sounds like he was in heaven. "Fuck, woman, *fuck*. You couldn't be tighter. Wetter." Then he drew my clit between his lips and sucked on *me*.

I tripped over the edge. As I started to orgasm, my scream was muffled again, this time by his thick girth. When I spasmed around his finger, he went crazy, sucking, setting in with a vengeance, his yell vibrating my clit.

Wave after wave rocked me, pleasure too scorching to be true. So strong that my vision flickered. . . .

When I grew too sensitive to take even another lick, I released him from my mouth to move away.

His answer was a slap across my ass.

"No, it's too much!"

"You'll take it for me."

As he started licking again, I shuddered and twisted atop his tongue. I thought it was a mercy when he removed his finger—until he began lapping directly at my core. "Sevastyan!"

He pressed my mouth back to his cock. "Take my cum from me. I'm about to give you your fill."

I groaned at his words, wanting it. Mouth locked on the head, I ran my palm up and down from the base to my lips.

His hips rocked to my fist, heels digging into the mattress as his massive body hurtled toward its release. His mighty thighs shook around my ears. "I want you to swallow me." His accent was so marked I could barely understand him. "You, Natalya."

"Umm," was all I could manage, now welcoming his tongue, knowing he was about to force another orgasm from me.

He took my pussy with a frenzied, openmouthed kiss, growling, "Every last drop, pet."

The idea of swallowing him sent me teetering on the brink of climax, with a rush of wetness for his awaiting mouth. He reveled in it, groans muffled. As he licked me for more, his shaft thickened between my lips, seed surging up his length.

The pressure he must be feeling as that knot of cum ascended! Readying to erupt . . .

"Imagine I'm pumping it into you right here—" He speared me with his tongue, breaching my core just as he began to ejaculate creamy liquid heat for me.

With that first shot of semen, he fucked me with his tongue and yelled into my flesh. As I went over the edge once more, my eyes rolled back in my head. Delirious with pleasure, I drank hot spurts of his cum, swallowing, swallowing.

Every last drop. . . .

CHAPTER 9

*W*ith a vicious curse, Sevastyan tossed me aside and exited the bed as if it were aflame, while I scrambled to the headboard.

What had just happened??

As he yanked up his pants, I pulled the sheet over me. Unless I was still dreaming, I was pretty sure I'd just been grinding this man's face while deep-throating him.

Who the hell am I tonight? When Sevastyan hissed as he tucked that beautiful semihard shaft back in his pants, my traitorous mind thought: *Whoever she is, I can't wait to be her again.*

I braced for a flood of anxiety. Instead, my body purred with satisfaction.

"That shouldn't have happened." He looked disgusted again— but this time with himself.

There were myriad emotions he should be feeling right now. Confusion, wonder, awe. *Not* disgust.

I was dazed, but in a good way, like I'd just defeated a fever and had come out stronger for it. I was different. I knew all about sex, but I'd never *felt* the power of it—the power of knowing that a man who obviously worshipped control hadn't been able to control his reactions to me. Just as my own had been uncontrollable.

He searched my face, studying my expression. For what? Disgust to match his? Regret?

The fear he'd faltered to deliver?

The worse he appeared to feel about this, the more comfortable I grew. I guessed I was contrary like that. Joke him if he couldn't take a fuck.

"So is this the part where you get mad and tell me to cover myself?" For good measure, I let the sheet drop as I stretched my arms above my head. To remind him of the breasts he'd just sucked and the nipples he wanted to pierce.

He swiped a palm over his face. "This was a mistake."

"Of course it wasn't. What we did was amazing." In this bed, my dream man had just rocked my world, making me come harder than ever before—*three* times—and my blow job hadn't been too shabby either. I was beginning to think I was a born fellatrix.

Out the window, I spied a glorious sight. The moon shone over the ocean. The ocean! My vacation was off to a promising start.

He sat on the edge of the bed, elbows on his knees. "It made you happy, to be used by me?"

Perhaps not so promising. I raised my brows with amusement. "I orgasmed three times; you did *once*. Who's using whom, Siberian?"

His lips parted in surprise. Well, that shut him up.

Tonight I'd realized something. I'd always thought that when I lost my virginity, I would be ceding something. Now I comprehended that with a man like Sevastyan, I'd be gaining something.

Pleasure to boggle my brain and memories to last my lifetime.

My entire mind-set about the deed was evolving. Insight: if a guy I had sex with ever carved a notch into his bedpost, I'd tell him to carve one into mine too—and then to go make me a fucking sammich.

Sevastyan said, "This was an indiscretion that must never be repeated."

"Because I'm taboo?" I frowned as a thought struck me. "Tonight wouldn't, like, get you killed by Kovalev or anything. Right?"

"Of course not. He's not a murderous tyrant."

"Then what is it?"

"I took advantage of his daughter. I can scarcely believe I've touched you." In the moonlight, I could see color tinting his cheekbones as he muttered, "Struck you."

"I ended up loving every second of what we did." I, Natalie Porter, had gotten my rocks off while being spanked. And I was going to roll with it.

I felt like a phone that had downloaded a new platform, but never been reset. When I'd orgasmed with him, I'd blipped, I'd blinked, and now I was ramped up.

He'd reset me, tweaking how I would feel about sex for the rest of my life. "Sevastyan, don't turn a positive into a negative." *Joke him, joke him . . .*

He faced me with a suspicious expression. "You were tight. Very much so. Surely you're not a virgin."

With a defiant look, I shrugged. "Guess you didn't find out *everything* about me."

He bit out a dumbfounded *"Blyad'!"* The word meant *whore*, but Russians said it like we might say *Oh, fuck!*

"This is not a big deal." It wasn't like I still had an intact hymen. My arsenal had taken care of that.

"Then why in the hell are you on birth control?"

So he'd seen the patch on my hip? "Various reasons." Mainly, I used it to regulate my periods.

But he wasn't listening to me. "It's bad enough to do this to a woman of experience." He shot to his feet, prowling the suite from one wall to the other. "It's another to despoil a girl who's never been touched!"

"Despoil? You didn't just say that archaic word! Well, it's only to be expected since we didn't have a chaperone and your man-root is so virile."

He scowled. "*I* might not look at it in such an 'archaic' way, but I don't know how others will react."

"Others? Like my father?"

Brusque nod.

"I thought you knew him so well. Well enough to tell me how great my new life is going to be."

"I do know him well. But he's never had a daughter before. I have no idea how he would take this."

"And what if I weren't his daughter?"

"You *are*." He stabbed his fingers through his thick hair.

"Answer the question."

He swung his head around, giving me a look so raw and primal that I gasped. "If you weren't, I'd be buried inside you right now. *Devstvennitsa ili net.*" Virgin or not. "What was supposed to sate my appetite has only whetted it."

Facts: He'd fantasized about me for the last month. He craved having sex with me, even if I was a virgin. He'd seemed to like certain things about my personality. He wanted more of me; I sure as hell wanted more of him—

"But this can never happen again," he added, his tone ringing with finality.

Was I going to be cock-blocked by some twisted kind of *mafiya* logic? I rose, walking on my knees to the edge of the bed, loving how his brows-drawn gaze followed the sway of my breasts. "I want it to happen again. And I usually get what I want. If you're not strong enough to resist me, then that's on you."

He narrowed his eyes at the challenge, seeming not to realize that he'd stepped closer to me. And then again. "If you tempt me, I won't be so gentle with you."

This had been gentle?

When I shivered with eagerness, he made a blustering sound. "You said I confused you? You *baffle* me. Is it me that you think you want, or merely the pleasure you crave?"

"I want the opportunity to find out."

"I believed that you would know better than this, that you had better instincts with men."

My eyes shot wide. "You didn't just say that. My instincts are untouchable!"

"Don't you get it? Your father intends to give you the goddamn world; even if I wanted it, a man like me will never be in your future." He turned toward the cabin door.

Staring after him, I murmured, "How strange."

He paused at the threshold without turning around. As if he couldn't help himself, he said, "What is strange?"

I tilted my head. "That you think *I* won't be deciding who gets to be in my future."

Shoulders bunched with tension, he slammed the door behind him.

CHAPTER 10

"My alarm!" I shot upright in bed, knowing I was late for work, wondering why the hell my clock hadn't gone off. "Late!"

Rubbing my eyes, I gradually comprehended that I was on a plane, that all the events of last night weren't a dream.

What had happened in this bed wasn't a dream.

I turned toward the door, found Sevastyan hanging up garment bags, a suitcase at his feet. "Relax, Natalie. You no longer have those worries."

Whereas I was naked, wearing nothing but a sheet over my lap and my wildly curling hair over my breasts, he was clad in an immaculate three-piece gray suit and a long coat. It fit his broad shoulders flawlessly.

I blurted out, "You look incredible." Like a billion bucks, like the dream man who'd rocked my world. No, he'd knocked it off its axis. It was as if I'd thought pleasure was only rated on a scale of one to ten, and then this guy had seductively whispered, "Didn't you know? The upper end is infinity."

And then this guy, let's just call him Sevastyan, had *demonstrated*. Surely that deserved an encore?

At my compliment, his high cheekbones grew tinged with color, but he said nothing.

Roll with it, Nat. "Hey, we've landed? I can't believe I slept through it." I frowned to see that the curtains were closed.

Had he come back in here after I'd fallen asleep again and drawn them for me? Awww.

"How much did I miss?" I'd slept like the dead—how long had I been out, anyway?—and now felt rested for the first time in weeks. A quick inventory of my body told me I was sore, but in all the right places.

"It's overcast, so you wouldn't have seen much."

When I leaned over to peek out the window, he glanced away sharply.

Outside, the skies were gray, the airport of no particular note. A limo was parked, cool and indifferent, on the tarmac near the jet. It looked like a car the British monarchy might favor.

"There are clothes here for you," Sevastyan said. "Everything should fit."

I gave him a saccharine smile. "Because you broke into my house and took down my sizes?"

He narrowed his eyes. "And then I personally confirmed your measurements." With that, he left me.

Oh, did you ever, I thought as I dashed into the shower. Minutes later, I returned to find steaming coffee and warm pastries left for me. I sipped the coffee . . . loaded with sugar and soy milk. Just as I took it, which he would know because he'd invaded my privacy.

Ignoring my irritation, I tore into the garment bags and suitcase. Jess would've had a clothesgasm over the selections. Even I appreciated the designer sweaters and slacks, the boots of soft, soft leather.

And the lingerie? The stylish bras and panties weren't overtly sexual—despite their see-through lace and coy ribbons—but farm girls in Nebraska just didn't wear stuff like this.

I wasn't in Nebraska.

So I shuffled through the undergarments, donning a matching pair in peach silk. I pulled on a form-fitting jade-green sweater of the finest cashmere I'd ever felt and a pair of black ponte pants. Normally I would've balked at the clinging material, but the sweater hit me almost at midthigh, so I wouldn't be flaunting anything. Flirty ankle boots molded to my feet, completing the outfit.

I checked myself in the mirror, surprised by the color in my cheeks. My eyes looked clear, the green more vivid. I appeared . . . well-loved.

Almost dewy-eyed.

If one session with Sevastyan affected me like this, I couldn't imagine what sex with him would do to me. *One way to find out.*

I packed the remaining clothes, then awkwardly rolled/carried the suitcase from the suite. If I'd expected Sevastyan to compliment me on my outfit, I was mistaken.

"You don't *carry bags.*" Once I'd dropped the suitcase like it was hot, he squired me to the exit.

At the head of the plane's stairs, I paused to inhale a deep breath, wanting to smell the country; all I smelled was jet fuel, and it was *freezing* here.

Anticipating my needs, Sevastyan said, "Here, I have a coat for you."

Fur, full-length. Decadent sable. "Oh, I don't do fur," I said firmly, even as I petted the silky expanse.

"In Russia, you do." I was opening my mouth to argue when he said, "It was your grandmother's. It's been altered for you."

My grandmother had worn this? Argument quashed. I slipped it on, not even surprised that it fit perfectly. As we descended the stairs, warmth enveloped me. "Why would Kovalev give me something like this?" He didn't even know me.

"Who else should this coat go to, if not the owner's only granddaughter?"

When he put it like that . . .

Down on the ground, a nondescript driver opened a door for me, but Sevastyan was the one who assisted me into the backseat.

Inside, a privacy screen separated us from the front. The tinted windows were so thick, I figured they had to be bullet-proof. Sevastyan sat across from me—as far away as possible. As we pulled out of the airport, he refused to look at me, just kept his gaze focused out the window.

"So where is Kovalev's place?"

"Outside of the city, on the Moskva River. Around an hour away."

We were going to be trapped in this car together for an hour? With him in that mouthwatering *GQ* suit?

When we turned onto a larger road, I pried my gaze from him, longing to experience this new country. I glued my forehead to the window to see the sights, but all we passed were warehouses that could've just as easily been in America. Only the Cyrillic lettering differentiated them. "Will we drive through Moscow?"

"Not today."

"I'm not going to see the city?"

"*Nyet*, Natalie." Hard no.

In a defeated tone, I said, "Not a single onion dome?" I'd always loved viewing pictures of those quintessential Russian domes, so brightly colored and bold—even before I'd seen the two tattooed on his bicep.

"Perhaps you will," he said in an enigmatic tone.

Silence reigned; industrial parks dominated for mile after mile. The ride was a special kind of hell. "It's warm. Can I crack the window?"

"Out of the question," he snapped.

I crossed my arms over my chest. If I'd had a flower in hand, I would have plucked its petals: *he wants me; he wants me not.* Last night I'd been convinced he desired more with me. Today, not so much. "I want to talk to you about what happened on the plane."

With a glance at the privacy screen, he lowered his voice to say, "We agreed to put that behind us." He sounded like he was trying to convince himself.

"No, we did *not* agree. You suggested it, and I vetoed. Besides, you're still thinking about it too."

"Why would you believe that?" he asked, his voice husky.

"Because you've been shifting in your seat, and you've kept your coat buttoned in this warm car. I'll bet you're hard behind that material."

He didn't deny it.

"You've got to be thinking about it, because I can't *stop.*"

"Try," he said dismissively, turning away from me once more.

"It's difficult when my every movement reminds me of what we did." Because of this delicious, *secret* soreness. I admitted, "My ass feels like I've been horseback riding for the last two days." And I wouldn't trade the experience, or the twinges, for the world.

Gazing out the window, he languidly curled his lips, his expression the epitome of masculine satisfaction.

Oh, that breathtaking grin. *Heart. Beat. Skipped.* Was that manly pride on display because I was still feeling his *corrections*?

His face was always so unreadable; he must truly relish what he'd done to me.

If he felt a fraction of the attraction that I did for him, then how was he denying himself a repeat? Maybe he routinely experienced that kind of pleasure with others. The idea made me seethe. "I guess you do things like that all the time with tons of different women? I suppose I'm one of many."

"You're not like the women I've been with."

He'd said as much to me last night. *Day and night.* "How so?"

Nothing.

"Tell me."

He shrugged. End of discussion.

Fine. "I need to talk to you about logistics. Now that we've sorted out my clothing selection—"

"It's not sorted. That was merely to get you through the day. An extensive new wardrobe will be provided for you."

When he said things like that, I wished I was more interested in fashion. And, well, money.

"Am I going to get a phone? I need to call my professors."

"I've e-mailed all of them, explaining that you had a family emergency and must travel. Duration unknown."

"You wouldn't!"

He raised his black brows. *Wouldn't I?*

He'd basically unenrolled me. Even though I'd already planned to arrange for incompletes, this high-handedness rankled.

"You've always been responsible with your department," he pointed out. "It would be unusual for you to disappear without a word."

"They won't buy it."

"They will when the e-mail came from your address."

"That's what you were doing while I was in the bath! I heard you come in earlier last night."

No denial.

So he'd been at my computer, steering my entire life, when he'd heard my *whimper*, deciding to check that out as well? Did he have no boundaries?

God, so much had happened since then. It felt like weeks ago that I'd been at that bar with my friends, probably because my life had changed more drastically in twenty-four hours than it had in the last six years—since my dad had died and I'd realized how short and precious life was. Since I'd started my quest.

My nervousness about this entire situation returned full-force. "Okay, what about my living arrangement? Where will I stay? And how long are we looking at?"

Sevastyan cast me a puzzled glance. "You will live with Kovalev at his home. Once it's safer, you'll come and go as you please."

"I'm supposed to live with someone I don't know?" I hadn't even had an opportunity to Google Kovalev.

"It's not as if you'll step on each other's toes there," Sevastyan said. "You'll stay encamped at his estate until the threat has been eliminated. Unless you decide to make your home there once the danger passes."

Voluntarily reside with a stranger? At the dingy Soviet compound? "But how *long* will it take for the danger to pass? A couple of weeks? A couple of months?"

"This is your life for the foreseeable future."

My lips parted. My fall vacay had just gotten extended—all because of a father I'd never met. "Tell me what Kovalev's really like."

One corner of Sevastyan's lips might've lifted. "He's nothing like you're expecting him to be." A little thawing from the Siberian?

"You genuinely like him. It's more than just, um, organizational loyalty."

He nodded. "Kovalev's the best man I've ever known. I respect him more than anyone."

"How did you meet him?"

"In St. Petersburg. By chance," Sevastyan said, with a twist of his thumb ring.

"Ah, that explains everything." Closemouthed Russian.

"Ask Kovalev for the story, if you like."

Maybe I would. "So what will I be expected to do all day, now that you've unenrolled and unemployed me?" Already I had much more energy than I was used to. "It's going to be difficult to go from hard work to hard leisure."

"You'll get to know your father. You'll enjoy the amenities at Berezka."

"Little birch? Is that the name of his compound?"

"*Da.*"

We fell silent. The landscape grew wilder, with more trees and larger properties. We passed gate after gate, each more elaborate than the last.

My nerves were getting the best of me. I fussed with my new coat. A fur one. My grandmother's.

What if I said something stupid or ticked Kovalev off? I didn't often put my foot in my mouth, but when I did, I tended to go big in that department as well.

What if the man wasn't even convinced that I was his daughter and this was some kind of test? I only had Sevastyan's word on everything. Shit. How much could I really trust him—

"Natalie, rest easy." He leaned forward and took my hands. "He's a good man."

Right when I'd decided Sevastyan was a dick, he had to go and be all understanding. A raw moment of insecurity from me. A raw moment of sympathy from him.

Then he frowned. "Your hands are cold." As I stared down, he took both of mine between his own. To warm them.

Just as I'd imagined my future, faceless guy would.

I blinked up at him. Had that only been last night?

"Weren't there gloves for you?"

"I didn't have a chance to look through everything."

"Don't be nervous." With utter confidence, he said, "You will take it all in stride."

"How do you know?"

"Because you have everything else." The car decelerated; he dropped my hands, clearing his throat to say, "We're here."

CHAPTER 11

*G*uard dogs and machine guns. Why was I even surprised?

At the beginning of the driveway, a pair of two-story white stone towers formed an arc over ornate iron gates. Uniformed men were poised in front of the structure, weapons at the ready, dogs snarling.

Our driver rolled down the window and spoke to a guard, who seemed to be trying to get a look at me. I supposed they must be curious about Kovalev's long-lost daughter.

A motor whirred as the gates opened. When they closed behind us, Sevastyan relaxed a degree, just as he had once we'd gotten into the air. His expression grew a shade less grim.

"Well." I exhaled a surprised breath. "That was different."

"The security has been increased for your presence. Kovalev will take no chances. But you shouldn't be frightened. We won't let anything happen to you."

"I'm not frightened, I've just never been out of the Corn Belt before. And now this . . ."

"I know, pet." I caught his glance at my lap, where I was twining my fingers together, and thought he had the impulse to hold my hands again. But he didn't.

The drive meandered through what looked like a park, with hill after hill of golf course–quality lawn. The sun began to break through lowering clouds.

I wanted to pay attention to everything, to memorize my first experience here, but again I was distracted by Sevastyan.

As we crossed a charming wooden bridge, I noticed he was analyzing me. Determining my reaction to this place?

The trees grew more numerous, dense forests changing colors with the fall. The leaves on the birches and other hardwoods were a riot of burnished orange, russet, and gold—gold like Sevastyan's eyes.

When we neared a colossal structure beside a lake, I cried, "Is that it?" The walls and columns were ivory, the tiled roof topped with three copper domes, green with patina. "Domes! Oh, it's gorgeous!" No dingy, Soviet-era monolith here. The lake was so glassy, the building cast a surreal reflection. I was in love, ready to declare myself home—

"That's the lake folly, a former church for the property." At my raised brows, Sevastyan added, "Now it's a place for guests to take tea."

"Oh." Onward we drove.

We passed a stable that must have had fifty stalls. "How many horses are there?"

"Dozens. Kovalev loves animals."

White tigers, anyone? Maybe he'd have caged Russian bears.

As we rounded a curve, a mansion came into view. No, not a mansion—a palace.

Jaw drop.

"*That* is it," Sevastyan said.

From a main three-story building, two wings stretched beyond my line of sight. It was the size of a freaking state building, but with so much more charm. I realized that the lakeside folly complemented the mansion, with the same colors and types of columns. The late afternoon sun cascaded over the scene. "I . . . this . . ."

"It's a former tsar's residence," Sevastyan said. "Twenty years ago, it was in bad shape, about to be renovated as a museum and Russian landmark. Kovalev bought it instead and painstakingly restored it."

"So it's historical." My heart was racing. "You didn't tell me I'd be staying in . . . in *history*."

The limo parked in front, near a line of high-end cars of all makes and models. Before the driver could reach my door, I scrambled out, Sevastyan following. I craned my head up. "Spectacular," I eventually managed.

He gave me a satisfied nod. *"Horosho."* Good.

"This must be Natalie Porter!" A young man about my age strolled out of the grand copper doors. When the sun hit his face, my lips parted. He was . . . stunning. His dark blond hair was rakishly cut, his features a study in symmetry. His vivid gray eyes were devilish and alight with intellect.

I'd just recovered speech after the sight of this estate. Now my brain was overloaded again.

"That's Filip Liukin," Sevastyan said in a tone rife with disapproval.

If Sevastyan was ruggedly hot and sex on a stick, this Filip was blindingly beautiful. While I was trying to form words, Sevastyan grated, "He's your *cousin*."

Awkward.

Filip was quick to point out: "Distant, far removed, and all that." His accent sounded British. He flashed me an easy grin, all dimples and flawless teeth.

Filip reached out as if to clap Sevastyan on the shoulder. "Welcome back, *bratan*!"

The look on Sevastyan's face deterred Filip from touching him. "Do not *ever* call me brother."

Whoa. Sevastyan acted as if Filip had just sliced an exposed nerve.

"You got it," Filip said easily, unperturbed. "Welcome back, all the same. I know you're glad to be relieved of this lengthy job."

Did everyone think I'd been merely work to Sevastyan? An onerous task that took him from home for a month? I hadn't been, right? Maybe I was misremembering his response to me. As icy as he'd been on and off today, I had to wonder. . . .

Filip opened his arms. "Come, Cuz, give us a hug."

Still stung to think of myself as a *task*, I let Filip embrace me. As I drew back, I glanced over at Sevastyan, saw that his jaw was clenched, that muscle ticking. He wasn't liking this whatsoever, as if he was *jealous*.

Attention fully on Filip—not a chore—I asked, "Do you live here?"

"I might as well," he said, adding in a flirtatious tone, "And with you here at Berezka, I plan to stick around. No one told me you were gorgeous."

My manalyzer sense began tingling, but I couldn't read it, for good or ill. If I felt a touch of unease, my opinion had probably been tainted by Sevastyan's reaction to him. I changed the subject. "Your English is so perfect." Sevastyan's was flawless as well, but unlike Filip, he'd retained his thick accent. "Did you grow up outside of Russia?"

"Yes, I was educated in England. Got my MBA at Oxford. Now I've returned." In an affectionate tone, he said, "I'm trying to update your old man's operation, dragging it into this century." At the front doors, he offered his arm. "Shall we?"

Was I being passed off, just like that? From Sevastyan to Filip? I'd been so excited before. Now I was out of sorts. Still, I eked out a smile. "I suppose so."

"I'll take her inside." Sevastyan's hand covered my shoulder in a possessive grip, sending pleasure through me. I wanted to sag against him.

Filip's smile barely faded. "I've got this. I'm sure you're tired from your stakeout."

Sevastyan didn't say anything more, didn't have to. One dark glance and Filip backed down.

"Easy on the trigger, Siberian." He chuckled good-naturedly. "I have something to take care of anyway. See you tonight, Cuz." He strode off toward that line of parked cars.

Sevastyan called, "Where's your own car?"

Without slowing, Filip called back, "In the shop."

I stared after the guy, because it was difficult to pry my eyes from him. Like watching a retreating comet.

When I turned back, Sevastyan looked like he was grinding his teeth. "Be wary of him. Appearances can be deceiving."

"If I didn't know better, I'd think you're jealous."

"That is not at issue," he said, spinning his thumb ring. "Come." He waved me across the threshold.

Inside, I gasped at the opulence. A grand staircase curved gracefully up from an immense foyer. Marble gleamed beneath our feet. Alcoves housed delicate statuary, and oil landscapes adorned the walls. Instead of the garish mishmash I'd anticipated, everything was refined and tasteful.

When we shed our coats, handing them to a uniformed servant, I felt like I'd lost a layer of comfort. Past the foyer, Sevastyan steered me into a long gallery. At the end were two solid wood doors. We paused just outside them. "Here's his office."

I faced the doors, filled with apprehension. Up until this moment, the idea of meeting my biological parents had been a distant dream, a farfetched hope. I smoothed my hair, then adjusted my sweater.

"Come. You will genuinely like him, Natalie." Sevastyan's strength seemed to permeate into me.

In a small voice, I asked, "Will he like me?"

He reached for the doors. Staring straight ahead, he muttered, *"On tebya polyubit."*

He will love you.

CHAPTER 12

*A*ll my *Godfather*-ish expectations of gloomy, dark wood paneling and clouds of cigar smoke vanished; Kovalev's study was light and airy. Numerous picture windows welcomed the fall sun.

Along most of the walls, a multitude of antique clocks ticked along happily. Others in various stages of repair covered a workbench.

Kovalev was *literally* a clockmaker? I felt silly for my comments on the plane, hoped Sevastyan wouldn't recall them.

I gazed to the right, finding the man himself on the phone. Pavel Kovalev was *so* not what I was expecting. He had black hair with gray at the sides, ruddy cheeks, and a slim build. No tracksuit—he wore a crisp navy sport coat with a blue button-down that highlighted his twinkling eyes. Zero gold chains.

Kovalev, the Russian mafioso, looked less like a Godfather and more like . . . a thin, dapper Santa Claus. He couldn't be further from my imaginings.

"Natalie!" He hung up the phone at once. With his blue eyes lighting up, he rose to hurry over to me. He was about five foot eight, maybe sixty years old. His arms were spread wide—like his infectious grin.

But for all that we shared DNA, he was a stranger to me. What should I call him? Mr. Kovalev? Father? Pops? I shuffled uncertainly, darting a glance at Sevastyan, who gave a brisk nod. His way of encouragement? In the end, I just said, "Hi." Lame.

Kovalev clasped my shoulders, leaning in to press a kiss on each of my cheeks. "You are the spitting image of my mother." He waved toward a portrait of a smiling woman proudly hung on a paneled wall.

I did look like her. My grandmother.

"How was your trip?"

Bewildering, eye-opening, occasionally wicked. "Unexpected?"

He gave me a sheepish look. "I do apologize, my dear." His English was as excellent—and accented—as Sevastyan's. "I assume Aleksandr filled you in on our current circumstances." Directing a proud gaze at Sevastyan, Kovalev added, "He speaks for me."

I remembered that phrase. It was a simple way of saying that Kovalev trusted him so much that he knew Sevastyan would say exactly what he would in any situation.

"Does he, then?" Was Sevastyan's face a touch flushed? Thinking about his "indiscretion"?

"Absolutely. He is a son to me, the only one I would trust to bring me my . . . *daughter*. I don't think I'll ever be able to say that enough." When his eyes got a little misty, I feared I might be a goner for this *mafiya* Santa.

"Sevastyan kept me safe," I assured Kovalev. "And the flight was pleasantly uneventful." *Burn, Siberian.*

"Good, good. Are you hungry? Shall we have tea?"

"Tea sounds great."

"I'll leave you two," Sevastyan said, all stiff and formal. "We need to speak afterward, Paxán."

Kovalev's gray brows drew together and a look passed between them. But I couldn't read it.

"Of course, Son."

Sevastyan turned and strode back the way we had come.

"He thinks the world of you," I told Kovalev. "He said he's been with you since he was young."

"Yes, I found him when he was just thirteen."

"Found?" How had Sevastyan been *lost*?

Kovalev made a sound of assent, but didn't elaborate. "Such a bright boy, and loyal above all things."

"What'd he call you as he left?"

"Paxán? It's his slang sobriquet for me, part *Godfather*, part *old man*. Believe it or not, it's meant warmly. Perhaps you could call me that as well, until we get to know one another. Just for now?"

Until I called him *Bátja*? Dad? The hopefulness in his tone tugged at my heart. I smiled. "Okay, Paxán, just for now."

He motioned me toward a pair of elegant settees, taking the one across from me. On cue, more uniformed servants delivered a tea service and a multitiered silver platter. Salmon and cucumber tea sandwiches were arrayed on the top level. Caviar and blini filled the second; cheese, pears, and grapes the third. Scones and pastries were artfully arranged on the bottom level.

As he poured, I filled my plate. The tea was a smoky, potent blend. Instead of sugar, he sweetened his cup with orange jam, so I followed suit. The combination was delectable.

We chatted about the weather in Nebraska and in Russia, and his past visits to the States (work trips to destinations like Brighton Beach and Las Vegas). He was surprisingly easy to talk to.

Then the conversation turned serious. "You must be wondering about your mother."

I nodded. "Sevastyan didn't say much, preferring for you to tell me."

"Her name was Elena Petrovna Andropova." Kovalev's demeanor changed. He looked years older, as if weighed down with regret. "From what I've been able to learn, she died shortly after you were born."

"Complications from the birth?" She'd died because of me?

Kovalev quickly said, "You cannot blame yourself. Health care wasn't what it should have been. The entire country was in turmoil in those years."

Had she ever even gotten to hold me? "I always thought she'd given me up."

"Never. Nor would I have. I knew nothing of this. We'd been . . . separated."

"Because of the Bratva code?" I asked.

"*Da*. I had no idea. I would have defied the code, searching heaven and earth for such a daughter as you!"

Though I thought I was pretty damned nifty, how could he feel so strongly? Just because I was his biologically? Or because of field reports from his enforcer? "You say that with such . . . surety. I know blood ties can be important to some people, but you can understand why I think other connections are important too."

"Of course! Yet I feel as if I already know you since Aleksandr has spoken so highly of you. It's very rare for him to give his approval, and never so wholeheartedly."

Highly? And wholeheartedly? "What has Sevastyan told you?" Would I live up to the hype?

"He told me that you're an honor student, with numerous

academic awards and scholarships. He sent me copies of papers you've written for journals; we've read them all."

I suddenly wished I'd put a little more effort into them. And I couldn't help but wonder what two gangsters would think about my subjects of discussion: depictions of women, gender, and homosexuality throughout history. Time enough to ask them, I supposed.

"I also got to see pictures of you at county fairs when young and more recent videos of you singing karaoke with friends."

I'd forgotten Jess had uploaded that video, from back in my enthusiasm-trumps-lack-of-talent era. *You told yourself that just last night, hussy.* My cheeks heated, and I sipped tea to cover my consternation.

In a wry tone, Kovalev said, "You come by your singing ability naturally."

The quip made me laugh into my cup. I was learning that he had the mischievous sense of humor that I enjoyed.

"Sevastyan told me how you've gone to school full-time while holding down three jobs." Expression gone grave, Kovalev said, "I know that you would often work so hard, you would stumble home in exhaustion."

I flushed uncomfortably. He made me sound like some Pollyanna Two-shoes. I'd had a goal, therefore I'd busted my ass to reach it. Simple. "To be fair, I *might've* just been drunk. 'Cause that's entirely possible."

Kovalev went quiet. All I heard was the tick-tock of a thousand clocks. Then he threw back his head and laughed.

He had a great laugh, giving himself over to it. I found myself joining in.

Once we'd quieted down, he wiped his eyes, saying, "What a treasure you are, Natalie."

As I grinned in reply, I told him, "About the jobs, Paxán, I don't want you to think my parents didn't provide for me. They always have, but I didn't want my mom to know about this."

"So to spare your adoptive parent pain, and to bring me great joy, you worked to the point of exhaustion. And you taught me an important lesson."

I raised my brows.

"Power comes in different forms, no? A syndicate like mine has power. But so does a twenty-four-year-old with fire in her belly and steel in her backbone. *You* found *me*," he added, repeating what Sevastyan had said last night.

I guessed my efforts could be considered a big deal, but I just looked at the last six years as . . . life. "Speaking of your syndicate"— I took a deep breath—"how did you get, um, started?" We might as well get this out of the way.

"Not by choice, that's for certain! I wanted to be a master clockmaker." He waved to indicate his collection. "Like my father before me, and his father before him."

I came from a line of clockmakers? Cool!

"When I was young, my family had a shop in Moscow, one of the many black market shops in the underground economy. It afforded us a comfortable living. Yet then these brigadiers— a *vor*'s henchmen—descended upon us, demanding money for protection from the gangs that ran rampant. The price to us was exorbitant. When we had no choice but to refuse, they made us pay in other ways."

"What happened?"

His eyes went distant. "My father died that night. My mother survived for a few years before eventually succumbing to . . . damage done to her."

My stomach churned, and I almost retched up tea. Then

an unfamiliar feeling came over me, a protectiveness for these people—and a quiet rage over what had been done to them. I knew the end of Kovalev's story—he'd obviously vanquished that *vor* and succeeded—but I wanted to hear *how* he'd done it. Sparing no details.

I wanted to relive his retribution. A startling idea. Maybe I was precisely where I belonged—in the middle of a turf war. "What did you do?"

"I was only a teenager when they struck," Kovalev said. "But guided by my mother, a fierce and proud woman, we avenged my father and outwitted that gang to stamp them out."

Yes, but . . . "How?"

He exhaled, giving me a sad smile. "Let's not speak of unpleasant things. Just know that we won the day. Yet not long after, a new gang arrived to demand money from us and all our neighbors and friends. My path became clear. I could allow a stream of jackals to prey upon us, or I could hire my own brigadiers to protect myself and our friends. Nearby businesses paid me what they could, and I expanded over and again."

In as even a tone as I could manage, I said, "I'm glad you defeated them, Paxán. I'm glad you avenged your parents."

Seeming to wake up, he said, "I have been worried that you wouldn't be able to accept what I am."

"Do you want to know something weird? I'm more upset that I don't get to hear how you defeated them than I am about what you do for a living."

He eyed me, saying in a softer tone, "What a treasure. . . ." Then he straightened, making his manner upbeat. "Let us talk of less troubling things, of the future. Tonight I've planned a banquet in your honor. You'll meet everyone in our organization, all our brigadiers. And your cousin Filip as well."

"I ran into him on the way in."

Kovalev looked surprised. "Most young ladies find themselves more starstruck after first meeting him."

Maybe if I hadn't already had eyes for Sevastyan.

"Filip's the son of my distant cousin and best friend, who died recently. The poor boy took it hard. Your being here is just what the lad needs. . . ."

After that, the afternoon passed companionably. Kovalev and I came up with things we had in common: dislike of slapstick comedy, love of animals and heist movies. "They're usually not accurate, though," he commented, reminding me that I was talking to a crime boss.

He told me stories about my mother—she'd loved to garden, loved plants; she would've been pleased to know I'd grown up on a farm. He challenged me to a game of chess in the morning and promised to teach me about clocks.

When they all struck five, Kovalev said, "As much as I'm enjoying this, I should let you go, so you can have time to get settled in before the banquet."

"Oh." Banquet, schmanquet, I was greedy for more time with my father.

In a confiding tone, he said, "I regret scheduling it, wish we could have a quieter dinner and carry on this conversation." He was as reluctant for me to leave as I was. "Aleksandr could join us."

A knock sounded. Speak of the devil.

CHAPTER 13

"*P*erfect timing, Son," Kovalev told him. "Will you see Natalie to her rooms?"

"I thought you would want to."

"No, no, you two go on. I'll see you tonight, dear." He pressed a kiss to the top of my head, and it felt natural.

As Sevastyan and I left the study, I couldn't stop smiling. The Siberian had been right—I hadn't known what I was talking about; Kovalev was wonderful.

On our way up the grand staircase, Sevastyan said, "You enjoyed yourself."

"Just like you said, Paxán is great." My prejudging of Kovalev had been off the mark to a laughable degree, and I'd been totally wrong about Sevastyan. Maybe it was time to take a hiatus from my manalyzing—which *must* be geographically limited.

Sevastyan raised his brows. "You call Kovalev a term of affection?"

"He asked me to," I said defensively.

"And you do, despite his occupation?" he said in a curt tone.

Though I'd expected a stereotypical *mafiya* kingpin, I felt like

I'd lucked upon this reluctant don, one who'd rather tinker with clocks.

I could overlook a lot.

"You were right, Sevastyan; I understand things better now." I held his gaze. "And I am so glad you forced me on that plane." *For more than one reason . . .*

I thought I saw his eyes growing heated, but he looked away, steering me along an art-lined hall. We must be heading down the other wing.

When we stopped in front of a set of white double doors, he said, "This is your suite." He opened them to reveal a huge sitting room, just as lavish as Paxán's office, but more feminine.

The décor was definitely intended for a chick. A really rich Russian chick. "It's so lovely. But, um, where do I sleep?"

With an exhalation, he started across the spacious area, leaving me to follow. We passed an adjoining study with a snazzy new Mac, then a media room with a wall-stretcher TV, before we reached the bedroom.

Stepping inside, I muttered, "This—is—the—tits."

"Pardon?"

"You've got to be shitting me." I twirled in place, taking in the massive four-poster bed, the hand-painted armoire as big as an elevator, the draperies with silk tassels the size of my forearm. Underfoot, oriental rugs warmed more shining marble. Above, intricate carved molding was gilded with gold. Jade green—my favorite—was the accent color.

"Paxán didn't decorate this for me, did he?"

"Of course. You're his daughter. He took great pleasure trying to imagine what you would like."

"And you knew green is my favorite color."

He inclined his head.

This reminder of his prying into my life didn't grate as much as it had before. "At least some good came from your spying, huh?"

Ignoring that, he said, "There are garments for you in the closets."

"Plural closets?"

"Naturally."

"Oh. Who picked out the clothes?"

"A stylist. She is on call for you, should you need anything else."

Near an extravagant display of welcome flowers, I saw a leather folio and several gift boxes. Inside the folio was a selection of credit cards and a list of phone numbers for Kovalev, the estate manager, the stables, my stylist, housekeeping, the kitchen. "Should I wait to open these presents with Paxán?"

With a raised brow, Sevastyan said, "Something tells me there will be more to follow."

Inside the first box was a smartphone that looked like it'd been transported back from the future. I'd be able to call Jess with my proof of life a week early—and eventually my mom as well. Though what I would tell her about all this, I didn't yet know.

The other boxes—from stores like Cartier, Harry Winston, Mikimoto, and Buccellati—were all filled with dazzling jewelry: a triple-strand pearl choker, sapphire earrings, an emerald drop fringe necklace with a matching bracelet. That bracelet was so heavy and substantial, I could deflect bullets with it, à la Wonder Woman.

Turning to Sevastyan, I joked, "There must be a million dollars' worth of jewelry here."

When he held up his palms in a *what're-you-gonna-do?* gesture, I cried, "Oh, my God. There is!" I inhaled a shaky breath.

This situation was too wild—and overwhelming. I now lived in a palace. I truly was not going back to school tomorrow; instead I'd be playing chess with my billionaire father.

This was my "new life" for the "foreseeable future."

I crossed to a set of balcony doors, opening them for fresh air. I drank in the sight as a mist began to fall over manicured gardens and landscaping lights came to life all across the property.

When Sevastyan joined me at the balcony rail, that feeling of connection swept me up again. But he was all coolness toward me.

"What's that building?" I asked him, indicating a two-story manor catty-corner to this wing. As with the lake folly, its colors and architecture complemented this palace. There was a sleek black Mercedes in the drive, much like the one he'd rented in Lincoln.

"My home," he said shortly.

"You live on the property?"

"*Da.* Though I have an apartment in Moscow," he said in a pointed tone, no doubt referring to my comment about searching his place—and doing other things. Such as watching him masturbate.

I swallowed, peering up at him, filled with questions about the man. What was he thinking at this moment? How'd he get that sexy scar down his lips? Who'd broken his nose?

Had anyone ever kissed that slightly askew bridge for him? "You must have missed this place while slumming in Lincoln."

Shrug. "I return downstairs now."

I followed him back inside. "What do you need to talk to Paxán about so urgently?"

Over his shoulder, he said, "I do have private concerns with him, Natalie."

I narrowed my eyes. "You're going to tell him about us, aren't you?"

He swung his head around at me. "There is no *us*," he said with such vehemence that I almost flinched.

"You know what I mean."

"I'm going to admit that I behaved inappropriately with you. I owe him that."

I had a great feeling about Kovalev, but the truth was that I didn't know him well. What type of punishment would an infraction like this bring? "How mad will he be?" I couldn't picture Kovalev losing his cool, but then I also couldn't picture him blackmailing politicians.

"At you? Not at all. As for me, he can't be more angry than I am at myself."

Sevastyan was starting to piss me off. I strode up to him. "Look, I just got here, and everything is wonderful with Paxán. Why rock the boat when you and I barely did *anything*? I held off on despoiling you. You were relatively safe from my clutches."

Stony gaze.

"Please, I'm asking you not to make a big deal out of something so trivial."

"Trivial?" He closed the slight distance between us until we stood toe-to-toe. "Maybe for two experienced adults. But you're hardly experienced, are you?" His breaths quickened along with mine. Tension sparked the air around us. Oh, God, his intoxicating scent hit me just as I recalled his fierce virgin-or-not promise and his admission: *What was supposed to sate my appetite has only whetted it.*

Chin raised, I bowed up to him until a sheet of paper wouldn't have fit between us. "Just because I haven't had sex doesn't mean I was a nun."

He cocked his head to the side, gaze flicking over my face, like he was trying to read me and coming up empty. I knew the feeling.

"And if my virginity is such a sticking point with you," I said, "that's an easy fix."

His fists clenched. "You mean with another man?"

That show of jealousy thrilled me, so I reminded him, "You could have done it." When I'd been wet and ready for him. Curiosity about how he would relieve me of my virginity seized me; I could only imagine what kinds of tricks this man had in his bag. A long exhalation escaped my lips, and I found myself saying, "You still could."

He took a step back, as if what I had might be catching. "Perhaps I want to tell Paxán so it doesn't happen again."

"You're that certain you don't want it to?"

"Yes," he said, but he'd started twirling that thumb ring. Maybe that tell also indicated when he was lying?

"Was I just a job to you, Sevastyan?"

He gazed to the right of me as he answered, "That's all you can be."

"Do you wish you'd never been sent to America for me?"

He faced me fully. "Every second of the day," he said, no longer touching his ring.

CHAPTER 14

*B*uzzzzzzzz.

My suite had a doorbell? As I hastened to the doors, which were a haul from my bedroom, I wondered if Sevastyan had come to get me. Though I'd been hurt at first by his parting words, I'd assured myself that he was trying to be a good enforcer, walking away from the taboo woman.

Spirits buoyed, I'd investigated my suite, getting ready for tonight. After taking a bath in a tub larger than most family pools, I'd gamely explored all the clothes, shoes, handbags, and cosmetics.

Though the lingerie on the plane hadn't been over-the-top sexy, the selection in my new wardrobe ran the gamut. I'd gone for daring—thigh-highs, a black silk thong, and matching demi-cup bra—just in case Sevastyan apologized for being a dick and admitted taboo was just his speed (*a girl can dream!*).

For the banquet, I'd decided to err on the side of dressy, selecting a formfitting wrap dress in royal-blue silk. The color made my eyes look more aqua than green.

I'd pulled my hair up, the better to show off my pounded-gold choker and chandelier earrings. Though I wasn't a makeup buff, I'd even opted for mascara and lip gloss.

At the door, I smoothed my dress, then opened up. "Filip?"

"I thought I'd escort you to the feast." He was dressed in the latest style, drainpipe pants and a slim-fit jacket. With his tie a little loose, his look said: *Ivy Leaguer who started the party early.* "You look ravishing, Cuz." He took my hand and kissed it.

If Sevastyan had done the same, I would've jumped like the man had live wires attached to his skin. But with Filip there was none of that spark. "Thanks, Filip."

Out in the hall, he offered his arm. "Were you disappointed to see me at the door?"

"What? No," I lied.

"I'm afraid our grim friend Sevastyan declined to come get you."

"Did he, then?" Burn.

It made sense, though. The man wished he'd never met me; why *wouldn't* he avoid me? How quick he'd been to tell me, "There is no *us.*"

Filip frowned down at me. "I've never seen him so put off by a pretty girl before. But all things considered, I suppose we shouldn't blame him."

"All things considered? What do you mean?" My black heels sank into the plush rug as we made our way down the hallway to the staircase.

"He was the boss's main heir before you came along."

I shrugged noncommittally, though I knew this wasn't the cause of Sevastyan's chilliness. *Manalyzing again, Nat?*

The truth was that I didn't *know* anything about him.

Filip continued, "Now Kovalev has taken such a shine to you, he called for his lawyers today to change his will. As of an hour ago, you're officially a billion-heiress."

"How do you know that?" We reached the stairs, descending. He grinned. "I have ways, Cuz."

Why the rush to change his will? "I never asked for that. I don't want any of Kovalev's money." Just thinking about having to deal with that kind of wealth, and the accompanying *responsibility*, made my necklace feel tight around my throat.

I liked the simple life; people with that kind of money didn't lead simple lives. "And I have no intention of horning in on Sevastyan's inheritance."

"Natalie, I never meant to imply that." He looked mortified, like I'd pantsed him. "I'm so sorry if I offended."

"Oh, Filip, I'm just being overly sensitive." I confided to him, "The money actually freaks me out."

"That's a good problem to have, no? Don't fret, you'll get everything worked out with Kovalev. He's a considerate man. He'll do whatever it takes to make you comfortable here."

"I'm sure you're right." Wanting to change the subject, I said, "You and Sevastyan don't seem to get along."

Filip gave me a *you-have-no-idea* expression. "He's like a vicious guard dog around Kovalev, not surprising since the man plucked Sevastyan off the streets."

That was where Kovalev had found him? The idea of Sevastyan living on the streets as a boy broke my heart. No wonder I couldn't get a sense of him. Sevastyan *was* a blend of street and privilege.

"He doesn't like anyone near Kovalev but himself." With a charming quirk of his brow, Filip said, "I'd probably admire the trait more if he didn't use it against me." When we reached the main floor, Filip steered me down an airy foyer.

"And why doesn't Sevastyan like you?"

"He resents my education. He never had formal schooling, you know. He hates any reminder of that. Chip on his shoulder the size of Siberia."

What must Sevastyan think about my advanced degree? Had he felt even a twinge of guilt when he'd unenrolled me?

"Just be careful around him, Cuz."

The same advice Sevastyan had given me about Filip. "Why?"

He gazed away. "The man's got some . . . serious issues."

"Tell me."

In a lower voice, Filip said, "He's been to prison and seems proud of it. He's got these two dome tattoos on his arm, which is *mafiya* code for doing two stints. One of those times was in a bloody Siberian prison camp. It does things to a man."

I was speechless. I'd seen those markings on his arm and had had no idea what they signified.

Yet knowing more about Sevastyan's checkered past didn't diminish my attraction for him. In fact, Filip's revelation had just given Sevastyan layers, making me want to peel them away one by one. Once I returned to my suite tonight, I'd fire up that Mac and learn more about the tattoos. Hell, about this entire new world.

"And don't even get me started on his bizarre relationship with alcohol."

"What do you mean?" I asked, though I'd already seen evidence of this. Last night, Sevastyan had consumed a drink, but only after abstaining from it again and again.

"Just watch him tonight. You'll see. But enough about him. Look, if you need anything, you come to me." Filip patted my hand on his arm. "You're Kovalev's daughter, and I owe that man my life."

"You do?"

He nodded. "I was in a bad place six months ago when my dad died suddenly. Kovalev gave me a lifeline."

"I'm sorry for your loss, and I really appreciate your offer."

I heard laughter and voices drifting from the room at the end of the foyer. I was eager to join the others, but just outside the doors, Filip stopped me.

"I'm so glad you're here, Natalie. It's nice to have someone else around who's Westernized. And who doesn't hold it against me that I've never been to prison!" He laid his hands on my shoulders and smiled down at me, a move that would make most women proffer their panties. "Kovalev has to go into the city tomorrow afternoon. Let me show you around the place—"

Before I could pull away, the doors opened, revealing the Siberian on the other side. My heart leapt—had he been coming for me?

He stopped in his tracks, expression growing lethal. *What'd I do now?* Then I realized it looked like Filip and I had been about to . . . kiss. I swung my head around to take in the immense dining room and the other guests already inside. About thirty brigadiers.

And all their eyes were on Filip and me, every conversation stalled.

I guessed it was pretty bad when dozens of Russian gangsters got scandalized by one's behavior. But I hadn't *done* anything.

At least, not with Filip.

When Sevastyan's fists balled, I marched away from both men. Squaring my shoulders, chin lifted, I made my way to Kovalev, my heels sounding abnormally loud in the silent hall.

He was standing at the head of a lengthy table that was covered with dazzling candles, china, and silver. He glanced uncertainly from me to Filip, so I gave him a ready smile. "This is incredible, Paxán. Thank you." My guiltless demeanor seemed to defuse the situation; conversations resumed.

When Kovalev pulled out the chair to his right for me, he said under his breath, "Anything amiss?"

I murmured back, "Not at all."

Filip followed, taking a seat beside me. With a laugh, he muttered, "That was awkward, huh?"

When Sevastyan returned to the table and took the seat opposite me, his face was his usual unreadable mask, but that muscle in his jaw was twitching.

Kovalev introduced me to the rest of our dinner companions, more than two dozen men in their twenties and thirties—Yuri, Boris, Kirill, Gleb, then I started losing track. They were a rough-looking lot, but they all appeared to hero-worship Kovalev. Only two other women were seated, Olga and Inya, long-term girlfriends of a couple of the brigadiers.

After introductions, what seemed like an army of servers began conveying platters, while others poured vodka into glittering crystal shot glasses. Though I wasn't used to being on this end of service, I forced myself to relax.

"A toast," Kovalev called, drink in hand. "To my lovely daughter. Who found me against all odds, who toiled and fought to get what she wanted."

Filip called, "The apple didn't fall far from the tree."

When the dinner guests raised their glasses, I did the same, then brought it to my lips to sip—

Everyone shot theirs, then turned to me. I recalled it was considered rude to put a glass with alcohol back on the table. With a shrug, I downed mine too, and cheers broke out. I couldn't help but grin, glancing at Sevastyan, who simply stared at me.

I could've sworn he'd been jealous of Filip earlier, but if he gave a damn, then why hadn't he bothered to come get me from my room in the first place?

In any case, I refused to let him ruin this for me. Here I was at an authentic Russian banquet, drinking vodka with my father's extended . . . clan. I was in the land of my birth, ensconced in a former tsar's home.

I gazed up, marveling at the frescoes above us. This absolutely looked like the dining room of a tsar. I realized I'd never *felt* history like this. Which took some of the sting out of my involuntary withdrawal from school.

Tonight, my good mood was bulletproof.

Another toast followed: *"Za vas,* Natalya Kovaleva!" To you. This time I got my shot down in time with the table. I savored the burn, pleasantly warmed.

When a *zakuska*—a spread of miscellaneous appetizers—was served, Filip leaned over. "This is called a *za-kus-ka.*"

Sevastyan said, "Natalie studied Russian—I'm sure she knows what it is."

I cast him a quick look of appreciation. Having every dish explained to me would've gotten old.

Filip's affable mien never faded, even as he said, "It's merely etiquette, Sevastyan. To be welcoming to a guest—escorting her from her room and such."

Thanks for reminding me.

The two men stared each other down. The tense moment was broken by another serving: oysters topped with plentiful caviar from the Volga Delta. Then a fish course followed.

I took a bite of heavenly baked sole, making a sound of delight; Sevastyan's eyes were on me.

I shot another vodka; his eyes were on me.

I listened to a story Filip seemed determine to whisper to me; Sevastyan clenched a fist beside his plate. He could assure me that there was no *us* all he wanted to, but . . .

Actions speak louder than words, Siberian. And his focus on me was warming me as much as the vodka.

When servers brought yet another dish, Kovalev announced, "In honor of Natalie's home of Nebraska."

It was corn soufflé! I grinned at him. "I love it." I was beginning to sound crazy tipsy.

Then I felt Sevastyan's dark gaze on me yet again. Was he remembering the cornfield? Pinning me in the dirt? Meeting his eyes, I downed another shot.

Kovalev turned to Sevastyan. "You're not eating, Aleksandr?"

He straightened. "Perhaps I'm feeling the trip."

Filip quipped, "Or your age."

With his quiet intensity, Sevastyan said, "I hold my own."

In a merry tone, Kovalev said, "There now, lads." He turned to me. "I think our clever Filip sometimes forgets the Siberian was a bare-knuckle prizefighter for many years."

I raised my brows. When I'd first seen Sevastyan, I'd guessed he was a fighter. That would explain the scars on his fingers, his broken nose. I recalled the many times I'd seen Sevastyan ball his fists. For a fighter, that must be the default factory setting.

When I thought of all the men who'd struck that noble face of his, I wanted to touch him, to smooth my fingers over his skin. I was trying to imagine him in the ring, dealing pain, when another course appeared.

Dessert. There were baked apples, fruit pastels—a kind of Russian Turkish delight—and *sirniki*, a cheese pancake with a side of honey for dipping. As soon as my first pastel touched my tongue, I rolled my eyes with bliss.

After dessert, drinks reigned and laughter grew boisterous. It was bad etiquette not to finish an opened bottle of vodka, so everyone politely pounded shot after shot—well, everyone except for Sevastyan. After the toasts, his glass went untouched.

Paxán recounted hilarious tales of his attempts at leisure. Sailing? The boat was now an artificial reef. Breeding horses? He'd find that wily escaped stallion one of these days.

I laughed until my eyes watered, admitting that I'd thought he would have white tigers and a bear—*and* a diamond-encrusted toilet, which made Kovalev double over.

The guy named Gleb taught me a Russian tongue twister. Everyone laughed at my buzzed rendition, but I was a good goddamned sport, so I feigned a quick curtsy. I saw that even Sevastyan's customary scowl had changed to a look of something like fascination, as if I were a creature he'd never seen in the wild before.

Every time I grew convinced I couldn't break through his icy reserve again, he'd show hints of the man beneath the enforcer façade. . . .

I wished I could freeze time—couldn't remember when I'd last had such a fun night—but before I knew it, a grandfather clock struck midnight.

Paxán stood. "Well, my friends and family"—he smiled at me and Sevastyan—"you'll have to excuse me."

A chorus of "One more drink!" rang out.

He shook his head. "Take pity on an old man! And continue—that's an order." Sevastyan and I rose at the same time, both intending to walk Paxán out.

"Sit, sit, you two. Enjoy yourselves. I'll see you tomorrow."

As I watched Paxán strolling away, I didn't want to let him out of my sight. I had the feeling that he might disappear. But then Sevastyan gave me a reassuring look, as if he understood what I was feeling. It helped.

After that, drinks continued to flow. The hour grew late, but I didn't care because I didn't have work tomorrow, didn't have to deal with first-year students spinning tales about why their papers were late.

My only complaint? I wanted Sevastyan to talk to me, to flirt with me. To touch me. I desired more of what he'd shown me the night before.

I wanted sex with him.

Craved it.

I'd been reminded of how relentless I could be; maybe I should pursue *him* relentlessly?

To my right, Filip and some brigadiers got into a heated debate about the fastest sports car—which gave me an opportunity for mischief. I was intoxicated enough that the idea of teasing Sevastyan seemed *brilliant*.

Though he'd warned me that he didn't like surprises, I slipped off one heel, then stretched my hosed foot toward his legs. I made contact with his inner thigh, right above his knee. He tensed, but didn't give me away, just cast me that menacing look.

Was it a good idea to play with an enforcer like him? Vodka said, *Hell, yeah, touch his badge!* I reached higher. With each inch closer I got to his dick, his breaths came quicker. He gave a forceful shake of his head.

With a lazy grin, I dipped my forefinger into a honey pot, then sucked it between my lips, my smug expression saying, *Whatcha gonna do, Siberian?*

His own lips parted. Recalling me sucking him the night before?

Higher, higher . . .

Contact.

God, he was burning hot, hard as iron. He tilted his head sharply, his nostrils flaring. And for a long moment, his chest didn't move at all.

With my lids gone heavy, I rubbed the ball of my foot along his length, thrilled when his cock pulsed in reaction. I grew wet in response, dampening the black silk thong I'd worn for him. My nipples budded in the demi cups of my bra.

When I stroked him from base to head, he cast me another look of warning—even as his gaze gleamed with lust. Now it was a battle of wills, a game of chicken. *Stroke.* He was refusing to react; I refused to quit. *Another stroke.* Who would blink first?

Wondering if I could get him off like this, I rubbed him with more pressure. The muscles in his shoulders and arms began to swell. The fighter must be clenching his fists beneath the table.

His eyes promised a hot and thorough punishment.

Mine must've been pleading for it.

If I retired to my room, would he follow? Apparently, I would be blinking first. I lowered my foot and slipped my shoe back on. As the sports car debate wound down, I feigned a yawn and rose. "I'm tired from the trip as well." Avoiding Sevastyan's face, I said, "Good night, everyone. It was great to meet you all."

"But there are more bottles to finish," Filip said with an irrepressible wink. Oh, dear, what if *he* tried to follow me?

To dissuade him, I said, "Stay and have fun—I'll see you tomorrow."

He brightened. "Tomorrow afternoon, then. It's a date."

Date? That wasn't what I'd meant, and I didn't want to get his hopes up. But all eyes were on us, so I decided to let it go for now.

With a last wave at everyone, I made my way out of the dining room. I took my time strolling back to my suite, pausing to regard the collection of paintings in the upstairs hall, wishing Sevastyan would come to me.

And then he did. Striding down the hallway, looking every inch a *mafiya* enforcer. Expression murderous.

Which for him could be literal.

CHAPTER 15

$\mathcal{A}$s Sevastyan prowled closer, I backed up a step, then another.

He grabbed my upper arm, dragging me down the hall. In a deceptively soft voice, he asked, "Did you enjoy playing with me?" He opened a side door, shoved me inside, then closed it behind us. I smelled fresh laundry and brass polish.

A maid's closet?

And it was in a tsar's residence? I could only imagine how many secret trysts had been carried out over the years within these four walls.

He flipped on a muted light, backing me farther inside. "You left me hard and aching, then planned a fucking assignation with Filip in front of me?" When my ass met a linen shelf, he clamped a hand on either side of my hips to cage me in, filling my head with his seductive scent. "Are we so interchangeable? Filip and I?"

"I don't like him that way."

"Do you not?" Sevastyan's voice was laced with rage. "You looked like you did at the beginning of dinner. When he was about to kiss you."

"What does it matter to you? You blew me off, remember?"

"It matters when you decide to stroke my cock under the table till I'm nearly strangling with need. It matters when you were drinking me down less than twenty-four hours ago." Without warning, he shoved my dress up over my hips.

I sucked in a breath.

He stared at my thong, then the black thigh-highs, fingering the lacy tops. "Who did you wear these for?"

I raised my chin. "You."

"So you planned for us to be together? After I'd said no? Tonight you've enjoyed playing with fire. But will you accept the burn you've earned?"

"Pardon—"

The word was cut off with a gasp when he lifted me up on the shelf. "I'm going to show you what I felt." He wedged himself between my thighs.

"What does that mean?"

He didn't answer, just unzipped his slacks to drag the heavy length of his cock out. The crown was damp with arousal. My body went electric when his shaft strained toward my pussy, as if hunting it on its own.

I'd loved on his dick with my mouth and taken his semen on my tongue, wanted to again. "Let me kiss you like last night." I tried to shimmy off the shelf, but he pinned me there, pressing that shaft directly against the silky front of my panties. Right against my swollen clitoris. I moaned when I perceived the heat of him, even through the damp material.

"Feel that," he rasped. "Teasing me got you wet? You like goading me until I lose control?"

"Yes," I whimpered.

He rubbed my upper thighs with his callused palms, higher and higher. With his thumbs, he reached under my panties and pulled my lips past the sides of the crotch. "This is what I felt." He thrust, as much as clothes-fucking me, with only silk between his cock and my clit.

I moaned low, my head falling back.

"No, you don't," he snapped, drawing my gaze. "You're going to look at me like you did when you teased me, Natalya. Like you would die if I didn't fuck you at that moment." He gave a second thrust, making my body vibrate. "Your eyes were begging me to bend you over that table and plunge into your pussy." Another thrust. "Is that what you meant to tell me?"

"Yes!" I was going to come like this, was already on the verge. "I want it now."

"Christ, woman." He rocked his hips again, gliding his shaft over me. More pre-cum clung to the head; he swiped a streak of it against the silk, then positioned himself once more.

The friction and heat were making me mindless. "Please don't stop that!"

"I *should* stop, leaving you as you did me." He leaned forward to rumble words at my ear, "Feeling like I'd explode, on the verge of coming in my pants. So close I wanted to; damn the consequences, I wanted you to bring my cock off in a room full of people."

When I shivered, his thumbs delved deeper. "Open your dress."

I untied the sash, then drew the sides apart, baring my bra.

"Very nice," he said with another thrust. "Now, take that off."

I snatched it up, wanting him to see my heavy breasts.

When they bobbed with his next thrust, he grunted the order: "Play."

My hands flew to them, cupping.

"Lovely Natalya." He rolled his hips again. The silk was now soaking. "You're going to wet me through your panties?" He ran

two fingers along the damp underside of his shaft before returning it against me.

I moaned. "Why won't you have sex with me?"

"Don't forget this is punishment." A crueler thrust. "And you're
not for *me*. Now, show me how hard those nipples can get."

I tugged at them.

"Harder."

I did, moaning when I felt his thumbs at my slit, opening me,
so close to breaching me with them. "Inside, Sevastyan. Put your
fingers inside me."

"Have you ever used one of those vibrators to penetrate yourself?"

My face heated, a ridiculous reaction considering what we
were doing. But I answered honestly, "Yes. I like to."

He groaned, bucking faster. "Then why were you a virgin?"

Between panting breaths, I said, "Hadn't met . . . the right
guy."

"Yet you think you have now?" He started a series of swift
pumps, sawing his shaft back and forth over my wet clit.

"Sevastyan!" I could almost pretend that he was fucking me,
his stiff rod pillaging my core. He'd fuck and fuck until I was
forced to come around his cock. Until he'd forced me to milk that
thick length . . . "Ah, God, I'm about—"

He covered my mouth with one of his hands, muffling my
screams. He slipped two fingers between my lips, treating me to
my own juices. "Suck," he ordered.

My head fell back and I sucked in delight, imagining those
fingers were his cock. Under his sharp thrusts, I began to orgasm.
I screamed, I sucked, I never wanted it to end.

Clenching, spasming, each wave brought unbearable pleasure—
and a frenzied hunger to be filled. . . .

When I was too sensitive to take any more, he pulled back and pressed my knees toward my naked breasts. With me rocking back against the wall, ankles on his shoulders, he yanked my panties to my thighs, baring me. Gaze locked on my swollen flesh, he fisted himself, masturbating that big cock.

Neck straining, arm muscles bulging, he grated, "Watch me come on you." He was aiming between my legs. The idea of him ejaculating there made me melt all over again, my pussy quivering and contracting as he watched—

"Fuck, woman, I see you!" Choking back a yell, he began to spurt heavy ropes of cum.

When scorching semen lapped against my sensitive lips, I moaned, spreading my legs in welcome.

Between gnashed teeth, he hissed, "My greedy girl wants more?" He squeezed his cock, and another ribbon lashed my mons. Over and over, he pumped himself until his shaft was spent, pulsating but empty. . . .

Dazed, wanting to kiss him, I reached for him.

But he pushed my hands away. "Ah-ah." He palmed me between my thighs—and began slathering his seed into my flesh.

Why? What? How could that be so sexy? As ever, I had no idea what he would do next. Though my arousal had renewed with a surge, I sat docile, allowing him to coat me.

After working my panties back into place, he used his whole palm to give the sodden crotch a good slap—which made me buck for another. With that same look of masculine satisfaction, he said, "You'll feel me tomorrow."

Wicked, sexy, domineering man. I couldn't imagine another male could excite me as much as he did. I needed to wrap my arms around him, to whisper in his ear how he drove me crazy.

But he simply zipped up and turned to go, to leave me like this. "Better focus your attention on someone you can actually manipulate. Speaking of which, have fun with Filip tomorrow."

When he reached the door, I gave my head a clearing shake. "That's all you have to say?"

Without turning around, he said, "Do not ever tease me again. I only play games when I make the rules."

"Rules, Siberian?" Now that I wasn't stupid with lust, I didn't love his domineering self. "You can make them, if only to watch me break them."

"If you tease me again, pet, you will not enjoy the consequences." He left me, shutting the door behind him.

Note to self: Tease Sevastyan at earliest opportunity, investigate "consequences."

In that closet, still warmed—and wet—from his attentions, I decided two things:

Aleksandr Sevastyan had to be my first lover.

And I'd let him *think* he made the rules.

CHAPTER 16

"You're Sevastyan, right?" I said with full-on sarcasm when I ran into him downstairs a week later. "Didn't I see you in the closet the other day?"

Since then, I'd made zero progress with my Sevastyan-pops-cherry plan, a plan that had since been *retired*. Which was only to be expected since he refused to talk to me, aside from superficial greetings.

He raised a brow at my comment, falling into step beside me as I made my way to Paxán's study.

I frowned at him. For the last seven days, we'd never been alone. He'd always been close by—yet achingly distant.

The morning after the maid's closet, I'd awakened smiling again, looking forward just to seeing him. I'd called Jess and told her all about him, about everything. She'd focused on one detail: "Nat, you've still got your skin tag?" I'd assured her *not for long, my friend.*

There'd been a bounce in my step as I arrived for breakfast.

Only to find Sevastyan was back to his aloof self, barely acknowledging me. While my body had still been feeling the aftereffects of what we'd done, his mind had checked out.

I supposed if he'd thought what we'd done on the plane was bad, then shoving me into a closet to have his way with me must have been awful in his mind. I'd tried to get him alone, endeavored to get him to talk to me. Nothing.

Disappointment had settled over me. During this lull, my disappointment had begun to feel a lot like anger.

I'd lived without Sevastyan for seven nights. I'd conceded defeat. My infatuation had faded.

It had! "Do you need something?" I asked him in a cool voice. *Now* he was going to pay attention to me?

Though he was dressed like a dream—dark gray slacks and a formfitting black cashmere sweater—he looked like he hadn't slept for days. "You and Kovalev are getting along well," he remarked in a neutral tone.

"He's easy to get along with." Paxán and I had been like two peas in a pod, appreciating the same jokes, enjoying the same books and food.

Growing closer every day.

Sometimes we spoke English, sometimes Russian. In both languages, he was sly and witty, and we often laughed to tears. Being with him was almost opposite to how it'd been with my dad. Though I'd never doubted he loved me and Mom, Bill Porter had been a quiet man. He and I used to work on his tractors, passing the time in companionable silence.

It was just as comfortable with Kovalev, only different.

Every morning, we played chess in an open-sided pavilion down by the Moskva River. Sevastyan remained in the background, usually on the phone conducting business, body tense, gaze alert for danger.

The security threat—which no one would talk to me about—obviously hadn't lessened.

Now Sevastyan told me, "You're easy to get along with as well."

Was he for real? "And how would *you* know?"

He hiked his shoulders. "I see you with him."

Sometimes when Paxán and I would laugh at something, I'd notice Sevastyan regarding us. At first, he'd appeared surprised. Now he would gaze at us with a satisfied look on his face.

Yet at other times I'd catch him surveying me with an expression that was far from satisfied—and it intensified more each day. I felt as if he was awaiting something. From *me*.

Like a hunter preparing to strike.

Even Filip had commented on it. "When you're not looking, he watches you like a stalker."

I'd scoffed, "A stalker would actually give me the time of day if I asked for it."

Yet something *was* building in Sevastyan, like a bomb clock ticking a countdown. But a countdown to what?

"Are you settling in?" he asked.

Was he going to query me about the weather next? I stayed him with a hand on his arm. "What's up with the small talk, Siberian?" I almost got the impression that he was trying—in his taciturn, enforcer-type way—to chat me up. When he peered down at my hand, I released him.

"Do you like it here?" he asked, his voice dropping a notch. "Enough to stay?"

We'd stopped in front of a rain-slicked window. Outside, fall rains drizzled. There hadn't been a break in the weather since I'd gotten to Berezka. Shadows from the drops coursed over Sevastyan's face, filling me with the mad urge to kiss each one.

Inner shake. "Why do you and Paxán and Filip get to leave, but I don't?"

He scrubbed his hand over his chin. "Because if anything happened to you . . . We simply can't take chances. You're so eager to leave?"

"Well, I have to admit I was getting stir-crazy whenever Paxán had to work—I'm not used to all this free time." Or this much energy. I'd been in desperate need of an outlet when Filip had suggested laps in the Olympic-size indoor pool. Every day, we went together. "But Filip has been doing his best to keep me occupied."

Those muscles on the sides of Sevastyan's jaw bulged. He took a step closer. As ever, tension brewed between us. I glanced up at his eyes, only to find his gaze on my lips.

"I told you to be wary of him."

"But not *why*." Once I'd shut down my manalyzing, I'd grown comfortable with Filip. Unfortunately, I felt nothing more for him than friendship.

Why couldn't I fall for a guy like him? He said whatever was on his mind, was easygoing, and acted like I hung the moon.

The opposite of Sevastyan.

If I were with Filip, I wouldn't have felt the just-in-case need to brush up on the finer points of BDSM, studying everything from corporal punishment to orgasm denial to dom/sub rituals.

Sevastyan had talked about obedience and discipline; was he interested in the lifestyle, the equipment, the paraphernalia?

Punishment bars and floggers, handcuffs and canes, nipple clamps and ball gags.

Recalling the way Sevastyan had slapped my ass, I'd watched online videos featuring grown women stretched over men's laps, spanked like they were wayward creatures in need of correction.

I'd been indignant and outraged!

I'd pictured Sevastyan forcing me across his lap for a similar chastisement; he'd once threatened to do exactly that. And as soon as I'd finished masturbating, I'd been indignant and outraged all over again!

Until I'd masturbated a second time. But that had been *before* I'd conceded defeat.

"What are you thinking of?" he asked me, his gaze riveted to my face.

I realized my breaths had shallowed, my cheeks heating.

He put his hand on my wrist, touching me with that live-wire grip. His brows drew together, until I could almost imagine he was about to kiss me.

Despite everything, I wanted him to—

Yuri exited Paxán's office.

I abruptly stepped back, tucking my hair behind my ears, resisting the urge to whistle. As the man passed, I tried not to notice the AK-47 strapped to his back. Even after a week here, I was still uneasy seeing guns everywhere. When the brigadiers took tea breaks, they would casually lay their weapons down beside their cups.

I kept telling myself, *Roll with it, roll with it.*

Sevastyan gave Yuri a chin jerk in greeting. *Carry on.* While the brigadiers revered Paxán, they seemed to uniformly fear Sevastyan. I'd overheard them talking about "the Siberian" in hushed tones.

Once Sevastyan and I were alone again, sanity resumed. I didn't need to be kissing a man who'd ruthlessly cut me out of his life. Didn't need to reward his shitty treatment of me.

Jess had an m.o. for dealing with badly behaving males—she called it *ABC: Always Be Crazier.* I was thinking my m.o. might be *kill 'em with kindness.*

When Sevastyan opened his mouth to speak, I gave his arm a

brisk pat. "Good talk, buddy! We should do this in another week or so." I strode off, leaving him looking confounded.

◆

*F*ifteen minutes later, Paxán and I were sitting in the pavilion at a table topped with tea, delicacies, and our chessboard. A fire in the pavilion hearth crackled, warming us. As usual, Sevastyan worked some distance away, fielding phone calls, his watchful eyes scanning for a threat.

The two of us sipped and snacked, wading deeper into our game. "Do you know who is a master player?" Paxán eyed our pieces. "Aleksandr."

"Is he?" I made my tone as uninterested as possible, even as my gaze flicked over to Sevastyan.

He was embroiled in a heated conversation, had begun striding outside into the drizzle. He made his way down to the nearby boathouse—which really should be called a "yacht house" considering the sixty-foot beauty housed inside.

I knew sub-nothing about boats, but I was pretty sure this one had been the villain's yacht in *Casino Royale*. Paxán had promised to take me out once the weather—and danger—broke, said we could motor all the way to the Gulf of Finland.

"You should play Aleksandr sometime."

I gave a shrug. Pass. I was trying to get over my fascination with him, not fuel it.

Yet when Sevastyan's words floated up, dimly echoing from the boathouse, I frowned. "Is he speaking . . . Italian?"

"Ah, yes," Paxán said proudly. "He speaks four languages fluently. He's a—what do you call it?—a self-learner?"

I nodded. The bruiser boxer, the feared enforcer, the professional hit man, was an autodidact. Fascination fueled once more. Damn it.

"If only I could interest him in the workings of clocks." Paxán had begun teaching me, and I'd geeked out, finding it addictive. "So have you given some thought to making this your full-time home?" He'd yet to exert any pressure on me, although I could tell how much he longed for me to stay.

In a dry tone, I said, "Gee. Maybe if you'd give me some gifts, you know, spoil me a little." I'd received countless pieces of priceless jewelry, another closetful of clothes, a red Aston Martin Vanquish that Filip had salivated over, and even my own thoroughbred, an exquisite dapple-gray mare named Alizay. I only awaited a sunny day to take her out.

In a matching tone, he said, "Next you'll be saying the Fabergé egg was too much."

With a laugh, I held up my thumb against my forefinger. "Just a touch."

He chuckled with me. "I can't help it. I have all this money and years to make up for. The birthday presents alone . . ." He tilted his head. "Sometimes I wish you were more interested in being rich."

The present that I'd adored above all the rest had been the least expensive: a framed portrait of my mother, Elena. How I wished I'd been able to know her!

She'd had strawberry blond hair, sparkling green eyes, and a coy smile. I might resemble my grandmother, but I saw similarities to Elena as well.

When I'd gushed over the thoughtfulness of the gift, Paxán had informed me that the idea had been Sevastyan's, which had surprised me.

"It's not that I don't appreciate everything, but at heart, I'm a farm girl. I like the simple life. Besides, you are the draw here—not the gifts." I hadn't gotten around to telling him that I wanted him to change his will back. The topic was morbid, and I got the sense that it would crush his feelings.

"But Berezka is pleasant, no?"

I gazed out over the surreal landscape. A green lawn sprawled to the edge of the river. Light drops of rain splashed the surface with notes like music. Otters frolicked in the current. Each day, Paxán would point out local species of animals. "Look! It's a stoat," he'd say. Or a shrew, or a raccoon dog, or a great crested grebe.

I admitted, "It's magical here."

"What can I do to convince you to stay?"

As little as I saw Mom, I could visit her twice a year at her new place. She was currently on a cruise around the world that she'd "won." Just a precaution, courtesy of the Kovaleva syndicate.

When I'd called to check in, I hadn't told her anything, figuring a reveal this major should be done in person.

Eventually Mom would be fine wherever I lived, but how could I leave Jess . . . and school? "Living here would be challenging, with school and all." I could let my master's stand as my ending degree; I didn't have to pursue the PhD. Yet somehow that felt like quitting.

"We are within driving distance of several renowned universities."

God, the hopefulness in his voice was killing me. I knew he was accustomed to having his way, just as Sevastyan clearly was, but Paxán was making the effort to coax me to remain—which made me respect him all the more.

"Starting at a new university is something to investigate, at least," I said, committing to nothing.

I was beginning to suspect that I was a commitment-phobe. Though I'd always considered myself decisive, I could see now that my decision trees were usually limbless.

If one completed a master's degree and didn't want to make a decision about one's future . . . well, get a PhD! Stay in the same chute. Start classes a week after the last ones ended.

Maybe that was why the money bothered me so much; in a way, it represented infinite choices.

Hell, I hadn't even *chosen* to come to Russia.

"It's your move, *dorogaya moya*." My dear.

I made a halfhearted play. "What about the danger, Paxán? What's happening with that other organization?"

"These are difficult times we live in. There used to be, well, honor among thieves. Now the areas I control are getting flooded with an element that frightens my people."

"What's going on?"

"I'll give you a mild example. My rival, Ivan Travkin, set up a parking lot in the middle of my territory. No one used it—there was no need to—so Travkin's men began smashing the windshields of any cars outside the lot, forcing people to pay for parking every day. They came to me to get this stopped, so I sent Sevastyan, who shut that operation down. Forcefully."

I could only imagine what the legendary Siberian had done.

"For years, Travkin has searched for small inroads like this, planning the death of my syndicate by a thousand cuts. But when he learned of your existence and sent two of his deadliest enforcers to America"—my twinkling-eyed Santa of a father grew steely-eyed and cold—"it was a declaration of war."

War. Was it any wonder that I worried about Paxán constantly? And about Sevastyan, his frontline general?

"Once we prevail, things will be different for you. We can

move freely." Paxán's expression softened again. "I will show you the country of your birth, your mother's hometown. We can find any cousins of yours!"

"I would love that. Other than this trip, I've never traveled."

He gave me an odd look, a *guilty* one, as if that was a failing on his part. "A fact that must be remedied as soon as possible. But in the meantime, it's not so bad at Berezka?"

As if magnetized, my gaze sought out Sevastyan. Though no longer on the phone, he remained on the dock, scanning the perimeter. I lifted my teacup for a sip, and a moment to gather my thoughts.

"So the interest runs both ways?" Paxán said slyly.

I nearly choked on tea.

"Aleksandr told me about the two of you."

I set down my cup, because it shook. "What did he say?"

"After you two arrived, he came to me, confessing that things with you had passed beyond what was . . . expected."

Had I gotten Sevastyan in trouble? "This is all my fault," I quickly said. "Before I knew who he was, I tried to pick him up in a bar—something I had never done before. And then later, I pushed him. He said no, that I was your daughter, but I pushed."

"I'm not angry, dear! I love Aleksandr as my son and want only what's best for him. He's thirty-one, and I'd despaired of him ever settling down. He's never even dated the same woman twice."

"S-settling down? Um, why are you speaking about that?" Had Sevastyan mentioned wanting to? With me? I couldn't tell if I was perversely thrilled—or about to bolt from the pavilion. "What did he say?"

Kovalev steepled his fingers. "When we first began to suspect that you might truly be my daughter, he grew excited at the prospect of having a sister. But then . . ." He trailed off with a perplexed expression.

"But then?"

"He saw you in person. He hadn't been in America for more than a week when I received a call from him. In his reserved way, he asked me to send a replacement, because his notice of you wasn't what it should be."

"What does that mean?" I asked as calmly as possible— even as my heart tripped over a beat. Along with my surprise at this development, a weird sense of power surged inside me. Sevastyan could barely control himself with me! He'd wanted to relinquish his job, knowing he'd disappoint the man he obviously idolized.

"Aleksandr confessed his interest in you was . . . dark."

Sevastyan had watched me and wanted me—*darkly*?

Paxán frowned. "And, well, deep."

That one was even more surprising.

Dark and deep sounded . . . stalker-y. Probably because Sevastyan had been stalking me at the time (though he'd been ordered to). Still, it gave me pause. "So he's not in trouble?"

"Honestly, this situation isn't ideal. If you two walked hand in hand into my office, wanting to get married, I'd throw you a wedding like Russia has never seen. But if it was known that my most trusted enforcer had—what's the word?—*trifled* with you, that would not be good."

I swallowed nervously, having no doubt he'd consider what Sevastyan and I had done trifling. "You'd be angry?"

"Only that you would be put at risk. If this continued, others would find out. I would lose respect for not keeping my men in order, and Aleksandr would lose respect for disloyalty to me. Unfortunately, our business—and our safety—depends on respect. With Travkin aggressing, we are already vulnerable. He would use this to undermine my authority with this organization."

"I don't think Sevastyan and I are in danger of any more, um, trifling." Though I might feel some inexplicable connection to him, whatever interest he'd felt for me had faded. Didn't know why. The only thing that had changed was that he'd gotten to know me better, so *ouch*.

"I would not even have approached you with this if I hadn't seen your own interest in him." Paxán looked troubled as he said, "Still, just as I want what's best for him, I must secure that for you as well. And I'm not convinced he is what you need."

"Why not?"

"Aleksandr lives a life of extremes." He exhaled wearily, gazing at Sevastyan with a look at once proud and a little mystified. "Extreme loyalty, violence, vigilance. I've known him for nearly twenty years and have seen him with scores of beautiful women"—*jealousy rearing its ugly head!*—"but I have never seen him respond to anyone the way he does to you. His interest *is* dark, and that's not necessarily a good thing."

Paxán hadn't exactly answered the question. "Are you warning me away from him?"

"I'm in an uncomfortable position. Do I hinder his happiness to secure yours? Or do I dare hope the two of you could make each other happy? Matches like this weren't uncommon in my day. It would make sense, no? A trusted right-hand man and a treasured daughter?"

Matches? Securing happiness? This all sounded so ominous— and permanent. My commitment-phobe self was on full alert. "This is really heavy. I hardly know him."

"Did Aleksandr tell you how we met?"

"He said I should ask you."

Paxán raised his brows. "That's surprising. He's a very private man."

"He did say you took him in as a boy. Will you tell me how you found him?"

Paxán nodded. "I was driving the slums in St. Petersburg, looking for a foothold in the city. And I saw this man in a back alley beating a boy of no more than thirteen, beating him bloody. This wasn't something unique. It was after the fall of communism. There were thousands of street children, and many were harshly abused."

Sevastyan had been abused? The idea left a hollow ache in my chest. I gazed at him, now a grown man, so tall and stalwart.

"But this boy," Paxán continued, "he kept struggling to his feet, facing the man with his shoulders squared. Why didn't the boy stay in the gutter? Why keep rising? I'd never seen anyone take so many hits. Eventually, the man wore himself out! When the boy landed his sole blow, the big man went down, and then the boy disappeared. I had to know why he'd kept rising. So I followed his trail of blood to ask. Do you know what Aleksandr's answer was?"

Spellbound, I shook my head.

"In a deadened tone, he told me, '*Pozor bolnee udarov.*' Shame is more painful than blows."

I swallowed. He'd been like that—at thirteen?

"Extreme, no? It's expected for each *vor* to mentor a protégé, to bring someone who shows promise into the fold. I'd never been interested in doing so until I met him."

"Where had he come from? Was he an orphan?" As I'd briefly been.

Paxán parted his lips, then seemed to think better of what he was about to tell me. "Perhaps he would confide in you if you two spent time together and got to know each other better."

And therein lay the problem. Anytime we were alone, we were in danger of fooling around. Which might explain why Sevastyan had been avoiding me.

"Paxán, I need you to level with me," I said, my face heating anew. "What would happen, if there was more . . . trifling?"

The dapper gentleman clockmaker pulled at his collar, utterly uncomfortable with this, reminding me that he was new at having a daughter. "Do you mind if I switch from English?" he asked, and I waved him on.

In Russian, using what had to be a record number of euphemisms, Paxán basically told me that if Sevastyan and I consummated a relationship, the man would be obligated to become *plighted* to me—a way of saying *bound*, fairly much forever—even without the wedding.

It all became clear. No wonder Sevastyan had distanced himself from me—he dreaded what might happen. Attraction to me was one thing, being plighted quite another.

Not that I wanted such an arrangement with him, but it still stung that he'd do anything to avoid getting saddled with me.

The first couple of days after the closet incident, I'd made excuses for his distance. He was too busy, had too much on his mind. *Stupid, Natalie.*

Not the guy to hold my hands and warm them when they're cold.

"I believe I'm bungling this." Paxán rubbed his temples. "You're so young. Too young to be given to another?"

"Given?" I said, voice scaling an octave higher. This was the way of the world here, a world I was now immersed in.

Gaze going distant, Paxán said, "Still, considering all the danger these days, maybe you need a man who would lay down his life for you."

"Will you tell me more about Travkin and the current threat

against us?" Paxán kept the specifics in the vault, so to speak, not wanting to burden me. "Do we all have glaring bull's-eyes on our backs?"

Paxán seemed not to have heard me. "It is a difficult situation, and perhaps it's not meant to be with you and Aleksandr. There are shadows in him."

"Shadows?"

Paxán focused on me once more. "I know Filip is also interested in you. You're closer in age and have much more in common."

"I'm not attracted to him like that. I almost wish I could be, but I'm not."

"No attraction at all? To *Filip*?"

I shook my head. "None."

"That is . . . unexpected. Perhaps you just need to give all this some time. Let things settle as they will?"

Sevastyan strode up the pavilion steps then, shoulders bunched with tension. A look passed between the two men, and Paxán immediately stood. "Now, my dear, it appears that I have pressing business."

I made my expression neutral. "Anything I should know about?" Whenever Sevastyan scanned for danger, was it because he was *extremely vigilant* or because danger was imminent?

Paxán absently kissed my head. "Nothing we can't handle. . . ."

Behind him, Sevastyan's restless demeanor called to mind that ticking bomb clock. His golden eyes darkened on my face—like an indecipherable warning, meant for me alone.

Sooner or later, the countdown clock would zero out.

And then what would happen?

CHAPTER 17

"*I* need answers, Filip." He and I were in the stables, awaiting the groom. The weather had finally broken after another week of rain, and I'd invited Filip to join me for a ride. "I need to know more about the threat to Kovalev."

Things around Berezka continued to heat up, and no one would explain to me what was happening. Not even when a photographer had arrived yesterday to take a head shot of me—for my new fake Russian passport. "Just a precaution," Paxán had assured me. "You never know when you might need to travel outside our territory."

To travel? Or to flee?

Since my talk with Paxán, I'd gone on a Sevastyan-fast, working to keep my mind off him. Sometimes I would catch his penetrating gaze on me—the clock ticking on—but he never said anything to me beyond good morning.

Still that tension simmered between us, mirroring the business tension pervading the estate. Both continued to grow, with no end in sight.

"Don't worry about it, Nat." Filip looked model-stylish in his boots, tan riding pants, and plaid equestrian jacket. Only a man of his physical perfection could pull off that outfit, a cross between voguish and swank. But he also looked exhausted. "Your father is a clever man. He's always one step ahead of the bad guys, even a ruthless character like Travkin."

I adjusted my own tailored coat with my warm gloves. Though the sun was out, the air was chilly. Fall in Russia had a definite bite. "I wish there was something I could do to help." I'd edited Kovalev's sparse Wikipedia entry, adding "allegedly" everywhere and implementing a "Contributions to Charity" section.

How had the syndicate lived without me all this time?

Strangely, there was no mention of Aleksandr Sevastyan anywhere online. There was a prominent family in Russia with the same last name, but they were in legitimate commerce and even politics.

"You *are* helping." Filip chucked me under the chin. "You make the old man happy. Each day you two grow closer. It's obvious to everyone. Let the menfolk take care of this."

I stiffened, then realized he was kidding. He was the most modern-minded guy here, and he loved to yank my chain.

"You're ravishing when you're all feminine and piqued." He tilted his head. "You know, you'd be amazing blackmail bait. That'd be one way to join the family business, Cuz."

"Are you trying to distract me?"

With his angelic smile, he asked, "Is it working?" He reached forward to grasp my ponytail, twirling the end around his forefinger. Just when I was about to step away, he abruptly dropped his hand. He had a knack for sensing how far he could push with the flirting.

He'd been having to pull back more and more—because he was *always* flirting. At times Filip's behavior made me wonder if he was aware of those plighted rules. I could swear there was an almost desperate feel to his attentions—which didn't fit with, well, everything about him. "There's nothing you can tell me?"

"Hey, I just work on the books. Sevastyan doesn't allow me inside the inner circle."

"Me neither." We were outsiders looking in.

When Filip brushed his hand over his tired face, I noticed that his watch was gone. Like Paxán and Sevastyan, he'd had an expensive wristwatch, but I hadn't seen it in a couple of days. I narrowed my gaze. "Something's going on with you." I looked into those guileless gray eyes. Too guileless?

"Nothing's going on, Cuz."

"Then where's your watch?" I demanded before I could bite my tongue. Hadn't I decided to eighty-six the overanalyzing? The prejudgment of men? Yes, but, damn it, I'd been getting some strong *gambler* vibes off him. Was his car really still in the shop after two weeks?

He averted his gaze as he said, "Went swimming with it the other day."

"Let me guess. It's in the shop too?" No watch: pawned? No car: hocked?

Was my cousin a gambler in deep?

"In the shop. You got it."

I peered up at him. He didn't seem to be worried about it whatsoever, so I supposed I had enough on my plate without fretting over my cousin's foibles. "You'd let me know if I could do anything?"

"Of course. You're a good egg, Cuz. You know that, huh?"

The groom brought out our mounts then. I fell head over heels for my mare all over again. With her glossy gray coat and black stockings, Alizay was stunning. The posh tack just highlighted her lines. Though western riding was preferred in Nebraska, I'd taken English riding lessons, and was thankful for it now.

I gazed into her lustrous eyes, seeing my own adoring reflection. Okay, maybe I did like money, if only for the horses it could buy.

When the groom brought out a third mount, I asked Filip, "Are you expecting someone?" I frowned to see a rifle stowed in a saddle holster.

Filip scowled, muttering, *"Bloody Siberian."*

As if summoned, Sevastyan entered the stables, his towering body briefly shadowed as he strode into the aisle. He wore black riding pants of a modern cut and a sharp all-weather athletic jacket that he could just as easily have worn to play rugby.

Filip's style: Barneys high fashion. Sevastyan's? Bespoke—and moneyed.

His gloves and clothes covered any tattoos, but that slim scar down his lips and the hardness of his features belied any gentlemanly appearance.

As he approached, he moved like an athlete; I could see the powerful muscles in his legs flexing with each of his steps, reminding me of when his thighs had quaked around my ears as I'd swallowed him down. . . .

Focus, Natalie. "Are you going with us?" I asked him, flushing at how throaty my voice sounded.

Sevastyan told Filip, "Kovalev wants to see you."

"Just taking Natalie out for a ride," he said smoothly. "I'll catch him later this after—"

"Now."

Filip's lips thinned. "Nat, let's go back to the house. We can come back for our ride when I'm done."

What if the weather didn't hold? I didn't bother hiding my disappointment.

Sevastyan said, "I'm taking her."

Why would he offer to be alone with me? Maybe he'd mastered his attraction to me, and was now in no danger of plighting. But why was he forgoing work? Had the difficulties been resolved?

Curiosity, my kryptonite, had me jonesing for answers.

The tension between the two men seethed. "You? Taking little sis out for a ride? How brotherly. But she's not interested." To me, Filip said, "Come, Natalie."

I stiffened, not liking his tone at all. Strange, since I'd loved when Sevastyan had ordered me around in bed. Or in a maid's closet.

Even after everything, I . . . missed the man. What harm could come from one little ride? I told Filip, "I've been waiting for this for two weeks."

He gazed from Sevastyan to me and back. In a disbelieving tone, he said, "You want to go—with him?"

Sevastyan bit out the words, *"Ona so mnoi."* She is with me.

Comprehension seemed to dawn in Filip's expression. Then a disturbing flash of anger surfaced on his face, reddening his cheeks. He turned that look of wrath on me. "Are you? *With* him?"

His words were rife with undercurrents that I found difficult to accept. Because right now, it seemed like the guy who'd ignored me for weeks and the guy whose face could make angels weep were in a pissing contest.

Over me.

"I just want to go riding, Filip."

He appeared to be grinding his molars to dust. Finally he told me, "I'll be waiting for you back at the house." With a black look at Sevastyan, he strode off.

Disquieted, I glanced up at Sevastyan, but his piercing gaze was trained on Filip's back. I said, "Do you want to tell me what's going on between you?"

"Nyet." That word—when spoken by him and addressed to me—might as well be translated: *Dead end, Natalie.*

"Why are you taking time off work? Has the issue with Travkin been resolved?"

He shook his head, repeating, *"Nyet."*

Dead end. He'd tell me no more—because I wasn't a member of the inner circle.

He brushed his gloved hand down the neck of his mount. "You wanted to go riding, so I'm taking you."

The stallion looked high-strung, and Sevastyan didn't strike me as a natural rider. Recipe for disaster? "Have you done a lot of riding?"

"Unfortunately, work precludes it."

"We don't have to go."

In answer, he moved behind me to help me into Alizay's saddle.

"Oh. Okay." Had he let his hands linger on my waist?

Then I watched, enthralled, as Sevastyan hoisted his muscular frame into his own saddle and brought his horse around.

My fears had been unfounded. Though he'd been plucked from the streets in his teens, he rode like he'd been raised in the saddle, with an arrogance that only came from excellence.

Again, the contradictions in this man were fascinating. As we set out, I stared at him with such absorption that I barely registered what a smooth ride Alizay was.

But how could I not stare? He was captivating, with the bright fall sun making his jet-black hair gleam. His physique when riding was a sight to behold.

A body like that was good for two things that started with *f.* And fighting was the other one.

Dragging my gaze from Sevastyan, I surveyed the breathtaking estate. A cool breeze finagled stray leaves from the birches surrounding the stables.

In comfortable silence, we rode, and as we gained distance from the manicured gardens and the tennis court, the guest houses and the garage, we saw more wildlife. A fox, two martens, numerous speckled squirrels.

When we crossed a babbling stream, Alizay gave a restless snort. Though I'd never ridden such a fine horse, I could tell she wasn't satisfied with this mild walk. I patted her neck. "This one's hungry for more." I bit the inside of my cheek; could that have sounded more suggestive? Wow, I might as well have pointed at my crotch as I said that.

"Then let's give her more." Sevastyan lightly swatted Alizay on the rump, sending her speeding forward.

He quickly caught up, and we galloped over what seemed like miles, the bracing air filling my lungs, invigorating me. I was unable to contain my laughter, and even Sevastyan's lips curled, almost a smile. Oh, yeah, if he ever did hit me with a real smile, I'd tumble off the back of this horse.

I caught myself wondering what it would be like if he were mine. In some mad moments, I could envision us together. It'd never be dull.

No, it'd be dark. And deep. I swallowed. In any case, the ball was no longer in my court. I couldn't have made it clearer to him how I felt, and he'd made no moves.

Until now? Or was this a platonic outing? He'd told Filip that I was with him. For the duration of this ride? For longer?

Our mounts matched paces, drawing even closer as we headed toward a distant birch forest. Once we'd reached that thick grove, we slowed to a walk. I loved watching the leaves flutter all around us, caught on the breeze like little kites. "This place is amazing."

"I used to explore here as a boy."

"It must've been an incredible place for a kid." Especially compared to what he'd known before then. Had he recuperated from that beating here? Gone from abject poverty to this wonderland of plenty?

From having no one to having a father in Kovalev?

"Paxán wanted me to feel that this was my home, so he made me read all about it." Gauzy light streamed through branches, hitting Sevastyan's face, his eyes. The gold was so vivid, it was like the sun had rendered them aglow from within. Spellbinding . . .

When I found my voice again, I said, "Tell me some of the things you learned."

In his gruff way, Sevastyan began describing the construction and renovation of Berezka. But as he talked about the people and the lands, he grew more animated, his passion for this place clear.

He caught me staring at him.

"What?" Color tinged those cheekbones.

Since learning he'd been a prizefighter, I'd longed to touch his face. Since Paxán had told me of his beating as a boy, I'd yearned to kiss this fighter from forehead to chin. "You adore it here."

He shrugged, but I could tell how proud he was. "Don't you?" When I nodded easily, he said, "Then why haven't you decided to stay?"

"It's a big decision. Living in a foreign country, changing schools." I knew nothing would make Paxán happier, and I wanted to give that to him. But not at the expense of my own happiness.

"Though you might not think I liked my old life, I did. I even liked working, just as you clearly do. I don't want to say I'm a hayseed or anything, but I enjoy a simple life." We'd slowed to a stop. "Enough about me. Why don't you tell me about how you came to be here?" Paxán had said Sevastyan might confide in me.

He studied my face. "Your father told you my history."

"Only how he first met you. You could tell me more." If Sevastyan and I could continue like this, talking, getting to know each other, would I fall for him?

Could he fall for me?

"I'm a good listener," I said.

Our gazes met. He parted his lips to speak. Then ire blazed in his expression. "Why did you invite Filip to ride with you?"

I was taken aback. "Why wouldn't I have?"

"You could have asked me." He gazed past me as he said, "Unless you specifically wanted time with him away from everyone else."

I rolled my eyes. "If I did, then that would be none of your business. You told me there is no us, remember? Maybe I took your words to heart."

"Did you take my warning to heart as well? I told you to be wary of him."

Sevastyan's anger was sparking my own. "And he told me the same thing—about you."

"Filip has a lot of success with women. That doesn't mean he's worthy of it."

"I get along with him. He doesn't *ignore* me, and he makes me laugh," I pointed out. "It doesn't hurt that he has a face that could make angels weep."

Sevastyan's gloved fists clenched on his reins. His horse nickered nervously. "I don't want you alone with him anymore."

This jealousy was so delicious, I decided to prime the pump. "Why? Scared I'm going to give it up to him?"

Something primal flashed in Sevastyan's eyes. "That will *never* happen."

"Is that why you're riding with me? To cock-block him?"

He simply answered, "Yes."

My toes curled in my boots. "Why?"

"I know what Filip had planned for you today." At my raised brows, he said, "He intended to seduce you."

"How do you know this?"

"Because any man in his right mind would be planning the same." He caught my gaze, held it. Was Sevastyan telling me that he was as well?

Was I back to being infatuated again?

I smoothed a curl from my flushed face. "Are you in your right mind?" *Say yes, say yes—*

Thunder rumbled.

As if waking from a daze, we both jerked our heads up. In these woods, we hadn't been able to see an approaching storm.

"We'll head back."

No, no, I never wanted this ride to end! Sevastyan was acting all possessive and jealous and had actually been flirting with me—in his terse, enforcer way. I couldn't get enough. What harm would a few more minutes do? "If it rains, we won't melt."

No sooner had the words left my mouth than clouds draped over the treetops like a suffocating blanket. A drop hit my face, then another. The sky continued to darken.

When a chill wind started to gust, batting leaves against us, Sevastyan ordered me, "Stay close." He started off, and I followed as he picked up speed, dodging around trees.

Lightning forked out above us, cold drizzle pinging my face. But this ride was exhilarating, made me feel so alive. I couldn't remember the last time my heart had pounded like this.

Oh, yeah. In a maid's closet fourteen days ago.

When lightning struck a tree not far in the distance, Alizay yanked against the bit, sidestepping. "Whoa, girl, easy. . . ." Exhilaration turned to apprehension.

Limbs raked my ponytail, pulling it from its fastening. Between the leaves and my whipping hair, I could barely see. Each bout of thunder grew closer. It sounded so much harsher than it did in Nebraska.

Sevastyan reined around and sped back for me. He seized my reins, forcing Alizay to trot alongside.

More lightning flashed overhead, and another bolt struck even closer. The drizzle turned to a freezing downpour with drops so big they thumped my head. The temperature felt like it was plummeting by the minute. Soon my breaths smoked through the curtain of rain.

Sevastyan narrowed his eyes in the direction of the stables. Then, as if making a command decision, he turned us in another direction.

Over the rumbling, I said, "The stables are the other way!"

"I'm getting you out of the lightning," he called back, spurring his horse.

Onward we rode. In movies, getting caught in the rain with a hot guy was always sexy. I was freezing, certain I looked like a drenched cat, and terrified of being electrocuted. To add insult to injury, my riding pants were creeping up my ass by uncomfortable degrees.

Once we emerged from the edge of the woods, the rain was so thick that I could barely make out a house in the distance.

As we neared, I saw it was about as large as the bungalow I'd shared with Jess. The rough-hewn style—exposed-beam walls and a wood-shingled roof—was completely different from every other structure I'd seen at Berezka.

To the side was an overhang for the horses. By the time we dismounted under the roof, my legs were so stiff that Sevastyan had to catch me. Steadying me on my feet, he barked, "Inside."

Leaving him to take care of the horses, I entered the windowless interior. I removed my soaked gloves, rubbing my hands for warmth as I glanced around me. The overcast light coming from the doorway illuminated a quaintly rustic room.

Realization dawned. This was a *banya*. A sauna house. I'd read all about them!

Russians took their saunas very seriously. There were rituals and social etiquette surrounding the *banya*. Creating the best mist—with the finest steam droplets—was considered an art.

The first room, the pre-bath, had pegs to hang clothes and a supply of towels, sheets, and liniments. Deeper inside was the steam room. Polished wood benches stretched along the walls. At one end of the room was a small blue pool. At the opposite end were a firebox and rock chamber.

A water bucket and ladle stood beside the rocks. *Veniks*—tied bunches of dried branches and leaves—hung from a nearby rack, like mini brooms. Wetted down, they were used to strike the skin to improve circulation.

For some reason, the firebox was already lit, spilling light across the area. The rocks radiated heat, making the air warm and humid. It smelled of cedar and vaguely of the birch *veniks*—like wintergreen, forest, and leather mixed together.

Realization dawned once more. I was going to be trapped in a *banya* with the most desirable man I'd ever imagined. A man I couldn't have sex with—without risking permanence. A man I wasn't even supposed to be fooling around with.

Though freezing, I whirled toward the exit, ready to brave the storm.

Sevastyan ducked through the doorway, rifle in hand. "Where do you think you're going?" Once he shut the door behind him, I could scarcely hear the thunder outside the insulated sauna, even as it rumbled the ground and walls.

It was as if we were within a moist, firelit cocoon, separate from the world.

As he shook out his black hair, he propped his gun against the wall, then placed a bar over the door.

Why would he lock it? Between chattering teeth, I said, "We n-need to ride back. Or call for someone to p-pick us up."

He discarded his gloves as he headed to a wall cabinet. I heard the clink of glass, and then he turned back to me holding a vodka shot. "Drink."

I accepted the glass but hesitated. Though I was eager to get warm, I knew better than to be in a sauna with this man—while drinking vodka.

"Natalie, drink. You don't even realize how cold you are."

At that instant, my teeth decided to chatter with a vengeance. With a mulish look, I chugged the burning liquid. When I set the glass down on a shelf, rim first, he gave me a satisfied nod and took my hand, leading me back toward the fire. While I watched, he stoked it even hotter, then ladled water over the rocks.

Steam hissed, floating through the air. It surrounded us, caressing my face. "If we stay h-here, something might happen." Something sinful.

Like the two of us stripping down to nothing, so we could lick droplets from each other's skin.

"Happen?" He strode toward me, removing his coat on the way.

I backed up a step. "You know, between us." He'd gone so long—why would he blow his perfect record now?

He raised his brows, eyes devilish in the firelight and mist. "Can't control yourself where I'm concerned?" His voice was a deep rasp.

Resist him, Nat. "Maybe I can. Doesn't mean I have to prove it by hanging out in a freaking sauna with you." When he stalked closer, I demanded, "What are you doing, Sevastyan?"

"Getting you out of those wet clothes," he said in a tone that brooked no resistance.

What the hell? Had the countdown clock finally zeroed out? My breaths shallowed as I recalled his restlessness, his piercing looks and mounting tension, as if he'd been about to strike.

Because he had been?

But why now? Why today? And in what . . . manner?

I pictured those indecipherable warnings he'd cast my way. Was I brave enough to face whatever it was he'd been warning me from? "And what if I refuse to take off my clothes, huh?"

"Pet . . ." Now every time he called me that it reminded me of his words: *collar and keep you.* He reached for my jacket, his gaze gone molten. "There's one thing you should know."

How could a single heated look make shivers dance over my entire body? "What's that?"

"I wasn't *asking.*"

CHAPTER 18

"Hold on!" I tripped back from Sevastyan as he advanced on me through the billowing steam.

Hanging out in a sensual sauna, naked, with an off-limits enforcer who happened to make my mouth water: what could possibly go wrong?

And Sevastyan had been all too prepared to take advantage of the storm. The sauna fire had been lit before we'd even arrived. He'd hinted around about planning my seduction, which made me wonder . . . "What's gotten into you, Siberian? I know the rules— we're not supposed to be trifling with each other."

In a low tone, with words like a promise, he said, "I have no intention of trifling with you."

I frowned. "But that's why you've avoided me, isn't it? Because you don't want to risk getting saddled with me. So what is this?"

"It's simple." He was almost upon me. "You're freezing when I can make you warm."

When I skirted away, he raised his palms, as if to let me know he'd never force anything on me.

I rolled my eyes. Like he ever would *have* to.

"Then I'll need to make it hotter in here." He returned to the fire. After coaxing more warmth and steam, he sat on a nearby bench and began undressing, his manner casual.

I was rapt as he unbuttoned his shirt with those ringed fingers. I didn't know if it was the vodka in my belly or a growing coil of excitement that was heating me more—just knew my chill had all but disappeared.

When he drew off the wet fabric, the muscles in his arms and shoulders rippled, those tattoos stark across his flexing chest.

I'd researched more about those markings of his. The two stars meant that he was a criminal aristocrat, a man who'd neared the upper echelons of the Bratva. The ones on his fingers signified that he'd been a thief and an assassin. But I also saw scars that I hadn't noticed on the plane—one from what must be a bullet wound in his side and another slash down the back of his arm that looked like a knife wound.

More reminders of how much pain his body had taken. Yet these scars didn't detract from his attractiveness; just the opposite.

He raised his chin proudly. The bastard knew how good his body looked.

How masculine.

How sexual.

I found my feet taking me closer to him, my hands itching to touch his damp skin. What woman would be able to resist him?

A better woman than I.

Before I knew it, I'd sat on the bench a couple of feet from him. I felt obligated to say, "I don't want this."

He raised his brows. *Oh, really?* "Take off your jacket."

With a swallow, I did. My ivory silk blouse was transparent, my stiff nipples and coral-colored areolas visible through my white lace bra.

When he made a low sound of appreciation, I admitted, "I'm scared."

"Of me?"

Never. I shook my head. "I'm scared of what this means. From what I understand, if we keep fooling around, you're going to get permanently stuck with me. Like you might as well slip a ring on my finger. Especially if we have sex."

"You let me worry about that."

Maybe the threat of mutual saddling had been exaggerated? Like when parents tell kids: "Go outside with wet hair, and you'll catch a cold."

Fool around with an enforcer, and you'll catch forever.

Sevastyan would never risk an everlasting future with me, right? And if I remained a virgin through this encounter, surely I'd be exempt from any *mafiya*-logic rules.

But maybe my brain was latching on to *any* excuse to keep this interlude going. Mist suffused the air, making everything feel dreamlike. And wasn't it easier to be reckless in dreams?

"What do you want from me, Sevastyan?"

He reached down to seize my ankles and pulled them over his lap, making me spin on my ass to face him. "Do you trust me, *milaya moya*?" My sweet.

Off went one of my boots and the accompanying stocking. "For some reason, I do." Off went the other.

Then he reached forward to unbutton my blouse with those tattooed fingers. I was still considering a retreat—until I caught his masculine scent.

Game over. I'd been drugged.

When he guided me to, I shrugged out of my clinging blouse,

leaving my bra—which highlighted my breasts more than it concealed them.

His gaze dipped, and he rubbed his palm over his mouth. "You control this situation, Natalya," he said, his voice lulling me until I was staring at his lips. "Tell me what you want."

Before I could think better of it, I'd gone and told him the truth: "More."

Cupping my face with both of his hands, he brushed his thumbs over my cheekbones. "Then I will pleasure you as I need to, as *you* need me to."

I didn't know what that meant, just knew it sounded necessary and critical. Like breath. "But I can't sleep with you."

He dropped his hands, narrowing his eyes with a blatant flare of anger. "All you can think about is preserving your way out? Then rest assured, I won't fuck you until you beg me. But if you're not strong enough to resist me, then that's on you," he said, repeating what I'd told him on the plane.

No begging equaled no sex? I could resist begging. Then I *would* be in control. "If not sex, then what do you have in mind?"

"I'm going to give you commands, and I want you to follow them to the letter." A gleam of pure lust accompanied his roughened words.

How much he needed this! The idea of my fulfilling his "particular interests" wiped my mind of resistance. Made my body pliant, my will weak.

He wanted to command me; I wanted it as well.

He pulled me closer to sit across his lap, until our faces were inches apart, our breaths mingling. He nipped my bottom lip, only to soothe it with his tongue. When he slanted his mouth over mine, I sighed with defeat and welcomed his sensual kiss.

As our tongues began to twine, I was dimly aware that my

pants had seemed to melt away. The shock of my bare breasts against his blazing hot skin roused me. While he still wore pants, I had only my panties left.

He broke from the kiss, lifting me off his lap. "Here, lie back."

My first order. The bench was about two feet wide, with polished slats. I could lie on it comfortably, but I suspected comfort was not Sevastyan's first concern. With a nervous swallow, I reclined for him.

He reached forward to tug my underwear off. Then he stared.

His golden eyes were lit with an animalistic intensity so strong it made my heart race.

I followed his gaze as he raked it over my naked body, wondering what he was seeing to affect him so strongly. My normally pale skin was flushed with excitement and dotted with mist, until it looked like it glittered. My restless hips couldn't seem to stop moving.

He wants me darkly, deeply, my mind kept repeating. What had unnerved me before now turned me on like crazy.

"Close your eyes, Natalie. Do not open them. And remain where you are."

"Sevastyan . . ."

"I give commands. You obey them. *Sdavaisya*." Surrender.

Trepidation surged—but it couldn't compete with my eagerness. Once I closed my eyes, he left the room. I heard him in the pre-bath. Had he gone for more vodka?

As I wondered what he was up to, I perceived a change coming over me. Any lingering uneasiness disappeared under an onslaught of sensations. I could feel those droplets of mist collecting all over my skin, to stream down my sides and pool in my navel. My nipples puckered tighter with each whisper of steam. The scent of the fire filled my nose.

The heavy fall of my hair spilled over the end of the bench. I bit my lip when I felt the rumble of thunder in the wood beneath me, a vibration from my heels to my head.

Every one of my senses was overwhelmed.

I grew even wetter, my lips swelling between my legs. I wanted to spread my thighs, to open myself to him. He'd said I was beautiful there, had licked every crevice and fold with a ravening hunger.

I needed him back! What was he doing? Curiosity plagued me—

Rip.

I tensed. That sounded like cloth being torn.

Rip . . . Rip . . . Rip . . .

What—the—hell? I thought I heard him running water as well.

When the sound of his footfalls approached, it was everything I could do not to peek.

"Did you do as I told you?"

"Yes." My voice quavered on the word.

"Good girl." He brushed his knuckles over my jawline. Of all the parts of me offered up to him, he caressed my face.

"Um, what were you doing?" I could imagine his eyes following the movements of his fingers.

"Preparing. I want your arms over your head."

Hesitantly, I stretched them back; he seized my wrists together.

I trembled when he tied cloth around them.

CHAPTER 19

"Sevastyan, I don't know." He'd described me being helpless. He'd told me he'd want to do filthy things to me.

Was I about to step off that trestle yet again? To plunge into this encounter?

"You can stop me at any time, Natalie."

You can't stop a free fall, you can't stop—

"But if you obey me, I promise I'll make you come harder than you ever have."

Though I didn't see how that could be possible, so far Sevastyan had kept all his promises. Which meant he intended to make me orgasm harder than on the plane, and in the closet?

I now had every incentive in the world to obey him.

While I shook with anticipation, he tied my wrists tightly together, then affixed them to one leg of the bench.

I sensed him moving again. When he reached across me, the plump head of his cock glided over my skin, tripping my stomach muscles. He was undressed? How badly I wanted to see him completely naked! Yet I squeezed my eyes shut, resisting the urge to open them.

He cupped me behind my knees, bending my legs until my feet were flat on the bench. "Let your knees fall wide."

When I did, I could feel mist dancing over my swollen pussy.

He sucked in a breath, and I knew he was staring at me there. I was tempted to close my legs, but he rasped, *"Ya sptryu na to shto prenodlezhit mne."* I'm looking at what's mine.

At this moment, all of me was his.

Was he going to tie up my legs? I now wanted him to. And then I wanted him to do filthy things to me.

I expected the feel of cloth around my ankles—instead, he knotted a strip around one knee. I couldn't tell what he was doing. Stretching the strip back past the head of the bench?

Once he'd fastened my other knee, I realized that both of my legs were suspended wide and spread, tied with one long band of cloth. If I pulled on my right knee, my left one would be forced higher and impossibly wider. Like a balance scale.

How to tell him to stop? That this was too much?

"Look at you. Red curls and plump pink lips—against those white thighs. Beautiful." My pussy quivered under his gaze, and he inhaled sharply. "Do you know how much I've craved to see this? My lovely Natalya bound for my use." His voice dropped an octave lower. "The things I will do to you."

My resistance perished with a whimper.

"Open your eyes."

"Okay." They went wide at the sight of him totally unclothed.

The fire bathed his body with light, flickering over the rises and falls of muscle. Droplets meandered down his torso, trailing over sinews. My mouth went slack, my lips needing to graze every inch of his glistening skin.

His muscular shoulders and pecs tapered down to unyielding

stomach ridges. Between his narrow hips, his cock jutted hungrily. I gasped to see the taut head and slit covered with beads of pre-cum, the distended length pulsing.

The sight of it wrought an answering throb within me. "Oh, God, oh, God." I'd never wanted anything more than I wanted that cock buried to the hilt inside me. But I couldn't *have* it.

I desperately needed to squeeze my thighs together or rub my clit to ease this ache. When I pulled against my bonds, I realized why he'd tied my legs like this. He wanted me to be able to move slightly so he could watch me struggle against my bindings, which clearly aroused him even more. His lips parted, his eyes seeming to glow with fervor.

Once I could tear my gaze from his, I noted the other tattoos on his body. On each of his knees was a mighty star to match the ones on his chest. I knew what those symbolized: he would kneel before no man.

Staring at Sevastyan's body was like staring at the sun.

"I want you to see the need I'll be battling." He fisted his cock, swiping his thumb over the head, glossing it with moisture. "Want you to see how badly I crave you."

With his other hand, he held up his last strip of cloth. Even my lust-stupid brain knew what he wanted to do with it. Sure enough, he cupped the back of my head, lifting it so he could tie the cloth over my eyes. "And then, I want you to see *nothing*."

"Wait!" To be fettered like this and sightless?

He finished tying the knot. "The better for you to feel. Trust me to take care of you. Tell me that you will."

I hesitated, then said, "I will."

"Good. Now, arch your back and keep it so."

Once I did, I heard a slosh of water. Then the ladle hitting the edge of the bucket?

Water streamed onto my chest. It was just shy of too-hot as my breasts channeled it straight down to my pussy.

I could feel the stream rushing over my clit. Could feel that sultry trickle directly over my opening. An intimate, liquid caress. I moaned, holding my arched position with difficulty.

Another stream danced over my throat. Like a collar.

I started to perspire. So hot—

"Ahh!" *Freezing* water licked across my breasts. He'd gone from steaming to ice cold. I struggled to keep my back bowed as he doused another cold line from one of my nipples to the other.

He poured more down my spread inner thighs. Goose bumps. Perspiration. Shivers. Panting. My body didn't know how to react.

Then cold directly between my legs.

"Sevastyan!" I futilely wriggled.

"Back flat. Open your mouth."

I was shuddering as I blindly obeyed. Cold water hit my tongue. I swallowed quickly, hadn't realized how thirsty I was.

"More?"

I'd never had such delicious water. "Uh-huh."

The stream returned, along with the tip of his finger, tracing my lips. I sucked the finger, drinking from it before he pulled it away.

Then nothing but sounds. The fire crackling. My panting breaths, his harsh ones. Moments passed. . . .

Against my lips, I felt the head of his cock. He was rimming my mouth as water trickled down his length. The visual of Sevastyan, funneling water along his shaft to my waiting mouth . . . *Oh, God, oh, God.*

I stretched my head up to suckle him, but he kept that lus-

cious crown from my tongue. I strained to free my wrists, needing
to drink him dry . . . yet he tormented me, daubing the head to
my lips, then drawing it away.

Another grazing contact, more cool water. The world began
to fade away until only Sevastyan existed.

Then absence. No contact. I was about to cry out when his
finger returned. I sucked it hard, swirling my tongue, letting him
know what I'd do with his cock. He must've gotten the message;
a growl broke from his chest.

When he withdrew his finger, I gasped, "Why are you teasing
me like this?"

"My greedy girl wants more?"

"You know I do!"

Pressure against my lips. His own?

Sevastyan was kissing me with light laps of his tongue against
my seeking one. I moaned into his mouth, but he kept the
pace slow, languid, laying his hand over the side of my face. He
broke from the kiss to brush feather-light grazes of his lips over
my cheek, my chin, along my jawline, then back to my waiting
mouth, to take my tongue with his.

The most tender, *romantic* kiss I'd ever received.

As if he cherished me.

He'd tied me up to use my body, then given me a lover's kiss.

Maddening man! As his lips and tongue leisurely claimed
my own, I thrashed against my bonds, desperate to grasp his
head, to bury my fingers in his hair so I could hold his mouth
to mine.

I feared I'd lose my mind before the afternoon was through.
And quite possibly my virginity. Did I trust what he'd said, about
not fucking me until I begged? Yes. But did I trust my promise to
myself not to beg?

Perhaps I *wasn't* strong enough to resist him.

He pulled away, brushing my hair from my forehead, adjusting my blindfold just so. "Lovely little Natalya."

I sputtered, "How do you have so much control?"

"I made you a promise that you'd come harder than you ever have before. I keep my promises to you. Now, open your mouth again."

I eagerly did, licking my lips for whatever he wanted to put between them. . . .

His cock. Without the water. Allowing me to better taste him. I eagerly lapped at the plump head, tonguing the moistened slit in the middle.

When he took it away, I thrashed anew. "Nooo!"

With one hand, he caged my throat; with his other, he thumbed a nipple. "Still."

I somehow calmed myself. Then another sensation against my mouth. Tightly rippled flesh. When I realized what he'd given me this time, I shot up, moaning against his testicles, my tongue swathing the ridges. In my frenzy, I sucked one wholly between my lips, trying for the other.

"*Uhn!*" He groaned long and low. "Greedy girl," he repeated.

Again he drew away, depriving me. Of his skin, his flesh, his sex, his mouth. He'd deprived me of this world he'd created—where he was everything. What would he do next? How would he touch me?

I felt his mouth on my breast, trailing kisses toward my nipple. Would he torment me as he had on the plane, avoiding the tips . . . ?

Yet as he licked the globes of my breasts, he pinched both nipples. Hard.

Harder. Tightening down on the peaks. It was painful—blissfully so.

He rasped, "You like that."

"Oh, God," I moaned as he pulled on them—

Only to abruptly release them.

He leaned down, mouth and tongue wrapping around a nipple, softly suckling as if to kiss away a pang. When he released it, I twisted to arch my other breast to him.

A dark chuckle sounded against my skin, but he obliged me. Once he began tracing his lips down my torso, he left both of my nipples aching and damp in his wake—and me already on the verge of coming.

He reached my navel, circling it with flicks of his tongue, then kissing it as if he were drinking from me. As his mouth dipped lower, he laid his hands flat over my upper thighs, his fingers stretching to my mons. Like he'd done in the cornfield.

Reading my mind, he said, "I've imagined that night ending differently. I fantasized that you wanted me to fuck you there, under the moon." He pulled my lips apart with such a sure touch. I could feel how soaked I was, how my folds flared.

His finger followed my wet seam, making me shudder. *"Ty takaya nezhnaya."* You're so soft. "So beautiful here." My hips thrust hungrily, my exposed pussy empty. "How could I not want to devour you at every chance?" He cupped my bottom. With his ringed fingers splayed across my ass, he lifted me like a bowl to his mouth, then ran the tip of his tongue from my core to my clit.

"Oh, God, yes!"

One finger entered me as he licked. Then he wedged a second one inside. But he removed them too soon, too soon—

"Do you want to know what heaven is for me?" Those fingers briefly dipped into my mouth for me to suck.

My taste! My taste was heaven for him. How could that turn me on so much? Again he took those fingers away too soon.

Attention fully on my pussy, he nuzzled me, then tugged my clit between his lips, nursing on it so softly. My entire body was quaking. He'd imprisoned me with his bonds—and his mouth—keeping me on the verge of coming with an expert cruelty.

When his suction finally increased, the bud swelled till it throbbed against his tongue. So close . . . so close . . .

He released it with a wet sound.

"No, don't stop!" It was a bundle of such unbearable sensitivity, I could feel mist alighting on it.

As if it was his toy, he blew on it. He played with it. Tormented it between his teeth. "So tiny, so luscious," he said in a gravelly voice. "And it will make you do things for me that you've never dreamed."

My toes curled, my fists clenched. How long had he kept me in this misery? I didn't know if minutes had passed or hours. "Too much!" How could boundless pleasure be so excruciating?

He drew on me even harder. At last! Should I tell him that I was about to trip over the edge? He would deprive me of my orgasm, just as he had everything else. *Hide how close you are. Don't let him know—*

"If you come before I give you permission, you'll be punished."

I writhed with frustration. Orgasm denial, just as I'd read about. "I-I need to come. *Please.*"

"Say that in Russian. I love that word from you."

"Pozhaluista!"

"Enjoy more of my kiss." I felt his ragged breaths against my spread opening. "But do *not* come."

Fierce licks over my clit forced a desperate cry from my lungs. Too late. I couldn't withstand this. The wave was crashing over me—

"You're coming?" With a growl of irritation, he sucked harder to finish me, tonguing me at the same time. My body twisted against my bonds, legs spread, hips bucking wantonly to his mouth. *Fuck. Fuck.* Sucking me so hard. Wringing from me the most powerful orgasm I'd ever imagined.

Just as he'd promised.

As before, my mind was . . . reset.

I lay, recovering from the staggering pleasure—but not sated. Instead of putting out the fire, that release had just taken the edge off, enough for my thoughts to briefly clear. The better for me to appreciate what he was doing to me.

To appreciate my submissive position. My helplessness. His mastery.

As I squirmed with after-shudders, he continued to lave me, savoring. "I taste your cum . . . could lick you forever." His voice sounded strained. "But you orgasmed before I wanted you to, *moya plohaya devchonka.*" That meant "my bad girl." As in naughty or . . . wicked.

And I was. For him, I was.

He pulled away. "I'm going to have to start over, to get you wild again. Are you ready for your punishment?"

In a dim part of my brain, I recognized that he'd set me up to be punished, that it was always going to fall to this—because he played games.

Was he playing for higher stakes than I could afford to lose?

CHAPTER 20

"I'm ready." *I think.* I didn't recognize my whiskey voice. Gone scratchy from my screams?

I heard a rustle and my eyes shot wide behind my blindfold. Was that a *venik*? One of those mini leaf brooms? What would he be doing with that . . . ? My questions faded when he ran it over my chest.

The wet leaves slithered over the contours of my breasts, the texture just this side of rough across my stiffened nipples. With a cry, I arched up—

Slap. He'd whipped one of my breasts! "Sevastyan!" Then the other. "What are you—"

And again! The sting continued to intensify, but my nipples hardened even more, as if to tempt another slap—which he promptly gave.

Over. And over.

I almost demanded that he stop—but everything he'd done to me in the past had been too earth-shattering to be missed. So I gritted my teeth and took the pain for him.

While my mind struggled to assimilate my . . . my *whipping*, he swatted those soft leaves over me repeatedly, the slapping sounds loud in the cocoon of the sauna.

As I gasped and shook, pain began to morph into a peculiar kind of pleasure. I couldn't . . . *crave* this? I'd ended up enjoying his harsh spanking on the plane, but having my breasts thrashed with an implement was seriously upping the ante.

So why had I started rising up to meet each stroke?

He lashed me until my tautened breasts ached, my nipples throbbing as badly as my clit had.

But I couldn't reach the brink like this. He was withholding any contact below my waist—more punishment for coming; I knew this as well as if he'd told me.

"Touch me, Sevastyan!" My inner walls clenched only emptiness. "I have to come again."

"Do you want me inside you?"

I moaned, barely recalling why it was so important not to have sex. "Oh, God . . . I don't . . . I can't . . ." My lust-stupid brain spun its wheels, gained no traction.

"If you became mine, I wouldn't let you go." His words were clipped, as if he was biting back frenzy. "Understand me, if I'm your first lover—I will be your last." The ringing tone of finality chilled me. "And I would kill any man who thought to touch what was mine."

Permanent.

"Beg me to fuck you." He lashed my right breast.

Trap!

In my mind, I saw him at the ready, about to capture me, to chain me forever. The hunter about to strike. *This* was what he'd awaited.

This. Why now? Why me?

"Beg, Natalya."

Can't think! "N-no?"

Silence. Finally: "What did you say?"

"I can't. Not unless you can tell me it'll only be sex. With no strings attached."

"I said you controlled this situation." Tone gone sinister, he grated, "But *I* control *you*. I can *make* you beg."

I whispered, "I know."

My admission seemed to temper some of his anger. "Then why deny us, *milaya*?"

"It's all too much. I just . . . can't."

"Then I won't fuck you till you beg me to—outside of this torment. Because I'm playing to win." *He makes the rules.* "This is more to me than just pleasure." Another slap of the *venik*.

"Sevastyan, I don't . . . I don't know how much longer I can stand this." Just when I was about to plead for mercy—or faint—I felt pressure at my core. A warm, bulbous object nudged against my opening. Despite what he'd said, *was* he going to fuck me?

No . . . that wasn't his . . . oh, dear God, was it the polished handle of the ladle? I whimpered, "Y-you can't." I couldn't think—because he'd begun to slowly penetrate me. "You're . . . you're doing this to spite me?" Diabolical man!

"I promised you unmatched pleasure, yet you took away my most effective means. Come now, pet, you said you needed something inside you."

I did. And I wanted it deeper, but he merely thrust with shallow pumps, until my head lolled. He avoided my clit completely—more punishment. Still, I was about to come.

Slap. Even as he fucked my pussy with the handle, he whipped my tender breasts. At that moment, I couldn't decide which stimulation I would kill for most.

I *did* crave the brand of pain this man delivered.

"Bend your will to mine." The strain in his voice made my toes curl. He lashed me; he thrust into my clinging channel. He maddened me. "When I order you to come, *obey*."

Thrust, thrust, thrust to the staccato sounds of my whipping.

I sobbed from the intensity. Gone light-headed. Euphoric. "Sevastyan, oh, God, *please*." A keening moan burst from my lungs.

"Ah, woman, your *sounds*! Come for me. Now."

I plummeted over the edge. Core-deep contractions made me scream with abandon, made me jerk against the ties as my body spasmed.

Lost in the throes, I heard myself confessing things: how I dreamed of him fucking me. How much I hungered to take him with my mouth. How I'd masturbated to fantasies of him.

Each admission was punctuated by his ragged groans.

When the pleasure finally subsided—even more heart-stopping than the orgasm before—I was left senseless, struggling to catch my breath. To *process* what he'd just made me feel.

With a loving kiss against my thigh, he gently removed the handle, leaving me empty once more. Yet I realized I still wasn't sated, that this need had only grown. Where would this insanity end? How could he make me into this mindless creature?

While he kept demonstrating such control, I was a slave to sensation. To *him*.

And hadn't he told me he wanted to make me his slave?

I felt him untying my blindfold. "Look at yourself," he commanded.

I blinked down. Didn't recognize myself. This was a stranger's body. Her pale skin was bright pink and slicked with sweat. Locks of stark red hair snaked over heavy breasts, coiling around lewdly protruding nipples. Her little clitoris was so swollen it jutted from her mons.

This stranger was a picture of wicked need. She looked like she'd been used. Just as Sevastyan had said.

Not a stranger.

Me.

Revelation. The blindfold had come off—and *I* had been revealed, a new me that I hadn't known could exist. I gazed at my abused nipples in wonderment, staring as if in a trance.

When his groan broke my stare, I twisted my head toward him.

He was revealed too. Just as my body had changed, so had his. His muscles were impossibly larger, corded with tension under his mist-slicked skin.

But nothing could compete with the view of his magnificent cock. His shaft was engorged, as if begging to be buried within hot flesh. In the firelight, moisture glistened atop the plum-colored head, making my mouth water.

He was . . . a *god*, with skin burnished by fire.

When I could drag my gaze from his body, I drank in the sight of his face. His lips were thinned, that scar a razor slash of white. His wet hair tangled over his lean, flushed cheeks. His noble face was filled with pain.

Pain earned while delivering my pleasure.

And in his smoldering eyes was his own madness. A bone-deep yearning that called to mine.

With his accent thick, he bit out one word: *"Obsessed."*

I didn't know if he was talking about himself or me. Didn't know if it was a question or an answer. Imagining it was the word foremost in his thoughts, I replied with the one foremost in mine: *"Revelation."*

His brows drew tight, and he hissed, *"Yes."* When he reached for the tie at my wrists, his cock slid across my sensitive belly and streamed pre-cum from the tip. It was like a taunt, a reminder of what I'd been denied, stoking my lust even more. I was still sizzling inside, seething like him.

"And we're not through," he promised. He loosened the knot—enough for me to eventually free my hands?—then stepped away. Leaning back against the nearby wall, he began to masturbate his mouthwatering cock.

I was transfixed by the erotic sight: a god, thrumming with need, self-pleasuring.

Then I realized he meant to deprive me yet again. "No, stop!" Crazed for him, I struggled to free myself the rest of the way—while he watched me with golden eyes.

Always watching me.

As he slowly fucked his fist, a shining bead welled from the crown. My eyes followed it as it slid down to the edge of his hand, and I wanted to cry. I strained harder, panic making my hands clumsy. "Please stop!" I was ravenous for him. Wild with hunger. I bit down on my lip, trying to stave it off.

He didn't stop, just continued torturing me with what I couldn't have. To be this close to him, yet kept apart? It was *killing* me.

"Please wait for me!" I wasn't merely stupid with lust, I was sick with it, fevered. "I *need* you!"

Then he spoke. "What you feel right now . . . I *always* feel. Since I first saw you."

The way I felt right now?

How had he survived it for so long?

But we didn't have to feel that way anymore. I clawed at the ties, freed my hands! Never gazing away from him, from his twisting fist and rippling muscles, I began to tear at the knots around my knees. "*Please*, wait . . ."

And then I was free.

Brows drawn tight, he groaned in anticipation, in . . . pain.

I could ease it. *Devour him. Drain him.* Ignoring the twinges in my muscles, I scrambled up.

A split second later I was on my knees before him, my nails embedded in his pecs, his length sucked deep into my throat.

His roar shook the room like thunder. As he continued yelling to the ceiling, I bathed his cock with my tongue, worshipping it. Impaled my throat with that broad head. Moaned with every hint of cum.

I raked my nails down his torso, then used one hand to clench his ass, the other to heft his heavy testicles.

He buried his fingers in my hair. In a voice so rough I barely recognized it, he murmured Russian to me.

Ordering me to keep milking him with my hungry little mouth.

Informing me that he would gladly do murder to possess me.

Declaring that my body belonged to him alone.

His unguarded words were about to send me over the edge when he grated, "You will wait for me . . . wait for my seed on your tongue."

His dusky sac tightened in my palm as his body prepared for release. I didn't think the meaty girth of his cock could get any thicker between my lips. Then it did. That swelling of semen was right below the crown.

"Look at me, *milaya*."

I peered up to find him frozen, his face a mask of agony, his body captured in perfect strain. As I tongued him, our gazes locked. For what felt like eternity, we were held suspended.

Then to the sound of his anguished bellow, heat jetted against the back of my throat.

He began thrusting furiously. I gripped his ass with both my hands to feel his muscles flexing as he worked to spend every last drop inside me.

"You"—thrust—"are"—thrust—"*mine.*"

With his cum on my tongue—my permission—I dipped my fingers to my clit and gave one sensuous slippery stroke.

Orgasm. Exploding. Clenching bliss. Fingers drawing it out, wringing more spasms. *Fuck. Fuck!* Tears streamed down my face as I swallowed him, drinking till he was emptied and shuddering, rubbing my pussy until I was too sensitive for more. . . .

Still gently sucking on him, I rested my cheek against his thigh. With infinite tenderness, he caressed my face. *Now* I was sated.

When his softening cock slipped out of my mouth, a drop of semen dribbled down my chin. He swiped it with his thumb. With an expression like awe on his face, he gave it back to my waiting tongue.

As I gazed up at him and sucked his thumb, his eyes darkened with possession.

Deep. Brutal. Never-ending.

He regarded me like I was a trapped thing, already his to enjoy.

Never-ending. Never-ending. *Never-ending.*

Dear God, what had I done?

CHAPTER 21

*A*s reality began to set in, I stood on unsteady legs.

I needed to get away from this man, who had more control over my emotions and desires than I'd ever had. This man who had altered me forever, showing me things I could never unsee.

Could never un*feel*.

I hadn't *decided* to become a slave; he'd made me one.

I'd almost had sex with him. Almost slipped the ring on my finger. Yet I didn't know him. I didn't know about his past, his family, or even what he liked to do in his free time.

I didn't know if we were compatible outside of sex.

"No, no, Natalie." He reached for me. "Don't wake up yet."

Some shadowy part of me didn't want to wake. I squeezed my forehead, torn. I was dizzy from the heat, from the life-altering pleasure.

When he grasped my hand and began leading me toward the small pool, I allowed it. He wrapped his arms around me, then dropped us in.

I shivered at the temperature, but I needed it, hadn't realized how overheated I was. He set me on my feet in the waist-high water, then leaned down to press his lips to mine.

I pushed against his chest, but he held me close, savoring my mouth with his, coaxing with his tongue to make me forget myself. . . .

Lost in bliss all over again, I was dimly aware that he was cleaning me, learning me. A big palm caressed between my legs. Another kneaded one of my breasts. Unhurried, as if he had all the time in the world.

Right when I was becoming chilled again, he carried me out. Before I could even formulate a protest, he was toweling me off. I wanted to tell him to stop, to leave me alone. To just let me process everything he'd done to me.

But I was distracted by his low growling sounds as he tended to me—drying my breasts, softly rubbing the curls between my legs. His shaft grew stiff again, swaying with his movements.

Were we about to start this all over again? Was I learning nothing? In all these interludes with Sevastyan, I hadn't been Natalie. I'd been *Natalya*. And that brainless hussy didn't seem to know better.

I stepped back from him, turned to search for my clothes. "I need to get dressed. *We* need to."

"Don't do this," he murmured from behind me.

"Another command?" Snatching up a robe for myself, I tossed him a towel.

He must've sensed I was about to freak out, because he covered himself, wrapping it around those narrow hips. "You *regret* this?" His voice was filled with disbelief. "You can't. I won't *let* you." As if he hadn't shocked me enough today, he scooped me up in his arms.

"What are you doing?"

He sat on the bench, cradling me, cupping the back of my head in a protective embrace.

Only fair, since he'd shattered me today.

In the cloak of the steam, I nearly broke down. "How can you change me so much?" I whispered against his ear. *"How?"* At one point I'd thought I would lose my mind.

"I haven't. I've just shown you a different facet of yourself."

Clasping him tight, using him like a lifeline, I buried my face in the spot where his neck met his shoulder. "*Why* are you showing me these things?"

He said nothing.

I pulled back to meet his eyes, found it impossible not to kiss his face. My lips touched upon the askew bridge of his nose, his chin, then smoothed over the lean perfection of his cheeks. He squeezed me tighter against him, seeming to relish this attention, this affection from me.

Between kisses, I asked, "What do you want from me?"

Silence.

"Did you mean what you said about obsession?"

He turned his head away.

"Ugh!" I disentangled myself from him and scrambled to my feet, searching for my undergarments. "You infuriate me!" I found my panties near the fire, half dry from the heat. Dragged them on.

Bra. Where the hell was my—got it. I turned from him, shucked off my robe, then strapped on my bra.

"Damn it, Natalie, I don't know what to say to you to ease the way you feel."

"Of course you don't." I whirled around on him. "Because

we're all but strangers! I don't know you!" With difficulty, I pulled my damp pants up my legs.

"What do you want to know?"

I had so many questions. How to decide on a first? "Those tattoos on your knees—they mean you'll kneel before no one, don't they?" According to my research. "Which would indicate that you're a *vor* yourself."

"That doesn't matter. I follow Kovalev."

Sevastyan was as much of a criminal aristocrat as my father. Yet another detail I'd had no idea about. "That's all you're going to say about it?" When I spotted my blouse, I pounced on it.

"I don't find it easy to talk about myself."

My fingers paused on my buttons. "Well, it wasn't easy for me to let you tie me up! But I trusted you in this."

"Would you take that back? Undo this afternoon, if you could?" He collected his own clothes, beginning to dress.

"I don't know," I admitted. "I don't understand it, or you." I shoved my wet hair back, knotting it at my nape. "You ignored me for weeks, then put on the full-court press today. Why now?"

"Paxán thought, and I agreed, that everything would be overwhelming for you here."

I'd never felt pressure like I had here. Never.

"When I confessed to him that I'd crossed a line with you, he asked me to give you room to breathe for a couple of weeks. He said you were young, and that I needed to let you find your feet. So I gave him my word that I would allow you space."

"For a couple of weeks." It all became clear. The countdown I'd sensed.

Today was my fourteenth day at Berezka. The clock had zeroed out.

"I was ordered not to speak to you in Nebraska; here I was forbidden to seek you out for that time."

I'd never thought about him having to wait to meet me over that month he'd spied on me. He'd already admitted that he'd fantasized about me sexually as he'd stalked me. How frustrating to watch and never be able to touch.

No, no, no, you're furious *with him, remember?*

"I think Paxán expected you to want Filip. Perhaps I did as well."

No wonder Sevastyan had been so angry when he'd thought Filip had been about to kiss me. "So what happens now?"

"Now?" He donned his pants. "Now I'm done allowing you space."

Was he joking? As I studied his face, I heard something outside. A truck? "Sevastyan, is someone here?"

He sat down to pull on his boots. "While I saw to the horses, I called the groom, told him to retrieve us in no less than two hours."

"Two hours? He'll know what we've been doing! We're going to walk out there and a steam cloud will billow out, and he'll know. Or he'll *think* he knows, and he'll tell everyone! It won't matter that we didn't sleep together. Everyone will believe we did."

"True."

My eyes went wide. "You did this on purpose. To force my hand. We didn't have sex, but we might as well have."

"You're *this* upset by the prospect of being with me?"

"I told you that I don't like making big decisions under pressure."

"Then we're fortunate that the decision's been made for you." While I gaped, he said, "I made a play for what I want." His expression so much as said, *Your ass is mine, and we both know it.*

"I made no secret of what I'd do to possess you. If this is the only way, then so be it."

I stiffened. Not exactly a ringing endorsement of me. He was so cold, so different from how he'd been earlier. *Because he's won. Or he* thinks *he has.* "What happens when the thrill of the chase wears off? And why me? Of all the beautiful women you've dated? I mean, you're in your thirties and never thought to settle down before."

Instead of answering me, he said, "This is a done thing, Natalie. Everything will work out if you trust me."

The groom's voice sounded outside.

Sevastyan tugged his wet shirt on, then reached for his coat. "I will tell your father that we are together. When he speaks to you, you'll tell him the same."

Simple. Clean. Permanent.

To live in a new country, in a new *world*, with a man I hardly knew. In a new life I wasn't convinced was better than my old one.

"Trust you and everything will work out? That's just another way of saying you know what's best for me. Or worse, that you know *better* than me."

"In this, I do. You don't have the experience to know that what just happened here—and in the closet, and on the plane—is the rarest exception, not the rule."

I was bristling. "Again, you're saying you know better than me."

"You're a smart girl. You're going to replay everything we've done, and you're going to reach the same conclusion I have." He moved in close, leaning down to kiss my jawline and lower.

"And wh-what conclusion is that?" When had he discovered how sensitive my neck was? With one spot in particular . . .

He pressed his lips directly to my pulse point, making my

knees weak. *"Eto ne izbezhno dlya nas."* You and I are inevitable.

Focus, Natalie! How could I still desire him when his high-handedness was unbearable? "An asteroid hitting the earth is inevitable! Or an active volcano erupting. Bad things are inevitable."

Drawing back, he gazed down at me. "No, *powerful* things are," he said as he captured my hand—to drag me out into the real world.

✦

*A*t Berezka's front entrance, Sevastyan walked me to the doors. I was suddenly aware of all the activity around us. Was it just me, or had the groundskeepers paused their raking to watch Sevastyan and me interact?

A couple of brigadiers emerged from the house. They stopped short and stared at my bedraggled appearance—before the warning in Sevastyan's eyes made them slink away.

Turning back to me, Sevastyan said, "I'm going to speak to Paxán after dinner."

I was still half-dazed. "I haven't accepted this. *You.*"

"Trust me, pet." He curled his forefinger under my chin, then leaned down to give me a kiss that anyone could see.

Which was his admitted plan. I thought it'd be a brief good-bye kiss, a toll I would grudgingly accept to get into the house as quickly as possible.

Instead, Sevastyan seemed bent on starting that fire in me once more. He took my mouth fiercely, giving me hot, seeking flicks of his tongue. It was a down-and-dirty kiss, with one objective: slay my resistance.

Which it did.

His hands descended to my hips, squeezing me against his body as his mouth consumed mine. Our tongues sparred until I was gripping his shoulders, wanting to get even closer to his unyielding heat.

As ever, his kiss had a way of blanking my mind, of filling me with a sense that all was well—even when I knew all was futher-mucked. . . .

When he finally broke away, leaving me panting and shaken, he smirked. "Lie to yourself all you like, but you've definitely accepted me." Masculine satisfaction emanated from him. His bearing wouldn't have been amiss on an Olympic podium.

Triumphant. Victorious male.

Was that why I couldn't shake the feeling that I'd been defeated?

When I opened the door with a wobbling step, he swatted my ass. I tossed a bewildered look over my shoulder, surprised as much by the unexpected love tap as by this playful side.

"Go inside and get warm, Natalie. And relax, this is a good thing."

Then he was gone, leaving my lips bruised and my mind in turmoil. Lost in my thoughts, I made my way up the stairs—

I started when Filip stepped in front of me on the landing.

There was fury in his eyes. "Have fun with the guard dog?"

CHAPTER 22

"I've been so worried about you!" Jess exclaimed when I called her that night.

"Really?" I'd kind of been worried about myself after Filip's meltdown just hours ago. "What's up?"

"Gee, I don't know, maybe the fact that some *mafiya* thug wants to off my best friend."

Oh, that. "Then why didn't you call me on the new number I gave you?"

"How the hell do you call Russia from Greece? It's like trying to figure out rela-fucking-tivity. And still, I gave it several shots. Of Ouzo. Seriously, you have no idea how much your situation is affecting me. I've been stress-eating my way across Greece."

I frowned. "You don't stress-eat—"

"Cock, Natalie. I was stress-eating cock. There, you made me say it, happy now?"

"Opa!"

"Twat."

"Bitch." Despite my foul mood, I had to check a grin. "I take it your trip was a success."

"Of course it was. But I don't want to talk about me, Richie Rich. I wanna know that you're safe."

Define "safe." "I've been perfectly fine."

She took me at my word. "So give me the details then! Tell me all about your gangster rumspringa."

How to begin? I sat at my vanity, staring at my reflection. I was back to my old Natalie self—no hint of Natalya—but if I were fanciful, I'd say my eyes were more . . . knowing. "It might not be just a rumspringa. Kovalev wants me to stay on." Any other woman would kill for an opportunity to live in a place like this, to get to know her father and study at a new university.

To be with a man as glorious and sexy as Sevastyan.

Radio silence from Jess. Then finally: "And you're giving the prospect actual thought?"

"I'm feeling, uh, a little pressure to stay." I told her about the last two weeks, the insane amount of gifts, my growing phobia of mass quantities of money, and the looming danger.

When I'd finished, she said, "You haven't mentioned the cage-fighter unicorn."

"I guess you could say we've gotten . . . involved." How to explain this confusing situation? Sevastyan's complicated nature? "With him, everything is extreme." Just as Paxán had said. "The man is extremely sexy, complex, infuriating. Sometimes I feel like I'm already in love with him; sometimes I feel like I should be running the other way. Bottom line, I am *extremely* confused." I detailed for her the highlights of our relationship and the specter of plight-hood, then gave her a blow-by-blow (har) of what had happened in the *banya*.

"That is so hot! You just gave me a wetty. *Fap, fap, fap.*"

"Will you be serious? Talk of bondage and whipping doesn't even make you raise a brow?"

"Please. *Nothing* between consenting adults fazes me." True to form, she zeroed in on her favorite detail: "You've STILL got your skin tag? Come on, Nat, this is getting ridiculous. Are you thinking with your vaj?"

"No!"

"There's your problem right there."

"Jess, I was hoping to get some real, unvarnished advice. I worry that I'm different because of that encounter, that I'm changed. But here's the thing: I think . . . I think he might be too."

"You really held out?"

"Somehow. The guy told me that if he was my first lover, he'd be my last."

She coughed. "That's seriously heavy."

"My thoughts exactly. I'd figured he was perfect for a vacay fling—but *mafiya* rules say that is not in the cards for Nat."

"Just so we're clear—you're talking about having sex with only one guy for your entire life."

"It sounds so bad when you put it like that. How many guys have you slept with, Jess? Really."

"Fourscore? Population of a small midwestern town? Horde?"

"But do you regret any of them?"

"Nope. Each one brought something different to the table."

I could admit to myself that Sevastyan had brought a banquet. Still . . . "It doesn't seem very progressive of me to get off on what we did. He ordered me around and basically trussed me up like a Thanksgiving turkey."

"Visual, Nat, visual. Now my *fap, fap, fap* fodder is no more. Anyway, I'm of the feminist school of thought that says 'If mama like, then mama fucking do.' Correct me if I'm wrong, but you are too."

I sighed. "I am." I'd never felt more pleasure, so how could I *not* view it positively? With one niggling misgiving neutralized, I moved on to a larger one. "I understand why Sevastyan doesn't want to talk about himself—he has a past, to put it mildly—but it leaves me with a whole lot of nothing to go on. A mail-order bride would know more about her intended than I know about my potential . . . plighted, or whatever. I just wish I had more time to sort out what I feel. Jess, tomorrow I have to talk to Paxán, and the pressure is killing me. The money, the danger, this enforcer—they're all about to make me pull my hair out."

"I've never heard you this freaked out."

Because I'd never been! "I signed on for this life"—somewhat—"and I suppose I'm obligated to pay the price when I screw up."

In a way, this crime microcosm was its own country, with its own boundaries and customs, and now I was bound by them. I tried to explain: "I entered into this world, and it's got its own laws. Doesn't matter how I feel about them; I tacitly agreed to them. Then on top of that, I was *explicitly* warned of the consequences. Yet I still broke the rules."

"Let's talk about how you entered that world! Some Russian threw you over his shoulder and stole you from our house! He tackled you in a cornfield, dick-glamoured you, and you still somehow resisted—at which point he forced you onto a *mafiya* plane. So don't give me this shit about how you agreed to some twatting laws."

Dick-glamoured? Kind of fitting. "But then I fell right into line." Dazzled by Sevastyan and Berezka. Lulled by laughter with my father . . .

"You know what? Fuck—this—noise," Jess declared. "You're *twenty-four*, Nat. Leave lifelong commitments to people who have fewer freaking years left. Fifty-year-olds and such. Anybody who tells a girl your age to make a commitment like this must think you won't live long." She caught her breath, then said, "Sorry. I forgot you might get capped at any time."

I swallowed. "Maybe I should view things with that in mind. Act like I only have a month to live. Despite everything, I know I'd want more time with Sevastyan."

But that didn't mean I wanted . . . forever.

"Listen to yourself! Put down the Kool-Aid and get some perspective, doll. Sneak away, and I'll meet you in Europe. We'll dodge bullets and break hearts."

"I wish." When I tried to picture how Sevastyan would react if I stole away, I kept hearing his promise: *If you run from me again, I will catch you. It's what I do. And then I'll spread you over my knees and whip your plump ass until you know better.*

Only now I knew he'd probably meant that literally. The thought made me shiver. "I'm stuck here for the duration."

"Say you accept the enforcer. Say the danger passes. Could you be happy there?"

That was the crux of it, huh? "Moving to a new country to be with a new guy while starting at a new school seems like a lot of variables all at once. A lot of choices to make," I pointed out. "And there's more. . . ." I told her all about Filip.

This afternoon, I hadn't even gotten a chance to ask the man what Paxán had wanted to talk to him about before he bit out, "Sevastyan was all over you at the front doors. The bastard as good as announced you're his."

Filip had looked harried, like this development had really affected him. But I hadn't sensed any deeper feelings from him. Yes, he'd flirted with me, but I was fairly sure he would flirt with a perfumed rock. "How is this your business?" I'd demanded, wondering if he'd been drinking.

"Because I care about you. *Really* care about you." He'd rubbed his hand over his wan face, drawing attention to his bloodshot eyes, to the deep-seated anger blazing from them. "Sevastyan teed you up. He played you. Now he's walking around this place with his shoulders back and a smirk on his scarred face—because he's a billion dollars richer. You're so naïve. You're not even his type—did you know that?"

Yes. Yes, I did. Still I said, "That's bullshit, Filip. Not that I owe you an explanation, but Sevastyan wants me." Except he hadn't given me a reason why it was *me* that he wanted above all others. He'd just said that he'd do anything to possess me.

"You got manipulated by a con artist, a hard-core prison thug. Well done, Cuz!"

Then Filip had added a parting shot that had made me cringe, driving me to the sanctuary of my room. I hadn't even gone down for dinner.

Had I believed what he'd said about Sevastyan? No. But Filip's accusations highlighted what I'd already accepted: I didn't *know* Sevastyan.

"What a scrote," Jess decided, dismissing Filip easily. "Normally I'd say you need someone over there, running point for you, skull-fucking when necessary. But then I recall how you react when backed into a corner."

"How's that?"

"You come out throwing elbows," she said. "You're nice, until it's time to not be nice."

"You're quoting *Road House*?"

"It was either that or quote from my latest torrid romance

novel." That was Jess's not-so-secret habit. As much as she loved the *idea* of love, her reading tastes made sense. Every now and then, she'd foist one on me. "You wanted my unvarnished advice, Nat? Here it is—do nothing permanent. And you damn well better not do anything until you fly my ass over there."

CHAPTER 23

I wasn't surprised when I got a summons from Paxán the next morning. I hadn't slept, was hardly functioning after two cups of strong tea.

For most of the night, I'd paced, wondering how I'd gotten myself into this mess. After alternately blaming myself and Sevastyan for this, I'd settled on Sevastyan.

He was more experienced than I was, and clearly more ruthless. But how had he manipulated me so easily? And to what end?

Paxán would want a decision this morning. He would lay down the law.

As I made my way to his study, I felt like I was marching to the gallows, my boot heels clicking along the marble. I adjusted the collar of my jade turtleneck, then smoothed my warm palms down the legs of my jeans. All I knew for certain was that I was bone-weary and so tired of being confused.

I passed Gleb, one of the brigadiers, sporting a pistol in an uncovered holster. Like Sevastyan wore. The man gave me a nod of acknowledgment, but nothing like the friendly greetings I usually received when I encountered one of the men.

Gleb's response brought to mind Filip's parting words: "All the brigadiers have been wagering whether the Siberian would lock you down. I should've taken that bet. But you told me there was nothing between you! And all that time, you let me think you wanted *me*."

I was now the subject of a bet. Paxán was right; my actions with Sevastyan had eroded my standing here. *Live in the crime country, then obey its laws. . . .*

When I entered the study, I was taken aback by Paxán's kindly expression. He'd been working on a clock, looking adorable with his magnifying glasses on. "Good morning, *dorogaya moya*! Tea?" Ever the gentleman. "You look like you could use some." He removed his glasses, setting away his tools.

Once I had a cup in hand, he motioned me to join him beside his desk. "I want to show you something." He opened a large glossy book, flipping to a page. "Have you ever seen this animal?" He pointed to a picture of a black wolf with vivid amber eyes, poised to strike from a snowbank. "Stunning creature, no? It's a Siberian wolf."

I nodded absently.

"This type of wolf is more likely to be a loner than other wolves. Some will roam the wilderness, hunting by themselves. But like others of their kind, they mate for life. They're vicious yet possess an undying loyalty."

I set down my cup. "We're not talking about wolves, are we?"

He shook his head. "The more I think about you and Sevastyan together, the more sense it makes. Then last night, he told me the two of you had come to an understanding?" The hopefulness in Paxán's expression killed me.

God, I didn't want to disappoint this man. "I . . . maybe we did? But I don't know if I feel that way now."

"Oh. I see." In a sad tone, he said, "Yet actions have consequences, my dear. On the bright side, your engagement could be a long one."

Except I'd never be able to break it. I was about to hyperventilate. "But . . . but . . ." I pulled at my turtleneck, beginning to pace the room. "I don't know him—not enough for this. I'm not saying I'd never want more with him, but I can't just sign on for this. Not yet."

Jess was right. *Don't do anything permanent. No lifelong commitments.* These men were expecting too much from me. This *was* too heavy. I couldn't be bound by this twisted *mafiya* logic. "Can't I just date him? In the States, we freaking date!"

"We do here as well, unless you're a crime boss's daughter who's gotten involved with his most trusted enforcer during a deadly war for territory."

When he explained it like that . . . Damn it, I knew I'd screwed up. But that didn't stop me from grasping for any way out. "Sevastyan and I didn't, um, consummate anything."

Paxán noted my panic, looking troubled in turn. "I won't force you to make a decision you're obviously uncomfortable with. He must have misread things with you. You shouldn't be punished for that. But my only other option is to separate you two."

He'd laid out an alternative, and like a drowning woman, I reached for it. "What do you mean?"

"I would need to send him from here, away from you. At least until things settle down."

"But this is his home. He adores Berezka."

"He has other properties," Paxán said. "These are difficult times. We must make difficult choices."

Difficult? Try dismal: make some kind of commitment to a

man who was a mystery to me, or send him away from his home.

I felt dizzy. "I don't want him to go." My eyes watered. "I'm the odd one out here. *I* need to go."

"Nonsense!" Paxán crossed to me to grab my shoulders. "You are my daughter! This is your home. It always will be."

I gazed up at him, surprised by this outpouring of emotion from my buttoned-up father.

As if discomfited by his reaction, he dropped his hands, backing up a step. "Make a decision, Natalie," he said, his voice sounding sterner than I'd ever heard it.

Nausea churned in my belly. "If I have to choose right now, this very minute . . ." So much pressure, confusion. In a rush, I said, "Then I don't want anything permanent with Sevastyan. Send him away from here if you have to, but I can't do this anymore!"

As soon as I said the words, I regretted them—even before I saw that Sevastyan had just crossed the threshold into the room.

He'd been *smiling* before he halted midstep, gorgeous lips curving over even, white teeth, his face all the more handsome for it. Something in my chest felt like it was shifting, *twisting*. Had he been happy to hear our voices, to join us?

I'd wiped that heartbreaking smile right off his face.

I had done that.

As comprehension hit him, the muscle in his jaw ticked. His fists clenched, his tattooed fingers going white.

Blood drained from my face, and I gasped at his expression; even Paxán took a protective step in front of me.

Because Aleksandr Sevastyan looked like he was about to do murder.

CHAPTER 24

*E*yes narrowed and cold, Sevastyan turned to stalk from the room.

"I will discuss things with him, and all will be fine," Paxán assured me, even as his face showed worry.

I started after Sevastyan, saying over my shoulder, "No, I need to go talk to him." I sped through the doorway out into the gallery, trailing after him. "Just wait, Sevastyan!"

Shoulders bunched with tension, he didn't slow. The panic I'd felt just moments before redoubled, now zooming in the other direction. What if I'd found the man who brought *everything* to the table? What if I'd just ruined things with him? "Sevastyan!" I followed him out the front doors onto the landing.

The last time we were here, he'd been kissing me possessively, laying claim. Now he was striding away from me, heading toward his Mercedes—to drive away. To disappear.

I rushed after him. Right when he reached his car, I grabbed his arm.

He flung it out of my grip. "What do you want?"

"You heard things . . . they were out of context."

"Then tell me you weren't just getting me kicked out of my own goddamned home, where I have lived for eighteen years."

"It sounded worse than it was. And in the end I never would have allowed that."

His expression turned even colder. "*You* wouldn't have allowed it? Only two weeks here, and you've assumed the role of princess so fucking easily."

I shook my head hard. "Paxán gave me two choices: sign up for something permanent with you, or see you leave. You tell me nothing about yourself, but expect me to make a commitment like that? I barely *know* you."

"You know enough. You know there was something between us."

Was. "Damn it, if you'd stop and let me explain—"

He whirled around on me. "I understand perfectly. You want me to make you come. You crave for me to fuck you, but only if it ends there. Beyond sex, anything with me doesn't appeal to you."

I pinched my forehead. "That's not fair!" I didn't feel like I was being backed into a corner; I was being tossed headlong. "I never asked for any of this, never asked for this kind of pressure!"

"This discussion is over. The situation has been made crystal clear to me." He opened his car, slid his big frame behind the wheel, then slammed the door in my face.

Corner, meet Natalie. "You asshole!" As he started the engine, I banged on the window with the bottom of my fist and launched my boot into the side of the car. *ABC, baby!* Always Be Crazier. "You rip me out of my life and then expect me to live up to your expectations?" Another kick. "Well, fuck you!" I leaned down so my head was level with his. "Go find some submissive bimbo who'll give you what I obviously can't."

He cast me a cruel smirk. "Planning to, pet." The engine revved, and he was gone.

✦

I looked like a bucket of fuck.

Felt like one too. Outside, another dreary, rain-filled day was coming to a close, dusk falling upon Berezka. Inside, I sat before my mirror, pinching my cheeks, scowling into the glass.

To brighten my outlook, I'd dressed in a royal-blue peplum top that looked sassy with a skirt of superfine merino wool and slouchy leather ankle boots.

It hadn't helped my outlook. Not even a little.

Deeming my appearance *good as it's gonna get*, I set off for Paxán's study to discuss some things with him.

My paleness and dark circles shouldn't surprise me, considering the last thirty or so hours of sleeplessness, confusion, and fury. Since Sevastyan had sped off yesterday morning, I'd run the gamut.

Dinner last night had been a miserable experience. I hadn't realized how much I would miss his company. No, he hadn't spoken to me much over the last two weeks, but at least I'd felt his presence, his palpable strength and protection.

Both Paxán and I had been out of sorts. Though he always politely turned off his cell phone during meals, last night he'd checked every message, every ring. He hadn't seemed to know what to do with himself, so unused to any conflict with the man he considered his son.

I'd felt a pang, wondering how much more Paxán could be expected to deal with. Aside from danger and unrest, he now had to live with this drama between his daughter and his enforcer?

Not to mention the tension between Filip and me. The guy must've heard I'd had a falling-out with Sevastyan, because he'd showed for dinner. Too bad that he'd been uncommunicative and drunk. Which had seemed to perplex Paxán.

After dinner had been just as miserable. All night I'd watched for Sevastyan's return. He hadn't come home, had probably spent the night in some other woman's bed.

At dawn, I'd clutched my balcony rail, anger ripping through me. He'd expected me to make all the right moves, all the time—though I had no reference to guide me. That anger had a way of clarifying my thoughts. I'd screwed up; he'd screwed another, removing himself from any chance of reconciliation.

He'd axed his limb off my decision tree. Which was a kind of decision.

With one decision down, I'd formulated others. Hence my meeting with Paxán this evening.

As I tromped down the stairs, I wondered if I'd see Sevastyan. I figured he'd be back today, if for no other reason than his undying loyalty to his boss.

Speak of the devil—I reached the gallery leading to Paxán's study just as Sevastyan did. On his way there as well? "You've returned?" My voice was scratchy, and I sounded as exhausted as I knew I looked.

"I still work with him," Sevastyan said in a low tone when we both slowed to a stop, as if by silent agreement. "I won't be kept away right when he needs me most."

Finally we were on the same page. "We need to talk."

Sevastyan canted his head at me, much as he had at that bar

the first night I'd met him. His pupils dilated, his eyes lit with more than simple interest.

Realization hit me. "You think I want to talk about . . . you and me? That ship has sailed."

He narrowed his gaze. "*You* are angry with *me*?"

Utterly pissed! But I needed to keep a lid on it, to calmly state my new proposal.

"You have a lot of nerve, Natalie."

"I've got . . . I'VE got nerve?" There went the lid. "Listen up, manwhore, you don't get to talk to me like that anymore. You revoked that privilege with your behavior yesterday."

"My behavior? You'll have to enlighten me."

"When you heard something out of context, flew off the handle, and headed out to bury your relationship sorrows—balls deep—in another woman."

He eased closer to me. "You're *jealous*."

I rolled my eyes. "Please. My shallow infatuation with you is done. As they say in the movies: you killed it dead."

That jaw muscle ticked away as he grated, "Then what did you want to talk to me about?"

In the dim light of dusk, rain pattered the gallery windows, casting shadows over his face. The face that I'd lovingly kissed. *Stay on topic, Nat.* "I'm worried about Paxán. He's got enough on his plate without all this."

"Agreed," Sevastyan said. "What do you suggest I do?"

"I suggest *we* go in there and tell him that we've worked out our differences and can be civil. We'll tell him that we've ended whatever it was between us, so you can continue to live here. I think if we present a unified front, it will ease his mind."

Sevastyan parted his lips, but I interrupted him: "This isn't up for debate." I turned away and strode toward the study.

He passed me to open the door, saying over his shoulder, "I haven't been with anyone else."

I stutter-stepped. My heart did the same. "Should I believe that?" For the second time in as many days, I found myself mentally urging him: *Say yes, say yes.*

"I don't care if you do or not." I'd never seen the Siberian this ice cold.

But I did believe him. Well, hell, then he *hadn't* been axed from my decision tree? Maybe that meant it *wasn't* over with him?

He added, "I was called away by work concerns."

In other words, he'd merely taken a rain check on the man-whoring. *So over!* "You're such a dick," I muttered. Yet when we entered the room, I pasted a huge smile on my face for Paxán.

He called to us, "Good evening to both of you. Aleksandr, it's good to see you here. And with Natalie!"

"Can we speak with you for a minute?" I asked, nearly wincing when his eyes twinkled even brighter than usual. He must think we'd come to announce something more than: *we're totes just friends!*

"Of course. Sit, sit."

Sevastyan sank back on one of the settees, resting an ankle over the opposite knee; at the other end, I perched on the edge of the cushion.

Wasting no time, I said, "Paxán, we want you to know that there won't be any future improprieties between us."

He raised a disbelieving brow at Sevastyan. In response, the Siberian stretched his arm across the back of the settee toward me, all casual. But I sensed tension thrumming in him.

Heedless, I carried on. "So it shouldn't be a problem for both of us to remain here at Berezka. I know you would feel more comfortable if Sevastyan was on site, helping to keep everything safe—and so would I."

Before I changed my mind, I plowed onward to announce one of my new decisions. "And there's more. I'd like to stay on here permanently. When this danger ends, I'll start looking into transferring schools."

I noticed Sevastyan stiffen beside me. Because he was surprised? Pissed? What?

Paxán, of course, beamed. "You mean that?" Then he slanted Sevastyan an expression that looked a lot like *I told you so*.

I nodded firmly. Over the long hours of the previous night, I'd grasped how much my indecision and hesitancy were limiting my life. I'd done a postmortem on my past and concluded that I needed to be bolder in my future. Yes, I'd acclimated to the new things Sevastyan and I had done with a certain cheek, but rolling with the punches was not the same as swinging first.

The utter joy on Paxán's face wrecked me. One thing I'd learned about him? It took so very little to make him happy. "This is good," he said simply, getting a little misty-eyed.

I glanced over at Sevastyan to gauge his reaction. Even more tension roiled from him. Which I didn't care about.

"This is cause for celebration!" Paxán said. "A true welcome, a permanent one, to your home. And we have some good news for you as well . . ." He trailed off, turning his head toward the entrance.

Sevastyan was already on his feet, peering in the same direction. I followed their gazes, spied Filip in the doorway.

The man's angelic face was crumpled in misery. His left hand was bandaged, seeping blood. In his other hand, he carried a machine gun—pointed at us. "Well, isn't this touching?"

CHAPTER 25

"What are you doing, Filip?" Paxán paled as he and I stood. "That's not a weapon you want to aim in close quarters." The gun was heavy for Filip, and he only had one hand to hold it. His arm was already quaking. "Much less with the safety off."

When Filip glanced down at the gun, it swayed in his grip. My heart lurched as the barrel's aim swept from me to Sevastyan to Paxán. "I'm taking you from here," he said to Paxán. "For the bounty from Travkin."

What?? Filip was working for that bastard? And there was a bounty? That was the heightened security risk no one would tell me about! Travkin had put money on my father's life.

"Just set the gun down and talk to me," Paxán said, his tone deceptively calm.

"No time to talk." Filip raised his bandaged hand, his voice breaking as he said, "The next go-round, my creditors won't be as merciful as three fingers."

They'd . . . maimed him? I covered my mouth, fearing I'd be sick. He had pawned his watch and car, and it still hadn't been enough. I'd wondered how deep in he was. I'd never imagined this.

Sevastyan grated, "Let Natalie leave."

Paxán added, "She's not involved in this in any way." He was all coolness on the surface, but I sensed his dread.

"She is!" Filip waved that machine gun toward me, making Paxán hiss in a breath and filling me with fear. "Natalie is the reason I'm in this situation. I was an heir! Then word got out that you were leaving her *everything*." Tears began to spill down his blotchy cheeks. "But when my creditors got wind of my courting her, they knew I could win over any woman. Suddenly they couldn't give me enough money." He aimed at Sevastyan. "Until they heard that the heiress is with the *enforcer*. They called in their debts."

"We spoke about this just two days ago," Paxán said. "I asked if you needed help."

That was what they'd met about?

"And I didn't need it"—he nearly spat at Sevastyan—"until he made his move the same day!"

"Then let's fix the situation," Paxán said, drawing Filip's attention away from Sevastyan. "Money is no object. For the memory of your father, I pledge to settle anything you owe."

"You don't understand. I need *more*." Tears continued to spill; the gun shook erratically as his fingers seemed to cramp. "The bounty Travkin posted is more money than I could ever see."

"Take me." Sevastyan's expression was filled with menace. "I'm a valuable prize for an enemy."

"I'm here for the old man."

Paxán swallowed. "Take your finger off the trigger, Filip, and I'll go with you."

"I give the orders! You send the bulldog away, then we'll talk about your long-lost daughter."

Sevastyan grated, "That won't happen."

"You don't give a damn about yourself, do you? But what if I threaten your precious Natalie?" Filip aimed—directly at me.

I was staring into the barrel of a gun—too terrified to keep my eyes open, too terrified to close them.

The weapon jogged in his weakening arm . . . only a matter of time . . .

"Harm her and your life ends today," Sevastyan vowed in a chilling tone. "I'm giving you one chance to leave this room alive."

Filip's bravado began to dissipate. "I-I don't have a choice." He lifted his free hand toward his forehead, then sniveled at the reminder that he'd lost his fingers. In a wheedling voice, he said, "Just let me take him, Sevastyan."

"Never." Had Sevastyan eased toward Filip? "This won't end the way you anticipated. The news hasn't had time to reach you, but there will be no bounty."

"What are you talking about? Of course there is! Why wouldn't there be?"

"Because just hours ago, I shot Travkin."

I did a double take at Sevastyan. Travkin was dead? That was the good news Paxán had mentioned?

"You're lying!" Filip's gaze darted. "Lying!"

Panicked, I said, "Filip, don't do this. It's not too late. We can still fix this."

Out of the corner of my eye, I spied Sevastyan inching even closer to Filip, until he stood between me and Paxán.

"Freeze, Sevastyan!" Filip cried. "I'll shoot, I swear to God I will!" Another shaky wave of that gun—

Sevastyan lunged at me just as bullets sprayed the room from wall to wall. Clocks exploded, glass shattering, chimes tolling like church bells. I screamed, the sound cut off when I hit the ground; Sevastyan was atop me, hand cupping my head. In his other hand, a pistol smoked.

Plaster dust clouded the air, but I could see Filip on his back across the room. He was shot in the belly, twisting in pain. Though my ears rang as if a siren was in my head, I could still hear his cries. And something else . . .

Paxán's breaths. They sounded *thick*. No, no, no! I struggled to rise, but Sevastyan had me pinned down.

"Are you hit?" he demanded of me.

When I shook my head, he lunged to his feet, charging for Filip.

As Sevastyan disarmed him, I scrambled to reach Paxán. He lay on the floor, blood gushing from a wound in his chest.

Sevastyan snatched the machine gun from Filip, then stalked around the room, checking the perimeter. "Natalie, put pressure on that!" He slammed the office doors closed, bolting them shut.

Kneeling beside Paxán, I pressed both of my hands over his wound. "You're going to be okay, you're going to be okay." Shock—I was going into shock. And then how could I help my father?

In between grimaces of pain, Paxán looked sheepish. "This is . . . not how I planned things."

"Don't talk, please don't talk." Blood skimmed past my fingers. Lifeblood. *He can't lose any more.* "You have to save your strength!"

Sevastyan dropped to his knees on Paxán's other side. He put his hands on top of mine, knotting our fingers to bear down with even more force. Sevastyan's expression was so hard, like granite under pressure. About to crack.

Paxán's wound wasn't fatal. It *couldn't* be. So why were they both acting like it?

What did Sevastyan and Paxán know about shootings that I didn't?

Everything.

Paxán cast Sevastyan a weak smile. "You know I couldn't have borne it if you'd saved me instead of her. Proud of you, Son."

The hazy scene replayed in my head. Sevastyan had been directly between Paxán and me when the bullets had flown. He'd made a choice, tackling me to the ground—instead of Paxán. "Stop this, both of you! Paxán, you have to hold on. You're going to make it!"

"Be at ease, *dorogaya moya*." With effort, he reached for me, brushing my face before his arm collapsed.

Then his eyes went to Sevastyan. "You are bound to her," he told him in Russian. "Her life is in your care, Son. Yours alone." He covered our bloody knot of fingers with his hand. "She belongs to you."

One sharp nod from Sevastyan. More pressure on granite.

With difficulty, Paxán turned his head back to me. "Aleksandr will protect you. He is yours now too." I stared down at our interlaced fingers, awash in crimson—it was like a blood oath. "My brave daughter."

My eyes filled with tears, drops spilling. "Don't do this! *Bátja*, please, just hold on."

"Bátja?" He smiled through his pain, somehow still evincing contentment. "I knew you would call me Dad." But the twinkling blue of his eyes was ebbing. Replaced by sightlessness? "I only wish I'd had more time with the two of you. I love you both."

To Sevastyan, he said, "Make her life better . . . for my having been in it."

Blood bubbled from his lips. His eyes went blank, his chest . . . still.

"No, don't go!" I sobbed. But it was too late.

Pavel Kovalev, my father, was dead.

CHAPTER 26

*"N*atalie, get up!"

The siren in my head was back. Sevastyan was standing beside me, but his words sounded distant.

He grabbed one of my blood-coated hands and hauled me to my feet.

"This isn't happening," I muttered as I stumbled along, glass from Paxán's beloved clocks crunching beneath my heels. "This isn't happening." My father couldn't be dead.

Sevastyan dragged me over to where Filip squirmed in pain, blood pooling from his gut wound.

In a broken voice, Filip told me, "I-I didn't want this. I came tonight . . . because others were already . . . on their way. It was going to happen. No matter . . . what I did. The bounty is . . . unthinkable."

Hatred welled up inside me, drying my tears. "Goddamn you! How could you do this?"

"Swear to you, I only came for Paxán." He reached his mutilated hand toward me. "If I didn't know about Travkin . . . others won't have heard yet either. They'll . . . be coming."

"What does that mean?"

"Travkin also wanted . . . *your* head."

With a furious yell, Sevastyan yanked me behind him, drilling a bullet into Filip's skull.

Two dead. Two. Slain before my eyes.

I couldn't catch my breath, my lungs seeming to constrict. I felt like the whole world around me was on fire, flames crackling ever closer. Like if I screamed, no one would hear. I was hyperventilating by the time Sevastyan snatched my upper arm in his punishing grip and started dragging me away. "Come on, Natalie!" Gun raised, he led me toward a door at the back of the office.

"We can't leave Paxán like this." I gazed back at his still body. His lifeless eyes. Why hadn't I closed them? *Stupid, stupid.* "We have to care for him!"

Sevastyan just yanked me along harder. "I'm taking you from Berezka. We don't know who can be trusted here."

I was speechless. As the siren in my head amped up, he shoved me into a garage I'd never seen, then tossed me into a dark sedan.

Haze.

A car ride down the wet shell drive, rain pouring from the night sky.

Sevastyan's bloody rings digging into the steering wheel.

Mud slashing over the windshield, wipers gritty.

The back of the car fishtailed; I remained frozen.

Sevastyan didn't slow until we neared the river, then slammed to a stop in front of the boathouse. "You're going to stay here and lock the doors behind me," he ordered as he reached across me toward the glove box. "The glass is bulletproof. You do not open these doors." He took out a pistol, cocked it, flicked off the safety, then held it out to me. When I made no move to take it, he laid it on the console. "If someone gets in anyway, you use the gun. Aim for the chest and pull the trigger."

Sevastyan was heading out into danger? Already the entire world was on fire; if I lost him too . . . "Where are you going? Don't leave! Can't we just stay in this car and drive away?"

He shook his head. "I don't know who's controlling the gates. Or who's waiting outside them. We need to leave by water." In the *Casino Royale* boat? "I'll clear the boathouse, then return for you."

When he opened the door, his own gun raised, I cried, "Please be careful."

He cast me an odd look. "Don't worry, your protection will return." He slipped out into the rain, swiftly closing in on the boathouse—

I spied a muzzle flash out of the corner of my vision. Heard a sharp pop.

Half of Sevastyan's upper body was wrenched back, as if he'd been punched in the shoulder.

Not punched. Shot.

Lightning struck as I screamed. By the time my eyes adjusted, Sevastyan and another man were grappling for a gun.

In the headlights' beams, I could see it was the brigadier Gleb. Sevastyan launched one of his anvil fists, connecting with the man's face. Gleb tottered, overpowered.

Sevastyan couldn't be hurt too badly if he could move like that, right? He wrested the gun from the stunned man, then pistol-whipped Gleb with it. "How many more are there?" he roared.

Gleb's face split into a macabre grin. Whatever he said sent Sevastyan into a deeper rage, his fist flying.

I scratched at my bloodstained hands as I watched Sevastyan beating a man to death. Another sizzling bolt forked out above, spotlighting a grisly blow.

I'd never seen anyone fight like Sevastyan. Fighting to *kill*.

This was Sevastyan at his most raw—and real. He was an enforcer, and killing was what he did.

When Gleb collapsed, unconscious, Sevastyan followed him down, dropping to his knees to continue annihilating the man. It was as if some demon had taken Sevastyan over. Gleb's face was a pulp; with each of Sevastyan's hits, blood sloshed up from it as if from a disturbed puddle.

When would this end? I opened the door, stumbling toward him. "Sevastyan, we have to leave!" Freezing rain drummed down. "You have to stop this!"

He peered at me, the headlights glaring in his eyes. I saw madness—and something more. Like he *wanted* me to stop him—because he was still beating the man.

Between bouts of thunder, I thought I heard bone crunch.

Then I heard something even more terrifying.

Gunfire in the distance. It sounded like a battlefield. The loyal and the disloyal waging all-out war? Sevastyan heard it too. His expression said he was desperate to join that fray.

If anything happened to him . . . if I lost both Sevastyan and Paxán in one blood-drenched night . . . ?

I remembered Paxán's words: Extreme violence. Extreme *vigilance*. "You said you keep your promises, Sevastyan. You swore to keep me safe."

He gazed up at me through rain-thickened lashes, his eyes aglow. I was drowning in them. We were drowning together. I held out my tremulous hand.

As if in a daze, he rose, seeming helpless not to come for me.

CHAPTER 27

"Will you let me look at your arm?" I asked Sevastyan for the tenth time. I figured I'd keep asking until he responded.

His clothes had dried on him, but he refused to move from the yacht's steering wheel. For hours, the engines had hummed unceasingly as he'd guided us upriver, our end destination unknown.

He sat on the captain's bench in the luxurious cockpit, his body rigid with strain. The muted instrument lights illuminated his weary face, those compelling features, his fathomless gaze.

This was the man who'd lunged in front of bullets for me. Who'd killed to protect me. On our first night together, he'd told me, "I will eliminate any threat to you, pitilessly."

He had.

The glow from the dash highlighted streaks of dried blood across his cheek, neck, and the ripped material around his injured arm.

How much of that blood was his? Gleb's?

Paxán's?

At length, Sevastyan said, "It's just a graze. I've had worse."

I knew. I'd seen the scars. Encouraged that he was at least talking to me, I asked, "Can't you take a break? Haven't we run far enough?"

I'd discovered that running was precisely what this boat had been equipped for. In one of the stately cabins below, I'd found new passports—for Natalya and Roman Sevastyan, a married couple—trunks of our clothing, and a trove of cash. Just-in-case precautions.

In case had happened.

Inside another cabin, I'd also discovered some of Paxán's things. After the events of the night, this inclusion had seemed . . . naïvely optimistic. Tears had stung my eyes like needles, but I'd tried to stem them, tried to be strong.

I'd managed to hold back as I washed off and dressed in slacks and a sweater. But now, imagining Sevastyan's own devastation, my eyes watered once more. Aside from me, he was the only other person alive who understood what the world had lost tonight. "We need to clean your injury and then you can rest."

"Later." Without looking away from his course, he said, "You're not safe."

"Who were you talking to earlier?" When I'd returned to the cockpit after changing, I'd heard Sevastyan on the phone, speaking in terse Russian: "I've never asked you for anything. Secure it." Then, in a lower tone, "Do you understand the importance of what I'm entrusting to you?" Before hanging up, he'd said, "Do not consider this a chance for something more."

What had that meant? And why had his very accent changed? It'd sounded like a different dialect.

Maybe a Siberian one? "Will you please talk to me, Sevastyan? I have so many questions, and I'm so sick of being confused."

He exhaled. "Then ask."

"What will happen to Paxán?" My voice broke.

Gaze fixed on the horizon, he said, "If those defending Berezka win, they will see to . . . they will take care of him." His voice was a rasp. "Once I feel it's safe enough for you to return, we would have . . . the funeral."

I'd never looked at a man and known he was dying inside. But how could I expect anything different? Sevastyan had chosen me to live—over the man he hero-worshipped.

He'd saved me over his own savior.

How conflicted he must be. For myself, I felt a deep welling of grief. But it was pure.

Sevastyan looked like he was slowly crumbling.

I reached for his good arm. "I only knew Paxán for a couple of weeks. If I loved him this much, I can't imagine what you must be feeling. I'm so sorry you had to choose."

"There was no choice," he said, but the guilt was plain on his face. "You heard his last words."

I tried not to think about that. About being given. A decree sanctified by blood.

I changed the subject. "Can you at least tell me where we're going?"

"I don't know. Don't know who we can trust. Everything is different now," he said. "And though Travkin is dead, there will still be danger until all the players know the bounty has expired. The snake still twists even after it loses its head."

Travkin. Just the name made my blood boil. I wanted revenge against that nameless, faceless thug, blamed him so much more than even Filip. My cousin had merely been the deceitful, ungrateful weapon; Travkin had pulled the trigger. "You truly killed him?"

Sevastyan nodded.

Then even from the grave, Travkin had effected my father's

death. "How did you get to him? He must've had an army of guards."

With a menacing look, Sevastyan bit out, "I was unexpected."

"That's all you're going to tell me?" I asked in disbelief. "Did you know that Travkin had put a bounty on me too?"

Sevastyan finally turned to me. "I found out five minutes before I walked into his customary haunt and plugged a bullet between his eyes."

I swallowed, trying to imagine this man striding into the lion's den like that. For me. "You could've been killed."

Gaze back on the water, he said, "You need to rest, Natalie. You were in shock earlier. Go below."

"I don't like below. I've never been on a boat like this." The farther we got from Berezka, the rougher the water had become. Hearing the waves slapping against the bottom of the boat terrified me. Surely it was only a matter of time before the hull cracked like an egg. "I've never been out on the water when there's no land in sight." Strange, even though I had no visual of the shore—no lights shone in the distance—I still felt like the world was burning all around me. Being close to Sevastyan made that feeling recede.

When we hit a larger swell, he muttered, "It's not a boat; it's a ship. And you're perfectly safe on it."

"All the same." I climbed up onto the spacious captain's bench beside him, sitting thigh to thigh. Maybe I needed to be near Sevastyan because of what we'd been through together. Maybe we needed each other because we'd both left pieces of our hearts back at Berezka.

Time passed. I lost my battle against tears. While I silently cried, Sevastyan stared out into the black.

✦

Boom. Boom. Boom.

I woke in one of the cabins, tucked under the covers. I had vague recollections of repeatedly jerking awake against Sevastyan's side, until I'd gone under for good. He'd moved me? And changed my clothes? I was dressed only in one of his undershirts.

It was still dark outside, but I had no idea what time it might be; fall in Russia meant limited hours of light.

I could tell we were stationary. Maybe Sevastyan had come down here to rest.

To grieve.

Boom. Boom. What was that hammering sound? I rose to investigate. As I made my way toward the source, I wondered how it would be with Sevastyan and me today. Would he expect us to abide by Paxán's dying wishes?

Would I abide by them? Accepting Sevastyan as mine? I remembered how I'd felt at the thought of losing him too.

As if barbed wire had been tightening around my heart.

Boom. Boom. I followed the sound to another cabin. When Sevastyan didn't answer my knock, I eased the door open. I heard the shower running in the attached bathroom—the booming was coming from within.

As a sinking suspicion took hold, I hastened into the bathroom. I sucked in a breath at the scene before me.

Naked under the spray of water, with his eyes glazed over and his teeth bared, Sevastyan was punching the stone shower enclosure with his battered fists. The steaming cascade hit his chest as he struck, over and over, as if at an invisible enemy.

If he'd been granite under pressure, now he was fracturing right before my eyes—just like the stone he pummeled.

"What are you doing?" I cried. How could he keep this up?

His fists bled; more blood trickled from a knot of cloth he'd tied tight around his bicep, his idea of a bandage for his bullet wound. It formed a groove between bulges of muscle. "Please stop!"

He didn't.

"Stop!" I tore open the shower door and scrambled inside, grasping his uninjured arm with both hands.

He was a killer, volatile and violent, but I felt no fear of him. Not even when he whirled around on me, black hair whipping over his cheek. He was breathtaking. Real. Raw.

Mine, my mind whispered.

That sense of connection to him flared like a blinding light.

Between gritted teeth, he said, "Leave." His eyes were bleak, his noble face filled with such pain.

I could ease it. "I won't leave you like this."

"Why? You don't give a fuck about me. Not beyond what I can do for you."

Did he mean beyond pleasure? Beyond his protection? I remembered his parting words after our fight: *Beyond sex, anything with me doesn't appeal to you.* "You're so wrong, Sevastyan."

He just stared at me. What was he looking for? Permission? Understanding? Finally he moved, placing his palms on the wall on either side of my head, boxing me in.

His star tattoos were at my eye level, mere inches away, beckoning me. I wanted to wrap my arms around him and press my lips to his chest.

Kiss him and kiss him and kiss him until all his pain disappeared.

Tentatively, I leaned forward to graze my lips over one of his tattoos. He flinched as if I'd struck him, but he didn't stop me. I chanced a brush of my lips over his neck. He was motionless, a statue on the outside, a brutal enforcer on the inside.

I nuzzled the rugged line of his jaw. I smoothed those locks of hair away, then kissed the chiseled cheek I revealed.

When I slanted my lips over his, he shuddered out a breath and drew back. Blazing in his gaze was that bone-deep yearning, the one that called to mine. "What do you want from me, Natalie?"

How to articulate it? *I want to kiss you until you forget your pain for a time, want to hold you tight against me because I can't seem to get my body close enough to yours.* In other words . . . "I want you to make love to me."

Before, I hadn't slept with him because of the future and consequences. I wasn't sure I would live long enough to enjoy the former, so I couldn't be bothered with the latter.

At my admission, his brows drew tight; he looked like he was unraveling.

I asked him, "What do you want from me?"

I gasped when he fisted the collar of my dampened shirt. "I want what's *mine*." He tore the material from me with one rip, stripping me.

I was trembling, bare.

As his gaze raked over my naked body, he couldn't bite back his anguished groan.

Sevastyan looked at me like a man plummeting toward death would look at a pair of wings. As if I were the difference between life or death for him.

I laid my palms over his star tattoos; he cradled my face. His forehead met mine. For long moments, we stayed like that.

When he took my mouth with his at last, I parted my lips in welcome, closing my eyes as he softly kissed me. God, I loved his taste, wanted to drink in the heat of his mouth.

As ever, I was struck by the contradictions of this man. He

was tender, yet carnal. His thoughts were a mystery, but his body told a story—of his restraint: rippling muscles, heaving chest, shaking hands.

With a groan, he flicked his tongue harder against mine, telling me that he was about to deepen this kiss. Telling me that he was about to claim this part of me, with the rest of my body to follow.

That he was about to conquer.

And when I surrendered utterly, he consumed me like he'd been suffocating and I was the sweetest air.

CHAPTER 28

*S*evastyan kissed me until I was dazed, boneless against his hardened body. I clung to him when he yanked my knee to his hip, clamping it there.

His cock pressed against my belly like a pulsating brand, and I grew wet for it, readying.

He used his free hand to grip one of my breasts, leaning down to lick its stiffened tip. I whimpered when he suckled it between his lips, still working that clever tongue, forcing more tension to coil low in my belly. He tended my other nipple in turn, tonguing, sucking, leaving both achy peaks straining for more.

Then his hand trailed down to cup me. He slipped his middle finger inside my spread lips, making me moan, "Yes, *yes* . . ."

When he felt how slick I was, a defeated sound broke from his chest and a second finger joined the first to open me.

Then he withdrew those fingers to his mouth, his lids sliding closed as he sucked clean my cream. Another dip, another suck. As if he was drinking me one drop at a time.

It was the worst torture to feel his strong fingers filling me, then emptiness. "Inside me, Sevastyan, please . . ."

He delved them deeper. "This is what you need." He pumped them into my core until I was clawing at his shoulders.

I felt light-headed, taken over by a kind of delirium. I was wild for him to lose control—because I was about to. My hands traveled down his wet body, my fingertips lovingly trailing over his sigh-worthy pecs.

On the way down, I brushed my thumb across one of his flat nipples, noting his sharp inhalation. As I sifted my nails through the crisp hair of his goody trail, his hand tightened on my pinned knee.

Once I reached the heavy weight of his cock, he rasped, "Use it."

I rocked my hips up as I pulled his shaft to me. When the head made contact with my pussy, he bit out a curse, his length jerking in my hand. Panting, I ran the crown up and down between my swollen, flaring lips.

"So slick," he growled. "So ready for me."

As I petted my clit with the bulbous tip, his towering body shuddered with need. "Enough teasing. Wanted this too long."

He covered my hand with his own, fitting the crown against my entrance, pressing forward just a fraction.

As soon as I knew without any doubt that I was about to lose my virginity, worries crept in. He was far larger than anything that had ever gone into my body. *This is going to hurt.*

He pulled our hands away, then began easing deeper, wedging the broad head inside. My gasp was cut off by his lips, hungry and insistent as he sank his cock farther. Each inch forced me to stretch more and more; where would it end?

Just as I felt a tendril of panic, he drew back. His smoldering eyes scanned my face, gauging my every reaction.

Though the hot water had long since run out, I began to

sweat. The stretch burned—*too big, too big*—so I raised myself up on my toes to buy some time.

He shook his head slowly. "Take it." His free hand seized my hip to hold me steady.

I inhaled for courage. Once I'd relaxed a degree, he murmured, "My good girl," then continued his inexorable possession of my body.

I felt pain—no surprise, considering his size—but I could bear it. When I'd accepted as much of his shaft as possible, when he was seated deeply inside me, he went still again. Though I sensed in him a ravenous lust—the urge to thrust must be *lashing* him—he somehow harnessed his aggression, battling his most primal drives.

Even as his neck corded with strain and his muscles shook.

Even as I could feel his cock throb inside me with every beat of his heart.

Voice a harsh grate, he said simply: *"Moya."* Mine.

At that moment I was completely his. I was joined with him, impaled by him, and there was no escape. Like I danced along the edge of a volcano about to blow—or gazed up at a rupturing dam.

"Moya." He drew his hips back, then eased them forward. The pain faded, and in its place came a hint of something so incredible—

He did it again.

My lids went heavy as wonder suffused me. Rapture. Fullness. Connection. With his next measured thrust, I breathed, "Oh, my God."

"You like that, pet."

Adore. "I never knew." My hands relaxed their death grip on his shoulders and began sweeping caresses over his sculpted back.

"My woman's getting so wet." Another roll of his hips had me sinking my nails into the rock-hard contours of his ass.

When I began to move with him, he bit out, "You want more?"

"Yes, God, yes!"

He lifted me with an arm looped around my back. "Hold on to me. Legs around my waist."

When I locked them there, possessive hands cupped my ass, forcing me to slip back down his slicked cock. His shaft hit me at a new angle, and my eyes went wide. The pinch was fleeting; the pleasure mounted.

"Surrender, Natalya."

I gave a cry, and did. Tonight I was his without reservation.

His golden eyes held me rapt as he surged against me, into me, cock thickening even more. When my nipples raked over his muscular chest, I tightened my arms around him, unable to get close enough.

He was inside me; I wanted to be enveloped by him.

His wicked, tattooed body was working mine, controlling my pleasure, heightening it in every way. The marble on the undamaged wall was smooth against my back. I slid up and down against it, slid up and down his throbbing length.

I was already racing toward my orgasm when his words ghosted over my ear: "You're giving me such a hot, wet clutch . . . about to steal my cum from me before I'm ready."

He was as close as I was? Even in this position, I began to meet his thrusts, writhing on his cock, grinding my swollen clitoris against him.

He gnashed his teeth. "Stop, *milaya*. Or I'll come."

I was too far gone to stop; surely we both were. I squeezed my legs around his waist so I could undulate faster, harder.

Water collected at the tight seal where our bodies met, my feverish movements sending it sloshing.

He splayed his fingers over my ass, grating, "Said . . . to *stop*." He dug into my curves to hold me in place, but his punishing grip just turned me on more.

Mindless, I panted, "Oh, God, oh, God!"

"Then moan for me, pet. Never get enough of that sound."

I did, until screams replaced my moans as I hurtled ever closer. "Sevastyan!"

He bit out, "I want to feel how hard my woman comes. Wring my seed from me."

At that, I crashed over the edge, my inner walls clamping down on his length. He gave a yell and ceased his thrusts; I knew he could feel me milking his cock with rhythmic contractions, demanding everything from him.

He held himself still as I clenched him over and over; spasms left me unable to do anything but repeat his name as my head lolled.

He wrapped my hair around his fist, forcing me to look at him. Between breaths, he said, *"Ty moya."* You are mine.

Then he threw back his head and bellowed, beginning to ejaculate into me. I could feel his semen jetting inside, like a scalding tide. Only then did he thrust again, bucking his hips in a frenzy to pump himself dry, yelling from the force of his release. . . .

Afterward, he clasped me against him so tightly, it was to the point of pain. I needed it, wanted him to squeeze me even harder.

I don't know how long we remained like that, hearts thundering together, his hips softly rocking. Hours might have passed. When even the cold water from the tanks began sputtering, he carried me from the shower, arm clasped under my ass, his semi-hard cock still inside me.

Hadn't I once dreamed that he'd taken me soaking wet to bed? Without separating our bodies, he sat at the edge, with me in his lap. He kissed water from my neck, nursing the skin above my pulse point in that way that made me melt. He nibbled on my bottom lip, tenderly sucking on it.

When he dipped his head down to tongue drops from my puckered nipples, I arched my back with a cry, glorying in the feel of him swelling within me.

Yet then he lifted me off his cock, turning me, easily positioning me with my back to his chest. "Want to see you better." He fisted his length to impale me once more.

"S-see me?"

He wedged his legs between mine, spreading me till my legs rested against his outer thighs.

"Look at you."

I gazed up. We were in front of the dresser mirror, our damp bodies reflected—as if two more people were in the room with us.

"Any man would kill for you."

My face was flushed, eyes glinting with passion. Behind me, he seemed even more massive and unyielding, while I appeared pale, small, and soft. The dusky shade of his cock was stark against the pink flesh receiving it so eagerly.

As he hefted my breasts, I gazed at his ragged, tattooed hands against my milk-white skin, at that knot of cloth around his brawny arm. He looked like a dark god, a warrior who'd just returned from battle.

Because he was.

He lifted me just enough to reveal his veined shaft glistening from my orgasm and his semen. When a pearly bead trailed down from my opening, he said, "You see my cum inside you?"

"God, I see it." The hot, rich essence of him. The evidence of

what we'd done. I moaned, beginning to tremble. In the mirror, I
watched my breasts bobbing with my shallowed breaths.

Against the hollow of my neck, he rasped, "I've never come
in another."

I was grasping at threads of this conversation. Never? Oh,
because he'd worn protection.

"Did you feel it inside you?"

I nodded. "It felt so hot, scalding. It made me want more."

He turned my face so our eyes could meet in the mirror, so I
could see how he regarded me, my body.

Like I was already a caught thing. His gaze was . . . sinister.
"In a way, I've marked you."

At the idea, I shivered against him. I'd expected a bruising,
frantic claiming in the shower, and even now. This was the man
who'd whipped my breasts, who'd slapped my ass so hard I'd felt it
the next day. Merely recalling how he'd plied me with pain made
wetness flood me.

Yet this relentless assault on all my senses was just as much
a demonstration of his dominance. He had control over himself,
over me. "This is where you belong."

"Belong?" I whispered. Such a loaded word.

"You belong against me"—he grazed his teeth down my
neck—"around me. Connected to me."

Connection. "Yes, yes."

His fingers made a cage over my throat. "You belong *to* me."
His other hand dipped down to stroke my slickened clit, eliciting
a gasp from me.

I spread my legs even wider, knowing he was about to make
me mindless again.

"I told you that if I was your first lover, I'd be your last," he
said, his fingers making slow, slippery circles. "I told you that

I'd kill any man who touched what was mine. Do you understand me?"

Though I could scarcely pull my thoughts together, reluctance stole through me. I understood he wanted to possess me. Darkly, brutally. But for how long? How totally?

Would there be anything left of me when a man like this had had his fill?

When I hesitated to answer him, he abruptly pulled out.

I was left cold, bereft. "What? Why?" Aching emptiness suffused me.

He positioned me back on his lap, his engorged shaft in front of my mons. It stood like an idol to be worshipped, making my mouth water and my hips rock. I couldn't keep myself from grinding against the damp base.

"Grasp it."

I did.

"Stroke it. Learn it. My cock is the only one you'll ever need—or know."

Enthralled, I put both hands on him, pulling, masturbating him in front of the mirror. "Oh, God, Sevastyan . . ."

"If you want it back, then beg me for it."

As I squeezed it in my fists, words fell from my lips: "Please give me your cock."

"Why?"

Why? *Honestly* . . . "Because I feel like I'll die without it."

"Then tell me who owns your exquisite little body."

Owns. *Owns.* Yet right now, he *did*—controlling it absolutely. He lifted me once more, poising me atop his cock, wedging just the head inside. I moaned, wriggling on him as he withheld what I so desperately craved. Fine! "You own it."

"Who owns *you?*" he demanded, upping the ante. Once

again, he was pushing me, forcing me to submit ever more completely.

But fighting him seemed . . . unthinkable. Like resisting the inevitable. So I murmured, "You own me."

"Good." His eyes gleamed with triumph. Satisfied that I'd surrendered, he dug his heels into the floor and thrust upward into my wetness.

"Sevastyan!" I cried, but he didn't slow, seemed to have reached the limits of his iron control.

His hips surged, pistoning between my legs. In the mirror, I could watch his gaze locked on my quivering breasts. I could witness his thick, shining cock plowing into me, swallowed by my hungry pussy. About to fill me with more of his semen.

My toes curled. I whimpered, tremors taking me over. Building, coiling, building, coiling—

Release.

My back bowed; I screamed helplessly as my body seized.

He tugged my hair to bare my neck, nipping me hard, snarling against my skin, *"Ty svodish' menya s uma!"* You madden me!

I felt his cock jerking inside me, then heat . . . burst after burst as I moaned his name—in a voice dripping with submission.

❖

After I'd collapsed back against him, limp with satisfaction, Sevastyan kept our bodies joined, taking the opportunity to soothe his bite with a tender kiss on my neck.

Soon he started hardening again. I was exhausted, but the feel of him growing within me once more turned me on so much that I was ready for another round.

Yet he lifted me from his shaft, moving me bodily to the top of the bed. "I don't want to hurt you. I forget you were untried before this night."

I could already tell how sore I was going to be. Probably a good plan to take a breather.

He lay on his back, dragging me against his side. As he held me securely in the cradle of his arms, I rested my head on his chest. With the sound of his heart against my ear, I traced a tattoo, filled with fascination for this man—and a lingering unease.

I'd once imagined that I would be surrendering *some*thing when I lost my virginity. With Aleksandr Sevastyan, I might have surrendered . . . *every*thing.

But fatigue was catching up with me.

As I was drifting off to sleep, he gruffly said, "I've got a thousand thoughts running through my head."

He was actually instigating a conversation? About what was on his mind? "Tell me. Even just one."

"Tomorrow, maybe," he said in a noncommittal tone. "Go to sleep."

"Just one, Sevastyan."

He exhaled. "This need I have for you . . . it should unsettle you."

I swallowed. It *did*. Still I asked, "Why?"

He pressed his palm against mine, studying our hands for nerve-racking moments. "Because it unsettles even *me*."

CHAPTER 29

$\mathcal{I}$ shot upright, waking to the sound of my own scream and boots stomping toward the cabin.

"Natalie?"

I was awake. On the boat. Just a nightmare.

In sleep, I'd relived those bullets spraying. I'd heard Paxán's treasured clocks shattering, thinking that he would be distraught at the loss.

Then I'd dreamed that Sevastyan had died by the boathouse, his mighty body felled. Raindrops had pelted his lifeless face, his unblinking eyes—

When he burst through the cabin door, I was already on my knees, reaching for him with a whimper.

He clasped me against him, tugging me into his lap as he sank down on the bed. "I've got you. Shh," he murmured, squeezing me against his chest. "Shh, *milaya moya.*" He began rubbing my back with his big, warm hand, soothing me. God, I needed him. His strength, his heat.

In his arms, with his heartbeat drumming through my consciousness, I wondered how I could possibly have thought of this man as sinister.

When he was like this, I couldn't make myself regret last night's surrender. As he pressed kisses against my hair, I felt closer to him than I ever had to anyone.

How could I have regretted giving him anything I could . . . ?

The sound of voices outside roused me. "Where are we?" I asked.

"Docked outside of St. Petersburg." He tucked me even closer. "Do you want to tell me about it?"

No need to ask what I'd been having a nightmare about. "I . . . relived it," I said in a broken voice. "Then I dreamed you died."

"I'm not going anywhere, Natalie. But you've been through a lot. You weren't prepared for any of this."

"I'd sensed something was off with Filip. Yet I ignored my instincts. I should've said something."

Sevastyan shook his head. "I'd told Paxán about my misgivings, but he was ever loyal to his friends. He felt like he owed more to Filip, wouldn't heed my advice. I should've fought harder, made him see reason."

I gave a bitter laugh. "We're both blaming ourselves. Maybe we should blame Filip? Or Travkin?"

In a low tone, Sevastyan admitted, "I wish I could kill Travkin again."

Reminded of what he'd done, I asked, "Why did you walk into the lion's den to assassinate him? Why not wait?"

"The minute he marked you for death, he ensured his own. No one will ever hurt you. No one . . ." Sevastyan's hand on my back paused; he tensed all around me.

"What? What's wrong?"

I followed his gaze, saw my reflection in the dresser mirror. There were fingertip-sized bruises on my hip and ass.

In a hoarse voice, he said, "I did this to you?"

I peered up, saw an expression I'd never seen on his face.

Fear.

Because the only thing that could scare a man like Sevastyan . . . was himself.

He set me on the bed as if I were made of porcelain, then stood to leave, his posture stiff. "I left bruises." He looked wrecked by this, which wouldn't do.

So I tried to lighten the mood. "Please. I bruise from harsh language. Besides, this is kind of the nature of the beast, no?" He'd whipped women before, bound them. "Surely you've seen this in the past."

He didn't relax whatsoever, conflict clear in his expression. "No. Not from my hand."

Because Sevastyan had never been with the same woman twice? When Paxán had told me that, I'd kind of thought he was exaggerating. But it was likely Sevastyan had never stuck around to see the aftermath of his appetites.

I sensed him slipping away from me. "I'm perfectly fine. You liked when my ass was sore," I reminded him. "How is this different?"

"It's different. Now." He handed me a robe.

With a frown, I donned it. "Now that what?"

"We'll discuss this later. We have a long day ahead of us."

He wouldn't look at me, was closing down right before my eyes. Now that we'd made love, I thought that we would be entering into a new stage of our relationship. In which, you know, we *talked*.

But it was as if a draft had soughed into the air between us. "In the *banya*, you told me not to wake up. I feel like I should be telling you the same. You're pulling away, and I don't know why."

"I have something for you." He withdrew an envelope from his jacket pocket, handed it to me. "It was in Paxán's cabin, in his safe." The back was sealed with a red wax circle. I recognized Paxán's fanciful calligraphic handwriting on the front.

For my daughter

He'd told me he would never tire of saying that.

"Read that, then pack a suitcase for five nights." Sevastyan gave a curt nod. "We depart soon. I'll leave you to it."

As soon as I was alone, I tore the envelope open. . . .

My dearest Natalie,

If you are reading this, then I am—how do you Americans so eloquently phrase it?—shit out of luck.

Even in those words, I could hear his wry tone, could imagine him writing it with a sigh.

However, you are with Aleksandr, and that is my consolation. He will walk into a hail of bullets for you.

He had.

Yet as loyal as he is, there is a darkness to him. Since the first winter I brought him to Berezka, he has not spoken about his childhood, but I know it was horrific. I never pressed him to talk about it, because I sensed he wanted to shed his past and make a fresh start.

This was a failing on my part.

Dorogaya, he's like an intricate clock, and some mechanism deep within is broken. He bears scars inside and out, and until he can trust another enough to confide about his past, I don't believe he will ever be whole. Coax him to entrust you with his burdens.

How? If Sevastyan hadn't learned to open up by now . . .

Not that I expected him to know how. He'd been raised from the age of thirteen in a domicile inhabited by men, rife with guns and criminals.

And who knew what had happened to him before that?

You're a wealthy woman now. Once you are out of danger, please see the world and live out your dreams.

With all my heart, I hope you and Aleksandr can build a future together on a strong foundation. But if you can't, my brave daughter, then eye the horizon. Life is short. Take it from someone who apparently knows.

Tears clouded my vision. Again his wryness permeated his words. But we would never laugh together again, would never share jokes.

You are my life's great surprise, treasured beyond words. However much time I got to spend with you was not enough—and never could be.

With all my love,
Bátja

Through tears, I reread the letter several times, until I was almost numbed to it, then placed it in the inner pocket of my suitcase. As I began to pack, I reflected on my father's advice about Sevastyan.

I wasn't a big fan of women trying to fix men, to change them. I always figured there were guys enough out there, so I should look for a total package that was already fully Ikea-assembled—or go without.

But getting Sevastyan to open up didn't necessarily involve *changing* him, it involved *getting to know* him. Like a scholarly investigation.

Our relationship needed work. *Work is what I do.*

Did I want Sevastyan enough to fight for him? Yes. Yes, I did. I'd wanted him since I'd first seen him.

I had to try.

I emerged from the cabin just as he was disconnecting a call. With the same mysterious person as before?

"Are you well?" His way of asking about the letter.

"Yes. Paxán wrote a beautiful good-bye."

Sevastyan nodded. "I've just learned that much of the danger has lessened. Word of the bounty's expiration has spread, and Berezka has been secured. Your father's funeral will be held there in two weeks."

"I see." I swallowed past a lump in my throat. "Are we going back there now?"

"Not yet. I've rented a car for us to head south to Paris. There's a secure property in the city."

"But if the danger is dwindling . . ."

"I trust the information about Berezka—but not enough to risk your life."

"Who's giving you the intel? One of the brigadiers?"

"A man named Maksim."

At the mention of this name, something tugged at my memory. "How do you know him?" When Sevastyan didn't answer, I said, "Let me guess. You met him in the north. By chance."

"Something like that," he said, twisting that thumb ring like a son of a bitch. Like my shady Siberian. "I've known him for most of my life. I do . . . trust him, up to a point, at least." Twist, twist, twist.

"Uh-huh." I didn't feel like he was outright lying, but he was definitely skirting around the truth. And for right now, I was just too drained to call him on it.

When he told me, "I'll get your bag," and set off for the cabin, it was almost a relief.

Once we were in the car, a Mercedes sedan much like his own, Sevastyan paused before starting off. Without looking at me, he squeezed the gearshift, rubbing his other palm over the wheel.

Finally he spoke: "A good man would reason that you were confused last night, traumatized, and couldn't be held accountable for your actions. A good man would release you back to your old life, now that everything has changed."

"But you don't consider yourself a good man?"

He faced me, enunciating the words: "Not in the least, pet." His answer sounded like both a promise and a threat.

How to respond to that? He'd basically told me he was a selfish bastard who wouldn't ever be letting me go. Just as he'd informed me last night, while petting me so divinely.

I let the conversation rest—but I wouldn't for long. Paxán's letter had just highlighted my own misgivings. I needed more from Sevastyan.

Yet what was I prepared to do to get it?

He put the car in gear. As we drove away, I gazed up at him, realizing I was starting off on an expedition into the unknown. With this trip, with this man.

I was a bystander in both cases—waiting for Sevastyan to switch gears or signal with a blinker, to open up or show some hint of trust.

And all the while, the hazard lights flashed over and over. . . .

CHAPTER 30

"*A*mazing," I breathed as I gazed out over Paris from the covered balcony of Sevastyan's town house.

His "secure property" was a four-story mansion from the turn of the century, with a to-die-for view of the Eiffel freaking Tower, the pinnacle of all my travel dreams. It soared, the top disappearing into a low bank of rain clouds.

"I'm pleased you like it," he said from the spacious open-plan sitting area. If Berezka had been all that was opulent, this place was nearly as lush, but the interior was more modern. In front of a crackling fire, he poured a glass of red wine for me.

I couldn't help but sigh at him, all dressed to perfection in a three-piece charcoal suit. Seeing him like this made me glad I'd dressed up today. This morning, he'd told me Paris was only a few hours away, so I'd forgone my most comfortable clothes for thigh-highs, kitten heels, a pencil skirt, and a fitted blouse of deep purple silk.

For the last five days, we'd driven ever southward toward Paris, giving me a passenger-side view of southern Russia, Poland, Germany, and northern France.

At night, we'd stayed in lavish hotels and made love for half of the hours we'd allotted for sleep. Though he'd taken me again and again, he always treated me like porcelain.

Over these days, I'd seen more of his fascinating contradictions. He knew wines, spoiling me with rare vintages, but didn't drink with me. When we dined in fine restaurants, he was such a gentleman, his table manners impeccable—yet I knew he was always carrying a very ungentlemanly pistol in a holster.

In addition to Russian, English, and Italian, he spoke fluent French and had a good grasp of German—but I could barely get him to communicate with me about anything meaningful.

He refused to open up. With every mile we'd put between us and Russia, distance had accumulated between Sevastyan and myself. I was beginning to see that Paxán was right: something was broken inside Sevastyan.

The grief we shared hadn't brought us closer; in fact, we'd avoided all mention of Paxán and Berezka. . . .

When he stepped through the balcony doors, I accepted the wine, asking, "Is this place really yours?"

"I bought it from a Saudi prince." That would explain the heavy security, the private entrance. A guard and servants were already installed here.

"Sounds expensive."

A hint of amusement. "I have money of my own, *milaya*."

Was that why Paxán had left his vast holdings to me?

Our first day on the road, Sevastyan had told me that when things settled down, we would need to discuss my inheritance, but I was in absolutely no hurry. Since then, we hadn't talked about expenses or money until now.

He joined me at the railing, the situation reminding me of the first time I'd looked out from my balcony at Berezka. Except that now, Sevastyan wasn't physically standoffish. He pulled me in front of him, my back to his front, and wrapped his warm arms around me. Resting his chin on my head, he locked me tight against his torso.

"When did you buy it?" I asked.

"Not long ago."

Another vague answer to put with the rest of them. I bit my tongue. Sometimes I bit it so hard it bled.

Since that night on the boat, there'd been no progression of emotions—or intimacy.

He'd claimed me again and again, praising me, bringing me untold pleasure. After each time, he'd let me explore his body as intently as he'd explored mine. Nights of breathless discovery. I would drift off to sleep with my hands still caressing him.

But he never took me as he so clearly needed to. I'd find his gaze on my wrists—because he needed them bound. He'd nuzzle my nipples, suckling them, but never grazing them with his teeth or pinching them up to the point of pain.

Yesterday, at a gas station in Germany, he'd been on the phone—again—so I'd wandered inside and made a purchase: a hard-core bondage magazine (it was just sitting in a rack of mags next to the motor oil!).

Once we'd gotten under way, he'd absently asked, "What do you have there?"

So I'd turned to a page I'd dog-eared while waiting for him, holding up one of the many pictures that had piqued my interest: a naked woman bound by her wrists and ankles to what looked like a padded sawhorse.

She'd worn these really cool nipple clamps; they'd looked like someone had placed one conductor's wand above the peaks, then another below, tightening the slim bars together with screws on the ends. Recalling how hard Sevastyan had pinched my nipples in the *banya*—and how I'd loved it—I wanted to be clamped like that. At the mere thought, my nipples had stiffened.

Once Sevastyan had registered what he was seeing, his pupils had dilated, his knuckles gone white on the steering wheel. Voice hoarse, he'd asked, "Is that what you think you want?"

I'd nodded. "You have a lot of experience with scenes like this, right?"

"Enough for both of us, so that we never have to descend to that level again."

Descend? "You should know—since *apparently* you're the only man I'll ever sleep with—that I want to try just about everything once. My curiosity demands it."

He'd swallowed, his throat working. "Like what?"

In as casual a tone I could feign, I'd said, "I loved it when you whipped me with the *venik*." When the stinging had turned to heat and the heat to bliss. "So maybe we should raise the stakes and try a paddle, or something like"—I'd shoved an ad for a flogger at him—"this."

My cool Siberian's upper lip had beaded with perspiration.

"Or this." I'd showed him a picture of a naked and gagged woman trapped in a pillory. A fully dressed man was behind her, smacking her between the legs with a *dogging bat*, which looked like a leather-covered bookmark that flared at the end. "That must feel . . . electric."

With a blistering curse, Sevastyan had snatched the mag from me, flinging it in the backseat.

I'd been certain he was about to pull the car over to ravish me on the side of the road. Yet he never had. He wouldn't even discuss what I'd shown him—as if it'd never happened.

Basically, my relationship with Sevastyan was emotionally

stunted and heading toward sexually frustrated. Two very big hurdles . . .

Now, as the lights of Paris twinkled in the distance, he turned me in his arms. "What are you thinking about?"

"The drive down. The magazine."

He dropped his hands and drew away from me. Crossing to the railing, he rested his forearms atop it. "I'm not discussing that."

I narrowed my eyes, filled with irritation and disappointment. But recalling his white-knuckled reaction to my choice of light reading made me realize I could wear him down. Tempt him to lose control. Maybe?

Of course, that would mean having to pay the piper. Was I ready to commit to a BDSM relationship with this man? Part of me wanted to, simply because it would at least be a *defined* relationship.

As we stood now, everything was up in the air, with zero stability. I was discovering that I liked stability. I'd liked living on one farm my entire childhood with steady-as-rocks parents. I'd liked settling in at one school.

Naturally, Sevastyan would feel differently after his hand-to-mouth existence as a child. But I needed more. . . .

"Talk about something else, Natalie, or we won't talk at all."

"Fine. We'll discuss other things. Such as how you made so much money." I'd had no idea he was independently wealthy to this degree, but it made sense considering he was a *vor* himself. Now I realized he'd lived at Berezka by choice, to be close to Paxán. The idea of that tugged at my heart. "Will you not tell me how?"

"I . . . fought." He fell silent. I guessed he knew he'd have to give me something more, because he tried again. "In my teens and twenties, I fought in underground *mafiya* matches. It was lucrative for me."

"I imagine you won lots."

"I never lost one of those match-ups," he said, not with conceit, but almost with . . . regret. In a lower tone, he added, "I am singularly suited to fighting, always have been."

"How so?" Superior bone density? High pain threshold? I recalled Paxán telling me that he'd never seen anyone take hits like Sevastyan, and he'd only been thirteen at the time.

Ignoring my question, Sevastyan continued, "A few years ago, I realized I wouldn't be able to fight forever. I had a business idea, and brought it to Paxán. He encouraged me to use my winnings to develop the scheme on my own."

"What was it?"

"A way to smuggle cheap vodka into the country."

"Isn't Russia the land of cheap vodka?"

"It costs significantly less to buy it from the States, but our alcohol tariffs deter most from importing it. So I came up with a way to disguise the vodka from customs."

"How?" I asked, fascinated.

"I had it dyed light blue with food coloring. Then we labeled the barrels as windshield-wiper fluid. Once in Russia, we reversed the dye."

I grinned up at him. "That's scarily brilliant."

He shrugged, but I could tell he was pleased with my assessment. "It made millions, still does," he said, again without conceit. Then he exhaled, gaze gone distant. "I help get cheap alcohol into the country. Ironic."

"How's that ironic?"

Attention back on me, he said, "Enough questions."

I tilted my head at him. I'd had a victory—he'd told me

more about himself than ever before. So should I let him off the hook?

I'd just decided I would when a lustful look arose on his face, the look I now recognized and breathlessly welcomed.

"I want to show you something." He led me up the stairs, then through a foyer to a palatial bedroom suite.

Inside, I saw our bags beside each other. "This is our room?" Staying in hotels with a traveling companion wasn't that big a deal. But it struck me that I was now *living* with a man.

At his place.

"You don't like it?"

The room was decorated in understated colors, dark blue and cream. The counterpane over the immense bed was lush but refined, the walls papered with a tasteful design.

The furniture was a complementing mix of masculine and feminine. There was a sophisticated dresser for cosmetics and jewelry—that I no longer had—as well as a weathered leather ottoman that looked like it'd been stolen from some duke's retiring room. Yet everything worked together. "What's not to like? Is this what you wanted to show me?"

He shook his head, leading me into an attached office with a bulky door. Inside were a desk, a cot, storage closets, and several monitors displaying camera feeds.

"Is this a panic room?"

"Precisely."

The feeds were from each area of the house. "The whole place is wired?"

"And one hidden outside." It displayed Parisians walking down a side street, most gazing directly at the concealed camera. "I can watch every feed on my phone." Sevastyan held up his cell, clicked an app, then showed me one. "So even when I'm not here, I can watch over you."

Always watching me. "Does it record?" I asked in an innocent tone, but he'd already sensed the direction of my thoughts.

"If we wish it to. Or you could watch a feed live as it occurs." He turned back into the bedroom, picking up a remote. A panel hummed, revealing a huge wall-mounted flat-screen.

With another press of a button, the TV came to life with a crystal-clear color view of the bedroom. The camera must be hidden in the molding on the wall opposite the bed.

He took off his suit coat, then moved to the bed, sitting back against the headboard. "Strip for me." He clicked another button on the remote, dividing the screen between the bedroom and the street. It was as if strangers were with us, gazing directly into the room. With his eyes darkening, he said, "Strip for them."

Oh, game on. This was the first even remote hint of kink since we'd had sex.

I pulled my hair down and shook it out over my shoulders; his gaze trailed over my mane, seeming to follow every curling lock.

With an indolent air, I unbuttoned my blouse; his hand headed south to rub the huge bulge already straining against his slacks.

I turned around when I shrugged off my top, keeping my back to him as I unzipped my skirt. The sound of his zipper joined mine. But I could see him on the TV, his gaze rapt on my ass as he fisted his cock.

God, that man aroused me beyond reason. I had a brief thought that he could be recording even this. The idea just turned me on even more. Any shyness I might have retained had been burned away by nights of his lovemaking, by his ardent gaze, his reverent touches.

This man liked my body and made no secret about it. So what was there to be shy about?

"Do you wish they could see you like this?" he asked as I shimmied from my skirt.

"I might." Off came my bra.

"My little exhibitionist." Just his rumbling voice had my nipples budding. "Are you a voyeur as well?"

Considering my wee addiction to porn, I had to say, "Odds are."

"Don't remove your heels and thigh-highs—I'm going to fuck you with those on."

I shivered at his words, reaching for my thong, the last item he'd let me slip off. I reveled in his heavy breaths as I inched the scrap of lace down to my ankles, stepping from it.

"Turn around so I can see what's mine," he commanded me.

As ever, any hint of his dominance sent a flutter through me. I slowly turned. Though he was still dressed, I flaunted my naked attributes for him.

He looked mesmerized, his brows drawn tight, lips parted. Relishing his obvious pleasure, I squared my shoulders and cocked a hip out. "Like what you see, Siberian?"

"And it's all for me alone. Come."

With a sassy grin, I sauntered to the bed, climbing up to walk on my knees toward him.

"Straddle me."

I situated one knee on each side of his hips and laid my palms against the high headboard—which put my crotch right before his face. Positioned like this, our gazes locked. His expression dared me to look away as he leaned forward to flick his tongue out. I gasped at the hard lash he gave my clit.

He did it again, burying his face deeper, not bothering to hide the fact that he was inhaling my scent. I raked my fingers into his ruffled black hair, rocking forward for more of his carnal mouth.

He licked my bud, tasting it till it was agonizingly swollen. His groans joined my moans as he ate me wetly, loudly—flicking and sucking with abandon until everything between my legs was sopping.

I perceived a droplet of my moisture trailing down my inner thigh, caught by the lacy garter-top of my hose. With a growl, he cleaned the lace with his tongue, sending my arousal spiraling. Then he set back in, ordering me, "Play with your nipples. Roll them between your fingers."

As I played, he spread me wider, nursing the hood of my clit until my legs trembled and my toes curled in my kitten heels. "Oh, God, Sevastyan, I'm close."

Right when I was on the verge, he broke away with a sweet kiss.

I peered down with confusion. "But . . . but you can't stop."

"Just did, pet." As he laid me back on the bed, I sputtered a protest . . . that fell mute when he rose to begin stripping. He made short work of his clothes, as if he didn't want to miss a nanosecond of this.

I gazed on adoringly, riveted to his body moving, all ruthless hardness. Each of those hollows and rises had known my lips. The gunshot graze on his arm was almost healed, another bravely earned scar to join the rest of them.

Another mark for me to kiss.

Back in the bed, he maneuvered himself between my legs,

fisting his shaft, aiming between my sodden curls. Even after all the times he'd taken me, I still went wide-eyed when he delved the head inside. He took care with his size, but I'd only been doing this for a few days.

"Any more protests?" he grated as he eased home.

I arched to him, sighing, "All good here."

As he began to thrust, I clutched the bedspread on both sides of my head. I saw his gaze flick from my hands, to my eyes, then back to my hands. When I stretched my arms over my head and crossed my wrists, his lids went heavy, and I felt his shaft pulse inside me.

"Don't hold back, Sevastyan."

"Not holding back."

"Don't you want to pin me down? Stop giving me pleasure at the expense of your own!"

He cast me a look like I was insane. "You think this isn't pleasurable for me? It's everything I can do not to come!"

"Then pin me down hard—because *I* need it."

"You don't know what you're asking," he said, bending down to kiss me, tonguing me with my own taste. He brushed my nipples over and over, then trailed his hand to my mons. His thumb worked my clit until I was moaning into his mouth.

When he finally broke away to drag in a breath, my head lolled, my gaze on the TV screen. I watched him from above, savoring the view of his powerful body as it toiled to sate mine. His back was lathered with sweat, the rigid muscles of his ass flexing as he plunged between my thighs. I could see his shaft disappearing into my pussy, his heavy testicles drawing taut.

As his chest rubbed over my nipples, even more moisture seeped down my cleft. He gripped the curves of my ass with both hands. His spread fingers encompassed the entire width of my ass, holding me steady for his taking.

Just as I wondered if he could feel all the slickness up and down my crevice, he grated, "So wet. My woman needed to be fucked, no?" I'd learned he tended to talk in the throes, and loved it when I talked back.

"I've needed it since this morning in the car. I kept imagining what you would do if I leaned over and started sucking you off."

His fingers dug in deeper, his middle one perilously close to my rim. But it felt *good*. How easy it would be to use my wetness to breach me with that finger. He squeezed even harder, spreading me, inching closer.

When I imagined him gently probing my ass while his cock pillaged my pussy, I wriggled to get his fingers there.

"Stop, pet. You'll give me ideas."

Anal play had always looked hot in the porn I'd watched. Just thinking about him readying me . . . "I told you I'd try just about anything once."

He hissed, "You want me to fuck your ass?"

When he said it like that? With such lust? "Okay!"

"That's not for you, beautiful girl. I'd hurt you."

Before I'd been a *dirty* girl. Or a *greedy* one. Now this tenderness was about to drive me insane.

I was sick of this! Frustration removed any remnants of a filter that had never existed in the first place. "I'll just imagine it then, fantasize about you forcing me to bend over the bed . . . spreading my legs and making me raise my ass so you can lube it up for your use."

"Unh!" His hips shot forward, his body bucking even harder. His ungoverned response shocked me. God, how badly he

needed to do these things to me—how badly *I* needed him to! I'd already planned to wear him down. How far was I willing to go?

In a throaty voice, I said, "My arms would be tied behind my back, my mouth gagged. You'd order me to be still, commanding me to relax." The more I talked, the easier the words came. "You'd penetrate my ass with one finger, opening me up with another."

"Goddamn, woman!" Another harsh thrust. My words were sending him over the edge—and myself as well. Was this fighter finally on the ropes?

"Then you'd slather lube over your throbbing cock, all over that thick head, giving me no choice but to accept it."

His breaths were heaving, his hips rocking. "You'd be so fucking tight around me, so hot."

Loving his response, I said, "I'd be nervous, might try to twist away—"

"Then I'd whip those perfect curves until you submitted to me. Because nothing would stop me from burying my cock balls-deep between them."

I moaned, so close to coming but never wanting this to end. "You'd start to move inside me . . . I'd go mindless . . . because it's you, possessing me completely."

"Your pretty screams would be muffled by that gag."

"Oh, God, oh, God." His sweat-slicked hips rubbed my inner thighs, the hair on his legs abrading my calves, adding to all the sensations.

I was panting, hovering on the edge when he said, "I'd pump my hot cum into you, flood you with it . . . never let you forget who you belong to—"

I exploded, arching off the bed. Grinding my breasts against him, I keened with ecstasy, clenching around him.

I was still coming when his back bowed, his chest rising

above me. The muscles in his straightened arms were bowstring-taut. Tendons strained in his neck as he continued to pound those hips. The power in his body was awing, the power he held in check for me.

When he ejaculated, he yelled, *"Natalya!"* His thick cock pulsated as it shot his cum inside me, coating me, filling me up.

Never letting me forget who I belong to.

He collapsed atop me, his body quaking with after-shudders—while I was reset once more.

I was barely capable of moving, of thinking. So I trailed my nails up and down his damp back as he ran his lips along my neck.

I didn't know how long we lay like this. Once I could process thought again, I reflected on what had just happened, wondering how long a need like Sevastyan's could stay bottled-up. If he couldn't fulfill his darkest desires with me, would he eventually go to another?

Would I?

I never would have thought I could come so hard and be so disappointed. During my first night with Sevastyan in that plane cabin, he'd told me, "You weren't supposed to be like this."

But I was.

I had "particular interests" as well. And I could now see how well we'd been matched. He'd once been my dream man, one who'd wanted to open my eyes.

Now he was like a mirage. . . .

❖

Later that night, Sevastyan and I lay on our sides, facing each other in the dim light of the room.

Through the open balcony doors, we could hear nighttime

Paris awakening. The resident cook had prepared a gourmet meal that we'd taken in bed—between bouts of more lovemaking.

I reached forward to trace a tattoo on his chest. "Sevastyan, why have you been so gentle with me?"

Shrug.

"I'm going to need a *verbal* answer from you."

Something in my tone must have alerted him that I wasn't playing around. He said, "Most women would want a man to cherish them, no?"

"That's evasive."

"Very well, then. Do you *not* want me to cosset you?"

"Up to a point. But not always." I pressed my lips together. "It's hard to explain. I want you to be like you were with me those first three times we were together. I want you to be yourself."

"What if this is my true self?"

"I don't believe that, especially not after tonight."

"Couples fantasize and talk about things that never come to fruition."

Damn, he was slippery. "Why fantasize, when we can have reality?"

His gaze bored into mine. "I will never hurt you. Now, change the subject."

Discouragement welled—until I realized he'd just given me an entrée. "The new subject is you."

He exhaled. "I told you that I have difficulty talking about myself."

"Probably because you never do it. I want to *know* you, Sevastyan. As well as you know me. And I don't think that's too much to ask, considering our circumstances."

He swallowed. This man had launched himself in front of a hail of bullets to save my life. He'd braved even more to fight off Gleb and secure our escape. Yet he dreaded opening up to me?

How to get him to understand I wouldn't judge him, wouldn't run screaming? "In case you haven't noticed, I'm pretty broad-minded. I wish you could talk to me, confide in me."

"Why?"

"Because we're in a relationship. And each secret confided between us is another stone in our foundation. Hey, let's just start with some soft-pitch questions. If you really don't want to answer, you can say pass."

He brusquely said, "Ask."

"What's your favorite color?"

"Used to be blue." He reached forward to twirl a lock of my hair around his finger. "Now it's red."

"What do you like to read?"

Still gazing at his twirling finger, he said, "History papers. On women and gender."

Clever. "Have you been to prison?"

"Twice. Neither time for too long. Paxán got me freed quickly enough." A flash of anguish crossed his face.

I forced myself to continue. "Those tattoos on your knees . . . you're a *vor* yourself?"

He dropped my lock of hair. "Yes." No explanation. No un-packing.

"Are you the head *vor* of Paxán's syndicate now?"

"Depends. I don't have enough information to answer that yet." He was starting to shut down again.

"Do you have any siblings?"

"No."

"Any family living?" I asked.

"None."

"What were your parents like?"

"Pass."

"Is there *anything* you'll tell me about your past? Look, I don't need to know things you did for your job, but I want to know about your childhood."

"Why is that so important to you?"

"I'm a historian, Sevastyan—I'm going to want to know your history." I scrambled for another question. "When did you know what your *particular interests* were?"

He shrugged again. "That's behind us."

I murmured, "Don't say that. You opened my eyes to all these new things"—for some reason, he flinched at that—"and now I want more. I can't go back, Sevastyan."

"Since you'll be only with me, you'll have to." The walls were coming up.

"Don't close me out."

He curled his finger under my chin, all tenderness, even as he said, "How could I close you out when I never let you in?"

As he rose to dress, I recognized a harsh truth: for Sevastyan, confiding in another would be akin to stepping off the trestle.

Which meant I was falling in love with a man who would never be emotionally available to me.

Corner, meet Natalie.

CHAPTER 31

*P*ressure.

I'd felt it at Berezka, still did. But over the last week, it'd transformed into something different: the pressure of two people who wanted each other—but no longer fit each other.

Because sexually, he'd changed himself; and emotionally, he remained the same.

I sensed it building inside him, inside of me. Some precipice loomed.

This morning, I was alone in the town house yet again. Sevastyan had gotten a text about two hours ago and rushed off to some undisclosed location. *Another meeting he won't explain.*

He had them daily, sometimes twice a day. I figured he was working long-distance on syndicate business.

After all, a multimillion-dollar operation had recently lost its leader, and I guessed the bulk of responsibility had fallen to Sevastyan. I could handle his long hours, but his secrecy grated on me. When would he trust me?

Maybe he was trying to shield me? Plausible deniability? If so, I knew nothing.

I was on the outside looking in, just like I'd been at Berezka. . . .

He'd taken me out to sightsee a couple of times, but his thoughts had been preoccupied, his piercing gaze assessing potential threats. Still Paris had been amazing, and I'd been able to check off dream destinations in my tourist guidebook.

I'd climbed the Eiffel Tower, sighed over the Arc de Triomphe, shopped for souvenirs along the Champs-Élysées.

Though he was convinced the danger to me was in fact dwindling each day, he didn't feel comfortable enough to let me go anywhere without him. So I was stuck here when he left to attend to whatever business he wouldn't tell me about.

When I'd informed Sevastyan that I needed to go shop for a new phone, he'd brought one back for me. When I'd told him that I wanted to go out and buy more clothes, he'd simply reordered much of what I'd left behind at Berezka—garments, cosmetics, shoes, hosiery, and of course lingerie.

He'd even started buying me jewelry. "Shouldn't I be paying for this?" I'd asked him. Shoulders gone tense, he'd replied, "You think I can't provide for my own woman?"

Though we had a maid, a cook, and a driver/butler/guard who could procure anything from a replacement birth-control patch to Le Chunky Monkey, this lap-of-luxury mansion was a gilded cage.

As usual, I was watching the feeds in the panic room, viewing Parisians going about their daily lives. This room was my favorite. I guessed I kind of liked spying on people. I'd imagine stories for their lives, speculating on what they might be talking about.

Or maybe I was just going crazy.

With a groan, I put my head in my hands. I was bound to a man who'd given me a glimpse of my true nature only to deny it. A man who wouldn't confide in me.

A man I still didn't know.

We were both dealing with our grief—separately—and seemed to be living satellite lives. If he was here, he was often on the phone with the mysterious Maksim. I'd overheard him saying enigmatic things like "Protect it with your life" and "She is with me."

I'd poured my heart out to Jess about how much I missed Paxán, but Sevastyan was the only one who could truly understand. I'd even told her about Filip. Her assessment: "If he was toxic in life, he'll still be in death. I *forbid* you to think about him. You're lucky to be alive."

Not lucky. Sevastyan had kept me alive.

Jess had also been ecstatic that Sevastyan and I had slept together. "You lost your skin tag! Now you enter into the fun stage of your life."

"Fun?" Not so much right now. If Sevastyan and I were going to have a viable relationship, we needed to work at it. But whenever I wanted to talk about his past or his thoughts or, God forbid, his feelings, he clammed up.

No true intimacy. No progress toward sharing.

And though the sex was always pleasurable, it was growing less satisfying. He dreaded hurting me or leaving a mark, and I could sense he was just as frustrated by his self-imposed limitations as I was.

Sooner or later he'd go to another to have such deep-seated needs met, unless I could entice him to partner with me. Sevastyan had told me he'd be my last; he'd made no such assertions about himself.

I felt like *I* was the one with a countdown clock. Tempt him before he strayed.

Emotionally stunted, sexually frustrated. Our two hurdles seemed to be growing taller and taller. . . .

Rising from my command central, I made my way to the bed. As I stretched out across the counterpane, I wondered if he was watching me.

The idea made me shiver. Maybe I should show him what he was missing whenever he left me behind.

He'd watched me masturbate once before, but I hadn't been able to appreciate it then. Now?

Even if he wasn't watching, I could pretend he was. Win-win.

Excitement rushed through me as I slipped off my shoes and hose, blouse and skirt, leaving me in only my underwear—a bra and panties cut from transparent nude material.

Lying back once more, I traipsed my hands up to my breasts to give them a squeeze, pressing them together and kneading them hard—like I knew he wanted to do to them.

With a sigh, I drew off my bra, twirling it on my forefinger before slingshotting it toward the camera. Breasts bared, I used one hand to tease my nipples, pinching them as he had; my other hand descended down my torso, dipping into the silk of my see-through panties. I left them on—because Sevastyan would still be able to watch my fingers stroking.

The phone beside the bed rang.

Flashing a smirk at the camera, I answered with, "You've caught me at a bad time, babe, ring you back in a sec?"

He sounded like he was calling from the car. "Stop what you're doing, you little witch," he grated in Russian. So our driver couldn't understand? "I'll be home in five minutes—you *will* wait for me."

"Or *what*?" I gave my clit a defiant stroke that made my hips roll. "You gonna make me sleep with the fishes?"

"Do not test me, pet."

I put him on speakerphone. "You left me home all alone. What's a girl to do?" Stroke. "Don't you want to know what I was fantasiz-ing about? It's you, fucking me senseless." Stroke. "Oooh. Wait, you don't do that anymore."

"What are you talking about?"

"You told me on the plane that women look at you and know they'll get fucked hard. I'm not seeing it." Burn!

I could all but hear him grinding his teeth as I continued to finger myself. "Natalie, you are *not* to come by your own hand."

"Was that in a rule book or something? I missed our relation-ship orientation. Come on, play along, Sevastyan. Ask me if I'm wet. No? Then I'll have to show you." I raised my knees to my chest, then slipped my panties to my calves. When I rested my legs on the bed, I spread my bent knees, giving Sevastyan a clear view of my soaked curls, which I continued to lazily pet.

He hissed in a breath. "Cease what you're doing *now*."

"Or you'll punish me? If a dominant like you doesn't want to see such disobedience—you should stop watching."

"I'll never stop watching you. This *started* with me watching you."

"That's right. This is the second time you've leered at me mas-turbating." Stroke.

"That's not what I meant. Damn it, woman, you do *not* want me to lose control."

"Oh, but I do!" Looked like it was time to bring my A game. Did I have the nerve to do this? What choice did I have? I was playing for keeps. "What if I did . . . this?" I went to my hands and knees before the camera, so he could see everything. I spread my knees, panties tight around my ankles.

"God almighty."

His reaction and this bare vulnerability—this *exhibition*—made my mind spin and my body heat, as if my arousal had just

downshifted to rocket forward. Apparently I *was* an exhibitionist—
my blood coursed from the thrill.

No longer was this a game; I was desperate to come.

When I bucked to my fingers, he made a choked sound, then
bit off some French command to the driver. Probably to go faster,
because a series of angry horn honks followed. "You have no idea
what you're doing to me."

I was lost to pleasure, flicking, flicking. . . .

"Then put your finger inside for me," he said in broken Russian. "Be my good girl, and fuck yourself with it."

With a cry, I snaked my forefinger along my clit toward my
opening, curling it between my lips; his heavy breaths on the
speaker filled the room, arousing me even more.

When I penetrated myself and began to pump, he rasped,
"I'll show you hard." The call disconnected.

Only a few seconds after, I heard him downstairs, his boots
pounding up the steps to this floor. And for the first time I
realized . . .

I should be afraid.

CHAPTER 32

$\mathcal{I}$ drew my fingers away, turning over on the bed. I'd just raised myself up on my elbows when he reached the threshold, seeming to take up all the space in the doorway.

I gasped at his appearance. His unsmiling lips. His clenched fists. His eyes glazed with sexual hunger.

When his straining erection jerked in his pants and a spot of pre-cum dampened the material, I couldn't stop a moan.

He looked . . . undone. Much as he had that first time he'd watched me in the bathtub.

Like he wanted to eat me up, bit by bit.

He strode toward the bed with a predator's gait, big hands un-buckling his belt—as menacing a gesture as I'd ever seen.

I steeled myself as he reached for me.

He snatched at my hips, flipping me over on my stomach, then shoved his pants to his thighs. Like an animal, he impaled me with one brutish thrust, mounting me.

His cock had to fight against my clamping walls because I was already coming, his rough invasion triggering my release. *"Oh, my God!"*

"Is this what you needed from me?" He seized my shoulders, yanking me back right as his hips shoved forward, sending his cock deeper than it'd ever been.

My cry was drowned out by his triumphant roar as he began to fuck.

His animalistic intensity called to my own, demanding another orgasm, stoking all my heat from before and then some. A new, unknown friction began to simmer deep inside me, until I was clawing the backs of his thighs, spurring him for more, more.

This position forced all my senses into overload. The sound of our slapping skin. The sharp sway of my breasts. The way his sac swung up to smack my wet clit with each buck of his hips.

He grated, "Is this"—thrust—"hard enough"—brutal thrust—"for you?"—*savage* thrust.

My teeth clattered on that last one, my arms giving out. I lay facedown on the bed, ass up, helpless to do anything more than receive his merciless fucking.

The idea of him using my limp body like this, a plaything for his lusts, hurtled me closer to the edge, my climax boiling up inside of me.

I panted his name repeatedly, half-afraid of the strength of my coming release. The pressure escalated and escalated. . . . Again I wondered, where would it end?

"This was what you wanted? A hard fuck?" he bit out, pummeling his cock inside me. "Then show me how you like it! Come again, pet . . . come all over my stiff cock."

He ordered; I obeyed.

My pussy convulsed around his girth, spasms racking my muscles. When the rapture hit and my mind registered the force of it, I emptied my lungs on a wild scream.

Screaming. Screaming. Until his roars joined mine and his

heat flooded me, his hips whipping against my ass for his final draining thrusts.

Dizziness. Remembering to breathe. Happily picking up the pieces.

He collapsed over me, murmuring my name as he nuzzled my hair. His lips brushed my nape, his breaths fanning perspiration there.

Yet then he tensed, seeming to wake up. He withdrew from me with a curse, climbing off the bed.

By degrees, I managed to make it to a sitting position.

"This wasn't what I wanted." He yanked up his pants.

He was acting like what we'd just done was wrong—when it'd been amazing and perfect and exhilarating.

He pointed an accusing finger at me. "You push and push. You don't know what you provoke."

I shoved my hair out of my face. "But I *want* to know!"

When he said nothing, I rose to snag my robe. Time to dig in my heels. Belting the garment around me, I said, "Sevastyan, something's got to give."

"What are you talking about?"

"I'm unhappy. With our relationship, with our sex life—"

"Are you joking? I make you come till you scream. Yet you're unsatisfied?"

"I want to explore what you showed me before. On the plane, you said I wasn't supposed to be like this, but I *am*."

He stilled. "You don't know what you are. You're twenty-four and have never had another lover."

"You are the one who said I loved it, needed it. You were right! I'm a flesh-and-blood woman, a *hot*-blooded woman—not some porcelain doll. So why have you changed with me?"

"You're under my protection. You're mine," he said simply.

"Please tell me this is not one of those Madonna-or-whore situations, where you think of me either as a pristine pedestal-topper or a slut."

He shrugged. No denial. *Oh, shit.* I pinched my temples. *No, no, no, he can't think that way.*

Because I knew such a belief couldn't be fixed. Not like a broken clock. Not with my sweet, sweet love. Not with all the magic of my vagina. Not with my inevitable ocean of tears. "Look, neither of us is getting what we bargained for. Maybe we should think about taking a break from each other."

He whirled around. His lowering expression made me back up a step. "You belong to me. There are no *breaks*." He swept his arm over the dresser, sending makeup and jewelry flying.

I tensed, ready to bolt for the safe room. Until I remembered that, for all his faults, this man would never hurt me. In spite of his balled fists, I demanded, "Then help me fix this!"

He put a hand to his throat as if he couldn't get enough air. "There is a need inside me—it's like a beast that howls. I need to do things to you. I need to control you, command you, punish you. In order to *madden* you." He stabbed his fingers into his hair. "I indulged in this before you, but never felt like I couldn't live without it. Yet now, with you . . ."

"Now what?"

"It's like a sickness inside me that I fight and fight but can never defeat." His voice was rising with each word. "And then you tempt me like this?" he yelled. "You gut me!"

I yelled back, "So stop fighting it!" I marched up to him, grabbing his face. On my toes, I met his gaze. "I'm *here*, Sevastyan. I'm ready, I'm willing. I *need* you." *I'm falling for you.*

For some reason, I held those words back. Maybe because I didn't expect him to respond in kind.

He'd talked about owning, controlling, and possessing me. He'd talked about obsession. But never about love. "Why would you fight something we both crave?"

With an eerie gentleness, he peeled my hands away, then strode over to the safe room's desk. From a false-bottomed drawer I hadn't known about, he retrieved a letter. Returning to me, he shoved it into my hands. "You weren't the only one who received a letter."

Overwhelmed with curiosity, I opened it. My father had written a final correspondence to him as well? The paper was crinkled. How many times had Sevastyan read it? Would he expect to read mine, still hidden in my suitcase?

My eyes widened as I scanned the lines:

She is precious, Aleksandr, treat her as a treasure, and above all things, respect her. . . . My Natalie's life is in your hands. . . . She's fragile, has been uprooted from a safe and sheltered existence, forced into the danger our world presents. Nothing else matters if she's not happy and protected. . . .

Oh, dear God. I gazed up at Sevastyan as everything became clear. "This is why you've been denying us?"

The man who'd been his savior, the one he felt like he'd failed, the mentor who'd guided his life for decades—had given his blindly loyal enforcer a final set of instructions. "Sevastyan, I respect Paxán's wishes. I do. But this letter has no bearing on what goes on between us." I handed it back to him.

He clasped the page with a shaking hand. "How can you say that?"

"We have to make our own way together."

"This letter reminded me of what you are. And then, right after I first read it, I saw . . . I saw the bruises I'd given you. I hadn't even *meant* to discipline you, not like I do in my twisted imaginings."

"Sevastyan, just wait—"

"He was your father. He was . . . my father. He expected me to treat you like a treasure. He didn't know about that part of my life. I took pains to keep it secret. If he had, he would never have chosen me for you."

"You're acting like that type of life is dark and dirty. Like only broken people do it."

He raised his brows: *No shit!*

"You don't have to be broken to like kink. Look at me. I had the most idyllic upbringing ever, and I can't stop thinking about it with you." When I saw he wasn't budging, I said, "You were instructed to keep me happy. Well, right now, I'm far from it."

He looked like he'd just stifled a wince. "Then that means I should succeed at least in protecting you. I don't want my past to taint you."

"Taint? Because I was so wholesome? Hate to break it to you, but I was already leaning this way. When I went online to order my 'arsenal,' do you think I didn't mosey over to the other pages on the site, the ones with braided black leather and shining silver chains? I was already curious."

For the first time, doubt flickered in his expression. Hope?

I pressed my advantage. "That's right. Maybe deep down you sensed it in me from the very start."

He shook his head hard. "This can't be. I don't want to discuss it further—"

"Shut up and listen to me! I'm fighting for us, and you're not even trying to meet me halfway. Do you think I'm stupid?"

"No! What are you talking about?"

"What you described as a sickness . . . you can't suppress something like that forever. You already threatened to find another woman the last time you didn't get your way with me. Since you refuse to see me as a partner, sooner or later you'll go to another to have those needs fulfilled."

With a sharp shake of his head, he grabbed my arms, about to speak, but I cut him off: "Did you never think that I might go to another too?"

He released me with splayed fingers, as if tossing a live grenade. With a vile curse, he turned toward the door.

On his way out, my fighter punched a hole in the wall.

✦

Alone, still pissed, I'd gotten myself dressed, then picked at some food I'd found in the fridge. Afterward, I'd called Jess—who'd been hungover and out of it. So I'd made my way into the panic room to idly survey pedestrians for mindless hours.

Or, more honestly, to wait for Sevastyan's return like a sap. What if he *had* gone to another woman? What if he was whipping her right now, dominating her with that compelling voice and magnificent body?

My eyes watered. I could get past anything, but not infidelity, not when I'd all but begged him not to do it—

I jerked up in my seat when I saw Sevastyan return. I blinked through my tears, watching him enter the kitchen with a large gift-wrapped package.

He'd been out getting me a present? My emotions spun wildly in the other direction. Giddiness. Glee.

As if he knew I was watching him, he glanced up at the camera as he set the box down on the counter. The look in his eyes was filled with warning. And maybe even a little . . . sadness. Then he left again.

Where was he going, and why leave the package? Was it a peace offering—or a parting gift?

I sprinted to the stairs, bounding down them to the kitchen. I tore into the box, finding an emerald-green beaded gown. Lingerie was included—a cropped black satin bustier with a matching thong. Thigh-highs and heels completed the ensemble.

There was even a long velvet jewel case with emerald earrings and a matching pendant.

I swallowed. What was this all about? I spied a card inside, snatched it up. As I read his handwriting, my excitement receded, my stomach giving a lurch.

Nine tonight. Be careful what you wish for.

S

CHAPTER 33

$\mathcal{I}$ finished pinning my hair up just before nine, then checked my appearance in the floor-length mirror.

The gown was nothing short of exquisite. The beading was sophisticated and asymmetrical, the design sweeping up my body, drawing attention to the high slit at the right leg, then to my flaring hips and finally my breasts, which were on full display.

At first, I'd thought the bodice didn't fit; then I'd realized my boobs were supposed to bubble up on top like this. The pendant he'd given me nestled right at my cleavage.

This look had called for makeup, so I'd put on lipstick, mascara, and even some shimmery eye shadow that made the color of my eyes pop. I'd snapped a selfie of my getup and texted it to Jess. She'd pronounced me a *stone-cold fox*. She'd pronounced herself *heteroflexible* and very interested in *sexy funtimes* with buxom redheads.

Still, having never dressed in anything like this, I was having qualms about going out in public. But then, I had no idea where Sevastyan was taking me, or even *if* he was taking me out. My dolling up could be part of some fantasy of his.

Was I nervous? Hell, yeah. That card had spooked me. Yet then

I'd reminded myself of what exactly I'd wished for: to explore our darkest desires—together.

And, man, was I *game*.

Plus, his concession signaled that he was *trying* to make me happy. I considered whatever he was about to show me as couples therapy, team building for two—

Sevastyan appeared in the doorway of our room. I sucked in a breath at his heart-stopping appearance.

He wore a traditional one-button tuxedo, obviously bespoke. The jacket flawlessly highlighted his broad shoulders and muscular chest. The material screamed *expensive*, but the cut said *conservative*.

Understated accessories—stoneless cuff links, a pocket square of dark silk with a barely-there design, a classic tie—completed his spellbinding ensemble.

His clean-shaven jaw made my hands itch to caress those chiseled edges.

He'd retained just one of his rings for the night, that sexy thumb ring. Along with his tattoos, it was a gritty counterpoint to the elegance of the rest of his outfit.

Even in a tux, he was still my street fighter. This man was on his way to becoming mine, was taking steps—albeit strange and mysterious ones—to advance our relationship.

Maybe in time he could feel something deeper for me too.

Studying my appearance as avidly as I studied his, he murmured, "Anticipation becomes you." He drew back to rake his gaze over me from the ground up. *"Ya potryasyon."* I'm undone.

"I could say the same."

"Come." When he put his hand on my hip to lead me downstairs, I could feel the heat of his palm even through the dress beading. Was he nervous? Or just that eager?

"Where are we going anyway?"

"Dinner first."

So we were heading outside of the mansion, and I looked like Jessica Rabbit. Oh, well. *See me, love me, motherfleckers.* "And then?"

"Patience," he intoned with a squeeze of my hip.

He helped me into a sleek new stole—*fur again, Siberian?*—then into our waiting limo. As we set out, tension rippled between Sevastyan and me. I had no idea what he was thinking, feeling. But when I shimmied in the dress and flashed my thigh-high through the gown's slit, his lips parted on an exhalation.

Our destination was a posh restaurant called Plaisirs. Its patrons were dressed to the nines—yet even they stopped and stared at Sevastyan as we walked by, forkfuls of food hovering in midair. They even stared at me.

The Nebraska girl cleaned up good. Feeling more confident, I squared my shoulders and lifted my chin, which seemed to please Sevastyan.

Dinner—at what had to be the best table in the house—was a light, sensual affair. Lobster, succulent fruits, delectable truffles, petits fours. The wine was so sublime I couldn't stop licking my lips.

Sevastyan ordered a vodka rocks, but didn't touch it.

I was just tipsy enough to ask, "If you don't drink, why order it?"

He released a pent-up breath, as if he'd known this question was coming eventually. "My father was an alcoholic. I do not wish to become one," he said in utter understatement. "But in Russia . . ."

"So many things involve alcohol?"

"Exactly. Maybe I do it to test my resolve."

He'd confided something to me! My heart gave a little flutter.

We were moving in the right direction. And suddenly his comment about the irony of smuggling cheap booze made perfect sense. "Is your father still alive?"

"*Nyet.*" Hard no. "It's a subject I'd rather not discuss." Softening his tone, he said, "Not tonight of all nights."

"Fair enough. So . . . any hint about where you're taking me next?"

"You're soon to see."

"Okay, Siberian." Reining in my curiosity, I took another sip of ambrosia/wine, grinning against the glass.

"You're . . . happy with me." He sounded surprised.

"Very."

"Because you think you've won in this, that I capitulated to you."

I set down my glass. "Not everything's a game, Sevastyan. Maybe I want us *both* to win."

"Then why were you pleased with me?"

"Because you listened to me. You acknowledged that I needed something from our relationship, and I believe you intend in some way to give it to me tonight. You're *trying*, and it gives me hope about our future."

"Whereas before you had nothing but doubts?" A dangerous glint flashed in his eyes.

"Sevastyan, you control whether I have doubts. It's in *your* hands."

"It sounds simple when you put it like that. But know that tonight is anything but simple for me."

And still he was going through with it. "I understand."

He frowned. "You expect much from me. In many areas of our lives. But perhaps I don't . . . recognize everything a young woman needs."

What to make of this perplexing statement? Then I remembered that, beyond sex, he didn't have a lot of experience with women. He'd never been in a relationship, had no siblings—so no sisters—and hadn't had a mother since he was thirteen, or younger.

Did he know a woman's body? Judges' scores of ten across the board. But her mind? Not so much.

In a wry tone, I said, "From now on, I'll speak up about what I need—you know, try not to be such a shy and retiring flower with you."

His expression turned to a look of fascination, again as if I were a creature he'd never seen in the wild before.

We stared at each other for long moments, while I attempted to imagine his thoughts. Was he trying to decipher mine as well?

He dragged his gaze away to check his watch, then signaled for the maître d'. He said something in French to the man, who promptly returned with my stole and a small box that I didn't remember Sevastyan checking at the front.

I turned toward the entrance, but Sevastyan took my arm. "This way." Box in hand, he led me toward the rear of the restaurant, right past the other tables . . . then out a back door into a cobblestone alley.

"Is something wrong?" I whispered. "Did you see a threat?" *So help me, if some mafiya thug ruins my fantasy night . . .*

"No. We go to our next destination," he said with an enigmatic air.

"Oh." Excitement rekindled inside me. "What's in the box?"

He surveyed the area. "I suppose you can have it now," he said, handing it to me.

With a grin, I tore it open, finding inside the most stunning mask imaginable. The material was a rich green that complemented my gown, the edges lined with what had to be real emeralds.

At the sides, silken flares jutted like a butterfly's wings. Beneath each of the slanted eye cutouts, the material curved down into a curlicue, a tapering wing.

"This is so gorgeous, Sevastyan!" I eagerly gave him my back when he moved to tie it on. "Is this for a masquerade?" In the last novel I'd read from Jess's collection, a historical romance by some author with a weird first name, there'd been a courtesans' masked ball. The French heroine and her Scottish hero had attended, naughtiness ensuing. "Are we going to one?"

"Of a sort," Sevastyan muttered.

Before I could ask about his odd tone, he'd tied my mask and turned me to face him.

"You're incomparable," he said with such solemnity that I blushed.

Who could resist falling for a man like this?

A better woman than I?

Then he pulled a silky onyx domino out of his coat pocket, tying it on.

My mind . . . went . . . temporarily . . . blank.

Once my brain sputtered back to life, a tangle of thoughts hit me. *Sexy. Rogue. Lava hot. Spontaneous orgasm.*

He couldn't possibly look more wicked. "Come along."

As he squired me forward, I kept sneaking glances up at his face.

"It's not far now, pet."

I was nearly overwhelmed with curiosity as we made our way toward the end of the foggy alley, the *click, click* of my heels echoing.

"Here." He stopped in front of an arched iron gate that looked like it was from the Middle Ages.

"What's behind there?"

"Our destination." He turned a lever and opened the gate, ushering me inside a damp tunnel. A torch lit the way deeper within.

"Uh, we're going in there?"

"Second thoughts?"

I'd asked for this. I was prepared for a free fall with this man. "You won't lose me that easily, Siberian."

Was there a whisper of surprise in his expression? Had he thought I'd back out? Or hoped I would?

"At least give me a *hint* about where we're going."

"It's a place I've been before."

As we followed the tunnel, I realized we were descending below the city. I'd read about catacombs underneath the streets of Paris and was itching to investigate my surroundings, yet he led me ever forward.

Ahead was a circular chamber with more torches. In the center, a fountain bubbled, flames dancing across the surface of the water. Firelight flickered over the rounded walls, illuminating mosaics. The tiles depicted lusty satyrs and maidens in coitus, the flames making it look like the satyrs were moving, *thrusting*.

Next to a formal entrance, a shining brass plaque was embossed with four words:

LE LIBERTIN

CLUB PRIVÉ

I murmured to him, "Is this some sort of . . . sex club?" Wasn't *sex club* synonymous with *swingers' club*? My heart fell. The idea of sharing him—or being shared—stopped me in my tracks.

"Lost your nerve?" he asked, detecting my tension.

"I don't want either of us to be with anyone else."

He backed me against the wall under one of those torches.

Firelight captured his face; behind his mask, his eyes were molten gold. "You are *my* woman. Mine. And I learned very early in life not to share what's mine. You think I'll ever let another touch you?"

I lifted my chin. "I won't be sharing you either."

This seemed to gratify him. "Then we're in agreement. Any other hard limits I should be made aware of?"

I thought he was amusing himself with me, so I rolled my eyes, grumbling, "Just take me into the freaking club before I die of curiosity."

Inside, a woman greeted us from behind a large secretary. She too wore a formal gown and a mask, an owl one. Though it obscured some of her features, her olive skin, lithe figure, and sloe eyes were arresting. "Welcome," she said with a thick French accent as she helped me from my stole. Once she'd stored it, she told Sevastyan, "Your private room is this way, Monsieur S."

How *many* times had Sevastyan been here?

He said something to her in French, then ushered me forward with his possessive hand back on my hip. As we followed her down an arcade, strains of lively classical music grew more distinct. We approached a set of double doors manned by liveried footmen, expressionless as they granted us entry.

Past the doors was a dazzling ballroom with a soaring ceiling, filled with formally dressed attendees.

We are no longer in the Corn Belt, folks.

Massive flower arrangements perfumed the air. Tapestries graced the walls, depicting more sensual scenes. Matching statues of Venus—which looked like they belonged in a museum—flanked a grand staircase. Along the steps, living human statues with skin dusted gold held candelabras to light the way.

The rich velvets, swathes of silk, and candlelit grandeur made me feel like I'd walked into a French period film. I finally found my voice to murmur, "How old is this place?"

"Centuries."

With that one word, he might as well have shot me full of adrenaline. Ah, the *history*—I breathed it in. Endeavoring to note every detail, I gawked all around me.

As we passed through the throng of attractive partygoers, I realized no one was getting down and dirty. There were drinks and laughter and flirting, but nothing different than you'd see in a regular club.

Was it just me, or were we collecting lots of stares? Sevastyan seemed to be growing increasingly agitated.

"What's wrong?" I asked him.

"They think you're available. That you don't belong to me."

"Why?"

"Because you lack a collar."

Collar and keep you. "Um, that's hot—in a totally appalling kind of way." But hey, this was all pretend, all gossamer fantasy and silken decadence, right? Noticing that many of the women did, in fact, sport collars, I asked him in a fake petulant tone, "How come I don't get a collar?"

But he was serious when he answered, "You haven't earned one." Right when I was about to flare, he added, "And I haven't earned the right to give it to you." He looked so conflicted behind his domino.

A fit, middle-aged man swept in front of us. He wore an elephant mask with an exaggerated trunk. *Subtle, buddy, reaaallll subtle.* He started to speak, but Sevastyan just gave him his signature killing look—the one that made men quake.

We weren't stopped again.

The owl woman was waiting for us at that grand set of stairs. We followed her up to a second-floor landing, then made our way down a hallway lit by gas lamps.

"Where are we going, Siberian?"

"Patience," he said again.

Not exactly my strong suit. After all, *im*patience was a sibling to curiosity.

A thought struck me. "Why did you pick a butterfly mask for me?" Of all the creatures he could have chosen.

"Do you think there has to be a reason?"

"I'm finding that you don't do anything without a reason."

"Perhaps there was . . ."

"Here we are," the woman said, stopping before an unmarked door. She unlocked it, and we entered.

An ornate candle chandelier cast subdued light over the space. In the middle of the room was a large settee upholstered in sumptuous-looking fabric. Antique chairs and tables made up a sitting area off to the side; a copper tub sat off to another. A plush theater curtain covered an entire wall.

The air was warm, smelling of candle wax and . . . newness. Which was odd, considering how vintage everything else had seemed.

It also smelled of leather.

The woman opened a waiting bottle of chilled champagne, pouring two flutes before she left. At the door, she gave me a knowing wink. What did she know that I didn't?

Maybe that a train was barreling down the trestle? Or how deep the freaking water was?

Keep cool, Natalie. I trusted this man to protect me, to pleasure me, to be what I needed him to be.

He motioned to the settee. "Sit."

I did, noting that it faced the theater curtain. Would we be viewing a movie? A bawdy play? We hadn't gotten to enjoy the masquerade at all, I thought with disappointment. In books, people always got to stay till midnight at least—not ten measly minutes.

Now that my eyes had adjusted to the dim light, I spied covered shapes throughout the room—shapes that could be anything. But I had an idea. My mind raced to those BDSM vids I'd devoured, the primer I'd inhaled, the magazine I'd shown him. Was there a pillory in here, or a spanking bench, or a swing? Would Sevastyan bind me up to torment me?

Part of me was terrified at the prospect. But I was woman enough to admit the idea got me wet. *Roll with it, roll with it.*

When he sat beside me, I said, "What is this room?"

"It's ours. One of the very few available to own."

Ours? "How long have you had it?"

"About nine hours. I had it renovated today and equipped to my specifications."

Since our fight this morning? That explained the new smell. I could only imagine the money he'd had to throw at this to get everything ready in time.

He picked up a multi-button remote from the table beside the settee. "You told me that you wanted to see more of Paris. Here's another slice of it." He pressed a button. The curtain began to open, revealing a wall of glass.

Behind the glass was . . . was . . .

When I realized what I was beholding, I breathed, "Oh. My. God."

Sevastyan's hand shot out to catch my champagne flute just before it hit the ground. . . .

CHAPTER 34

*W*hen my shock lessened a degree, I was able to comprehend what I was seeing beyond the room's glass wall.

Sevastyan had brought me to this private club to witness . . . an orgy.

And it was going on *strong*.

There must have been three dozen participants, attractive ones. They were all in a center ring, as if in a circus, with sex apparatus everywhere.

Masked men and women were strapped to X-frames, caged in pillories, or suspended from chains in the ceiling. One woman was fettered to what looked like a body-shaped massage table. Females and males were bent over crimson boudoir chairs. Strong hands gripped splayed ankles.

Once I'd recovered enough to react, my hands flew to my mask. "They can see us watching them?"

"They can't see inside," Sevastyan assured me. "They only see a mirror, unless we push a button on the remote. And, Natalie, they're fully aware they're being watched."

Then I'd just been taken to voyeur heaven. "This—is—the—tits."

"Indeed."

One naked woman was perched on a trapeze with her ass atop the bar, her feet resting on either side. The trapeze was lowered until she was mouth-level with a guy who buried his face between her legs, while a brawny man slowly took him from behind.

Not everyone was naked. Some wore leather accessories. Others wore elaborate lingerie: shimmery corsets, intricate garters, and striped hose as if from *Moulin Rouge*. One man's entire body was encased in some kind of vacuum-sealed black sleeve, with only an air tube and his erection protruding—the latter of which was promptly utilized by a nubile female.

I wanted to examine every little detail, every act in the ring. It was as if there were scenes from all of my most erotic dreams. I wished I had ten sets of eyes! Or that I could record this.

Every lash across upthrust breasts made my own swell against my bustier. When the trapeze woman began screaming her way to ecstasy, bucking against that man's mouth, my panties grew wet.

Without dragging my gaze away, I said, "There are other rooms like this?" I'd noticed all the walls surrounding the orgy were mirrored.

"There are six total."

"You told me you've been here before. Were you down there?"

"On occasion."

One woman was tied backward over what looked like a huge barrel. Men lined up to use her mouth, while others took turns licking her. She seemed starving for more.

Had Sevastyan been one among those men?

Just as jealousy flared, he pulled me into his lap, curling his finger under my chin so I'd face him. "And I hungered to be where I am now. With a woman in my keeping. I'd wager most of them in the ring would envy us our position."

"You'd want a single woman over all those beauties?" The closest one to us was model fine, on her hands and knees and spitted by two men—a shaft in her mouth and another between her legs. They were railing the hell out of her, to her blatant delight.

Sevastyan said, "Considering that you are the woman in question, yes."

Smooth. "Do you want *us* to be down there now?"

"I told you. I learned very early not to share. No one else touches what's mine." His gaze flicked over my face. "Can you handle this?"

Did he think I'd beg off? "Since they can't see in, it's like watching porn. Which I excel at. So all good here."

He dragged me against his chest. Once I'd settled comfortably on his lap, he handed my glass back to me.

Sipping champagne and watching unabashed sex while his scent permeated my mind.

In fact, all of my senses were heightened. There was music, even laughter, but the rest of the sounds were erotic. Moans, groans, and rampant screams. Crackling leather, clanking chains, and snapping floggers.

Against my ass, I could feel Sevastyan's heavy cock like a red-hot brand. I found myself squirming against it, rubbing my thong against my wet labia.

Even the bubbling champagne tickled my tongue. I imagined pouring it down his body and licking him clean. . . .

Yet aside from all I was seeing and feeling, I couldn't stop thinking about the fact that Sevastyan had chosen me to bring here, had purchased this room with me in mind. The idea of him taking such care to get every detail right moved me.

He truly was trying for us.

I finished my champagne, vaguely aware that he took the flute from me.

Then his hand wandered up the slit of my gown, which had ridden up well above the top of my thigh-high. "Spread your legs as much as you can."

Never looking away from the spectacle, I did, bending one knee over his legs. I wanted my thighs wider; I wanted to be rid of this confining dress. I needed his skin against mine, as much as I needed to see everything happening in the ring—every new knot, kiss, whipping, and release. My gaze bounced from one scene to the next.

"You can't even decide where you want to look," Sevastyan observed with dark amusement. Using his forefinger, he started to draw lazy circles on my inner thigh. "And your heart's racing."

The champagne and wine I'd consumed, combined with my constricting bustier, were making me light-headed. My breaths were shallow, breasts quivering above my bodice.

They must have attracted his attention—with his other hand, he began tracing those same circles over the tops of my breasts. Then came an electric shock. Part of my areola was peeking out above the bustline of the gown, and he was lightly scraping his nail over it.

If he kept this up, I'd probably orgasm. "Sevastyan, before I forget . . . no matter what happens, I want to thank you for bringing me here."

"You thank me? What does my taking you here say about me, Natalya? To win a woman, I am willing to defile her?"

"Defile?" My tone was incredulous as I regarded a couple at the far right of the ring. The man was tied down to a spanking bench while a woman in thigh-high boots caned him. His skin was sweating, muscles straining, expression ecstatic. "This is one of the most glorious things I've ever witnessed."

Sevastyan followed my gaze, then frowned as if we couldn't be looking at the same thing. "You consider this so?"

"Without a doubt." There was pageantry all around. Between participants, there was ceremony.

He reached my thong and found it soaked, a groan reverberating in his chest. "What are you enjoying most?" he rasped. "The men? The women?"

"Both." When I'd watched same-sex couples online, it'd always been crazy hot. But tonight?

Mercy.

I admired one pairing toward the back of the ring. Two unclothed women were sixty-nining, so caught up in each other they were oblivious to the sex all around them. The top one had luscious ebony skin and the bottom one was even paler than I was. The tableaux they presented was so surreal, I didn't think I'd forget such a divine sight for the rest of my life.

Once I could finally break my stare, I found Sevastyan studying my expression. Determining what turned me on?

"You're not going to watch?" I asked.

"I'm looking at what arouses me most." He regarded me with such intensity that I had to avert my gaze.

I surveyed the room behind him. More light spilled in from the glass, highlighting those draped shapes. There was apparatus in here as well. Solely for our use.

Leisurely petting my wet panties, he said, "We aren't here just to watch."

"Good." I felt like I was on the cusp of discovering not only what made Sevastyan tick, but myself as well, unveiling our most forbidden fantasies. At last I would alleviate my sexual curiosity, which had grown like an inferno inside me.

"I'm going to push you tonight, Natalie. To determine whether this is truly what you need. You'll be given three tests, and if you pass them, this life will be yours as you desire it."

"Tests?" He had my full attention.

"The first is that you obey me absolutely—and readily—in every command, even ones outside your normal comfort zone. The second is that you accept any tools I decide to use on you." *Tools?* "The third is that you become aroused by everything I do to you."

Merely talking about this was arousing me. "How will you know whether I'm turned on by you and your tools—or by the freaking orgy taking place right in front of me?"

His lips curled. "I'll know. Now, up you go." Once we were standing, he took off his jacket and undid his tie. With a careless air, he cast them both away. "Give me your jewelry."

I removed my earrings and pendant, handing them to him.

Such a guy, he *pocketed* them. "Slip out of your heels." When I did, he turned me to unzip my gown. "You still want an introduction into this world?"

"Yes." I had to suck in so he could get the zipper down.

"You're certain?"

"One hundred percent." I was ready to partake, to enjoy—and to make progress in our relationship. We'd had two hurdles—sexual frustration and lack of emotional intimacy. Tonight we would dismantle the first, paving the way toward fixing the second.

Once I'd stepped from the gown, he balled it up and lobbed it in the direction of his jacket. *Men.*

With me still turned from him, he knelt to roll down one of my hose; then off went the other one, leaving me in only my mask, thong, and bustier.

Before he stood, he nipped the cleft of my ass with his teeth, sending a thrill through me. "Turn around." When I did, he bit back a groan to say, "My God, you are lovely."

A guttural yell from the circus ring drew my attention, but he pinched my chin, bringing my focus back to him. "Pay attention only to me. I'll tell you when you can look again."

So I'd be able to hear—yet not see? My imagination was going to run wild.

Releasing me, he crossed to one of the room's draped shapes. He uncovered a table topped with an extensive assortment of toys, paddles, and various bondage gear. There were a lot of items I'd never seen—and couldn't determine a purpose for.

He returned with four leather cuffs, tossing three on the settee. They were thick, lined with padded cloth, each with a large metal ring sewn into the middle.

With a kiss to my right wrist, he buckled the first cuff. A kiss to my left wrist preceded the next.

Dropping to one knee, he lifted my right foot to rest on his thigh. He caressed my ankle as he coiled leather around it.

This process was a foreplay all its own, whetting my arousal even more. As he buckled the last cuff, I peered down at my body, at my striking leather bonds. This was truly happening! When he stood, I went to my toes to give him an adoring kiss across his lips.

I drew back, gazing up at him, letting him see all I was feeling.

Desire, affection, excitement . . . and more.

"I think I see the hope you spoke of earlier." *You do.* "My

Natalya comes to such a place and feels *that*? I wonder what else you feel. What you feel for me?"

Too much! I pressed my lips together.

"I'll get that answer from you soon enough. Now, come." He led me over to a dais beside the tool table. I glanced up with a thread of trepidation to see a chain dangling from the ceiling.

He smoothed his palms down my arms, then raised them over my head, locking the cuff rings to a loop in the chain. Though he hadn't suspended me, I was definitely held fast.

"Spread your legs," he said, kneeling beside me.

Trust him, Nat. I tentatively eased my feet apart.

"Wider." He put pressure on the inside of a cuff.

Once I'd spread my legs wide, he attached the right cuff to a recessed bolt in the floor that I hadn't seen. He affixed the left cuff to another hidden bolt, each click and snap only heightening this spine-tingling anticipation.

He rose, stepping back to admire his handiwork. Behind his mask, his golden eyes roamed over me.

I was well and truly bound. I had to choke down a spike of panic. *I might've gone too far.*

No, no, no. Nothing could signal my trust more than giving up total control to this man. And, in turn, he would trust me more.

Right?

His gaze narrowed intently on my bustier. With his attention distracted, I could have peeked at the orgy. The glass stretched before me, a tantalizing portal, but I refused to look until he told me I could—even when I heard the crack of a bullwhip slice through the air.

With great relish, Sevastyan began unhooking each individual eyelet of the bustier from the bottom up. When I'd donned it earlier, I'd noticed that there was a profusion of hooks. Now I realized why; unwrapping his belonging was part of the ritual for him—one he obviously savored.

As did I. Soon his roughened hands would replace the material. . . .

When he unfastened the last taut hook, my breasts spilled free, the sight earning a groan from him. He discarded the garment, then turned to my thong, ripping it on one side.

Over the sound of my gasps, he rent the other side, letting the wet material land between my legs.

Except for my mask, I was nude; he remained dressed.

Raking his gaze over my body, he yanked on his shirt collar, popping a few buttons free at his throat. "I did choose your mask deliberately."

"Why a butterfly?"

He met my eyes. "Because you're elusive to me. Because I haven't caught you yet." He reached forward to roll my nipples between his fingers until they jutted lewdly, until I was arching up for more.

Before leaving me, he gave each of my breasts a light slap— which I found almost reassuring. He returned with two slim metal bars. My pulse quickened when I recognized what they were: the clamps from the picture I'd shown him, the two conductor's wands—except these had a sexy chain attached to the ends that would loop down toward my navel.

"Are you ready to be tested, Natalya?" He began screwing the bars down over my straining nipples, as far away from the tips as possible.

The pinch was biting, but I didn't shy away. Hadn't I specifically asked for this?

Once he'd secured the bars, I looked down, startled by how

turned on I was by the view. Seeing it in a magazine was provocative. Seeing my own nipples like this was . . . sublime.

"Look at you. Bound and clamped for my pleasure. How long I've imagined this."

"Is it everything you hoped it would be?"

"Better. *Ideal'naya.*" Unimprovable.

His husky compliment only added to the stimulation, so I aired a very real fear: "Sevastyan, what if I come before you want me to?"

"You'll be punished." The gleam of anticipation in his eyes made my hips roll, pulling on my already stretched thighs.

He lifted the delicate chain that hung from the ends of my clamps. "This chain goes in your mouth between your teeth. If anything happens that you don't want, all you have to do is drop it for the night to end. Period. And you know I do as I say I will."

I frowned, thinking he was much too cavalier about ending this night. While I appreciated that he'd set up the equivalent of a safe word, *nothing* could end this. Least of all my botching it!

When he offered me the chain, I took it into my mouth and bit down—which tugged my nipples even more. Still, I could stand it. I could stand anything.

"You can look at the ring now, Natalie." Something in his tone made my ears twitch.

"But for this to continue, you must be vulnerable." He moved to my side. "Revealed. I told you that no one else will touch you; I said nothing about them beholding you."

What was he talking about?

"I intend to clear the glass so everyone can see my beautiful prize. . . ."

CHAPTER 35

What?? My jaw slackened, and I almost dropped the chain.

To have dozens of people see me strung up? While I was naked, clamped, and about to have who-knew-what done to me?

It was one thing to flash guys at the creek near home. This was a different world.

Sevastyan picked up that remote, his expression inscrutable. "If you don't want me to reveal this room, all you have to do is drop the chain."

Realization hit me. He thought I would balk—that we would go no further than this! And then he could say he'd tried.

So he *hadn't* been taking pains to please me? No, he'd been setting me up for failure.

Bastard! To hell with that. I had on a mask; no one knew who I was, and I'd never see these people again. This was one night of my life, a few hours of gossamer fantasy.

"Drop the chain—or prepare to feel their eyes on you, coveting every inch of your pale skin."

He was trying to unnerve me. It was working! Did I actually have the mettle to do this?

"Come now, we'll go home." He was like a devil on my shoulder, tempting me away from what I needed—from what *we* needed. "All this will be like a dream."

In my mind, moving forward with this equaled moving forward in our life together. And I yearned for that. When I wanted something badly enough, nothing could stop me.

Not even the leering eyes of thirty strangers.

I refused to drop the chain. I refused to stay on the ground and not climb up to the trestle. Once I broke the surface of this, it would all be worth it.

When I knew my mind was made up, I began to shake—like a fledgling. Like a girl about to free-fall.

Sevastyan's brows drew together. "You're trembling?" He laid the backs of his fingers against my cheek, as if to check for a fever. "Drop the chain, *milaya*. That's all you have to do."

I gritted my teeth, set my jaw, and turned from him to stare at the glass. *Bring. It. On.*

I heard him exhale a stunned breath. He'd never thought I would do it. He'd set me up to take a fall. *Sometimes I'm quite all right with falling, asshole.*

"Very well. They'll see my woman." I got the sense that he hated the idea of displaying me. Caught by his own trap?

I had been ogling those in the circus ring; soon they'd return the favor. Tit for tat. I almost laughed hysterically.

"It's not often that one of these rooms is revealed," Sevastyan said. "This will be a treat for them, and for the other rooms as well."

I'd forgotten about the other rooms, with their hidden occupants who would *not* be giving me tat. But there was no going back; he'd pressed the button.

I heard a whirring sound, braced myself for their stares.

As attention fell on me, participants elbowed others, heads craning. Like starving pack animals who'd just scented a meal.

My shaking grew worse.

Still a devil in my ear, Sevastyan murmured, "You know what to do. And then I'll conceal you once more."

Partners were turning mid-sex, adjusting positions for better viewing. *Don't lose your nerve, Nat!*

"I told you that you'd feel the bite of leather across your breasts, its sting between your legs." *Yes, oh, yes.* "You'd let them witness your first descent with me?"

Descent? I refused to look at him, just stared at the frolicking in the ring.

"You must want this very badly indeed." In a wondering tone, he mused, "For a submissive, you can be extremely aggressive."

He had no idea. *You* will *be dominating me tonight, Siberian. Why fight it?*

"You've made your decision." He strode out of my sight line. Back to the table of tools?

He returned with a large dildo made of steel. I'd seen those on the site that I'd ordered my own arsenal from, but they'd been pricey. "Do you want this, Natalie?"

It was almost as big as his dick. As wet and empty as I felt, I did crave it. But to have everyone out there see my penetration?

His eyes were challenging behind his roguish mask. "Drop the chain if you don't want me to work this inside you—for their pleasure."

He began chafing it between his palms, warming it for me. The sight of his dexterous hands and tattooed fingers working that steel phallus made my hips buck.

By the time he ran the head of it down my belly, the metal was hot to the touch, seeming to burn against my skin. He trailed it lower, past my navel, then through my small thatch of curls.

The tip briefly rolled over my tingling clit. When he fixed the head against my needy entrance, I forgot to breathe. There was no give to this dildo, total rigidity, and it looked as heavy as a hand weight.

Yet he meant for me to take it all?

He twisted the crown right at my soaked opening, as if he were screwing the huge thing into me. "Take this—I'm *giving* it to you." He positioned himself so everyone could see him wedging the shining cock inside me. "Or drop the chain."

Embarrassment scalded me, as hot as the thing itself.

But as I scanned the crowd—I saw parted lips, captivated expressions, increased tempos—my shame morphed into . . . stimulation. Yet another stimulation.

Just as it had aroused me to bare myself to the camera in Sevastyan's bedroom, this was turning me on beyond anything I'd imagined. As he used my wetness to force the dildo inside me, inch by stretching inch, I basked in their stares.

Sevastyan followed my gaze. "My little exhibitionist. They covet my woman almost more than I can bear." He leaned in until his face was beside mine. "There's a need in me—to destroy them for desiring what's mine. Never forget that."

His jealous possessiveness only made me wetter.

"I want this deep inside you, Natalya. Open and accept it." I tried to relax my muscles, taking it, taking it. . . .

When the phallus slid into place, he pumped it a few times until I was nearly drooling around the chain. Then he fitted slim leather straps around my waist to lock the heavy thing within me. Once it was secured, he gave the base a decisive slap that made me—and others—moan. "Do you thank me for it?"

I nodded, adjusting my wrists and ankles in their bindings, readying for whatever was to come next.

I noticed one rangy man near the glass seemed to be riveted to my crotch as he pounded his partner, a voluptuous woman bound atop a silken cushion on the ground.

When I circled my hips a few times to get used to the intrusion inside me, the man shuddered, gave a loud yell, and pulled out. His heavy-lidded gaze met mine as he spurted onto his partner's mound.

Had he wanted me to see him come? To react? Interact?

"Now, now, Natalya," Sevastyan chastised. "No need to taunt them with what they will *never* have."

Had I been? Well, hell. Maybe?

Sevastyan strode away. Seconds later, I felt strands of leather slink down my spine. A flogger. As I'd suggested to him on the drive to Paris.

"Are you ready, pet?"

I'd been ready. I bit down on the chain and nodded—

Leather snapped across the backs of my thighs.

The sting made my eyes water. But when he moved beside me to assess my reaction, I gave him a *that's-all-you-got?* look.

His brows rose above his mask. His lips curled.

The flogger landed harder. And again. Even as I whimpered around the chain, I found myself jutting my ass for more—which earned me groans from the audience, especially from those who were similarly bound.

What submissive wouldn't want a man like Sevastyan to dominate her?

A man so dark and dangerous. So compelling and powerful.

And he was mine.

Sevastyan snapped the flogger against my thighs, my ass, even the top of my back, then repeated the rotation. With each blow, the pain mounted and mounted, until it . . . didn't.

Instead of twitching agony, all I could feel were areas of heat; my pain receptors were still pinging, but must be confused. I arched for more, shifting the weighty cock inside me.

When Sevastyan's lashes rained down harder, passions seemed to escalate in the ring. I had to fight the force of the strokes to remain in position. Soon perspiration dotted my skin.

"My lovely Natalya bucks to meet her punishment." His tone was thrumming with pride.

Every inch of my flesh was growing hypersensitive, as sensitive as my aching clit. When Sevastyan struck me, it became sexual. A sexual stroke. He knew exactly how far he could go to heighten my arousal without dampening it.

He'd wanted me to endure his tools. I wasn't just enduring, or even accepting; I was *exalting* in them. When he paused to gauge my response, I faced him with widened eyes. *What are you doing to me?*

He narrowed his, then seemed to hold his breath as the flogger flashed out to catch my clamped breasts, my trapped nipples. *The bite of leather against your breasts* . . . I writhed in shocked delight, silently begging him for another.

Was he going to make me come like this?

When his hand descended between my legs, fondling roughly, I undulated to his touch, sending that dildo even deeper inside me. Nearly wild with the need to climax, I didn't care who saw me wantonly riding his fingers, wetting them.

He groaned with satisfaction to find me soaked around the base of the dildo. "Do you know how hard I'm going to make you come?" He seemed like a boy with a new toy. Excitement sizzled in him. "Ready yourself, beautiful." His focus was all on me.

I recalled his words from our fight earlier today: *I need to control you, command you, punish you. In order to* madden *you.*

Everything he was doing was for the ultimate goal of my pleasure, with his own as secondary.

My reaction was what turned him on most.

And he intended to make me *react* as I never had before.

"I might not recognize everything a young woman needs," he bit out. "But this I know. *This* I can give you. Of the rest . . . ?"

What was he trying to say? My question was forgotten when he moved in front of me to bring his hot mouth down to one of my pinned nipples. I could feel his rapid breaths against the tip.

When he licked the peak, I thought I would faint with pleasure. Against my flesh, he said, "More lashes, love?" He suckled my other nipple, leaving them both glistening for our audience.

I nodded eagerly as dual needs welled up inside me, like lava about to erupt: my crazed urge to come—and my desperate hunger for more of the flogger.

He returned to his task, singling out my ass for his attention, his blows forcing me up on the balls of my feet. When I jerked back to meet the flogger, the dildo lurched, propelling me even closer to orgasm.

The frequency of the lashes had been scattered, but now the speed increased to nearly constant. Sweat dampened my hair and slicked my skin. The moistened flogger tails laid fire across my nerve endings, sending my mind into turmoil.

What should have been pain morphed into delirium and then into euphoria—and Sevastyan was fueling it with each stroke.

My vision blurred. No longer could I see the orgy. No longer could I hear anything but his choked groans that accompanied each thwack of leather. It was as if all my senses had receded so I could better perceive each individual flogger strand—and the kiss of breeze preceding a lash.

To better appreciate the steel cock he'd had the foresight to give me.

To float higher and higher until I was flying.

High. I was . . . high. My eyes rolled back in my head, my lips curling with delight, my teeth gritted on the chain so he wouldn't take this feeling away.

Never take this away. Boneless, hanging from my restraints, I *soared*—just as my release ripped through me in raw, shattering shock waves. Through clenched teeth, I keened my pleasure.

Tears streaked from my eyes as my sheath milked the dildo again and again. . . .

"Natalya?" I dimly heard Sevastyan calling. "Natalya!"

Calling for me? Where have I gone? Want to go there again.

Once the last of those shock waves had passed, I blinked, turning to him with a dreamy smile.

For some reason, my response made his eyes glint.

Then he rested his forehead on my shoulder, as if over-whelmed by what he'd discovered, as if this was more than he could believe. *"Ty sozdana dlya menya."* You were made for me. He licked sweat from my neck, nipping my skin as he ground his erection against me. At my ear, he said, "You were right—I've never seen anything more glorious."

He tossed the flogger aside and began running his hands all over me. The roughness of his calloused palms over my abused flesh made my toes curl.

When he unfastened the strap around my waist to remove the dildo, my inner muscles tightened around it, didn't seem to want to let go. He insistently tugged until it slipped out. Behind me, it too vanished.

"You like to display yourself, *moya plohaya devchonka*." My wicked girl. "Do you want to reveal more to them?"

I frowned—how much more could I possibly show them?—but nodded anyway.

I heard him rustling through items on the tool table. When he returned, he unfastened my left ankle restraint.

Had our audience eased the pace of their pleasures? Wondering what he had in store for me next?

Around my free leg, he wrapped a leather strap, using it like a sling to hoist my knee, until it was level with my waist. He fastened the strap to the same chain that secured my wrists above.

I was balanced on one foot, even more exposed and vulnerable to him, to others.

I heard his zipper descending. Now would he fuck me? Against the fiery skin of my thighs, I felt his length pulsing.

"Do you want them to see you?" He ran the damp head against the cleft of my battered ass. "Really see you. Inside?"

He reached around me to spread my lips. Even after all that had happened, blushes painted my skin. I could feel cool air on my entrance—could feel their desirous eyes centering on me there.

That didn't stop me from growing even wetter, from my lips swelling against his fingers.

He cupped me wholly. "Offer this to me," he commanded. "Present it."

I arched back as far as I could, jutting my ass against him.

"Very good." He pinched the tips of my nipples in reward, making me light-headed. "Do you want them to see you come again?" Before I could answer, he'd grabbed me, one hand below my raised knee, the other clutching my hip. With one sure thrust, he entered me from behind.

I moaned around the chain, already on the verge. I felt as if I'd never come at all, as if my arousal had been stoked for days with no release.

He gave me long, hard plunges that jostled my body. My breasts bounced, my trapped nipples screaming each time the chain tightened.

As he drove into me, he grated, "You thought I was going out to find another woman that day you spurned me." He moved in closer, tongue flicking out to taste my sweat. "How could I replace you? Even then I knew it was impossible."

Can't think. He'd already felt that strongly for me?

"Am I irreplaceable to you? Drop the chain if I am."

Irreplaceable? Right now he was *everything*. A giver of pain and ecstasy, with a godlike body he used to pleasure mine.

With effort, I slackened my jaw, pushing the chain out with my tongue. It fell with a soft tinkling sound.

I licked my lips and worked my jaw, wondering what he would do next, craving it.

He covered one side of my face with his big hand, pulling me back to accept his kiss. Even as he plowed between my legs, his lips were tender on mine. The combination of brutal thrusts with the reverent caress of his tongue was as mind-blowing as anything else from this night—

I heard a sudden snap of leather, felt its sting across my mound. I whimpered into his mouth. Was that a dogging bat? Like the one I'd shown him in the magazine?

I couldn't look down to see because he still cupped my face. He continued kissing me—letting me know that it wasn't for me to see what he struck me with. It was for me to feel, to accept his lover's kiss, to come as he tormented me and fucked me from behind.

Another strike paddled my mons and clit, smacking against my sodden curls; there was a bite, but it wasn't pain, just friction and pressure where I so feverishly needed it.

Maybe I was desensitized, because I was rocking my hips for more as his cock continued to plunder.

Against my lips, he commanded, "Surrender everything to me, *milaya*." Another strike.

And another. I was so close. "Sevastyan," I whispered. *"More."*

He thrust—"I want to hear you scream your surrender"—and slapped.

Lost to him, I did surrender everything. To the beat of my whipping, I threw back my head and screamed. Thrashing helplessly in my bonds, I came for him, drenching him with cream. With each core-deep tremor, my sheath clenched his thickened shaft.

"I feel you milking me," he growled at my ear. "Give you what you want!" He fucked with all his might—

Scorching cum erupted inside me; my steely-willed, controlled Sevastyan roared *un*controllably for all to hear . . . over and over . . .

Abandoned, shuddering, he emptied the last of his semen into me.

With a ragged groan, he continued softly thrusting through our mixed orgasms, while I was left dazed.

All my senses zeroed in on him, only him: his pounding heartbeat, the cool fan of his breaths on my skin, the warmth of his cock still joining us.

When my head lolled back against his shoulder, he pressed kisses to my neck.

I roused somewhat when applause broke out, peppered with catcalls and whistles. I expected a blistering wave of embarrassment, but I was still too overwhelmed to react. A quick scan of the ring showed out-of-breath lovers, silks and velvets wetted from releases, glistening mouths and chins.

As we stared at the glass, Sevastyan wrapped one muscular arm around my neck, another around my waist, squeezing me close to show his claim.

Sensing his fury blazing out at the others, I peeked up at him.

No, he hadn't liked displaying me; now that the heat of the moment had passed, he was baring his teeth. "Given them far too much of you." He reached over to the table and pressed a button on the remote.

We were concealed once more.

CHAPTER 36

*T*he thunderous applause continued, even after the glass was blacked out.

Yet I couldn't regret anything once I heard Sevastyan's voice suffused with pride: "My fantasy made flesh. I should never have doubted you to know your own mind." He gingerly pulled out of me, zipping himself back up as he moved to face me.

He brushed damp hair from my brow, his expression alternately possessive and . . . awed.

But when I shivered, he turned all businesslike. With swift, efficient movements, he released my raised knee and removed my ankle cuffs, then reached for my breasts, for the clamps.

He unscrewed a bolt, loosening the metal at one end. "This will hurt, love," he murmured as he eased it off my left nipple.

Blood rushed into it. I had to choke back a cry.

He took the throbbing peak into his mouth, stroking with his tongue to help with the pain. The right one was worse because I knew what to expect. The instant the clamp was off, he moved to that nipple. "Shh, love," he soothed against the tip, "there, it's almost over. . . ."

With my next shiver, he broke away, returning with a white, fluffy robe over his arm. He held it at the ready as he freed my cuffs from the ceiling chain. I collapsed into his waiting arms, cocooned by the pillow of the robe.

I trembled against him as he removed one wrist cuff and kissed the damp skin beneath it. He repeated his kiss with the other. "You're free now."

Such loaded words; I'd already been freed. He'd described this kind of behavior as a descent. It was just the opposite. With this man, I had flown. I'd *soared*. In a way, to submit . . . was to ascend.

Maybe I was still flying. Everything seemed muted and soft, the lights dimmer.

"How do you feel?"

"Little dizzy," I said in a scratchy voice. "What happens now?" There would be time enough to disbelieve what I'd just done. But tonight I was just going to roll with it.

"I'm taking you home." He guided my limp arms into the robe sleeves. "I expect you to relax and worry about nothing while I cosset you."

I could deal with that.

He bundled me up, cradling me against his chest, then carried me from our room.

Would we have to see those people? Go through the ballroom? When I stiffened, he said, "We're going out a private exit, love. The car's waiting."

Even when we were ensconced in the back of the limo and under way, Sevastyan didn't release me, keeping me on his lap. He removed my mask and his own, then reached into the cooler for a bottle of orange juice. "Drink." He held it up to my lips.

I quirked a brow. "No warm milk?"

"You have no idea how hard your body worked tonight. I want you to come down softly."

I took a sip of the juice—had to be the best I'd ever tasted. It was everything I could do not to chug it like a frat boy on a keg nozzle. "What do you mean by coming down?"

He eased closer to lick a drop of juice from my lip, making my lids grow even heavier. "Your blood is flooded with endorphins. That's why you felt—"

"High?"

"Precisely. But what goes up must come down."

"You'll be here to catch me when I fall?"

He curled his forefinger under my chin. "*Vsegda.*" Always.

Tonight we'd gotten one thing figured out. Surely hurdles had been cleared. Now we would make strides together.

I kissed the crooked bridge of his nose, then buried my face against his chest. I ran my fingers through his thick hair, clutching it as I hugged this big, brave man close. I'd never felt so cherished. So protected.

He was my guardian angel, my friend, my dream lover.

Aleksandr Sevastyan was everything. *Everything*.

He pulled me back to meet my gaze, his hooded eyes like gold coins. "Revelation?"

I whispered back, "Obsessed."

✦

At the town house, he kept me in his arms, sweeping me inside and up to our bathroom. The light was low, the whirlpool bath already bubbling.

When he peeled the robe from me and lowered me into the

water, I wanted back in his arms. As if he disliked the distance just as much, he hastily stripped, then slid in beside me. He sat on the submerged bench, pulling me back into his lap, my shoulder against his chest.

"I could get used to this," I sighed. I'd read about kink after-care and how important it was, but hadn't grasped how much I would need it. I felt like I'd been broken down to the most primal levels and now had to readjust to everything.

It was like lingering at the edges of a drug-induced high, produced from the cleanest-burning drugs imaginable.

He started kneading my shoulders. "I intend for you to get used to it. Tonight, I take care of you."

I felt his shaft stiffening beneath me and grinned to myself—more of him, this very night? And his massage! Kneading . . . kneading . . . *So. Freaking. Good.*

Once his big hands had rendered me into a heap of bliss, he began shampooing my hair, massaging my scalp until I was on the verge of drooling for the second time this night.

After rinsing the strands with a sprayer, he worked conditioner through them. I turned to watch him over my shoulder. His face was drawn with absorption, as if he truly wanted to get this right, to bathe me and care for me, just so. That melted my heart.

He caught me staring up at him like a fool. "Are you enjoying this part?"

"I *loathe* it."

He chuckled. I'd actually made him laugh? His lips were curling. Still not a full smile, but close.

His lightheartedness signaled so much to me, and I grew even more optimistic about our future. "You never thought I'd go through with it, did you?"

"I admit it." Finished with my hair, he smoothed the length over one of my shoulders, then grazed bath oil over my sore upper back.

"Any regrets?"

"I decided that if you were willing to go through that—your first real time—then you must want it badly." His cock pulsed against my bottom—because he was replaying those scenes? "I took you to a place that I thought of as sordid. And you saw beauty everywhere and felt hope. Maybe that club is what you make of it? What you *bring* to it."

"I believe that, especially now."

"I meant what I said earlier. You know your own mind. I'd forgotten that along the way."

"What do you mean?"

He lifted one of my arms, washing it from fingertips to shoulder before bathing my ticklish underarm. "In Nebraska I witnessed your drive when you set your mind to something. I saw how hard you worked; at everything, you tried so damned hard." He saw to my other arm. "I wanted to know how you could keep at it, with no guarantee of success."

"But you couldn't talk to me to ask."

"Could only watch you from afar." He reached for one of my breasts, thumbing my nipple. "Are these sore?"

I could barely keep my eyes open as he stroked me. "A little. But I kind of like it. A constant reminder of the things we did."

He made a sound of approval. "We've established that you're hot-blooded—and you know your own mind. Yet you were a virgin?"

When he moved to my other breast, my lids slid shut. "I had some bad experiences."

Dropping his hands, he tensed around me, gritting out one word: *"Names."*

My eyes went wide. "No, no, not like that! I had some unfortunate, clumsy experiences, I should say."

"I don't understand."

So I told him about the guy who spooged into his condom. "He *fled* after that, never to be heard from again. I wasted weeks on that guy."

"Now that I know what he'd been so close to experiencing, I could almost pity him."

Awww. "I dated another guy for a couple of months, but I'm pretty sure he was a subbie. There were a few others who just weren't worth the bother."

Looking back, I could see that I'd been waiting for a man's man—one older than me, a lot more dominant, with some rough and dangerous edges. In other words, not your typical UNL student.

"Their loss is my gain."

I trailed my nails over his forearm. "I didn't *want* to be a virgin. Do you know how challenging it was to be sex-positive and progressive on a college campus and still be virginal? At my age? It was like a dirty little secret."

In a grave tone, he said, "I'm glad I was able to be of service with that."

Grinning, I turned to face him better, hanging my legs over his outer thigh. "So what's your story?"

"Story?" He seemed disconcerted that the conversation had steered toward him.

"This is where we trade dating tales."

He gave me an *I-got-nothing* look.

"You really haven't spent a lot of time with women outside of sex, have you?"

"Not at all." He began massaging my feet, working bath oil up my surprisingly sore calves.

"How did you usually find, well, bedmates? I don't suppose there were *mafiya* mixers?"

He raised his brows at that. "I would go to a bar or a scene club and wait for a woman to approach," he said without conceit, just stating the facts. "I'd stay for the time span of a few drinks; the situation would either resolve itself or not."

My face flushed when I realized I'd been one of those approaching women. "So when I hit on you that first night, you equated me with them?"

He shrugged.

"You didn't date any of the women you slept with? No going to a movie or out for coffee?" I couldn't picture him doing either.

"Never."

"Aside from our dinners on the road, was tonight your first real date?"

"Yes." As I hid my surprise, he added, "How am I doing?"

My heart fluttered. "Judges' scores of ten."

He frowned. "I shouldn't have admitted that to you, I suppose."

"No, you should have. I love"—*everything I learn about you*— "hearing new things about you."

"My first date, your first flogging," he said with amusement.

"I adored what you did to me."

"Tonight I realized that I can torment you and treasure you. For you, it can be one and the same." His hands began ascending my legs. "And there's much more to show you."

My breaths shallowed. "I want to see it all."

"I'm having supplies delivered tomorrow. We'll take it slowly, but be prepared for wherever this leads us."

"You really knew your way around this stuff." Though I spread my thighs in welcome, he simply teased me with those light circles. "How long have you been doing it?"

"Awhile."

Evasive much? "Now will you tell me about your particular interests?" With his fingers at work, I fought to keep my concentration. "When did you recognize them?"

He opened his mouth to answer, then closed it.

"Please tell me. I'd like to know, since I benefited from those interests so much."

"I will, one day. For now, I don't want to think that far back into the past." *How* far back? "Know this: before you, I participated, but now I see those encounters for what they truly were."

"What?"

His gaze held mine. "Practice."

"For me?"

"For you."

I couldn't stop the slow grin that spread over my face.

His eyes dipped to it, darkening. "There will be rules, Natalie." He reached between my thighs at last, palming me with a sure grip. "This is mine. I'm the only one who gets to pet you here. I plan to keep you well pleased, but if you ever need to come, you wait for me—or for my command."

"So I'm never to play with myself in front of a camera for you?" I wriggled over his erection, making him inhale sharply.

"I'll order you to do that again—at a time when I can properly enjoy it. I was in a meeting that day when I stole a look at you." Against my damp neck, he said, "I shot hard as rock, had to rush out of the building. The phone shook in my hand the entire way back to you."

His words sent a thrill through me. "Then I'll await your command."

"And my permission. You're not to come at all until you ask for—and receive—permission from me."

"I can live with that. Any other rules?"

"Yes, one." He pinched my chin. "Don't ever look at another man with lust, unless you want him dead."

I knew he meant that literally.

"You belong to me alone. No man could feel more possessive of a woman than I do you." His eyes mesmerized me, as if he could see into my soul. Right now, I felt more vulnerable with Sevastyan than I had in front of an audience of dozens. "Do you understand me?"

Gazing up at him, I nodded.

"Horosho." Good. "I think that deserves a reward." He settled me on the submerged bench—alone. Before I could protest he'd risen from the water.

Drops sluiced down those magnificent muscles, over his entrancing tattoos. Just the sight of his body made my achy nipples grow even harder, my pussy wetter.

After spreading another plush robe over the flat marble expanse at the edge of the tub, he lifted me to my feet. "Go to your knees and forearms on the robe." He helped me climb up.

Even out of the water, I felt floaty and boneless, letting him guide me into the position he desired—one that left me bare to his gaze.

"Now rest on the side of your face and straighten your arms back alongside your body. That's it. Ease your legs apart." Even more exposed? "Good. Keep this position." He moved behind me. "Just relax and accept what I'm going to do to you."

Which would be what exactly—

He grazed the head of his cock along the crease of my ass.

I gasped. Surely he wasn't going to do *that*?

"So sensitive." Another graze. "Why am I even surprised?"

Right when I was resigned, arching up for him to do whatever he wanted, he leaned down and began to kiss one side of my ass, light nips and licks where he'd whipped me.

"You're going to be sore here too." The other side of my ass received the same attention. "You were so exquisite with these bright pink lashes over your pale skin." He ran his face against the backs of my thighs. "I imagined how each one must have made you feel and nearly came just from the sight."

He moved his face between my legs, leaning in to my pussy. To kiss from this angle? That was so hot. . . .

With his first lick, I couldn't bite back a cry.

"You sound surprised." He teased my entrance with the tip of his tongue, then said, "You didn't think I'd let a day go by without tasting you here? There's a reason I call you *milaya moya*." My sweet. "I'll be irritable any day I don't get my fix of this." He kissed me like he would french kiss my mouth, with his tongue sweeping and seeking between my lips.

I moaned, already close. I wanted him to continue—but I was on fire for him inside me. "Sevastyan, please fuck me again."

"Can't. You must be tender. I don't want to hurt you." He parted me with his thumbs, setting in with even more hunger.

Panting, I said, "I-I can take it."

He moved lower to my clitoris. "This isn't enough?"

"Oh, God!" My hands curled into fists.

A dark chuckle sounded against my flesh. "Relax and accept." He kept licking and sucking, until I was in a crisis: not wanting to come without permission, but tripping along the brink.

"Sevastyan, can I—"

"No."

"Please let me come!"

"How?" he demanded.

"Wh-what?"

"How do you want to be made to come? Be more specific when you beg me. And hold your position if you want my mouth."

I forced myself to go limp. "Please keep doing what you're doing. Harder." My words were throaty with passion.

"Where? Be very specific." He was so domineering that my thoughts got scrambled for the thousandth time tonight.

"Please . . . lick my clit . . . until you make me come."

"Umm. Better." He was lording his sexual power over me, and I didn't know which one of us enjoyed it more.

As he bent down farther to better tongue my bud, he spread the globes of my ass, his fingers nearing my ring.

I couldn't believe I was about to say . . . "A-and touch me there at the same time."

All innocence, he asked, "Here, love?" just before his stiffened tongue speared inside my pussy.

I stamped the tops of my feet with frustration. "You know what I mean!"

"Ah yes, this." He gave me another frustrating/blissful thrust of his tongue.

Half out of my head, I whimpered. "Please lick my clit while you touch my ass."

Tone wry, he said, "Better still, then."

In a dim part of my brain, I comprehended that my ruthless hit man was *playing* with me, enjoying himself! And I loved it.

He took my clit between his lips and drew wetly.

"Ah, God, ah, God . . ."

The pad of his thumb found my center—

I exploded, startling myself with my sharp scream. *"Sevastyan!"*

The pressure between my cheeks and around my throbbing clit wrung wave after wave from me as he suckled and played. . . .

Once he'd coaxed every last ounce of my release, he stood behind me, rasping, "Greedy girl. You came without permission? Tomorrow I'll punish you for that. Tonight you get a pass because you've pleased me so well."

Between breaths, I asked, "Now will you fuck me?"

"You can't tonight." He was stroking himself? "Besides, seeing you like this . . . I won't last long."

"Really?"

"If I donned a condom right now, I'd be sure to come in it."

Even in the midst of this, I couldn't choke back a laugh. Maddening, fascinating man!

I rested on my forehead, tucking my head under to watch him. Those tattoos on his arms rippled over his muscles as he worked his thick length.

He bit out, "If you knew what I was imagining right now, beautiful . . ."

My toes curled from his wicked tone, from his wickeder eyes.

"Do you want my cum to mark you?" He squeezed his fist even tighter, as if to hold back a flood of it.

In answer, I arched my back down, spreading myself wide—

He loosed an overpowered bellow. An instant later, a ribbon of heat landed across my ass. Hips working, he fucked his fist, striping my flesh with semen.

Each heavy lash was as scalding as the leather he'd used to whip me. He yelled out his pleasure over and over . . . until finally spent.

Breaths heaving, he said, "Look at the sight of my woman."

My face flushed. I could only imagine what I looked like— spread, vulnerable, my reddened bottom coated.

"I'm committing this to memory."

Heartbeats passed; his gaze lingered until I was squirming. "Sevastyan . . ."

Then we were down in the water again, and he was washing me off, lavishing kisses and praise—which I lapped up, a kitten to cream.

He rose, toweled off, then scooped me from the water, lifting me as if I weighed nothing.

As dazed as ever, I let him towel me dry and carry me to bed. Beneath the covers, he lay on his back, pulling me against his side. Once I'd curled into him, he gave an exhalation—pure masculine satisfaction.

My ear was over his heart, its strong beat lulling me to sleep. I couldn't remember the last time I'd felt so relaxed, so . . . at peace.

I'd never felt so in love.

He tugged me even closer, saying against my hair, "You have pleased me above all things. I never knew I could feel such pride."

Just before I drifted off, I smiled sleepily. Tonight, we had taken a wrecking ball to the walls between us.

Tomorrow everything would be different with him. . . .

CHAPTER 37

Nothing is different, I thought as I paced the room. *Not a damn thing . . .*

Today I'd slept until after lunch—a full ten hours!—waking with a big grin on my face and the words *man, my ass is sore* on my lips. Only to realize I was alone.

Sevastyan hadn't left a note or a text, hadn't called.

I'd been completely out of sorts, feeling hungover, chilled, and jittery from my endorphin withdrawal. Despite having few residual marks, I'd felt like I'd been through the wringer.

Still did, even three hours later. And his absence continued to baffle me. Yes, I'd figured he was out doing secret syndicate business, but couldn't he have taken a day off? I never should've been out of the bed, should be snuggled up with him!

Why isn't he here for me? I paced faster as my imagination ran away with me. What if he did regret taking me to the club? What if he was filled with second thoughts? *Why can't I get warm?*

What if I'd disappointed him somehow?

Normally, panic would not be my go-to emotion. But after the physical and emotional extremes of last night, I felt like a spinning top.

I reached for my phone, even as I told myself, *Not going to call him.* I didn't want to come across as some needy chick who couldn't go without reassurance—merely because she'd been whipped, screwed, and forced to come in front of dozens of people just the night before. . . .

Earlier, I'd been staring at the phone, waffling, when Jess had called. After my tepid greeting, she'd demanded, "Where'd he take you last night? I'm dying to know—so bad I figured out how to call France!"

Once I told her all about my experience, she'd said, "You really let him string you up? In front of an audience? Aw, Nat, I'm just so darned proud of the woman you've become!" After a pause, she'd said, "Wait, you're lapping me sexually? I want my own membership to Cirque du Cock! Come on, you durrrty hussy, buy me one, huh, huh?"

I'd been in no mood for humor. "He wasn't here when I woke, and he left no word. Jess, why would he pull a nail-and-bail?"

"He's probably out racking his brain for his next play. One-upping Cirque du Cock won't be an easy feat."

After we'd hung up, I'd attempted to distract myself by watching the camera feeds, but it'd been no use. Here I was pacing again, marching from wall to wall across the plush carpet.

I'd paced more since I'd met Sevastyan than in all the years before him.

Each minute that he remained absent, my mood continued to plummet. *Not going to call . . .*

Pride—mingled with anger—gave me the strength to toss the phone on the bed.

Still freezing and achy, I took a steaming shower, then headed to the walk-in closet. Skirts and delicate blouses, heels and hose. If he'd reordered items from my vast wardrobe at Berezka, he must have cherry-picked these clothes.

I scowled at his selections. Sometimes I just wanted to veg out in sweats and a pizza-stained T-shirt. Sometimes I would prefer to wear jeans and clunky boots while trapped in my gilded cage.

When kink-hungover, I didn't automatically reach for a gauzy teddy. . . .

The sun was setting by the time Sevastyan returned. The first thing I noticed—his gaze was shuttered.

"Where were you?" I sounded remarkably calm, considering the fact that I wanted to bum-rush him with waif-fu.

"Meetings." He wasn't cold, but there was a marked difference between the dream lover of last night and the detached man standing in front of me now.

"So how was your day?" (*Dear.*)

"It was fine."

I stared at him with bewilderment. "Mine was fine too. Dandy really." *This* was how he was going to treat me after all we'd shared? How naïve I'd been; just because we'd overcome our sexual hurdles didn't mean we could overcome our emotional ones too.

"Good." He turned away, removing his jacket and holster.

I got the sense that he was trying to distance himself. And if I were paranoid, I would even have said that he was . . . uneasy around me.

After we'd gotten on the same page at last? That couldn't be right. Forcing a laugh, I said, "Have you been avoiding me today?"

"No," he answered, but he was twirling that ring.

CHAPTER 38

"You're quiet," Sevastyan remarked.

"Just thinking." I stared out the limo window as we navigated the streets of Paris, passing lines of flickering gas lamps and chestnut trees. He'd said he had a surprise for me tonight, some unspecified destination.

It'd been four days since the club, and while Sevastyan and I had continued to make progress in bed, we'd been stymied in other areas. Namely: every single one.

We'd crested that night, and now seemed to be bottoming out.

"You're pensive." He drummed his tattooed fingers on the armrest. "I've never seen you so."

"Guess I have a lot on my mind." Misgivings. They were flooding in.

There was no denying it any longer—Sevastyan was avoiding me during the days.

Which was so different from the nights, when he would spoil me with pleasure, commanding me, guiding each interlude. Again and again, he'd demonstrated that our kinks were breathlessly well matched.

As promised, he'd had a collection of tools and gear delivered. It came stored in a sizable wardrobe—basically a BDSM closet. Though he hadn't broken out any hard-core gear yet—true to his word to take things more slowly—he had used different toys on me.

He seemed fascinated by my orgasms: how quickly he could force one from me, how long he could deny me, until I was pleading for permission.

At night, he was perfection. But during the day, *if* he was around, he was quiet and closed off. Which sucked in more than one way. Sevastyan was pressing for more sexual vulnerability from me, an ever deeper surrender, which left me raw the next day—just in time for him to be an ass.

Like running to catch a fly ball—with my face.

He drummed his fingers again. That *drum drum drum* was grating on my nerves. The night of the club, we'd meshed seamlessly. Now friction chafed between us.

"Tell me what you're thinking about," he said.

Oh, that was rich. "No hint of where we're going?" I asked, deflecting, letting him know how it felt.

"I meant this as a surprise."

Another sex club? *Not really in the mood, Sevastyan.* Yet I had to admit he'd put my curiosity on a slow boil. "For someone who hates surprises, you like delivering them well enough."

"Would you rather have stayed in? It is getting late."

My emotions were in such tumult that I might've balked at going with him, except for two things: I was desperate to get out of the house. And earlier, he'd acted differently with me.

When he'd returned from his meeting, he'd taken me in his arms without a word and held me like I was the only thing keeping him afloat. Like he was crossing a finish line to reach me.

It was so confusing!

He exhaled a long breath. "Sometimes you're an utter mystery to me." If he kept drumming his fingers, I was going to snap them like dry kindling.

"You're one to talk. Besides, I tell you everything that's on my mind."

"Not tonight."

"Maybe not," I conceded.

"I asked you to tell me what you needed. You agreed to."

Where to start? "You really want to do this?"

"Yes."

Here goes . . . "When you bailed the day after the club, I would've expected you to leave a note or a text. To reassure me."

"Of what? There can be no doubt of how I felt after that night."

"It would've been nice to receive *any* acknowledgment."

Drum drum drum. "Very well. And . . . ?"

"I want to know where you go every day."

"I have business concerns that I'm able to address from here."

"Syndicate business with that Maksim guy?" I asked. When he nodded, I said, "I know he gave you information about Berezka. I know you talk to him as much as I do Jess. Who is he to you?"

"Nothing more than a temporary ally. He's assisting me with work obstacles I've run into."

Again, I got the impression that Sevastyan was shielding me. Plausible deniability?

"What else is bothering you?" *Drum drum.*

"I can't stay cooped up and alone in the town house any more."

"Which is one of the reasons I'm taking you out tonight."

I glared. "How much longer will we stay here? I'm used to being around people, talking and laughing. I'm used to having goals and working toward them. I need an end date; this indefinite shit doesn't work for me."

"We'll return to Russia at the beginning of next week. Things will be different there, Natalie."

Why did I have the sinking suspicion that I'd be hearing that line a lot? "How?"

"You'll meet new friends. Your days will be full, and I'll feel more confident in your safety. For now, I need you to be patient."

I inwardly grumbled. I supposed I could make it another couple of days. . . .

When the limo slowed, I asked, "Are we there?" My voice sounded ridiculously expectant; *curiosity killed the Nat.*

Sevastyan drew a silk cloth from his jacket pocket. "As I said, it's a surprise."

"Fine." I let him blindfold me. Once we'd parked, he helped me outside into the blustery night.

As he guided me up a flight of concrete stairs, I asked, "Oh, so we're going *above*ground this time?" Snark.

"I wouldn't get used to it," he snarked back.

We crossed a threshold into a warm interior. Aside from the echo of my heels, it was quiet inside.

When he removed my blindfold, I blinked my eyes, adjusting to the soaring area. Recognition hit, and I twirled in place.

We were in the Musée d'Orsay! I'd read all about this museum in my tourist guidebook, had seen pictures. It was a renovated train station housing galleries of famous French impressionists and other artists of the period.

Van Gogh's *Starry Night over the Rhone*, my favorite of them all, was . . . *here*. It blew my mind that I'd soon be viewing it in person.

I glanced around, saw not another soul. The lights were dimmed.

This was just for us? My irritation from before dissipated to a whisper, and I felt guilty for my impulse to snap his fingers.

In a dry tone, Sevastyan asked, "Is this the tits?"

A laugh burst from me. "It is! You're redeeming yourself, Siberian. How did you get us in after hours?"

"Called in a favor. This museum's smaller and more personal than the Louvre, better suited for one night's exploring. Come."

One of the first sculptures was of lovely Sappho with her lyre, her expression contemplative. "She composed her poems to be accompanied by the lyre," I said. "You could say she's the first lady of lyrics."

The autodidact looked impressed. "You know ancient Greek poetry?"

"You don't study the history of sexuality without getting to know Sappho." *Natalie Porter, history student.* Did that designation even fit any longer?

Maybe I should take Paxán's advice and travel the world, living out my dreams. With the man beside me . . . ?

As Sevastyan and I strolled on, passing one wondrous statue after another, I sneaked glances up at him. Though he'd pulled off this museum coup, he seemed a little less confident than his usual proud self.

I recalled his attentive expression when he'd washed my hair, how badly he'd wanted to get it right. He looked the same tonight, as if it was critical to impress me.

In fact, he was gauging my reactions more than he was admiring the exhibits. Just as he'd watched my face—instead of an orgy.

"You're not interested in art?" I asked.

"I'm more fascinated by how you respond to it."

Irresistible Siberian. When he made comments like this, how could I stay mad at him?

One of the last exhibits on the ground floor was *Woman Bitten by a Snake*, a life-size sculpture of a female writhing naked across a bed of flowers. Her body was voluptuous, her curves on display for eternity.

Even in the midst of such a sensual sight, I could feel Sevastyan's burning gaze on me. When I peered up at him, his eyes darkened, letting me know whose curves he wanted to see for eternity.

I'd gotten accustomed to that sensual look of his—in bed, in the shower, in a sex club. But in a museum, I grew kind of flustered. Like I'd been when I'd first tried to pick him up.

I girlishly tucked my hair behind my ear—*uh, can I buy you a drink?*—and moved on. We climbed the stairs in silence, each lost in thought.

But on the second floor, I hastened past other masterpieces without due reverence to get to *Starry Night*. And then . . .

There it was. Right in front of me. "I can't believe I'm looking at it."

He remained silent by my side, allowing me take it in.

The copies I'd seen had never conveyed the elaborate texture of the piece, the exaggerated brush strokes. Those gaslight reflections over the water were bold daubs. Each star was a cluster of deftly layered paint, creating height from the canvas.

I blinked up at him, having no idea how much time had passed. With a blush, I explained, "It's my favorite of the era."

"Why this one?"

"The boats, the lights over water . . . this scene is a world away from the fields of home, from all I'd ever known. I'd never seen these kinds of blues in the Corn Belt. For a girl like me, the colors were exotic, calling to me." Not to mention that I'd secretly sighed over the two lovers in the foreground, sharing such a night.

Sevastyan eased even closer to me. "When you get excited, your cheeks flush pink, and your eyes become even brighter against that flame-red hair." He reached forward to twine a lock around his finger. "Your colors call to me."

A breath escaped me. Seeing him like this, I told myself that life-altering sex, admiring looks, and earnest compliments could tide me over.

Until what?

Until he saw me as a partner, a confidante.

He drew back. "Again, I speak too freely with you." Now color shaded *his* cheekbones. "Whenever I'm around you, I say more than I mean to."

"Then we should spend more time together." I let him lead me by the hand to another gallery room.

"Or less," he said, even as he appeared displeased by that prospect.

"Would it be so bad for me to know more about you?"

"I don't think you would like what I revealed."

Was that the reason for all his secrecy? He didn't want to scare me off? That didn't bode well.

As I perused another exhibit, I remembered my first semester at UNL. Jess and I were just becoming friends, and she'd been dating a "promising" new guy. Yet one night he'd told her with a mysterious air, "I don't think you'd like me if you really got to know me."

Much to his dismay, she'd kicked his ass to the curb. To me, she'd explained, "When a man tells you something like that, honey, you better take him at his word."

Jess and I had made each other a promise: when men talked about themselves negatively—*"I'm no good for you," "I have trouble committing," "I'm not going to settle down anytime soon"*—we would listen to them.

Sevastyan had told me he wasn't a good guy. I'd thought he meant because he was a hit man. So what was he hiding from me?

"Perhaps I would tell you more about myself," he said, "if I were more certain of you."

The finish line was still between us, a glaring line of chalk. "Then we're right back in the same catch-22. I find it difficult to throw all-in when I know so little about you. You give me a crumb of information only every few days. At the rate we're going, by the time I'm ready to sign on, twenty years will have passed."

Speaking of time . . . We'd drifted to stand in front of the great d'Orsay clock window. Between the roman numerals, I could gaze out and see the misty Seine below, the lights of the Louvre and the Tuileries Garden.

Faced with this view, my current friction with Sevastyan faded, giving way to memories of my father, the Clockmaker. When the minute hand ground forward, I had to stem my tears. "How are you doing, Sevastyan?" I didn't have to be more specific.

His face was granite under pressure. "I grieve, as you do. I think about him a lot."

I took Sevastyan's hand in mine. "Thoughts of him come all the time, sparked by so many different things." Tonight, I'd reflected on his letter, on his hopes for me. Earlier this week, I'd seen white tigers on a street-side billboard, and my mind had snapped right back to laughing with him. "Will you tell me a story about him?"

Sevastyan was opening his mouth—doubtless to decline.

"Just one," I hastily said. *"Pozhaluista."* Please.

Looking like he was about to speak in front of thousands, he cleared his throat. "When I'd been with him for a few months, he took me to a summit meeting. Another *vor*'s son said something about Paxán that I took as an insult. I got into it with the older boy—which meant the two of us were sentenced to fight in the middle of a packed warehouse. 'You're too smart to be taking blows to the head,' Paxán told me as he walked me through the crowd." Sevastyan frowned. "He was always telling me that I was smart. So I told him I would 'fight smart.'"

I could imagine this exchange so vividly: Paxán shepherding him through a throng of *mafiya*, tough Sevastyan with his chin jutted—even as he soaked up the attention from Paxán. Because no one had given it to him before?

"As I headed toward the makeshift ring, men were yelling all around us, placing bets. I was just fourteen, and it was . . . a lot to handle." Understatement. "Paxán looked so concerned that I'd get hurt. I told him he shouldn't worry about me."

"What did he say?"

"He sighed and told me, 'Best get used to it, Son.' The first time he'd called me Son. Something clicked in my head, and I finally accepted that I would have a home with him, that it was permanent."

Had he been worried for months that he would have to return to the streets? To leave a place like Berezka? *Oh, Sevastyan.*

"After that, I was determined to make him proud, to win."

"And you did?"

"It took three men to haul me off my unconscious opponent."

At fourteen. "Paxán let you continue fighting after that?"

"I convinced him I'd do it for no reason at all—or for money and respect. He had no choice but to agree."

"You didn't go to school?"

"I was learning from him," Sevastyan said matter-of-factly. He didn't have a chip on his shoulder about schooling; no surprise, Filip had lied. It was clear Sevastyan was confident in his intelligence and learning. It was also clear Paxán had nurtured that confidence.

"Each week, he bought me books. Mathematics, economic theory, philosophy, great Russian literature. And history," he said. "He never told me I had to read them, but the reward was discussing the books with him, usually while he tinkered with those damned clocks."

Sevastyan's unmistakable affection made my eyes water anew. "Thank you for telling me that story." He'd opened up to me about something! Every time he showed me these glimpses of himself, I fell a little bit more in love with him.

He raised his brows. "I think that's the most I've ever spoken."

I couldn't tell if he was kidding or not.

At that moment, the clouds parted for us, revealing the moon. Its light spilled down over the river and illuminated the numbers of this clock, making them glow.

The full moon. Had it been a month since Sevastyan had taken me to Russia? Since he'd first kissed me?

I wondered if he realized this. It seemed that everything he did was by design. Might Sevastyan be a closet romantic? In a casual tone, I said, "This is an anniversary of sorts for us."

He didn't look surprised at all. "Yes. It is."

"Are we commemorating the first night we kissed?" Before I'd had any idea what this man would mean to me.

"I want to." He drew me against him. "You can't imagine how badly I'd wanted to claim that kiss."

"You claimed far more than that on the plane."

His lids grew heavy as he obviously thought back to what we'd done. "I was a very lucky man that night."

"And now?"

"I'll consider myself lucky, my elusive girl, once you consider yourself taken. Every man has a weakness; you are mine. I've accepted that. Now you must accept me."

No, every *person* had a weakness. Aleksandr Sevastyan was my own.

"I need you all in, Natalie."

He *had* opened up to me tonight, and we could build from that. I smiled up at him. "I haven't ruled anything out, Siberian."

"I suppose that's good enough—for now." He rubbed the pad of his thumb over my cheek. "Do you want to see your painting again? We can go back."

Back? When the minute hand ground on once more, I didn't feel sadness. This time I felt a tiny bloom of optimism.

Maybe we were at last moving *forward*.

CHAPTER 39

"The plighted life's not treating you well?" Jess queried a couple of days later. "I thought you guys were lovey-dovey all the time after the museum."

"If possible, he's even more distant." This morning he was once again MIA. And, *shocker*, he'd left no note, belatedly texting me: in meeting

Gee, thanks. I'd thought talking about Paxán would be our common ground. Yet that story about my father had been the last I could coax from Sevastyan.

"He sounds like a downer to me," Jess observed.

"We're supposed to go to Russia in two days. He promises everything will be different there."

"And?"

"I'm leery. Jess, I'm not sure if I want to return with him." In some dark moments, I didn't know if I *could*—not without sacrificing some part of myself. "How can the sex be so good when other parts of our lives are so lacking? I know without a doubt that no other guy will fit me so well in bed. I found him on my first foray."

"You sound like you're in love with him, Nat."

"I am," I admitted. "But it's complicated. This love might have a razor's edge to it. And it's exhausting. I don't remember the last time I was so tired."

Perhaps I needed to get out from under his influence and process everything that had happened. His personality was larger than life, the things he'd shown me as well; it could be that I'd overloaded.

Sometimes I thought a break from his intensity might be welcome. Other times I shrank to think of parting from him.

"You've got to bring this to a head," Jess said. "If you want answers out of him, then demand them. Speak to him in the language he understands: Unicorn. Or Glock, or whatever. Dig until you get the splinter out of the lion's paw."

"And if I *can't* dig it out?"

"Then let him get fucking gangrene—alone. Put a cap on this, girl. Give it one more shot, but then you're done."

Maybe she was right. He expected me to do all the adjusting—while he stubbornly remained the same. Maybe I should stop compromising and making excuses for him.

"You know you're probably going to have to cut this one loose, Nat. I think you're hoping that I'll tell you to stick it out through thick and thin, through all his wank moppet damage. Wrong. Sometimes self-preservation means preservation of self."

"That's deep, Jess." And it was exactly where I was failing: keeping the Natalie in Natalie. "Where'd you hear that?"

"Read it in a twatting romance novel."

I gasped. "You can *read*?"

"There's my Nat! I missed you. Lose the downer unicorn and come home."

I recalled his reaction the last time I'd suggested a break; he'd trashed the dresser. "Taking time off will be difficult with a guy like him."

"Then remember my advice. *ABC, baby.*"

After we hung up, I dressed, readying for battle. What I wouldn't give for a pair of jeans and clodhopper boots—or any garment at all from the bottom of my Nebraskan laundry basket.

I settled on a satin-weave blouse in cobalt blue and a black pencil skirt. I knotted my hair atop my head as I slipped into a pair of pointy-toe heels.

It wasn't until later that afternoon that he returned, making his way up to our room. Weariness emanated from him.

Not just weariness—distance. It was worse than it'd ever been. And I could swear I even saw resentment in his expression.

Resentment toward . . . *me*? What the hell did I do? "We need to talk."

He shucked off his gun holster, rolling his head on his shoulders. "I don't want to do this right now."

"You're not going to put me off any longer. I'm done whiling away here when you go out for your mysterious meetings—that you keep secret from me. I'm done being shut out of your life."

His eyes were full of warning. "You need to learn patience."

Patience? He was putting this back on me again? "When do you intend to let me in? When do I rate high enough to get to know your business? To actually discuss things with you? After we sleep together? Already did that! Once we're living together? We *are*." I tapped my chin. "Hmm? Maybe after you whip and screw me in front of an audience? How much more personal can things be than that? Yet you won't share what's going on in your life? In your thoughts?"

"Maybe it will *never* happen," he said, filling me with alarm. "Did you ever think about that, Natalie? How about *never*?"

"If I'm not your partner in this, then I'm no better than a doll, a toy you bring out and store away whenever it suits you." Like I'd done with my arsenal. "How do you think that makes me feel?" To him, I was merely a belonging—which he'd *told* me.

Should've listened to him, honey.

He scrubbed his palm over his mouth. "Maybe you expect things from me that I do not know how to give."

"You know how. You just refuse!"

"So I'm to shoulder all the blame? Why should I tell you anything when I can sense you're pulling away from me?"

"Oh, no, no, no, Siberian. I'm not pulling away—you're shoving me out of the fucking door! You keep this up, and I will bolt. Do you understand me?"

Though I sensed a weird kind of panic in him, his demeanor was all confidence. "There's no leaving, sweet. You're as addicted to me as I am to you."

Under the influence. I couldn't deny this. Not to mention that I was stupidly in love with him. Yet if he wasn't good for me, *to* me . . . "It's true, I am addicted to you. But maybe it's time to kick the habit—"

A commotion sounded downstairs. Sevastyan lunged for his holster, had his gun out in an instant. "Stay here. Lock the door behind me."

My heart slammed. "Who's here? Is it another *vor*'s men?"

He cocked his head. After a moment, he said, "No, and that's a problem."

"How? Why??"

"Because I can kill an enemy's men."

CHAPTER 40

*A*s I locked the door behind him, I wondered why Sevastyan hadn't told me to go to the safe room.

But didn't I know? He didn't want me to watch the camera feeds. Which meant I *had* to.

At the desk, I scanned screen after screen as he made his way downstairs. My eyes widened when I saw the monitor that covered the parking area. Our guard was laid out on the ground. At least he looked like he was still breathing.

In the kitchen, I spied a black-haired man as tall as Sevastyan, flexing the fingers of his right hand. One guy had knocked out that big guard with a fist?

Could he be the mysterious Maksim? He dressed as well as Sevastyan did, maybe even more conservatively. Despite decking somebody, he'd managed to keep his dark suit crisp and flawless.

In the color screen, I could see that his eyes were a piercing blue. And for some reason, this stranger looked familiar to me.

He helped himself to a bottle of vodka and snagged shot

glasses, as if he was just waiting for Sevastyan to join him. Yet he set out three glasses. So where was the third guy?

Sevastyan entered the room. Despite looking like he was about to blow, he'd stowed his gun, tucking it into his waistband at the small of his back.

Amazingly, the other man had no fear of him. He smirked as he made some comment, his bearing aggressive.

Could he not see how close Sevastyan was to violence? It was simmering right beneath the surface, waiting to be unleashed.

After another exchange—were they speaking Russian?— Sevastyan inhaled and exhaled, as if for control.

I had to hear what they were saying! I took off my pointy heels, carrying them with me as I sneaked out of the room. I crept down the steps, then paused outside the kitchen doorway. Now I was a peek-freak—*and* an eavesdropper?

If he would have talked to me, I wouldn't be forced to stoop to this!

"Answer me!" Sevastyan demanded in Russian. "What the hell are you doing here?"

The man replied in the same, "This is the welcome I get? After all the work I've done to help your fiancée, you won't even let me meet her?"

Fiancée? Why would Sevastyan have told him we were engaged? And what had this man been working on for me?

"You haven't been helping because you're honorable, Maksim. You only wanted something to occupy your disturbed mind."

A puff of breath escaped me. Maksim. In the flesh.

"A game maker at rest is a dangerous man," Maksim said in a tone of agreement. "As the old bastard always told us, 'Life grows long without schemes.' In any case, you're one to talk—you're playing a treacherous game right now."

What game? Was he talking about sorting out syndicate business? *Outside looking in.*

"When I asked for your assistance," Sevastyan said, "I told you not to view this as an opportunity for more. You agreed."

"You assume we want more from you, Roman?" *Roman??* "Don't flatter yourself. I merely want to meet the woman who's at long last brought my big brother to his knees."

I sagged against the wall. Maksim was Sevastyan's *brother?*

I could see it. Both men had coal-black hair and towering, muscular frames. Though Maksim's eyes were blue to Sevastyan's gold, and Sevastyan's nose had been broken, the rest of their features bore a resemblance.

But that wasn't why he looked so familiar. Finally I remembered. I'd seen his picture online, when reading about another Sevastyan family—the mega-rich, connected Sevastyans.

This man was Maksimilian Sevastyan, the politician.

Hadn't I read about *three* brothers? I cast my mind back to that article. I believed the youngest one was named Dmitri and was a CEO of some company. There'd been no information on the eldest, other than his name. Roman Sevastyan.

The same name that was on his fake passport. Except it wasn't fake. His real name was Roman. And he'd been born into wealth and privilege.

No wonder his manners were impeccable. No wonder he'd seemed like a born rider.

What else hadn't he told me about? I gazed up at the ceiling. The better question: What *had* he told me about?

And the meager crumbs of information that I'd worked so hard to get weren't even true! When I'd asked him if he had any family—and specifically any siblings—he'd answered none. He didn't have just one; he had *two.*

Somehow he'd gone from an affluent, respected family to the slums. If he'd been on the streets, it hadn't been for long before Paxán found him.

Unless that was all a lie. Maybe he'd scammed Paxán. Who the hell knew?

Remembering my boasts, I felt my cheeks burn. *My instincts with men are untouchable. I can figure out men easily—*

"Get the fuck out, Maks. I won't ask you again."

"You took her to the club last week, but won't even schedule a dinner with me?"

I put my hand over my mouth. Sevastyan's brother knew about Le Libertin? Had he seen me?

And why in the hell would Sevastyan take me to a sex club his brother also frequented? How . . . *ick*!

"Don't look so surprised," Maksim told him. "I know everything you do. You forget—I'm in the business of information. Now, call my sister-in-law down to meet me, or I'll force my way up."

Sister-in-law! I needed to put a stop to this insanity. I slipped on my shoes, smoothed my hair, then entered the kitchen.

Sevastyan shot forward, inserting himself between Maksim and me. "Natalie, go upstairs. *Now*."

My feet were rooted to the spot. "You told me you didn't have any family left. And *no* siblings."

Maksim tsked, sidling around Sevastyan. "Roman has two brothers. I am Maksim, the more handsome one. And you, Natalie Porter, are even lovelier than I expected. Evidently I need to schedule a trip to Nebraska." He held out his hand, so I offered mine. He turned my hand to place a startling kiss on the pulse point at my wrist, glancing up with his penetrating blue eyes. "It's a pleasure."

Sevastyan didn't like that at all. So joke him. I smiled back at Maksim. "Very nice to meet you."

Sevastyan snatched my hand, using it to drag me back. "You will wait for me in our room."

Dismissing me? He wasn't even going to act guilty about the fact that he'd lied to me and been busted?

"No, Natalie will remain for drinks," Maksim said, pouring shots. I supposed he didn't have the same hang-ups over alcohol as his brother. "We'll order in." He was just as domineering as Sevastyan! "I refuse to leave until I get to know my sister-in-law."

"I am *not* married to Sevastyan."

"Details. You will be soon. Roman considers you engaged."

"You mean plighted?"

"Oh, no, I mean on the cusp of a legal, binding marriage."

Did Sevastyan just assume I would? The asshole hadn't even proposed! I felt *my* fists balling.

I'd asked him when I would get to know his business. He'd considered us engaged and still hadn't deemed me worthy of his trust?

How much more twisted could this "relationship" get? "I wouldn't put money on a wedding."

Sevastyan ground his teeth until his jaw muscles twitched.

I turned to Maksim. "I heard you say you've been helping me. How?"

"I'm a politician in Russia. A powerful one." He grinned, buffing his nails charmingly. Still, I sensed pain lurking inside him. Did he use his charm as a concealment, his own mask? "At present, a few of us politicians share the same resources as the *vory* in the *mafiya*—and even tactics. Roman knew I had men on hand to secure Berezka for you."

"Then, in that case, *spasibo*." Thank you.

Voice deep, he murmured, *"Vsegda pozhaluista."* You're quite welcome. This man's charisma was off the charts. He gave me another grin that revealed white teeth. I recalled the one time I'd seen Sevastyan truly smile, and realized the two men looked even more similar than I'd thought. "You still call my brother by his surname?"

"That's what he told me to call him."

Maksim turned to him. "You're no longer a mere enforcer. Your fiancée should call you something more personal."

"I'm not his . . ." *Oh, forget it.* Neither man was listening to me.

The two stared each other down, *Roman* seeming on the verge of blows. Before the shit hit the fan, I might as well try to get answers out of one Sevastyan. I asked Maksim, "Why have you been meeting with him all week?"

"He's been using me to help extricate you from the *mafiya*— trading syndicate holdings for clean ones of equal value. Like a billion-dollar game of Monopoly. He has power of attorney, and I have the means to get these things done secretly and quickly. So I have—without even a single thanks, I might add." Maksim cast a pointed look at his brother, but there seemed to be an underlying amusement in him, as if he found this situation humorous.

I whirled around on Sevastyan. "You could have taken me to those meetings, or at the very least *told* me about them. They concerned my inheritance!"

"You've shown no interest in this money—"

"You're one to talk, brother," Maksim cut in. To me, he said, "Roman could have made himself a billionaire this week. But for reasons I don't follow, he refused to rob you, refused to break his word to your father. He's worked on your behalf to disentangle Kovalev's legacy from crime. And once that's complete, Roman will step in as *vor* in the territory."

My eyes narrowed on Sevastyan. "I asked you about this! Seems like that might've been a decision we made together." He'd signed on for a new position without even a mention to me. Because I wasn't a partner; I was a possession.

One didn't ask one's favorite toy to discuss potential career paths. *Ugh!*

Scowling down at me, he bit out the words, "Natalie, upstairs—now."

"You did not just bark another order at me." In front of his brother? Blood heated my cheeks. Did he think he could command me like this simply because he did in bed?

Why wouldn't he believe that? Dear God, I hadn't made things better by trusting him sexually—I'd made them worse.

Weeks ago, I'd asked myself what I was prepared to do to get more from Sevastyan.

My definitive answer: not this.

I needed to accept that nothing I could do was going to move the needle with this man. He would always be closed off. And I deserved more than a satellite's orbit and a collection of lies.

I deserved preservation of self. Or I'd rather be alone.

It was as if a neon sign was slowly crackling, clicking, popping to life in my brain. The lights spelled: *This relationship is doomed, dumbass!*

I had steel in my backbone and fire in my belly. My time was valuable; I didn't reward shitty behavior with more of it. *I can't fix him, Paxán.*

Maksim told me, "Don't listen to him, *dorogaya moya*." My dear. "You need to teach him that orders—outside of some . . . situations—are unwelcome."

How much did this man know about my sex life? If they went to the same club, did the two brothers share similar interests?

You know what? That is none *of my business.*

"Roman is a handful, no?" Maksim continued. "A silent, brooding handful. If it's any consolation, he has always talked this little, sharing nothing of himself. When we were children, quiet was rewarded. The opposite was . . . not."

I didn't have time to puzzle at his words before Sevastyan growled, *"Zatknis' na hui!"* Shut the fuck up! Clearly about to go ballistic, he told me, "Leave now! Or I will carry you to our room."

When I told Maksim, "It was a pleasure to meet you," he flashed me a look of disappointment, as if he'd thought I would fight more. "I'll be upstairs," I said. A lie, to put with Sevastyan's.

I won't settle. I'm going to keep my eyes on the horizon.

In our room, I packed a messenger bag with my new passport, my cherished letter from Paxán, and some cash. I grabbed my wrap coat, my cell phone, and nothing else.

On my way out, I flipped off the bedroom camera. ABC, baby.

Do svidaniya, Siberian.

CHAPTER 41

"Your flight is about to board," a French security guard told me as he inspected my ticket and fake passport.

In a matching fake accent, I said, "I'm surprisingly quick." Especially if properly motivated.

An hour ago, I'd used the maid's entrance to slip out of the town house, sneaked past the groaning guard, then hailed a cab. On the way to the airport, I'd used my phone to buy an economy ticket to Nebraska.

I'd chosen my flight based on one criterion. It departed, like, *now.* I just had to hope that this passport would work.

I stifled a sigh of relief when the man handed it back. "*Mademoiselle*, you'll have to run to make your plane."

"Thanks!" I called over my shoulder. Run? In heels and a demi-cup bra? Beautiful. My heels clicked along, boobs bouncing—to the delight of a pair of males I passed. *This is why I preferred to wear minimizers!*

As I rushed down the concourse, I called Jess.

She answered on the first ring. "How'd the splinterectomy go?"

"I left him to die on the table." I darted glances around me, wondering how much time I had before Sevastyan noticed I was gone. "I'm at the airport right now." Leaving him was for the best. I needed to go home, to see my friends and my mom. To sort through everything that had happened to me. To get back to my old self.

"He'll come after you?"

"You have no idea—"

A text chimed on my phone. With a grimace, I read it.

Get your ass back here or I will whip it raw

"Shit, Jess! He knows I'm gone. He's going to assume I came here and follow me." To catch me and bring me back.

How had I gotten myself into this monumental mess? This had all started because I'd wanted to find my biological parents. Both were dead, and now I was saddled with a fortune that was still in the rinse cycle—along with a lying, stalker ex-boyfriend, who also happened to be an assassin.

Fuck!

"You've got a good head start on him, right?" Jess said. "And there's got to be security everywhere."

"If I can get away now, do you think we could hide out at your parents' lake cabin for a couple of weeks?" Months? Years?

"Hide out? Nat, what did he do to you?!" She sounded on the verge of skull-fucking something.

"Nothing like you're imagining. But he isn't who I thought he was."

"Skeletons in the closet?"

"Boneyard. And I still don't know the half of it. He told me he had no family, but I just met his brother a little while ago! A big-shot politician. And their family is rich."

"I thought you said Sevastyan was a street kid."

"That's what he led me to believe. You can imagine my shock. Jess, I didn't even know his real name."

"Holy shit, that's serious. So to the cabin we go. I'll make Jell-O shots for our trip, pick you up at the airport, and then we're off. Quick question of no particular import: was the brother hot?"

"Jess!" I slowed, swiping my palm over my nape. The first night I'd met Sevastyan, I'd had a sense that I was being watched; I had that feeling again.

Wary, I surveyed the terminal—

Sevastyan! He was here, on the other side of the security checkpoint, charging through milling travelers.

God, even now I found him breathtaking to behold, with his powerful body and determined demeanor.

His intense golden eyes swept the area. Because he was hunting. For me.

"Gotta go. Fucker's here." *Click*. How had he found me so quickly?

Our gazes met. Confusion flashed over his face. As if he truly had no idea why I'd left?

Too bad, Sevastyan, I am done.

I had to hope that he couldn't get through the long line at security. What were the odds that he'd already bought a ticket— and lost his ever-present pistol?

His confusion was turning to fury. His body language said he would murder anyone who got between him and me. For me, his eyes were filled with warning. *Don't you dare run.*

My expression told him, *This dumbass can* finally *read neon signs.* I gave him a pilot's two-finger salute, then made my way toward my distant gate. They were boarding! If I could just get on the plane . . .

I was out of breath by the time I filed into the slow-moving line. "Excuse me," I said to a group of sweet-looking elderly ladies in front of me, "do you mind if I skip ahead?"

They gave me *bitch, please* looks.

Out of the corner of my vision, I spied the crowd parting for a very tall black-haired man. Shit—he'd cleared security! My line snailed forward. . . .

Panicked, I scurried away from the gate down the terminal, knowing how this would go down. He'd catch me and I'd have to scream and fight.

And then he'd still never let me go.

When I had nowhere else to run, I spun around, squaring my shoulders.

His eyes were crazed as he stalked up to me. "Come." He snatched my upper arm.

"Let—me—go." I tried to wrench free of his viselike hold. "I'm not leaving with you."

"Natalie, *now*."

People were staring at us, whispering behind hands. Under my breath, I snapped, "Why can't you just leave me alone? You've been doing it for weeks!" At least during the days.

"Fight me, and I go to jail. Because nothing short of that will keep me from you."

Damn it! I'd seen his body language, promising pain to anyone who got between us. In the *banya*, he'd told me he'd do murder to possess me.

I didn't want anyone to get hurt. And I didn't want him to go to prison. Again.

"Interpol would love to take someone like me into custody."

I glanced past him, saw a gate attendant reaching for a red phone. To alert security?

Talk about making a major decision under pressure: My freedom for his?

I recalled how Sevastyan had been last night, in our bed. My dream man.

Damn, damn, damn! It seemed I could leave him—but I couldn't send him to prison. Not after everything he'd done for me.

This man saved my life.

His grip tightened, and his frenzied gaze pinned mine. His pupils were blown, his eyes appearing almost black. "I won't be taken from you. Do you understand me?"

I swallowed, hoping very much that I did *not* understand him. I had a flashback of what he'd done to Gleb, and pitied any guard who confronted this enraged enforcer. I had no choice but to go with him. For now. "Let go of my arm, and I'll come with you."

Instead, he dragged me along, my wishes ignored yet again.

"You can't do this!"

"Doing it."

Okay, so he could force me back—didn't mean I'd stay. He couldn't watch me every hour of the day and night. I promised him, "Short of your locking me in a cage, I *will* return to Nebraska."

"I'm not above using a cage."

"You dick!" As soon as we were outside the airport, I launched the toe of one of my pointy heels at his calf, booting him as I had his car back at Berezka.

He didn't seem to feel it whatsoever. So I kicked his ankle.

Nothing. And then he was tossing me into the back of his limo, signaling for the driver to go.

Apprehension overwhelmed my anger. The privacy window was up; I was at Sevastyan's mercy.

What was he going to do to me?

As if even a foot was too much distance between us, he yanked me across his lap. He squeezed me against his chest, those massive arm muscles rippling around me.

On the way back from the club, he'd held me like this. Never had I felt more cherished and protected.

Now? I'd never felt more conflicted. Had some traitorous part of me clamored for him when he'd scanned the crowd for his woman? Had some part of me thrilled earlier to hear myself called his fiancée?

What is wrong with me??

As I sputtered protests, he stripped off my messenger bag and coat—still too much between us?—then he clasped me harder, inhaling the scent of my hair, like we'd been parted for ages. In a distant tone, he asked, "Why would you leave?"

"You know why! I didn't sign on for a one-sided relationship, didn't sign on to be treated like a thing. You don't confide in me, you order me around, and you lie to me!"

As if he hadn't heard me, he grated in Russian, "You're not to leave me, Natalya. I'll never let you go."

"My God, are you hearing me at all? You sound like a freak! You can't keep me if I don't want to be kept!" I managed to draw back a couple of inches to glimpse his face—then wished I hadn't.

A professional hit man had fixated on me, and now seemed to be experiencing some kind of mental break because I'd left him. It was as if he couldn't make out my words because some bomb blast was repeatedly going off in his head.

Realizing how futile it was to try to communicate with him, I fell silent. But he wasn't done.

"For now, I'll discipline you."

I swallowed. "Putting the D back into BDSM?"

Against my hair, he said, "I told you that if you ran from me again, I'd catch you. I told you I'd spread you over my knees and whip your ass until you knew better."

His text had said he'd whip it raw. At the thought, I tensed even more in his iron embrace.

"And don't I always do what I say I will?"

CHAPTER 42

Sevastyan kept me trapped in his arms as he climbed the steps to our suite. He only let me go to slam the doors behind us.

As his threat replayed in my mind, I wondered if I should make a dash for the safe room. Yet even now I couldn't manage to be afraid of this man.

"Never run from me again!" He couldn't seem to catch his breath. "The thought of not having you . . ." He punched the wall near the hole from his last show of fury. As his fist made impact, he loosed a short, violent yell. Like an animal in pain.

"Sevastyan, just wait."

Flexing his hand, he twisted around to face me. "Strip."

"No, I don't want to."

"STRIP!"

I snapped, "Sure thing!" and stepped out of my shoes, scooping them up. "Here we go!" I flung the first one overhand like a dagger. Missed. He batted away the second.

"Why don't you arm yourself with your shirt next, sweet?"

"Fuck—you!"

"Fuck me?" Though his pupils were still blown, his sexy lips curled. "We're getting to that." Underneath all this pain and frenzy, Sevastyan was still Sevastyan.

Seductive. Undeniable.

He prowled closer, running the heel of his palm over the straining bulge in his pants. I'd been conditioned by him; seeing this man's erection would always make me grow wet to receive it. When he was just before me, his body heat and addictive scent wreaked havoc on my senses.

"You won't remove your clothes when I command it? I think you don't want me to discover what you're hiding."

Hiding?

He seized my hip with one hand. His other hand was climbing under my skirt. "Will I find you wet? If so, you're going to get whipped. If not, I won't touch you."

Not fair—I couldn't control my response! I squeezed my thighs together, but he forced them apart.

When he felt my damp panties, he grunted with satisfaction. "I think you want your punishment very much."

Was I already so lust-stupid that I . . . *did*? He rubbed me with his slow, hot fingers, sending my thoughts into chaos.

Maybe I should use him for the pleasure he always gave, then figure out what to do afterward. So what if he was going to spank me? It wasn't like he hadn't done it before—with a flogger. I could get through this.

Or maybe I was making excuses for him—yet again! I shoved at his wrist and twisted away from him.

He let me get a step away before his hands landed on my shoulders to jerk me back. He leaned down, his mouth descending on mine.

My cry was his access.

His tongue flicked . . . deliberate, sensual. Leveling my resistance. Even as he tore my blouse from me like it was tissue paper, he was giving me his mind-numbing, toe-curling lover's kiss—as if he couldn't help himself.

As if his mind was saying *Discipline her*, while his heart was saying *Kiss her*.

Though my mind screamed *Resist him*, my heart told me . . . *Surrender*.

With a defeated moan, I kissed him back, twining my tongue with his. He was caught up, and now I was too. I might hate myself afterward, but I couldn't stop this.

Whatever happened tonight would be my grudging toll, to buy my break from him.

He cut short the kiss to snatch at the fastening of my skirt, rending that material as well. He shoved what was left of it down my legs, all but clawing away my hose at the same time. His overt aggression was turning me on, the wild edge to his touch. . . .

As he ripped away my bra, he kissed my neck—licking and sucking right over my pulse point, knowing how that drove me crazy.

"Tell me to give you the punishment you're so wet for," he said against my skin. "Or tell me you never want to feel my hands on you again."

Never to feel those tattooed fingers on my skin, playing me like an instrument?

Can't.

"Tell me no"—he scraped his teeth over that spot on my neck—"or tell me you want this."

I choked out, "I want this."

With one brutal yank, he ripped off my thong. Once I'd been stripped down to nothing, he released me, moving to sit on the leather ottoman. "Come here." Though he sounded like he was on the very brink of losing control, I crossed to stand before him.

"Turn around," he ordered me. "Then go to your knees and forearms."

As I had in the bathroom that night? It was such a vulnerable position to be in. Was he about to go down on me again?

"Now, Natalie." His face was unreadable.

What would he do to me? Curiosity flooded me as I followed the command, kneeling on the plush carpet—

He seized my ankles, yanking me back until I was in a wheelbarrow position over his lap, leaving me to balance myself on my hands.

"Sevastyan!"

"Lean on your arms."

Breathless, I did, resting on my forearms and forehead, which put my ass in the air.

"Wrap your legs around my waist."

I had no choice but to comply. With my legs circling his torso in reverse, I could feel his hard cock pressing against my mons and belly. He'd told me he would spread me over his knees; he'd never specified how.

Positioned like this, I was totally bared to him, my pussy and ass on display for him. Perfect for whipping, for exploring and tormenting. The exposure only fueled my arousal—

His palms came down, cracking over both cheeks. I hissed in a breath, but the soreness from the club had long since faded. I could take his . . . correction.

Soon, I'd no doubt beg for it.

As the sting morphed into that prickling heat, I had to bite back a moan.

"My sweet Natalie craves this." Could he see how wet I was getting?

I cried out at another sharp crack. He was punishing me, and it was a pleasure. When I raised my ass for more, I could feel my flaring lips opening for his gaze, my clitoris jutting against the fly of his pants.

"Do you have something you want to show me, love?" With a low groan, he spread me even wider. "So—fucking—beautiful." He delved a finger, screwing it into my slippery core.

I almost came spontaneously—without permission.

He wedged in another finger, increasing the pressure. Then . . . another? He was mercilessly working in a third. I wasn't sure I wanted it, until he rumbled the words: "You can take it for me."

With a whimper, I did. "Ah, God, *yes*."

While I panted, he fucked me with those fingers, growling at the view. All the while, he spanked me, rocking his straining shaft against my mons and clit.

I was so close to coming for him. . . .

Over and over, he rocked and fingered and slapped—until I couldn't stand it anymore. "I-I need to come."

"Why should I give you that? You were leaving me." *Slap.*

"Please!"

Slap. "If you want to come so badly"—he shoved his bulging cock against me—"then use me, greedy girl."

Gone shameless with need, I did, grinding against his hardness, taking his wetted fingers and his stinging correction. Even before he groaned, "My God, woman, look at you," I knew the picture I presented. I knew his darkened gaze was rapt on the most private part of me, stuffed full with his fingers.

And I was turned on all the more for it, hurtling toward my orgasm.

"I could watch this all night." *Slap.*

Right on the verge, I moaned, "Oh, God, oh, God—"

He abruptly removed his fingers. "Your punishment's not over."

I sputtered, "Sevastyan, no!" He'd never gotten me *this* close, only to deny me. I was quaking with need.

He grabbed my hips, lifting me to my feet, holding on to me as I swayed. "You really think I'd let you come so easily? Reward your running?" His rage didn't seem tempered whatsoever, merely . . . delayed. "From now on, you have to *earn* your pleasure from me. And you're about to." He steered me toward the gear wardrobe, turning me to face away from it.

I heard the whisper of leather and the clinking of metal from within, could only imagine what he was searching for. I tried to summon up fear, but only felt that burning curiosity. What would this man do next?

"Bend your arms behind your back, and cross your wrists," he said. "Keep them there for me to bind."

He hadn't restrained me since the club. "I don't know—"

"You always think I'm *asking*, pet." He gave my ass a smack. "Obey me now."

To be bound and helpless with this man? How could I want that so much?

I had to feign hesitation as I crossed my wrists behind my back. I kept them there for him to wrap with leather cuffs. They were attached to each other, trapping my arms in place.

An instant later, cool leather met my throat; I startled, but he'd already stretched a collar around my neck.

Collar and keep you. The leather in the front dipped down to a V, reaching the hollow above my sternum. The interior was lined with what felt like cushiony silk. As he buckled it in place, I shivered.

He attached another strap of leather to the cuffs, pulling up-ward. What would he—

Click.

He'd connected the cuffs to the back of the collar. When I tried to move my arms, I felt a definite tug at my throat, which—I could admit—only added to my dark thrill.

Without a word, he lifted me, depositing me on the bed. I shifted onto my side to watch him stride back to the wardrobe.

He returned with a black drawstring bag, a ball gag—and a bottle of oil. "Facedown, Natalya. I'm going to gag you, then open you up. Just as you described for me when we first got here."

He wanted anal sex? Now? "Sevastyan, you can't." I maneu-vered myself to my knees. As horny as I was, and as curious as I'd been . . . "You're too angry. You're going to hurt me."

With silky menace, he said, "I won't hurt you—not like you did me when you ran."

"Will you just listen for a second?"

He tossed the gear to the bed and seized my upper arms. "Submit to me!" He crushed me against his body, my nipples raking the cloth of his shirt. He kissed my neck again, his hands descending to grip the cheeks of my ass. He ground me against his pulsing cock—until the idea of him taking my ass didn't fill me with alarm.

It filled me with need.

He released me, grating, "Open your mouth for me." He held up the ball gag before my widened eyes.

I could have clenched my jaw; I could have screamed at him. Instead, I found myself parting my lips.

"That's it, *milaya*. Now look at me when you lick it."

Lick? When I gazed up at him and swiped my tongue over the ball, his lids went heavy with satisfaction. So I did it again.

He rubbed the moisture over my lips, tracing the outline of my mouth, then fitted the ball between my teeth. While I tried to get used to the foreign sensation, he fastened the straps behind my head.

Though I'd been gagged, collared, and bound—he wasn't through with the gear. He moved me to lie on my front, then began pulling something else up my legs. Whatever had been in the drawstring bag?

I thought I felt more straps. These didn't seem to be leather—more like . . . elastic? He shimmied them past my calves and knees, then higher, until one hugged each of my upper thighs.

What is this? What could it be? God, the curiosity . . . Maybe it was another dildo like the one he'd used at the club?

When he secured a third strap around my waist, I felt something spongy between my legs. I realized what it was with the first vibration—one of those wearable, remote-control vibrators.

Fitting it snugly over my clit, he turned it on at a frustratingly low speed. "You'll enjoy this." The sensation made me moan against my gag. "But not too much." He set it to pulse on for a brief period, then off for much longer, then on again at that slow, slow speed.

"On your knees," he ordered.

This was really about to happen? Could I actually do this? If I was honest with myself, I'd admit that I trusted him to keep me safe, to take care not to hurt me. Hands still locked behind my back, I made my way to my knees.

"I want you facedown." I heard him stripping behind me.

He could have positioned me to receive him, but he seemed determined to make me participate, to submit at every opportunity. Did he assume my aching horniness would compel me to obey him?

If so, he was right.

Heart racing, I leaned forward to rest my forehead against the bed, leaving my ass up in the air. That vibrator came back on, making my hips roll.

"You always get what you want, don't you? But I hadn't given you your way in this."

He pressed the backs of his hands against my inner thighs. "Spread your legs."

My mind whispered, *Step off the trestle*, just as he commanded, "Submit to me, *milaya*." I couldn't resist both my will *and* his.

The anticipation of what he was about to do to me was maddening. The mere idea of this act . . . with him . . .

When I worked my knees wider, I felt the head of his cock brush along the back of one of my thighs, leaving a distinct trail of dampness. How badly he must want this!

"Do you trust me not to hurt you?"

I had to nod.

"Good." He slapped my bottom again, but this time his palm was wet. With oil? He drizzled a line along my crevice.

When I felt drops trickling directly over his target, the gag muffled another moan. He grazed his forefinger up and down, scarcely making contact with that needy part of me.

Each pass of his finger, he applied a tiny bit more pressure. As the vibrator fired up again, continuing its slow assault on my clit, he pressed hard enough to breach me, just barely.

My groan of frustration made him hiss in a breath. "My greedy girl wants more?"

I nodded my head against the bed, arching my back. The vibrator stopped, and I wanted to cry. By this point, I would have begged him to fuck me there.

With one hand gripping my hip to hold me steady, he started

to circle the pad of his finger over my opening, making me drool around the gag.

Waiting . . . waiting . . . Right when the vibrator came back on, he dipped inside to his knuckle.

At last! I moaned at the exquisite sensation. With the vibrator humming, he pumped his finger.

Against the gag, I cried, "More!"

"As you wish." More oil. Deeper penetration. "You think I would hurt you like this? That I wouldn't prepare you?" Another finger joined the first, wedging inside, stretching me.

For what felt like agonizing hours, he gave me shallow pumps. More oil. *Deeper.* More oil. *Wider.* Vibrator buzzing on and off.

I was glad of the gag when I began to babble and beg. *Please, please, please.* I was ready—couldn't be more ready. By the time he removed his fingers, I was nearly insensible.

I heard him squirting more oil. To slather over his heavy length? I could all but see him oiling himself, gliding his big hands across the taut head, the thickened base, along those prominent veins.

I wanted so badly to stroke him, to lick him, *anything*, but I was helpless. Even without the gag, my mouth would've been ajar, starved for something to suck. Every inch of my body was empty and open, receptive to whatever he wanted to give me. . . .

When the crown kissed my hole, I shook from the jolt of sensation.

"Don't fight me," he groaned. "Let me in." He pressed forward, entering me—just as the vibrator ramped up once more.

Once the entire oiled head was inside, I moaned because it was so good. Better than good.

He delved farther, his girth difficult to accept. Even still, pleasure suffused me the deeper he went.

Between gnashed teeth, he said, *"Teper' ti prenodlizhish mne vsetselo."* Now I've possessed you. Completely. He sounded as crazed as he'd looked earlier.

I twisted my head around and chanced a look back. His gaze was riveted to where our bodies joined. *If eyes could incinerate . . .*

Was he overwhelmed like me? How strange; I was bound, vulnerable, impaled—yet *he* seemed overpowered by this act taking place between us.

He withdrew a couple of inches. As I writhed, trying to adjust to him, I felt him drizzling more oil. "Relax, love. Surrender to me."

I willed myself to relax as much as I could.

"Good girl." Then he gave his first thrust into my ass, bellowing with satisfaction. The force of it rocked my body, pulling on my collar.

I could do nothing but cry his name against my gag—accepting the fact that I had leather strapped around my neck, that my arms were immobile, that I'd been wired to a device meant to drive me out of my mind.

That the man I loved had completely dominated me, and I was melting for him.

He drew his hips back, then rolled them forward, sending his cock even deeper. After another measured stroke, he fucked harder, grunting with pleasure. His sweating body slapped the oiled curves of my ass—more punishment against flesh that had already been whipped into submission. Conquered.

But I reveled in the sound of our skin colliding, knowing he was about to make me come. And then he would follow. He'd told me he would fill me up with cum. . . .

Yet then he stilled. "Up on your knees." He lifted me so I was kneeling with my back to his torso. He wrapped an arm across my chest, seizing my left breast in a possessive grip, trapping my bound arms between us.

His free hand trailed down my belly. With the heel of his palm, he cupped the humming vibrator tighter against my clit, then he stretched two fingers farther between my legs. He plunged them inside my hungry pussy right as he bucked behind me—and it was . . .

Cataclysmic.

He wrenched an orgasm from my core, screams from my lungs. As the pleasure rolled on and on, fierce contractions overtook my lower body.

"I feel you!" With a savage bellow, he joined me, beginning to ejaculate. His fingertips dug into my curves, his hips jerking with each palpable shot of hot cum—one after another as he grated, "Never forget . . . who you belong to!"

Long after he'd emptied himself inside me, he kept thrusting, as if he didn't want to relinquish his new prize.

Finally, he collapsed over me. In a hoarse rasp, he told me in Russian, "There is nothing left of me. . . ."

CHAPTER 43

Sevastyan freed me.

He hadn't nuzzled my neck as he used to, hadn't shown me his usual affection. He'd merely pulled out of me, leaving me limp on the bed, then started on buckles and straps.

Once he'd removed everything, my arms and jaw were sore. I didn't know what I was supposed to do or say.

Without a word, he scooped me up and into the bathroom, turning on the shower. In the tangle of my mind, one thought stood out. *Nothing has changed.*

I was still stuck in this hopeless relationship, devoid of trust and sharing. Except that now, he seemed even more distanced.

There is nothing left of me. What had he meant by that? Did he mean that he'd come his brains out and was empty?

Or that this was all I'd ever get from him? Beyond sex, there was nothing?

I plumbed my emotions and recognized that I was feeling . . . despair.

He carried me into the shower, easing me to my feet to stand with him under the spray of hot water. He poured bath oil into his palms, washing me with his bare hands. "Let me tend to you," he murmured as he laved my body with such familiarity, as if we'd been together for years.

As a husband would a wife. Like two people who trusted each other.

His detachment dwindled—he couldn't seem to hold on to it—and soon soothing Russian endearments spilled from his lips. With zero hesitation, he saw to every inch of my body, inside and out, even my bottom.

I would be sore tomorrow, but he hadn't hurt me. At least, not *physically*. My eyes pricked with tears.

Once he'd finished with me, he turned to soaping his own body, giving himself a cursory rubdown.

Tears kept forming. I didn't cry often; God knew I was an ugly crier. I squeezed my eyes shut, resenting every drop that escaped, cursing the tremble in my bottom lip.

"Natalie?" His tone aghast, he demanded, "What is this?" He grasped my cheeks, lifting my face. "Why are you crying?"

I opened my eyes but said nothing. *Let him see how it feels.*

"I've . . . hurt you?" He looked furious with himself, releasing me to ball his fists. "It was too much."

Tears continued to spill.

"Ah, God, *milaya*." He dragged me against his chest, coiling his arm around my nape. Locking me against him, he launched his other fist against the marble. Again and again.

Trapped like this, I could do nothing but wait. Nothing but *feel* . . .

His muscles moving against me. His chest shuddering with breaths.

I sensed his need to punish, to deliver pain. And for the first time, I realized that the invisible enemy he wanted to strike . . . was himself.

I whispered, "Stop, Sevastyan."

To my amazement, he did. "I would rather die than hurt you like this."

I believed him. "I'm not h-hurt." Tears continued to spill, belying my words. "You didn't hurt my body."

"Then I scared you. I've made you cry. Tell me how to fix this, and I'll do it. Anything except letting you go. That I can never do."

"No, you won't fix this. You had chances to, but nothing has changed." I pushed away from him. "Just leave me alone."

Of course he wouldn't. He took my wrist, drawing me out of the shower. Reaching for a towel, he began drying off my shoulders and arms, my belly. He knelt, rubbing my legs as if I was the most precious thing in the world. With a kiss against my hip, he said, "It's been decades since I've felt shame like this."

Shame is more painful than blows. That only made me cry harder.

He rested his forehead against my belly. "You are gutting me, love. You want to leave—you have reason to—but I can't let you go any more than I can quit breathing."

Now what was I going to do? *Nothing has changed.*

I twisted from him, then grabbed my robe, donning it on my way out of the bathroom. I was heading for my closet when he took my hands and gently urged me toward the bed. As he drew back the cover for me, my shoulders slumped with exhaustion.

Maybe I should take a breather for a minute or two. I didn't remember eating today, and all the emotions I'd experienced over the last several hours had drained me.

What he'd done to me had drained me.

Yet when I acquiesced and climbed into the bed, I felt like a failure, crying even harder.

He drew his pants back on—to be less threatening to me?—then paced at the foot of the bed. "I don't know what to do with this." Back and forth, he paced. "I have no idea what to do, Natalie. I need you to help me figure this out."

He moved to sit next to me, but my watery glare stopped him. He backed up to sit on the end of the bed. "Talk to me."

"That's all we ever do. I talk to you. I'm laid bare. You go unscathed, sharing nothing of yourself. Do you know how messed up it is that I didn't know you have a living family?"

"I should have told you. I see that now."

"Too little, too late. You expect us to be in this relationship, but we're not—"

"Yes, we *are*."

"Then you don't know the meaning of the word. If we'd started as a normal couple—regular girl meets regular guy—maybe things could have been different. We would have gotten to know each other, revealing details of our lives on an equal playing field. But it wasn't like that. You knew everything about me, and I knew nothing about you. Nothing except lies. Our dynamic was ruined from day one."

His breaths shallowed. "You're talking like this is done, over beyond salvaging."

I sobbed, "Because—it—is!"

He swiped his palm over his haggard face. I'd never seen him so shaken. Not even when Paxán died in front of us. "I . . . don't accept that."

"I thought that if I gave you my trust, you'd return it. But you won't. You never will."

"What if I did? Could I fix this?"

"No. Because if this is what I have to go through to get a crumb of information out of you, I'll pass. It's too exhausting! Besides, you warned me of this. You told me point-blank that I expected too much from you. You told me earlier today that trust might never come for us, and that you couldn't give me things I needed. I'm such an idiot. I know better than this. I know that when a man tells you he's no good for you, then you listen to him."

Stupid, Nat, falling in love with an emotionally unavailable man.

When my tears quickened, Sevastyan looked like I'd slapped him. Which just made me madder. There were emotions inside of him—he wasn't deadened—he'd just decided to keep them from me at all costs.

"If it's my fate to chase you, then I will. I will do anything to keep you." He put his head in his hands and rocked back and forward. "After you ran . . . imagining my existence without you . . . I realize . . ."

"What?"

He raised his head to me. "Concerns beyond you no longer matter. You're at the center of my life"—he frowned—"no, you *are* my life."

"Then why don't you treat me like it? I didn't even know your real name!" In a cutting tone, I said, "Isn't that something a fiancée should know?"

"Aleksandr was my grandfather's name. I cast off my first name when young. Maksim calls me Roman to goad me."

"Why did you tell him we were engaged?"

"Already there is troubling interest in you as an heiress. You'll be safer if it gets out that you're marrying a man who can protect you."

So Sevastyan was just putting up a front to keep me safe, to fulfill his promise to Paxán—

"And . . . I expected to wed you." He admitted, "I *want* to."

An answering want bubbled up inside me! Then I remembered all the reasons it would never work. "Earlier, you ordered me from the room like a dog—in front of your brother."

"You're not to be around him, Natalie. He's dangerous."

I wondered what it took for a man like Sevastyan to deem another *dangerous*. "Why?"

"Because I can never predict what he'll do."

"What would it have hurt for you to tell me what you and your brother have been doing for me?"

"The plan is risky. At any moment we could fail. If I tell you I will do something, it's because I'm confident I can. Not so with this. Plus, the less you know, the safer it is for you."

Plausible deniability. And to be fair, I couldn't see him telling me, "I have an idea—probably won't work—but I'm giving it a shot anyway."

He added, "Besides, if I disclosed this to you, then you would have asked about Maksim, forcing me to continue my lie to you. I don't want to lie anymore."

"What about your becoming the *vor*? Don't you think that's a decision we should have made together?"

"You might have talked me out of it, though I can see no way around it."

"You didn't even give me a chance to come to the same conclusion? I've surprised you before. I'm not *il*logical—well, except for being with you."

Pain flared in his eyes. "It's not that I don't want your opinion. But I know that the more I talk to you, the more you will expect me to."

"You're right. I would have liked for you to tell me at least the most basic things about your past!"

"Maybe I haven't wanted to reveal these things because I know it will drive you away! The more I want you, the more I dread this. You've seen my dread."

"What are you talking about?"

"Each night, I've been tempted to talk to you. A couple of times I came so close. Then, in the morning I would curse my stupidity, my weakness." He turned away. "I've never been so weak with another. And maybe . . . maybe I blamed you for making me feel like this."

"Like what?"

He whirled around on me. "Like I'll die without you! And if my past drives you away, then where does that leave me? Fucking *dead*! So why have I also been feeling the need to tell you of the past? It makes no sense!"

"That's your excuse for your coldness?" After every blissful night, he'd awakened even more resolved to shut me out, blaming me because he'd almost folded? "Let me get this straight. You've been a dick to me because you wanted me more than you did before?"

He didn't deny it.

"God! Again, you're not giving me a chance. You're driving me away by *not* talking to me. You know what? I—give—up. If you dreaded every time I asked about your past, you're really going to now that I've stopped."

"What does that mean?"

"It means you get to keep your secrets." Fresh tears spilled down my face. "I don't want them anymore!"

"You want me to confide in you because you think it will fix things in me, heal me. It won't!" Voice rising with each word, he said, "I will always have these shadows inside me!"

I yelled back, "Damn it, Sevastyan, I never wanted the shadows to disappear—I wanted them to be *our* shadows!"

His lips parted, eyes filled with bafflement.

"I wanted to *know* you; not fix you."

He recovered enough to say, "And what if these shadows show you that you can never have what you want of me? That my past makes it impossible for me to offer you the future you crave."

I dashed tears away with the back of my hand. "What kind of future do you think I want?"

"A life with a good man."

I couldn't argue with that.

"But a man is defined by his past," he said. "Which means I'm a killer. I always will be. There's nothing I can do to erase that for you. No matter how hard I work or how much I sacrifice, it follows me and always will. How do I keep it from tainting you?"

"I already know about your occupation. I accepted it. I've seen you kill twice. Is there more?"

He shot to his feet, pacing again. Why would he answer that? If he equated his revelations with the end of our relationship, he wouldn't. Not unless he accepted that it would end if he *didn't* tell me.

"You don't know what you're asking of me! I never told Paxán these things, and he came to trust me. To love me. Why can it not be the same with you?" Sevastyan was angling for his own self-preservation. "Why can't you just pretend my past is a blank void?" Under his breath, he said bitterly, "That's what I do."

"I can't pretend. I have to know."

He stabbed his fingers through his hair, yanking at the ends. "Natalie, I need you . . . I need you *not* to know me. And still stay."

"I swear to you that will not happen."

He dropped his hands. "Goddamn it, it must!"

I shook my head, my tears drying. "Sevastyan . . ."

He faced me and stood motionless, as if awaiting a gallows drop.

". . . I'm already gone." I rose to dress.

He clutched at his throat as if starving for air. "Don't speak like that!" He lunged forward to clutch my shoulders. "Look at me. Look at me!"

His eyes appeared full black. "I will tell you that I've killed many sons, many fathers. I started at the age of twelve."

I held my breath.

"The first father I killed was my own."

CHAPTER 44

*S*evastyan's admission rocked me. Not only because of what he'd said, but because of the shame emanating from him.

He released his grip on my shoulders. "Say something, Natalie." He was waiting for my disgust—and he had zero doubt he would receive it.

Little as I knew about Sevastyan, at least one trait had been made clear: his unwavering loyalty toward those he loved. Considering that he'd been only twelve when this had happened, and he'd hinted that things had been bad with his alcoholic father, I had to believe he'd been defending himself. "Your father must've left you no choice."

Sevastyan did a double take, seeming shocked that I hadn't run from the room. "How can you say that? Did you not hear me? I've just confessed to . . . patricide."

"I saw how you were with Paxán. You would've been devoted to any father who was worthy of it."

Sevastyan sat at the foot of the bed, then stood abruptly, only to sit once more. The pain inside this man! *Some mechanism deep within is broken.*

"Tell me the circumstances."

Narrowing his gaze, he bit out, "I got my father to the top of the stairs in our home, looked him in the eye, and pushed him, knowing he would likely die."

"What happened before this?"

"Are the facts not damning enough? As a boy, I made a decision to kill. And I've been doing it ever since."

I pressed on. "What happened before your father died?"

Sevastyan's brows drew tight, as if I'd just confounded him. "I . . . I never got this far when I imagined telling you. I always expected you to back away, fear in your eyes."

Instead, I took a seat on the bed, settling in with my back against the headboard. "Tell me now."

Looking anywhere but at me, he began, "My father was violent when he drank. My earliest memories are of blocking blows. He was a massive man, with these fists . . . they were unyielding. They were weapons."

His earliest memories? The idea of Sevastyan as a little boy, abused by the man who should've been protecting him from harm, burned inside my brain.

I remembered his words: *I am singularly suited to fighting, always have been.* Paxán had witnessed him taking a beating and had puzzled how someone so young could continue to rise.

Sevastyan had been able to take blow after blow—because he'd been so *used to them.*

Oh, God. Trying for a steady tone, I said, "Please go on."

"He considered himself a disciplined man, bragging to others that he only drank when it was dark out. Which meant he never stopped during the Siberian winters. Even now, I hate winter. Autumn just as much."

"Why?"

"It will always be a time of tension for me, a season to anticipate pain. Each day the sun sets sooner. Anticipation can be as hard as enduring."

All of this had been going on during these fall weeks that I'd shared with him? And I'd never known what deep-seated pain he'd been battling. "Was your mother with you?"

"For a time, but she couldn't protect us from him. She died two winters before he did. Supposedly she fell down those same stairs. A tragic accident, they said. Yet I have no doubt he pushed her. He just left her body there, mottled with bruises, cast away like garbage. Dmitri found her the next morning. He was too young to handle that sight, was inconsolable."

Who could handle seeing something like that at any age?

"Though I loved my mother dearly, I remember being angrier about my brother's suffering than I was sad over her passing."

"I'm so sorry." Sevastyan had lost his mother at ten. How much of her abuse had he and his brothers witnessed before then? "Please tell me about the night your father died."

I saw the exact moment Sevastyan decided to step off the trestle; he swallowed thickly. "My father knew all of his sons' hiding places inside the manor. No matter how quiet we were, he would find us, seeming to delight in our fear. So my brothers and I often hid outside when he was drunk."

Now I knew why Sevastyan hated surprises. Now I understood why he'd nearly gone ballistic when Maksim revealed that "quiet was rewarded."

"The last night I saw my brothers as boys, I was scarcely twelve. Maksim was eleven and Dmitri seven. Over the years, we'd all suffered concussions, broken limbs and ribs."

How casually Sevastyan related that—life-threatening abuse reduced to background information.

"Yet on this night, my father's rage seemed even sharper than usual. Though it was the dead of a Siberian winter, we had no choice but to flee outside." Sevastyan's eyes went vacant, as if he was reliving it. "I dressed Dmitri as warmly and as quickly as I could, then we waded through snow to reach the closest out-building, a drafty toolshed. We waited there, freezing for hours, staring at the shelter of our home. The manor was aglow with light, the windows fogging from the warmth inside. Our family had such wealth, but we were about to die of exposure."

I could imagine the scene so clearly: three traumatized boys yearning for that brightly lit manor, while fearing the monster within it.

"When Dmitri's lips started turning blue, I knew I had to go inside, to see if the old bastard had passed out. . . ." Sevastyan's eyes flashed toward me. "I don't want to remember any of this. I never did! I've never told another about this night."

"Please, trust me with this."

Seeming to steel himself, he began again, confronting this agony for *me*. "I hadn't gotten past the kitchen before he spotted me. I ran, but my legs were so stiff from cold it was like my feet were trapped in quicksand. He caught me, repeatedly bludgeoning my face. One of my eyes swelled shut, and I could barely see from the other."

Sevastyan had started sweating, his chest sheening with it. Was he aware that his own fists were clenched till his knuckles were white? I wanted to touch him, soothe him, but feared he'd go silent.

"He demanded to know where his other sons were, vowed he'd beat me to death if I didn't tell him. Somehow I managed to get loose, fought my way up the stairs. On the landing, he caught me again."

Eyes watering, I whispered, "Go on."

"For the first time in my life, I did more than brace for a blow. I . . . I *hit back*." Even after all these years, Sevastyan's tone was filled with astonishment. "He was stunned, but hurt too. I was big for my age—and all of the sudden *my* fists felt unyielding. I'd never struck another, not even Maksim in play. When my father recovered from his shock, his gaze turned lethal. I knew he was about to kill me."

"What happened then?" My heart was in my throat.

"Years' worth of rage welled up inside me, and I . . . beat him. Over and over. He'd backed to the edge of the stairway, swaying there unsteadily. Our eyes met. I'll never forget the uncanny feeling I had at that moment—I knew this was exactly what had happened to my mother. He'd beaten her, driving her to the brink. Stranger still, he . . . he *registered* my comprehension. And he had this bloody smirk as he said, 'You'll grow up to be just like me. Whenever you look in the mirror, you'll see my face.' The idea was so horrific—I launched my fist, knowing he would fall, hoping he would die. He snapped his neck against the first-floor wall." Sevastyan slid another glance at me.

"I'm here. What did you do after?"

"I knew I'd be sent to prison for murder. So I covered his body and retrieved my brothers. Afterward, I gathered what cash I could find and ran into the night. I had enough to reach St. Petersburg, to get lost among the other children there."

"How long was it before Paxán found you?"

"A year and a half. Long enough for me to suspect Paxán was some sort of deviant when he offered to take me in. Long enough to be mystified when I recognized he was a good man."

"How had you survived before then?"

Sevastyan rubbed a tattoo on his finger. I remembered that

one signified thievery. "I stole. But as I got older, it became more difficult—I was getting taller and couldn't slip away in a crowd as easily. There were times I was caught." His voice broke lower. "If you crossed the wrong protection gangs and couldn't fight your way free, things were . . . done."

He'd been attacked by street thugs?

"Your father told you about how he first found me. But what I never confessed to him was that I didn't always win on those streets. And when I didn't"—he stared down at his fists—"I lost . . . much."

Oh, God, no, no, no. I'd read about preyed-upon runaways in the States, read things that made my skin crawl; what had those men done to Sevastyan as a boy?

He glanced up. "Do you understand what I'm saying to you?" *Shame is more painful . . . ?*

But he had *nothing* to be ashamed of! Did he not understand that? Tonight, I might not be able to overturn twenty years of thinking, but so help me, ultimately I'd convince him.

His eyes went hazy once more. Was he reliving those agonies as well? I didn't want him to, only wanted to comfort him.

In a hollow tone, he repeated, "I lost much."

"Will you tell me?"

He closed his eyes. "I will. Just not today. Don't ask that of me today." His eyes shot open. "But you don't leave."

My heart was shattering, shards all around me. "I won't," I assured him. How easy it'd been for me to demand equal disclosure about our pasts when I had nothing shocking—or even noteworthy—to disclose. I'd wanted us to be equal, yet I hadn't realized that our histories weren't. "Why don't you tell me what happened to your brothers?"

Clearly relieved to move past that topic, Sevastyan said, "We had no relatives, so they remained at the manor, with conservators brought in to arrange for their upbringing. I stayed away, fearing prosecution, but also because I look so much like my father, more with every year. I wanted to spare them the sight of me. I didn't know until years later that Maksim had convinced the authorities that he and Dmitri had witnessed our drunken father's fall, and that their older brother was missing because I'd become crazed with grief. Even then, Maksim could spin a tale like no other."

Fondness for his brother had crept into Sevastyan's tone, at odds with the chilliness between them earlier.

"I thought I had saved my brothers from an abusive tyrant, that they'd be free. At least I could wear that badge." He clasped his forehead. "Yet just this week, Maksim admitted to me that the caretakers who came in to raise him and Dmitri were . . . worse than our father."

"How?" I asked, but I could guess. His brothers had been abused, just as Sevastyan had—as if that was always going to be their fate, no matter what they did or how much they fought it.

"I won't speak more about it, because that's not my secret to tell."

I recalled that day of the museum when he'd returned to the town house. He'd said nothing to me, just wrapped his arms around me as if I were the only thing keeping him afloat. Had he just learned of this from Maksim?

"I understand, Sevastyan. But you can't take the blame for that. You were just twelve—you couldn't have known."

"I abandoned them. That's how they see it, and they hate me for it. Maksim less than Dmitri, because he remembers me more. But deep down, they both want me to suffer for their fates. Why would I ever want to reveal my family to you, when I know they despise me?"

"I don't care how anyone else feels about you."

"Would you not? I didn't want anything to affect your opinion of me. Sometimes you look at me as if I'm some sort of hero. I can't explain . . . there's no explaining what that feels like to me." The look of longing on his face gave me an idea. "What would happen if you found out that most of my life has been everything *un*heroic? What if you discovered that I'm hated—and that I hate myself for every time I lost?"

He moved closer to me, shaving off the distance, and I wanted him to.

"Then, after finally managing to win—in work, in life—I was losing you."

Not trusting myself to speak, I offered him my hand.

He stared at it in disbelief, then all but lunged for it. He absently took my other hand and began warming them between his own. Because they were cold.

At length, I said, "Thank you for trusting me with this."

"You aren't disgusted with me?"

"Of course not." I wanted to wrap my arms around him, but I thought this moment was too tenuous. "With your father, you acted in self-defense. I think things got mixed up for you because you were so young." Over time, his mind must have confused his memories, guilt overwhelming the reality of that night: if he hadn't protected himself, he would have died. "You didn't have a choice."

"Every day, I look in the mirror—and my father stares back."

"You're nothing like him," I said vehemently.

He scowled at me. "How can you say that when you tell me you don't know me?"

"Would your father have harbored this guilt for nearly two decades? Would he hate himself for things he had absolutely no control over?"

Sevastyan swallowed. "And what about the other . . . ?"

"I'm just grateful you survived. I'm grateful you told me."

He looked like he seethed with emotion. "You can't expect me to believe that you're willingly here with me after I confessed what I did—and what was done to me. Much less *because* I confessed it!"

"You have to believe it, because it's true. What I know of you only binds me to you more."

He fell silent for what seemed like an eternity.

"Tell me what you're thinking, Sevastyan. What you're feeling."

"Feeling?" He made a caustic sound. "You've just felled me. No, you've *slain* me. I'll never want another, yet you were ready to give up on me." He dropped my hands, his ire mounting. "You can't think that all this is random! Paxán found me all those years ago. Across the world, you somehow found him, and then he sent me to you. At any point, you could have been lost to me."

Sevastyan had told me in the *banya* that we were inevitable. Now I realized why he believed that.

Now I did too.

He reached out to grip my upper arms. "I went through my entire life, never knowing that I was starving for this beautiful, brilliant redhead. Then I saw her. I watched her. All the while, she had no idea that she went about her days and tormented me every one of them."

I gasped. "Sevastyan . . ."

"The first time I saw you, you nearly put me to my knees. I wanted to invade your thoughts as totally as you had mine. When I did manage to sleep, I'd dream of you and wake up fucking the sheets." His grip grew harsher, as if someone were trying to take me away from him. "I'd will you to look at me. And then, in that bar, you did. You showed interest in me, and amazingly Paxán approved the match. All he asked was that I give you time." He released my shoulders to pace. "Time—while goddamned Filip moved in on *my* woman!"

"I didn't choose Filip."

"You didn't choose me either! Not until you were alone and confused, reeling from Paxán's death. I took advantage of you that night, and every night after."

"No," I said firmly, "I wanted you."

"Because you didn't know the real me. Can you understand now why I didn't want to give in to my perversions with you, to give you pain? I feared becoming like my father. I fought so hard, but the thought of you going to another . . . it sent me over the edge."

Was I hurting *him* by putting on pressure? To engage in sex he wasn't comfortable with? Considering all the abuse I knew about—and the abuse I could only imagine—I had to wonder.

He might enjoy what we did together, then be appalled at himself.

He was talking to me now; I needed to dig deeper with him. "Will you tell me when you first realized your particular interests?"

His voice was so grave when he asked, "I'm to reveal even more?"

"Yes, Sevastyan," I answered. "There's no word limit here."

His brows drew together. "It didn't start out as a sexual thing."

"I don't understand."

He exhaled. "I'd always had my brothers in my life, but in St. Petersburg, I suddenly had no one. Though there were other children, I couldn't connect with them. Not with my background. Yet I hated being alone. Even at that age, I decided that I needed a wife—who would belong to me."

I tried to picture Sevastyan as a boy, mulling marriage of all things. Yet decades later, he'd never wed. *He wants to marry you, Nat. . . .*

"I was young enough to make ridiculous plans, but old enough to realize I was homeless and penniless. I knew I had nothing to offer anyone. Until a year later . . ." He trailed off.

"Tell me."

With reluctance, he said, "There was a back-alley prostitute that all the boys used to watch. I could tell she was feigning passion with her clients, faking screams—desperate just to be done for the night."

I cringed to think of all the things he'd seen when living on the streets.

"Then one night, a man came to her, touching her in ways I'd never seen before—exacting, even cruel ways. He made her put her hands against the wall as he whipped her. I couldn't believe he was striking her. I was ready to kill him for hitting someone so much smaller. I started for the man, but then I looked at her face—really looked. Her eyes were glassy, and she couldn't catch her breath." Sevastyan's gaze flicked to me—to see if I was still with him?—then away. "She was . . . she was in heaven."

"Go on."

"Once the man finally fucked her, this jaded woman melted for him. In those moments, she would've done anything for more. She *belonged* to him absolutely." Sevastyan faced me, holding my gaze, as if he needed me to fully understand him. "He had something to *offer* her—something that other men didn't. I realized if I could learn how to do the things he'd done, I could master a woman like that. *I* could make her melt. I didn't crave the acts as much as I did the result."

I'd suspected that kink for this man had more to do with

a woman's pleasure than his own. Now I was learning that he'd imprinted the day he'd seen a woman taken to heights he'd never before witnessed. "And then later?"

"As I told you, it always felt like practice. After I met you, I understood why. But then when my needs grew fiercer with you, I feared I was interested in pain for the wrong reasons. Maybe because I'd received so much of it. Maybe because I wanted to control it like alcohol, meting doses of it. I was terrified that I would scare you away—or lose control and harm you."

And all I'd done was push him. Regret weighed on me. "Then I've pressured you into things you're not comfortable with."

He shook his head forcefully. "When someone like *you* had those needs . . . what I did to you didn't feel sordid. You made it . . . clean. I went to a place like that club, and I felt hope too."

I must have looked unconvinced, because he added, "I was right all those years ago. That night of the club, *you* looked like you were in heaven—and I knew you were mine."

I recalled how his eyes had glinted, how he'd rested his forehead against my shoulder. He'd told me I was made for him.

"On the ride home, you curled your little fingers into my hair and shivered against me. You sighed like you loved me." His gaze bored into mine. "I will do *anything* for that reaction."

He'd seen how tastes of pain could affect a woman, and he'd internalized that want. This man only yearned to madden me, to take me to new heights. Which meant I wasn't hurting him!

And he was actually communicating with me.

Right when I was growing convinced that we could make this work, his eyes turned bleak. "But you weren't mine, were you?"

"I was. I am!" I made a sound of exasperation. "Do you know how frustrating it's been to fall in love with every facet you let me see—even when I believed you'd never let me see more?"

"Love?" His Adam's apple bobbed.

"Yes, Sevastyan. I'm willing to work on us, if you are too. If you'll just keep talking to me, I believe we can handle anything."

He eyed me suspiciously, as if he couldn't fathom this turn of events. "You're giving me another chance?"

"If you'll give me one too. I do need to learn to be more patient, just like you said."

He eased closer. "I know I'm not right. But if you help me, I can be better. That's what I want. Natalie, understand me: I'm . . . *asking*."

I was already reaching for him. When he swung me over to straddle his lap, I wrapped my arms around his neck. Against me, his body shuddered as if a weight had been lifted from him—like an overworked muscle finally allowed to rest.

I whispered, "You let me in."

He could only nod.

"Please don't shut me out again. As long as you talk to me, I'll never leave you."

"I'll do whatever it takes."

For what might have been hours, he held me like this. "Sevastyan, what happens now?"

In a voice hoarse with emotion, he said, "Now we go home."

CHAPTER 45

*T*he Moskva River was almost frozen.

From the pavilion, I watched otters frolicking on blocks of ice. I'd seen a stoat, several hares, and a snowy owl. They were all thriving in these bitter temperatures—a damp cold even more biting than I'd known in Nebraska.

The pavilion was one of my favorite places on the property. I would come here whenever Sevastyan was working.

All around me, Berezka was covered in snow, pristine. Which helped me to forget the fight to the death by the boathouse, the war for control that had raged over these grounds.

Paxán's untimely death.

Seamless white reminded me that wounds heal.

Though Paxán's grave site was beautiful—a clearing atop a hill, surrounded by birch trees—I felt closer to him here.

His funeral had been somber, attended by so many who'd loved him. In front of others, Sevastyan hadn't allowed himself to show grief. Later that night, in front of me, two tears had slid down his face, which might as well have been a thousand for a hardened man like him.

Every day that passed we could think of Paxán with less pain. I was thankful that I'd gotten to spend even that short amount of time with him. In just weeks, he'd changed my fate forever.

His dying wish had been fulfilled: my life was better because he'd been in it.

I glanced over and saw Sevastyan striding toward me, his long charcoal coat whipping about his legs; my heart sped up at the sight of him. I knew that it always would.

The winter sun caught his face as he neared. To look at him now, I would say he'd found some measure of peace. He appeared younger, that weariness I'd first sensed in him lifted. He smiled more often, and I could even make him laugh on occasion.

"Ready to go in?" He offered his arm for the walk back to the main house. We'd redone my wing for the two of us, moving his things from his house on the property.

"All set." I took his arm with a gloved hand, glancing up at his flushed cheeks and brightened gaze. Sigh.

Over the last month since we'd returned, Sevastyan had been able to disentangle Paxán's legacy from *mafiya* concerns; then he'd taken over as *vor*, though in a scaled-back capacity. Now he focused on protection for Paxán's territory and people.

And, *damn*, did the job of protector suit Sevastyan.

"Your gifts for your mother and Jessica arrived from Buccellati today." Boxes of extravagant jewelry.

Okay, okay, so the money was growing on me.

For Christmas, Sevastyan and I planned to visit Nebraska. I could only imagine what my family and friends would think about my ex-enforcer.

"Thanks for letting me know about the presents," I told him with a grin. I was pretty sure he sometimes talked just to make some kind of mental "word quota." I razzed him about that all the time. "Have you thought any more about your brothers?" I'd floated the idea of Sevastyan calling them on Christmas, a tentative start toward something more.

"I . . . haven't ruled out anything. Though Maksim might think I'm leaning toward his proposal."

"You have a point." While I was angling for a mere holiday call, Maksim was angling to unite his might with Sevastyan's and take over, well, Russia.

Sevastyan hadn't agreed to anything, but his rivals had caught wind of the potential alliance and backed off considerably. Which meant he didn't have to work so much.

Maybe he could leave his post this spring and take me around the world?

Or perhaps I'd enroll in school over here. No surprise: I hadn't decided yet.

One thing I was certain of? I was determined to make this winter different for him, to have him associate it with our warm bed, our wicked lovemaking, and our hopes for the future.

"Oh, before I forget, Jess has kind of called dibs on your old place. She wants to fly back with us after the holidays." And she might've vowed never to leave. As she'd put it: "If I get to live in my own mini palace, Imma be one borscht-eating bitch."

"Then it's hers," Sevastyan said, surprising me. "As long as I get you to myself during the nights."

"You've got yourself a deal, Siberian." For the first time in his life, he was enjoying the long nights. We swam together, read together, and played chess by the fire. Or we tried to. Last night, we'd scattered the pieces when he'd tossed me atop the board to have his way with me.

Never had a queen been so happy to be taken.

Often, we talked into the night as he shared more of his burdens. With each one, I marveled at the loving and honorable man he'd become. He'd also been telling me all about Paxán, and I could see the kindly clockmaker's hand in guiding him.

Sevastyan still had shadows; now they were *our* shadows.

As for me, I'd been working on becoming more patient. To help with that, I was repairing my *bátja*'s clocks. Clock-making demanded patience.

When the wind whipped, Sevastyan said, "Come here." He tugged me closer, shielding me with his big body. He always did that, just as he warmed my hands whenever they got cold.

I snuggled up to him, even though I was warm in my luxurious cashmere coat and sweater—that I'd paired with jeans and clodhopper boots.

I'd been making an effort to preserve my *self*; Natalie was back—hopefully a little more patient and accepting. Maybe, just maybe, a little wiser . . . ?

When a white hare crossed our path, I murmured, "It's so beautiful here."

"Wait till you see it in the summer." He'd started talking about the future, growing increasingly confident that I wasn't going anywhere.

Probably because we'd taken to living together like a house on fire. "Hey, maybe we'll have gotten rid of Jess by then."

He flashed me an amused look.

The only thing missing between us? He hadn't told me he loved me. Though he showed me every day, and he'd certainly convinced me of it in Paris, I needed to hear the words. Yet this was one thing I couldn't ask him for; it had to come naturally. . . .

"Tomorrow we should visit the *banya*." As he peered down at me, the sun struck his eyes, setting them aglow.

Molten gold: my new favorite color.

"I agree. It's important. For our health." Had I thought I would miss the thrills to be had at Le Libertin? Wrong. Sevastyan had already made me fly on several occasions since we'd been home.

Other times, he would make love to me with touches and kisses so worshipful, I couldn't decide which side of him I craved more.

"And until we can get to the *banya*," he said in a husky voice, "what should we do for our health?"

"A chess rematch? Or maybe a hot shower for two?" We conserved water whenever possible because we were responsible citizens. Who liked sex in the shower.

"I have an idea. But it'd be better if I showed you. . . ." He trailed off, his expression filled with sensual promise.

At that look, a puff of breath escaped me. "Can we walk faster, Sevastyan?"

Instead, he stopped, drawing me even closer. "As much as it pains me to say this, my brother was right. You should call me by something other than my last name."

"What are you thinking?"

"Anything. Pick something out of a hat."

"Wow, so many options." Decades ago, he'd chosen Aleksandr for himself. Maybe I'd shape it up a bit. "It could be that I've got a name already picked out. Perhaps I'm just waiting for the right time to tell you."

"Why wait?"

"Are you being . . . impatient?" In a saucy tone, I countered, "Okay, then why are you waiting to propose to me?"

Sexy grin. "I can't much longer—I know you're going to want to marry when we go to Nebraska."

Busted. Our first night together, he'd mentioned my wearing "his gold." Who knew I'd first wear it in the form of a wedding ring? I quirked a brow. "Pretty confident I'll be your wife, aren't you?"

He removed his glove to smooth the backs of his fingers over my cheek. *"Eto dlya nas neizbezhno, milaya."* It's inevitable.

♦

*W*e lay in our bed that night, catching our breath after a round of bone-melting sex. Sevastyan was still softly thrusting, brushing kisses over my face.

I was utterly sated, basking in heavy-lidded bliss as the nearby fire crackled. Outside, snow pelted the windows and winds howled, but all was cozy within.

Tonight, I'd decided that there was nothing better than watching his body move by firelight—and that this man possessed a never-ending bag of carnal tricks.

When he trailed his lips down to my neck, I threaded my fingers through his thick hair, arching to his mouth.

Between kisses, he rasped against my damp skin, *"Ya lyublyu tebya."* I love you.

A log popped in the fire; I grinned like an idiot.

He tensed when I didn't answer, raising his head with an alarmed expression. "What is it?"

Still grinning, I said, "It's nice to hear those words." I leaned up and kissed the bridge of his nose.

His lips curled. "I can only imagine."

With all my heart, I told him, *"Ya lyublyu tebya,* Aleks."

"Aleks?" He cupped my face with his rough palms, eyes lively. "Of all the names, this is what you've decided to call me?"

"You don't like it?" I asked, though I could tell he did.

Molten gold. "I like it." Then he leaned down to give me a lover's kiss like no other. . . .

The night I'd met Aleks Sevastyan, I'd wished for someone to snuggle up with through the winter.

I'd never imagined that the winter nights would be this cold—or that the warm arms around me could be so strong.

EPILOGUE

You are cordially invited to
celebrate the wedding of

Natalie Marie Porter

&

Roman Aleksandr Sevastyan

Saturday, the twenty-ninth of December
at six o'clock in the evening
Fontanelle Manse, Nebraska

R.S.V.P

Name: __Maksimilian Sevastyan__

- [X] Would be delighted to accept
- [ ] Must decline with regret
- [2] Number of people in party

R.S.V.P

Name: __Dmitri Sevastyan__

- [ ] Would be delighted to accept
- [X] Must decline ~~with regret~~
- [ ] Number of people in party

AUTHOR'S NOTE

*F*or this story, I envisioned the clockmaker/repair shop that Natalie's grandparents owned as one of the many underground enterprises that flourished in Russia outside of State control in the '60s, '70s, and '80s.

While researching Russian organized crime—facets of which grew apace with the underground economy in those decades—I dug into the backgrounds of various crime bosses. They ran the gamut. Some had advanced degrees; others were political activists. One had even become a TV producer. With such real-life variety, I felt comfortable portraying a gentleman clockmaker (one with a violent and dark past, which he specifically glossed over for his newfound daughter).

Lastly, I can't take credit for Sevastyan's vodka/wiper-fluid import idea. This scheme was based on true events.

I hope you enjoyed *The Professional*. Thank you all so much for your readership! And play on . . .